RUNNING FROM SHADOWS

Book 2: Shadows of Synd Series

E. ABRAHAM

ISBN-13: 979-8-9857684-4-2

For the ones like me who never knew how to save themselves, but figured it out anyways.

Special Thanks to @chelseaflewellenauthor for the Reapers motto and the #latenightwritersclub for keeping me on task to finish!

Trigger Warnings:

Violence: Guns and Knives
PTSD from abuse
Anxiety
Panic Attacks
Murder
Physical Abuse (not by MMC)
Threats of Sexual Assault
Stalking
Criminal Activities
Drugs
Kidnapping

If any of these are triggers for you, please visit the author's website for other works.

Content Warnings:
Explicit Sex
Adult Language

ONE

Ryker

I'm pissed. Royally pissed.

The last six months were a shit show, but at least the last couple weeks have been quiet. Too quiet. It's like all of Synd has been holding its breath, waiting for the Guild to hit back, to punish us for fucking up their plan to steal our people and sell them to the highest bidder. When they snuck in six months ago, trying to take over our city, I thought we were done for. So much so that I called in reinforcements from the Vipers.

It's been ten years since I've seen MacKenzie. She tagged along with her older brother, Dante, to help drive the Guild out of Synd. It was a punch to the gut, since Dante failed to mention she was going to be here. He knew exactly what he was doing. Dante might not know why I've avoided her since I took over for the Reapers, but he knew something happened, which makes his tactics all the more suspect.

Being pulled from a meeting I actually wanted to attend, I'm now racing across the city, all because little miss Kenzie doesn't understand boundaries. I have no idea why she randomly showed up, but when I get to Reaper territory, I'm sending her ass straight back to Rima. I don't want to hear her fucking reasons for randomly showing up.

I needed to be at the meeting with the leaders of Synd. The discussion on resetting protocols between our territories is something we've been putting off for weeks. Between the two mafia gangs and the Reapers leading the city and its underbelly, we need to get our shit together. Getting back on track hasn't been the easiest, especially with Mason Byrns basically ghosting everyone. I don't blame him after taking out his second to save his sister Sam and then her moving in with the Kings to live happily ever after. That would send me into a tailspin, but the back-to-back hits are taking its toll on him.

There's a clear difference around me when I cross the line between Byrns territory on the east side of the river and the Reapers' area tucked away in the north of Synd. Several men are hanging around outside Trigger's, the bar sitting right on the boundary line. It's plastered with the Reapers' red-and-black colors, with a giant golden hippo from a Gala tucked under the awning. I still can't figure out if one of the Kings or Mason Byrns had it delivered, but it had to be one of the mafia leaders. My money is on Alex King. Bikes line the lot alongside members proudly displaying our patches. Usually, I get a rush of pride when I see them gathered but not today. Today I'm just pissed.

I pull in, searching for Doc, my Sergeant-at-Arms, but he's not there. Cursing, I make my way inside, ignoring the members nodding to me. I don't have time for their shitty complaints right now. It's dark, and biker flags cover the windows. I squint into the dim space.

"Trigger," I call out to the owner behind the bar. "Where's Doc?"

He nods to the end of the counter tucked around the corner. I make my way over and lean next to his beefy arm. He takes up two spaces, double the size of other men. Doc is almost the same height as me when he's sitting, which reminds me why I'm glad he's in our club and not working against us.

"You got something for me?" I ask, shaking my head when Trigger puts a beer in front of me.

"Uh, no? Should I?" he asks, eyes widening.

Coming from his large frame, his soft spoken voice is jarring, even after having known him for seven years. He's never raised his voice around me, even when we've had to strip someone of their colors. I think the members respect him more for it.

"Apparently, we have a visitor at headquarters?" I prompt, eyeing him.

"Haven't heard about it. Who's here?"

He calls after me as I walk away. Hawk, my VP, will call him soon enough to gossip. They're like little hens, particularly when it's about me. The only reason I don't bother beating their asses is that they keep it to themselves, with the exception of Blue.

I blast across the river that curves through our territory, and my gaze drifts to the water. It's not as wide here. If I followed the river south, deeper into Synd, it would widen, allowing all sorts of things to be dropped into its depths with most of the city none-the-wiser. The people living along its edges in the Barrens deal with most of the riffraff, including the bodies that float by.

When I pull into headquarters tucked along the tree line at the north of our territory five minutes later, I'm still pissed. Every time MacKenzie would open her mouth six weeks ago, she'd spout sarcastic comments or asinine suggestions. She always was a spitfire, saying whatever the hell she wanted, whenever she wanted, regardless of the consequences. Not much has changed.

Storming through the double doors, I bellow Hawk's name, but he doesn't answer. Scanning the empty space, I wait. I'm not about to search this entire fucking building for them. I pull out my phone to text him. I'd like to say I'm calm and collected, but there are more than a few F-bombs in my message. I don't think I can get any more pissed, but it happens when his response comes through.

Your house.

I burst out the door, storming down the block. My place is the largest one for several blocks, but it's only a two-story. As I reach the back porch, I'm submerged in childhood memories of the Raines kids and me playing in the back yard, the revving of motorcycles making up the background of our childhood. Not much has changed since Dad died, except the paint on the covered deck and the bullet-proof windows I had put in when I took over the Reapers MC. I glance to what used to be the Raines' house. It's run-down now, the deck sagging and the paint chipping. Hawk didn't want to move in when he got elected

VP, and Raymond, MacKenzie's dad and the Reapers old VP, left it to the club when he took his kids and moved to Rima, running from his memories and a regime change.

"Hawk," I roar after I swing open the back door.

His muffled reply comes from upstairs. I can't believe he not only brought her here but paraded her around. He probably gave her a fucking tour. I'm sure MacKenzie waltzed right in, Hawk trailing behind. She never did understand boundaries, at least when it came to me. She did whatever the hell she wanted, including slipping into my second-story window whenever she felt like it. I push the memory of the last time she pulled that move from my mind. The last thing I need is to stroll down memory lane.

When I hit the top of the stairs, Hawk steps out of *my* fucking bedroom, hands up in supplication, as if that will stop me from throwing him out the window. He's the quintessential biker, tattoos running up and down his arms. He runs his hands through his short-cropped brown hair. Usually, I wouldn't care if he was wandering around my house, but the guilty look on his face puts me on edge.

"Helms, calm down," he says, trying to stop my forward momentum, but I'm hell-bent on getting through that door.

"Get the fuck out of my way. Why the hell did you let her cross the line, much less bring her to *my* house and set her up in *my* room?" I try to brush past, but he pushes my chest.

"You don't understand. You can't go busting in there, ready to throw her ass out!"

I shove him into the wall, then slam the door open. I expect to find her standing there, hands on hips, with some sassy remark, but it's empty. I sweep the space again and finally find her in my bed, straight dark hair spread over my pillow. She's curled up on her side, facing me, fast asleep. I'm about to spin back around and confront Hawk, but my mind registers what I saw, and my stomach drops.

Her face is a myriad of bruises and cuts. Her hand is curled under her cheek, discolored skin where there isn't a bandage wrapped around her palm. Mottled marks wrap around her wrist and arm, looking suspiciously like fingerprints. I freeze, not able to process what I'm seeing. She's so black and blue I barely recognize her.

"Helms, come on." Hawk grabs my arm and gently pulls me from the room.

Shock floods me as he leads me downstairs before collapsing on the couch and rubbing my hands over my face. Behind my lids, I keep seeing her injuries. Bruises covered every inch of exposed skin, and her shuddering breaths pointed to many more I couldn't see under the comforter. As the numbness seeps out of me, I turn to my second.

"What the fuck happened?" I ask in an ominous voice.

My anger at Kenzie has sunk into rage for whoever touched her. I'm going to take my wrath out on him if he doesn't start talking, and from the look in his eyes, he knows it.

"I don't know. MacKenzie showed up at headquarters, stumbling through the back door. I got there just in time to catch her before she passed out in my arms. I didn't know who the hell she was at first. I didn't recognize her. But whatever did happen, it's bad."

"Explain," I growl, but he shakes his head.

"There are wounds all over her body." He holds up his hands as I glare. "I didn't go looking for them, but she kept wincing when I carried her over here. Mac's in a bad way, Helms."

I nod, staring off, my mind racing. Dante and I may have been best friends growing up, but we didn't keep in touch much after Ray moved the family to Rima. It wasn't until their dad died five years ago that I heard from him. When Dante took over, we talked a little, but I don't know what's been happening in his territory. Calling for aid from the Vipers two months ago was hard enough. Trying to bridge the gap between all the years we missed was harder. I can't imagine Dante had a hand in this. We always agreed on how we wanted to run our clubs, and it wasn't beating the shit out of women, especially Kenzie. She's the one bright spot in Dante's life in a world that's hard enough already. Talking about the changes we wanted to make in front of our dads wasn't an option, but in the dead of night or hidden away in the woods, we agreed we didn't want to rule through fear like them.

"Call Ren King. Maybe he can get footage of her coming into the city, at least figure out where she was before she crossed the line. I want him to call me directly," I say, pushing to my feet.

"You trust him with this?" Hawk questions.

He's not trying to be disrespectful, but I bristle.

"Just fucking do it," I reply without a backward glance, making my way back upstairs.

I push on the door, which creaks slightly, and slide inside before it clicks shut again. The front door slams as Hawk leaves, hopefully to follow my instructions. Seeing

MacKenzie's state again stuns me, cementing my feet to the floor all over again. She winces in her sleep, and I jolt, swinging a chair to her side. When she winces again, I shush her, but it doesn't stop her eyebrows from drawing down. I want to gather her up in my arms, but I'm afraid it will hurt her more.

"Kenzie, what the hell did you get into?" I murmur, rubbing my thumb against her ebony hair. I smooth the strands down but stop when I hit a bump, and she jerks.

Slipping my phone from my pocket, I text Ink, our doctor, to come check her out. The only thing I can tell him is her nose isn't broken. It may be swollen, like the rest of her face, but it's still straight. I send a text to Hawk to keep this shit to himself. He's not one to go blabbing to the members, but I'm sure someone out there saw MacKenzie making her way through the streets and is liable to ask. The fewer people who know, the better.

Staring at my phone, I hover my thumb over Dante's name, unsure of why I'm hesitating. He can't be responsible for this, but what if it was someone in his club? How would I even explain how she looks? Her face is so swollen I can barely make out the features I memorized growing up. I focus on her closed eyes, holding my breath, silently begging to see the bright hazel sparkling back at me.

Rima is over three hours away, and I haven't heard from Dante in a couple of weeks. Kenzie is obviously running from something—or someone. To out her would only bring whatever trouble she's fleeing straight to our doorstep. I text him instead, asking him how things are. I try to keep it vague, but I'm itching to call and ream his ass for letting this happen to his sister.

I wait, staring down at the message. Five minutes, ten . . . and it still sits on unread. Shaking my head, I get up, heading for the door, but I turn around to gaze at the sleeping woman in my bed.

What are you running from, Kenz?

TWO

MacKenzie

My face hurts. Like, a lot. It's the first coherent thought in my mind in who knows how long. The last thing I remember . . . the train station . . . stumbling out the doors and a guy catching my arm when I tripped. I had my hood up, but when I looked up to thank him, he recoiled and then asked if I was all right. I don't remember much after that.

I shudder, keeping my eyes closed. I don't want to face whatever new hell I've found myself in. A fluffy pillow is under my head and a warm blanket over my shoulders, so I doubt I'm in the hospital or a serial killer's house, unless they want to fix me up before they kill and eat me, but that seems like a lot of work.

I could just stay in this little bubble, pretending I'm safe, but that's not feasible. My lids flutter up, but only one eye opens. My right eye is swollen shut. I try to shuffle on to my back, but my muscles protest, and a groan leaves me. Every single one hurts, like someone's used me for a punching bag, which is precisely what happened, but I'm trying not to think about that.

Glancing around the dimly lit space, I instantly recognize where I am. I've played and slept in this room as a kid. I threw rocks at the window to my right. I had to pay for a new one when one of those rocks was a little too big, when I was a little too upset at . . .

Ryker Helms.

I have no idea how I got here. The memories of my flight blur together, making my head pulse. I need pain meds. I need water. I need a shower. *Fuckin'A, I need help.* It was the only thought I had when I ran. *I need help.* Ryker was the only one I could think of, though he's made it clear he no longer wants anything to do with me. I thought a whole-ass decade was long enough for him to get over the bullshit he was going through, but when Dante and I got here to help with the Guild, it felt like he hates me now. He'd pushed me away before, but the hard look in his eyes when I walked into headquarters made it clear there would be no reconciling. It hurt more than I'm willing to admit.

A single tear flows down my cheek, gathering in my ear and making me shudder. I try to lift my hand to brush it away, but pain reverberates through me, and I stop with a gasp. Instead, I turn my face to the side, rubbing my ear into the pillow gently. My gaze catches on the chair next to my bed, but it's empty. Ryker must have been here.

He's clearly off doing whatever it is he thinks is so damn important. Biting back a groan, I roll my stinging eyes, sending a bolt of pain through my temples.

I'm halfway through pulling myself up to lean against the headboard when the door clicks open, and there he is. I have no idea how he'll react. Hell, on the best of days, he growls at me. Now that I'm black and blue, he'll recoil, like the man at the train station. Having experienced that enough throughout my life, I'd rather not go through it again.

"For fuck's sake, MacKenzie, what the hell are you doing?" Ryker's harsh voice rings out, making me wince. Voices shouldn't be that growly after someone gets hurt.

His tattooed hands reach for me, but I flinch. His touch will hurt, he'll be pissed, and I'll want to fight back, but I don't have the energy. I can't handle the lectures and judgment, especially from him. I glance out the corner of my eye, catching a glimpse of deep blue eyes, before he tucks his chin to his chest.

"Just don't. I got it," I say in a raspy voice, sounding pathetic, despite my attempt to come off strong. Even to my own ears, I sound pathetic.

He sighs and runs his fingers through his wavy black hair. I renew my efforts to move without really moving, but it's slow going. Every time one muscle moves, another protests, and another tear falls. It's no longer worth it to swipe them away.

Ryker steps closer, wraps an arm around my back and under my knees, and scoots me against the headboard. I still cringe, but it's less painful than I had expected. He collapses in the vacant chair, scrubbing his hands across his face and then pinning me in place with his intense stare. His full lips are distracting, but he's scowling. Of course he's fucking scowling.

"What the fuck happened, MacKenzie?"

Hearing my full name, I crinkle my nose, which, in turn, further stings my face. I wonder if my nose is broken. That'd be absolutely fan-fucking-tastic. Wondering what he'll do if I say nothing, I stare at him and wait. He'll stomp around and make a fuss, which will only make my head hurt worse. Totally not worth it. *What the hell am I supposed to say?*

"You got any water? And maybe something for the pain? Something strong?" I ask.

I shouldn't have brought my problems to his doorstep. He's got a sweet deal here, never having anyone contesting his territory, starting wars, shooting at him. Between the Kings, the Byrns, and the Reapers, they've got this place locked down tight. Even the hubaloo with the Guild—while not exactly great—wasn't all that bad. They got out of it virtually unscathed in the end.

Ryker hands me a bottle and some pills. It looks like regular pain meds. Dick. Of course he couldn't break out the strong shit for me. My bandaged hand can't grip the cap, and I grunt. He snatches the bottle, opens it, and thrusts it into my hand. Oh, he's pissed. When I tip my head back, the blood roars in my ears, pooling in the base of my brain. It's not until the water hits the back of my throat that I realize how thirsty I am. Ryker grabs the bottle, spilling some on my shirt, and I squawk.

"Don't even start. You chug this, and you'll be puking all over my bed."

I lean back, closing my eyes.

"You going to tell me what's going on now?" he asks.

"No," I say, belligerent.

"No? Seriously, Kenz, you stumble through the back door of headquarters, pass out in my VP's arms, looking like you got run the fuck over, and you're not going to tell me what happened? Why did you come here, then?"

Standing next to the bed, he's seething, clenching and opening his fists—open, closed, open, closed. Trying to get my thoughts in order, I stare at his hands, but when he lets out a strangled noise and lifts his closed fists, I flinch. He'd never hurt me, but after what I went through, my body reacts without my say-so. I thought I hid my reaction, but Ryker quickly steps back, and my gaze flies to his face. Pain, guilt, and something else mixes together in his eyes.

"Sorry," I whisper, at a loss for words.

"Fuck, Kenz, don't be sorry. Just tell me what happened. Please."

The 'please' almost breaks me. I could tell him everything. I could tell him about them and what they did. But what will he do then? I'm not ready for the answer. Either he'll hunt them down and kill them all, and I'll have brought more problems on him, or he'll do nothing and that'll break my heart—he'll break my heart, all over again. I need more time to figure things out.

"Can I stay here? Until I can move without wanting to die?"

It kills me to ask, but I don't have another option.

He chokes out what sounds like a sob. "Let's not talk about dying when you look like you do."

"You didn't answer the question."

"I'm not going to throw your ass out, but if you won't tell me what's going on, I'm calling your brother," he threatens.

My mind whirls with all the information I'm keeping from him.

"You can try, but Dante won't answer."

"I'm not going seven rounds of ammo with you, MacKenzie," he snaps, throwing me back into a memory so forcefully my eyes slam shut.

All us kids, lined up along the tree line. We took turns playing a stupid game of Russian roulette with cans filled with small explosives, hoping we made it through our seven rounds. I couldn't have been older than seven when I followed the boys all the way out there, hoping they'd let me play, too. It didn't last long before Dad found out and cussed us out for being so stupid. From what I remember, the boys had to clean headquarters for two months, while I didn't get punished at all. That was the year Maddox started treating me differently. I shake away the memory, forcing myself back to the present.

"Can I stay or not?" I ask, swinging my gaze to him.

We stare at each other, neither of us wanting to back down.

"For now. Get some rest. We'll talk in the morning." He strides away and shuts the door firmly behind him.

The meds are starting to work, so I can move without feeling like I'm going to pass out again, and I make it to the attached bath before I throw up. I swipe my hand across my mouth, barely registering the ache it causes. I flush, then flush again after I pee, thanking whoever kept me in my own clothes. The last thing I want is to be running around in Ryker's shirt. It'd fit, but with my breasts, I'd stretch it out for sure. I want to take off my bra, but I don't think I could reach without retching again.

As I splash cold water on my face, I hesitate. I don't want to know what I look like, but I slowly lift my eyes. I don't recognize the woman staring back at me. She's beat the fuck up, black and blue, eye swollen shut, blood matted along the hairline. I never had what one would call sharp cheekbones, but now my face is twice as big as it usually is, puffy and unrecognizable.

"What do I do now?" I ask the woman in the mirror.

She merely stares back at me, anguish and fear reflecting from her dull hazel eyes. My hands shake, and before I know it, I'm curled up on the tile, my body crying out. I'm spiraling, but I can't snap myself out of it. I can't tell Ryker what happened.

I can't.

I can't.

I shove myself up, grimacing through every motion. Stumbling into the bedroom, I search for my shoes, then find them shoved under the bed. With the state my body is in, I won't be able to make it out the window like I had so many times as a kid. Even if I wasn't a ball of pain, I couldn't fit through it anymore. Knowing my luck, my ass would get stuck, and I'd have to yell for help, only to be met with more of Ryker's growling and snarling.

Passing the night stand, I swipe the pill bottle and water, clutching them close since I don't have any fucking pockets in these pants. Easing the door open, I think up excuse after excuse if I run into Ryker, but the house is silent and dark. I can't tell through the ringing in my ears if I'm being quiet. Creeping down the stairs, I slide my foot to the right on the third step as to avoid the creak, and a bike passes by the house, rumbling through the silence.

When I have my hand on the knob of the front door, I freeze as Ryker's deep voice drones through the wood panes. Someone else answers him, but their voices are too muffled to make out. Knowing I should flee out the back, I press my ear to the door.

". . . Dante still hasn't replied. Hasn't even read it. Something's not right," Ryker grumbles, frustration seeping into his tone.

"Doesn't she have another brother?"

I recognize Hawk's voice, the Reapers' VP. I met him when we were here last.

"Yeah, Maddox. Never was very close with him, but if MacKenzie won't tell me what the hell happened, I'll have to call him."

"There's got to be a reason she doesn't want to talk about it. Maybe you should wait, see if shit works out."

Ryker barks out a laugh. "You don't know MacKenzie Raines. That woman will go to her grave with it if she wants. She's stubborn, bullheaded, sarcastic, and doesn't listen for shit. Good with a secret, bad with sharing. I'm going to have to call Maddox sooner or later. I'll just have to figure out when."

"Wait until the morning. She's not going anywhere in the state she's in," Hawk replies.

"Yeah, we'll see."

I have to get out. Now. Silently, I back away and turn when I'm sure they're not going to come in and bust me. I don't know where I'll go, but I have to get away before Ryker turns me in. The back door is open, letting in the cool spring air—*Thank god*—and I run. Not actually run, since I'm pretty sure I'd die if I tried running, but I make my escape, with Ryker and Hawk, none the wiser.

THREE

Ryker

For the second day in a row, I'm pissed. I like to think I usually keep my cool when shit goes down, but apparently not. Not wanting to wake Kenzie up, I waited for her, but when noon rolled around, and I still didn't hear her stirring, I checked and found the fucking bed empty. The pills, water, her shoes—all gone. The bathroom has smears of blood on the cabinet, but she's disappeared. Kenzie vanished from right under my nose.

"Fuck!" I yell, the only thing coming from my mouth in the last hour.

All my top guys are searching, but I doubt they'll find her unless she's passed out somewhere. Hawk convinced me to stay here, in case she came back, but she won't. She was probably out the window ten minutes after I left her alone. My phone lights up, and I swipe my thumb over it four times before it connects as I stare at my trembling hand.

I shake my head, ignoring the tremor, and bark into the phone. "What?"

"No dice, Prez. If she's in Reaper territory, she's hiding somewhere," Hawk states calmly.

He's lucky he's not standing in front of me. I might've bashed his face in.

"Did you check the woods?"

"Yeah, but if she went in there, there's no way we'd find her. You guys spent a lot more time there than the rest of us. I checked the spots you told me about, but there's nothing there. I think it's time we call it."

My mind moves to the next option. Whatever shit Kenzie got into doesn't matter. I'm going to find her. I pull up Ren's number. He told me he prefers to text, but this is an emergency, so he can deal.

"Helms, what can I do for you?"

"I need your help," I say, trying not to freak out.

"I am helping you. I don't have the information yet, though," Ren contends, annoyance slipping into his tone.

"This is related. The woman I had you looking for isn't in Reapers territory anymore. I need to find her."

"Oh. Well, in that case, I can help you. However, you'll have to refrain from divulging where you acquired this information."

"What?" I snap.

He sighs, and I hear a door close before he says, "Don't fucking tell them I told you, dumbfuck."

I rear back, peering at the phone. I've caught glimpses of who I think Ren is under the mask he wears, but it's entirely different to experience it.

"Understood. Where is she?"

"Before I tell you, I have some questions. And before you freak out, yes it's important. Because as soon as you have her location, you'll be tearing off to get her, and I won't know what the hell is going on."

"Fine," I hiss, pinching the bridge of my nose.

"What happened to her?"

"You've seen her? Is she there?"

"Answer the question, Helms," Ren demands.

"I don't know. She showed up black and blue. Won't tell me what happened."

"Has a doctor checked her over? And why the hell is she hiding from you?"

"Yeah, Ink did. Said there wasn't much to do until she woke up and told us what hurts. He didn't want to do anything with her passed out, since she didn't have anything serious."

I'm not about to admit to Ren King my suspicions on why she took off.

"Helms, why is she hiding from you?"

"Fuck, Ren, I don't know. I told her to tell me what happened, or I'd call her brothers to get the story if she didn't. I don't know what else you want from me."

During the silence, I glance at the phone, making sure he's still on the line. I wait, knowing whatever verdict he makes will be the difference between knowing where she is or not. I assume she's at the Kings' estate, but how she got there is beyond me. She's only been there once for the meeting months ago. Pacing back and forth, I'm about to snap if he doesn't talk.

"She's here—with Sam," he murmurs, and I stomp out the door, heading for my bike.

"I'm on my way. Did you find out how she got there?" I ask, swinging my leg over and shove the keys in.

"Car service. Helms, listen, she won't tell us what happened either, although maybe she's said something to Sam, but whatever she's running from, she's terrified."

"Of fucking course she is! Someone beat the shit out of her," I bellow, drawing stares from headquarters down the block. I don't fucking care.

"Yes, I understand, but if you come in here demanding answers, she's only going to run again. Plus, I'm fairly certain Sam will kick your ass. And as I like being in *her* good graces, I will back her up," Ren says.

"Understood." I hang up, trying to calm my racing heart.

The drive over doesn't help, though I try to take it easy. Every time I blink, Kenzie's battered face flashes, asking me if she can stay. I'm not pissed anymore. Fear has replaced the anger. I've tried to keep her at arm's length, but she keeps barreling back in, intent on disrupting my life.

The driveway is clear when I pull into the Kings' estate, but the door swings open as I bound up the stairs, and I'm face-to-face with Shane King, mafia leader of the west side of Synd. His scowl isn't anything new, but the disappointment in his blue eyes is.

"King."

"Helms. What the hell is going on up there?" he asks, crossing his tattooed arms over his chest.

I itch to match his energy, but I don't have it in me.

"Your guess is as good as mine at this point. She showed up black and blue and wouldn't talk about it when she finally woke up. You going to let me in?" I ask.

"You intend on dealing with it?" he counters, raising an eyebrow.

"Damn right I am. Now let me see her."

He nods and leads me in, heading toward the kitchen in the back of the house. It's more of a mansion, with wings, secret tunnels, and more. I'm surprised they don't have a butler.

Six months ago, I hadn't spoken more than ten words to these guys, much less seen their house. After the shit with the Guild, I realized how divided we've become. I didn't want to retreat to my territory, content to merely react the next time a crisis hit our city. The first time I had dropped by for dinner, Shane thought another disaster was on our doorstep. The last six weeks—hell, the last couple of months, has drastically changed how we interact with one another, and I can't say I'm mad with how things are turning out.

"Mac is okay, by the way. Doing better than when she showed up last night. I told her I was going to call you, and she flipped, tried to run out the back door until Sam calmed her down. I called our doc, talked to him about her injuries. Might want Ink to examine at her again once you get her home," Shane says as we weave through the maze of hallways.

"He came over first thing this morning, told me to let her sleep. Once lunchtime passed, I went to go check on her and found her gone. What time did she show up?"

"Late, past midnight. The guards almost didn't let her in, but Sam came home right around then and recognized her. Don't know how with Mac's injuries, but Sam brought her in."

"Anything else I should know?" I murmur.

I want to push past him; rush to where she is, but any information I can get from him will help.

"We need to meet soon. We've got some problems with our shipments. Nothing big, but it's fucking up our lines, which bleeds into your shit. Oh, and Mason's being a little bitch again."

"Not surprising. He looked like shit at the meeting. You talk to him lately?"

"Sam has. She's keeping shit to herself. We can't let him fall apart, though. That shit will trickle into our territories," he grumbles.

"Try again," I mutter.

Shane's a little less of an asshole now but not by much. Getting him to care about the leaders instead of equating things to business hasn't been easy.

"Fuck you. He's pissing me off."

"Why? Because he's being a little bitch?" I smirk, but it falls off my face when I remember why I'm here.

"He's treating Sam like she fucked off and abandoned the family or something. It's bullshit. I wanted to confront him, but Ren said it would hurt Sam. So, now I'm stuck calling him a little bitch. So, shut the fuck up and try to get his ass in line."

Even though he's right, I roll my eyes. The Kings won't get in the middle of it, which leaves me to pick up the pieces of Mason Byrns and put him back together. As if I don't have enough on my fucking plate. We walk the rest of the way in silence, both lost in our thoughts.

Shane pushes open the door, and I crane my neck to see over his shoulder. I spot Mac's straight dark hair spilling forward, covering her face, at the table. Sam and Alex are laughing, but Mac's head stays bowed. I nod to Ren, leaning against the island, and he lifts his mug, staring at me before casting his eyes back to Sam.

"Ryker! You missed one helluva end to the meeting yesterday. I thought Shane's head was going to explode," Alex booms, making Mac flinch.

Sam's hand shoots out, backhanding him in the arm, and he shoots her an embarrassed smile.

"Not sure there's a time when I've seen him when his head doesn't look like it'll explode, so . . . ." I reply, but my eyes are fixed on the woman who still won't lift her head.

"Princess, time to go," Shane says, grabbing Sam's hand and then pulling her up.

"Sucks to be you, Bug," Alex says, taunting Sam, about to take a bite of what looks like the world's worst pasta, but Ren yanks him out of his chair. I didn't even see Ren move.

"What the hell? I was eating."

"We're all going. You're not going to stay in shape if you keep eating all the pasta and never working out, dumbfuck," Ren replies, frog-walking Alex after Shane and Sam, who disappeared out the door.

My eyes track them as they bicker until they're cut off from view before I swing my gaze to Kenzie. Stepping closer, I try not to startle her. Her hands twist around themselves in her lap. This isn't the woman I know—or knew, the one I remember, the one who I saw almost two months ago. My Kenz would be spitting fire, sarcastic comments and confidence flying everywhere, with little care to what others thought of her.

This woman is meek. Quiet. Terrified. Even during the attempted coup that took my dad out ten years ago, she didn't look like this. She was pissed then for our club, for me, for the city. She'd wanted to deal with the traitors herself. She would have, too, if her dad let her. I lower myself in the chair opposite her to give her space. The way she reacted to Alex's loud, sudden voice was a bucket of cold water, icing my lungs and making it hard to breathe.

"Kenz?" I whisper, leaning forward, trying to peek past the curtain of hair.

"Hey," she whispers.

"Baby, why'd you run?"

"I don't know," she mutters, tilting her head.

She's lying. She was never very good at deception. We always got caught because MacKenzie couldn't lie.

"You ready to tell me what happened?"

"You going to call my brother?"

"Not if you don't want me to, but I can't help if I don't know what's going on," I say, frustration leaking through. I tip my head back to regain control. I almost don't catch her reply it's so faint.

"I can't."

"Where's Dante?"

I figure asking about him is a safe topic, but she's shaking her head.

"I don't know." She sniffles, wiping a tear and flinching, like she forgot her swollen face is a mess of bruises.

"Fuck." I scrub my hands over my face, trying to come up with a plan, some way to get her to open up to me.

When I drop them in my lap, MacKenzie's hazel eyes are staring at me, fear and guilt radiating from them.

"He's missing. He was supposed to be home a month ago, but he never came back, never answered his phone. I don't know where he is."

Her voice is trembling. A tear falls from the corner of her eye, still swollen shut.

"Who's running the Vipers, then?"

I need her to keep going. I'm afraid she'll clam up again, refusing to speak, and we'll get nowhere. Mac ducks before glancing to the side, eyes tracking the guard, who's making rounds along the tree line on the outer edge of the property.

"Maddox." I grimace, hearing the bitterness lacing her tone.

There was a time Maddox and Kenz were inseparable. But, one day, he wanted nothing to do with her. At the time, I figured they had a fight, they'd make up, and things would go back to normal, but that never happened. It only got worse the older we got—until neither of them could say two words in the other's presence without some biting remark.

"Kenz, you need to tell me who did this to you." She shakes her head. "I can't help you if you don't tell me."

Her shoulders tighten, and her jaw tics before she whispers, "I can't."

I heave out a breath. "What am I supposed to do with that, MacKenzie?"

I don't expect an answer, and none comes. We sit, me watching her, and her staring at the world outside, not seeing any of it.

FOUR

MacKenzie

After almost an hour of sitting in silence at the King estate, each of us waiting for the other to break, Ryker announced he was going home. I was welcome to come with him or stay there. He didn't say, but I could tell he was annoyed that I wouldn't tell him who was responsible for my current state.

Thankfully, Ren offered to drive me back, since my body couldn't handle sitting behind Ryker on his bike. Ren slipped a phone in my hand as I got out, nodding when I stared at him with a questioning look.

I'm pacing in the room Ryker stuck me in at Reapers headquarters. It's empty, like a tomb, with white walls and nothing but a bed, a small closet, a desk. It's usually occupied with an initiate waiting to be admitted as a member of the

Reapers, but for now it's just housing me. I grip the phone in my hand tighter, listening to the sounds of laughter in the background.

"I'm fine, Sam, really," I say, keeping the waver from my voice.

"Say the word, and we'll come get you. Promise," Sam says, and I shake my head.

I hardly know her, but when she found me last night, lurking in the shadows, hesitant to approach the guards blocking the way, Sam ushered me right in. She'd put me up in a room and stayed with me long after I expected. She didn't ask any questions about where I got my injuries, content to bandage me up, and respected when I told her I didn't want to call anyone. She merely nodded, an understanding in her eyes.

"Thanks."

I want to say more, ask more, but I don't want to be a bother. I don't want to drag her and her family into this any more than I want Ryker involved, but I'm running out of options on what to do.

"Of course. Don't worry about it. Call me if Ryker gives you any trouble. He can get real bossy sometimes." She puffs out a laugh, and I chuckle along, even though I don't feel like laughing.

"Listen, Sam, I don't want to burden you with my problems, but if Ryker is anything like he was when we were younger, he'll be stubborn. I think he might throw my ass out if I don't tell him what's going on soon, and I can't. I just . . . I can't tell him," I confess.

"Sweetie, you don't have to tell him a damn thing. He's not going to throw you out. I don't know what happened between you two, but . . . you know what—never mind. I think he's got your back. In case he does pull a bonehead move, though, just call me. You got our numbers. We'll come pick you up."

As tears gather in my eyes, I choke back a sob. I expect relief but guilt floods me. I'm not this weepy, weak woman who burdens others. I'm not someone who needs to be saved.

"Thanks. I'll talk to you soon," I choke out, hanging up before I lose it, and she comes barreling through the door to rescue me from my own emotions.

I spin around at the sudden knock, my heart jumping in my chest. The room spins until I close my eyes to calm my racing heart and even out my shuddering breaths. I try to tell myself it's nothing; I don't have to fear whoever is on the other side, but my body doesn't listen. Rational thought is not in control. Forcing myself to move, I angle my body behind the door before I crack it open and see Hawk, concern etched on his face. I step back, pulling it open the rest of the way.

"Hey, Hawk!" I say brightly, pasting on a forced smile.

I don't think it works, though, as the lines on his face deepen, and he glances down the hall, then back to me.

"Hey, Mac, how you doing?" he asks, eyebrows drawing together.

"I'm fine. Did you need something?"

I can't keep up this charade much longer, or I'm likely to shatter into a million pieces, leaving him to sweep away the remains of who I am.

He nods, looking away. Bringing his gaze back to mine, he thrusts a bag in my direction. When I don't immediately take it, he shakes it a little, leaning in slightly.

"Here," he says, shoving it into my hands, forcing me to grab it.

"What's this?"

"Clothes. Alex dropped them off," he says, his focus on the bag.

"Umm, okay?"

"He said it was some of Sam's stuff. For you. She didn't think you had any." Hawk's cheeks redden.

After holding it in as long as I can, I chuckle, then burst into laughter. Groaning, I clutch my stomach when the muscles in my stomach tighten and pull, sending an aching wave through me, but I can't stop snickering. Hawk's alarmed expression tells me I look like I've lost my mind.

"I'm sorry." I gasp, trying to pull myself together. "But she can't honestly think I'll fit into anything of hers. I'll look like an overstuffed sausage."

His face flushes a deeper red, and he clears his throat. "I'm sure it won't be that bad."

"Oh, it definitely will be. It's fine. Thank you. I needed that." I chuckle, peering in and seeing a whole mess of black.

I haven't spent much time with Sam, but I don't think I've seen her in anything other than black.

"Well, let me know if you need anything else," he says, shuffling his feet.

I'm a walking horror show, so I'm not surprised he wants to escape this conversation.

"Oh. Do you have a toothbrush? Shampoo? You know, hygiene-type stuff? I need a shower badly."

"Yeah, sure. I'll talk to Helms, see what we can scrounge up."

"Oh, don't bother him with it. I'm sure I'll figure something out." I grimace, imagining *that* conversation.

The longer I stay, the more I wonder if I should have gone somewhere else. I could go back to Sam's place, but I'll be a burden no matter where I end up. I'll only bring more problems and the unknown to their door. I would have hopped a train and changed my name and ran as far as I could, if I had the money. Lost in my thoughts, I search for another solution.

Hawk stares at my feet, and I clutch the bag filled with clothes I'll never fit into.

"If you need something, MacKenzie, you should ask." Ryker's voice echoes down the hall, making me jolt.

Sucking in a breath, I think about answering with a retort, but I don't have it in me to play the part today. I can't put the confident face I force on each morning, the one broadcasting to everyone that I don't give a damn what they think or what they say. Battered and bruised, both inside and out, I'm exhausted.

"I'm fine. Thank you, Hawk," I say before pushing the door closed and dropping the bag on the bed.

Ryker apparently has other plans, as he shoves his way into my room, slamming the door behind him, making my muscles tense. I hate this feeling of terror that flows over me every time I'm startled. Ryker isn't scary to me, but convincing my body of that every time he bellows or slams things is a useless endeavor. After everything that's happened, I don't blame myself, but I wish I could convince my brain I'm not in danger—at least not right now—not from him.

"What the hell is going on with you? You're flinching at every little noise. You're turning down offers of help, and I haven't heard one sarcastic, bullshit comment from you since you've been here. What the hell happened?"

An edge of desperation seeps into his voice. He reaches for me before curling his hands into fists and letting them fall to his sides.

"Ryker . . ." I sigh.

He tracks every tiny movement, from the tension in my shoulders to the trembling in my hands, before turning away and walking out, this time closing the door with a soft click.

I stand there for a long time, contemplating where to go from here. I can't keep putting him off. He won't take my silence much longer, and I'll be forced to decide to give up my secrets or run again. I'm still trying to come up with an answer when I crawl beneath the sheets. Giving up the battle, I let weariness overtake me.

The darkness throws me into a momentary panic when I don't recognize where I am. I have no idea what woke me up. My dreams were a chaotic jumble, and I must have been thrashing in my sleep, since the covers are tangled around my feet. My body is sticky, goosebumps dotting my skin, and I itch. A shower is exactly what I need. I want to let the hot spray heat my blood. I've been cold since I left Rima; since I was sent away from Synd ten years ago.

Angry voices boom from the hall, and I lurch up, swallowing the sob of pain desperate to escape. A sour taste sits at the back of my throat, almost making me gag. I can't understand the words over the roaring in my ears, but I scramble from the bed. Eyeing the door, I crouch on the opposite side. The noise tapers out, and I suck in deep mouthfuls of air to tap down the panic rising in me.

I hate this. I hate everything about what I've become, what they've made me. I wish I could rewind time, back to where I only had to worry about whether people were nice to me because my brother might kill them if they weren't. It wasn't normal by any means, but I was safe. This? This is anything but safe.

"You can't expect me to settle for that bullshit." Ryker's voice rings out in the silence, violence lacing his tone.

"Well, that's all you're going to get. So, get the fuck out of my way, Helms."

My heart freezes. All the calm from a minute before flees in the wake of the voice still echoing in my head. Maddox, my half brother, come to take me back. Black spots dance across my vision, threatening to blind me. The spell is broken when a clap of thunder rings out, followed by a sudden downpour of rain lashing against the window. I can't go back. Only one thought reverberates through my mind . . .

Run.

I pull myself up, barely feeling the aches and pains from the beatings I took days ago as I throw myself toward the window. My fingers hit the sill and an arm wraps around my waist, yanking me back. I go feral, kicking and shrieking. My feet leave the ground, and whoever is holding me tightens their grip, yelling something in my ear, but I'm so far gone I can't decipher it. I claw at the limb holding me captive, gouging deep and leaving lines of red. Blood seeps through the tan skin, and a grim satisfaction envelops me, feeding the savage beast rearing up within me. I won't go back. I'd rather die. I lunge toward freedom, thrashing until the arm around me draws tighter and the window, my only hope, swims as my eyes fill with tears. I'm going to pass out. It's creeping up, and I double my efforts, kicking my feet back but meeting only air. All at once, the fight leaks out of me, my body sagging, accepting my fate. I welcome the blackness with open arms. At least I'll be safe within the shadows.

FIVE

Ryker

"MacKenzie is sleeping. So, no, you can't talk to her," I grind out between clenched teeth. I should have known calling Sam would only complicate things more, but I didn't know what else to do. Between Hawk giving me the side-eye and Ink telling me she's traumatized, not to mention Maddox throwing a tantrum, I didn't have any other options.

"Helms, I'm two seconds away from slipping in your window and smothering you with a pillow. Tell me what the fuck happened," Sam sneers.

"She was trying to get out the window. There's a fucking hurricane happening out there—if you didn't notice. I stopped her, and she went crazy." I gaze at the white bandage Ink insisted on wrapping around my arm.

They'll scar, but I don't care. I'll tear them off tomorrow, anyway. I'm more concerned with what made her go feral.

"Was Mac running from you? What did you say to her?"

"I didn't say a damn thing. I'm not doing this with you, Sam. MacKenzie will call you when she wakes if she wants, but until then, I'm not going to be the go-between. I don't owe you shit," I snarl.

I hang up and immediately regret it. Slipping it into my pocket, I hope she understands and doesn't try to shoot me. The door to my bedroom is cracked enough to see Kenzie still asleep in my bed. The blankets are bunched around her hips, revealing every dip and curve of her body, but I glance away. I have no idea what happened before, but I'm getting used to being in the dark when it comes to her situation.

When the stairs creak behind me, I turn. Hawk is coming up, a grim look on his face. I can't take any more news. Turning back, I let my eyes roam over her sleeping form, taking in the bruises still covering her face. I rub at the ever-present ache in my chest. Hawk clears his throat, and I walk to the spare room, gnawing agony dogging my every step. Hawk shuffles in, glancing out the window.

"Maddox is demanding to see her still."

"What'd you tell him?" I grunt, crossing my arms.

"I laughed in his face. He didn't like that much. He did mention this was a misunderstanding, though." He snorts.

"Her entire body covered in wounds is a misunderstanding, huh?"

"Apparently. Made it seem like she got herself in this situation."

"Well, let's go. I'm interested in seeing how he thinks she's at fault, regardless of the circumstances behind it."

Hawk leads the way, but I stop when he reaches the front door. At his questioning look, I peer back up the stairs.

"He's at headquarters," he says.

"Yeah, I know," I answer, eyes still fixed behind me.

"Blue is outside. He can sit with her."

I don't dwell on it much, but when Hawk showed up a year after the coup, it was a godsend. He was young, running from something, and had a chip on his shoulder ornerier than my own. No one wanted the VP position after Raymond left, and it sat unfilled for a lot longer than I should have let it, but Hawk never balked. Knowing I can trust him to do what I can't or won't deal with makes my life easier.

Headquarters is usually quiet this time of night, but for some fucking reason, half the club is milling about, playing cards or trying to appear busy. With the storm raging outside, I'm not surprised there's more than usual gathered, but why they've all congregated in the main meeting area is beyond me.

Hawk leans in, whispering, "Some of the guys saw you carrying her out."

Sighing, I spot Mac's half brother stuffed in a corner, having what looks like a heated conversation with himself, but when he turns, a phone is pressed to his ear. He spots me across the room, holding up a finger. Sucking in a breath, I narrow my eyes, and Hawk chuckles behind me.

"Not funny," I snap, swiping the water dripping down my face.

"Oh, I was just imagining what his face will be like when you rearrange it. Won't be so pretty then, huh?"

Maddox Raines does look like a pretty douchebag. He was always more concerned with dressing like he was in an MC rather than actually being a part of one. He used to have a leather jacket, no patches, since we were too young. He wore the thing every day. Maddox would strut around, telling the younger kids off, threatening to beat the shit out of them. The rage in his eyes when I told him he looked like a goddamn moron should have been a clue, but I thought I was invincible then. I thought he'd jump me, we'd beat the shit out of each other, and things would go back to normal. Instead, he took it out on Kenzie. I never understood his logic, but I started paying attention after that.

Maddox's brown eyes never leave mine as I weave around the tables scattered about the room. The members' eyes swing between us. Having an audience doesn't bother me, but if Hawk was right in what Maddox was implying with Kenzie, he might regret doing this in the open.

"Five seconds," I say gruffly when we reach him.

He holds his finger up again and turns away as I tower over him. Hawk plucks the phone from Maddox's hand, earning him a squawk.

"What the fuck!" Maddox leans toward me, but jerks back when I don't move.

"I don't wait, Raines. Tell me what the fuck happened with Kenzie," I demand, crossing my arms.

Maddox rolls his eyes—whether at my demands or my nickname for his sister, I don't particularly care.

"She got herself in this mess. I don't know what she told you, but she's lying." He scrubs his fingers over his dark scruff.

I can't figure out if he's trying to grow a beard or thinks he's badass for having a little stubble, but I notice the spots where hair refuses to grow.

"Why don't you answer the question, Raines?" Hawk says.

"Oh, she got involved with some guy. His girlfriend didn't like that much, and neither did her brother. I told you, Mac's at fault. I'll bring her home. They won't bother her anymore, but maybe she learned a lesson about touching something that isn't hers." Maddox smirks, about to run his fingers through his over-gelled hair, but stops at the last second.

My eyes narrow and my head tilts, studying him. I raise an eyebrow at Hawk, and he subtly shakes his head. Relief floods me again, knowing he's my second, quickly followed by the stabbing ache in my chest returning.

"Get out," I announce, loud enough for everyone to hear, and turn to stalk away.

"Excuse me?" His voice drips with disbelief.

I swing around, storming back before shoving him against the wall. It takes everything within me to not put my fist through his throat. Somewhere along the way, Maddox morphed into this sack of shit.

"This is Reaper territory. I choose who comes and goes. Be thankful I'm letting you walk out with your life," I snarl.

Maddox's eyes burn into mine, but I don't back down. Confident one of the others will make sure he leaves, I push off the wall and swing around. I need to get back to

Kenzie. I don't want her waking up in my bed without me there. She'll probably try to slip out the window again.

"Ryker," Hawk calls.

I glance over my shoulder while he catches up. The rain has let up at least, but now we're left dodging mud puddles in the parking lot.

"Who's taking care of him?"

"Doc is seeing to it. A couple of them wanted to, but Doc pulled the enforcer card," Hawk says, shaking his head and falling into line with me.

"Good. Put out the word I don't want him back in our area until I say otherwise. Call Mason and get him in the loop. I'll call King."

"You think he was lying?"

"What the fuck do you think?" I cock an eyebrow at him.

"I think what he said was shit, but the other stuff? I don't know. I don't know Mac, not really. Does this seem like something she'd do? Hook up with someone who had a woman?"

I want to say no. I want to deny she'd ever put herself in that kind of situation, but I can't. She seems like the same girl I knew before, but ten years is a long time. The reality is, I don't know who she is anymore, no matter how much I want to refute it.

"I don't know," I say when we reach my door.

"Ryker, whatever happened . . ." Hawk peers off toward headquarters, where a cursing Maddox is being stuffed in the back of a car.

"I'll figure it out."

"Not what I was going to say. Don't push her. I know you wanna know what happened, have her trust you, but bullying her into it will only push her away more."

"When did you turn into a fucking therapist?" I snap, mostly because he's right, even if I don't want to admit it.

Hawk meets my gaze, brows pulled low.

"Don't fuck it up."

I watch as he walks back to headquarters to get their asses back inside. The rain has stopped, but my entire front yard is a mud pit, just like the parking lot. Slipping inside, I realize my boots are filled with water. I strip, leaving me in only my boxer briefs before gathering up my sopping clothes to throw in the laundry room to deal with them later. A soft yelp has my head snapping to the top of the stairs, and Kenzie's hazel eyes widen, fixed on my bare chest. I clear my throat, and her eyes skip to my face.

"Sorry," she whispers, swinging around.

"Nothing you haven't seen before, Kenz," I say with a laugh.

"You're naked." Her voice quivers in either pain or embarrassment.

"If you think this is naked, we might have to revisit Sex Ed, baby."

She swings back around, glaring as she purses her lips. Her chest above her tank top is flushed, but it disappears under the bruises still covering her neck, and I hold back a wince. Every time I see them, pain stabs my chest, knowing I couldn't prevent her from going through that suffering.

"Saying you did a poor job at educating me, Helms?" Kenzie plants her fist on her hips, and I wince again.

"We're not talking about that," I growl, stomping to the laundry room off the kitchen.

I hope she'll go back to bed, but moments later, her bare feet slap on the stairs as she rushes after me. I pull on a T-shirt and sweatpants before stuffing the wet clothes in the machine.

"What, I didn't give you enough time to get over it?" she huffs.

Taking a deep breath, I close my eyes, bracing my hands on the washer. I want to believe she'll wander away if I pretend she isn't there, but it never was her way. I spin to face her, leaning back and crossing my arms as I eye her. Bruises encircle her neck, like someone had their hands wrapped around her throat. Red rings circle her wrists, and Ink said something about a boot print on her ribs. Kenzie glances away as I study her, and her shoulders slump, the fight from minutes ago ebbing away.

"Maddox was here."

She whips back to me, grimacing at the move. Her hands are trembling now.

"Was?"

"Threw his ass out."

"Why?" she asks, shoving her hands under her arms.

I sigh, turning back to finish starting my laundry. "I don't tolerate lying."

"What'd he say?"

"Doesn't matter. You ready to tell me what type of shit you're in? Or are we still pretending you can handle it on your own?"

The washer starts up, filling the small space with a thumping noise, reminding me I need a new one.

Mac is quiet for so long I turn back to see if she slipped away, but she's still here, staring at my bare feet. A tear falls when I open my mouth again, leaving a spot on her shirt. Shocked, I stare at the wetness. She's not a crier, never was. For some reason, she got it in her head that we wouldn't let her run with us if she did. I suspect it had something to do with Maddox. When another one falls, I pull her in my arms and cup the back of her head. A strangled sob escapes her, and she's clinging to the back of my shirt, nails digging in. Her body shudders, gripping me tighter, and I hold her, whispering into her hair, praying she'll finally let me in.

SIX

MacKenzie

For the third day in a row, I wake up not knowing where I am. My eyes are gritty from losing my shit last night, and I groan when I remember how I broke down. I couldn't hold the tears in anymore. Ryker kept asking questions, and it was just too much. My life is falling apart around me, and I can't find my way out. I thought I would come here, stay awhile, heal. Then I'd run again. I thought Ryker could access my money and smuggle me out. It was a dumb plan, though. Of course he'd ask questions. Of course he'd want to know what happened. Of course he'd be a stubborn ass about it. He doesn't know how to be any other way.

Another groan leaves me when I sit up and swing my legs over the side of the bed. I'm alone again, but the same chair sits next to me, a blanket draped over the back. A stabbing pain hits me, and I press on my ovary, doing math in my head. I'm still trying to figure out what day it is when the door squeaks open, revealing Ryker, fully clothed. Thank god.

"What the hell are you doing? Get back in bed."

I roll my eyes—both of which I can finally see out of now—and heft myself up. A sharp pain shoots through me, but it hits me: I haven't peed in god knows how long. As I shuffle toward the bathroom, my muscles protest when he scoops me up, making my stomach roll.

"Oh god, put me down," I force out between my fingers.

"No."

I swear, if I throw up on him, it's his own damn fault. I close my eyes to stop the room from spinning and jolt when he leans to put me on my feet. I stumble, but he grips my hips, making me yelp.

"I'm fine," I say breathlessly when he lurches back.

"Shit, Kenz. We've got to get you to the hospital."

I glare over my shoulder. "I'm not going to the hospital. You're ridiculous. Now, get out so I can pee."

His eyes focus on my stomach, where a strip of skin is showing. I yank it down, scowling. I'd think he was checking me out, but he's probably focused on the bruises. He shakes his head and backs away, closing the door behind him.

I do my business, barely making it off the toilet without crashing to the ground. I wash my hands as Ryker hammers on the door. The bruises on my face are fading. Actually, they're morphing into splotches of greens and blues. Dropping my head, I pull deep breaths into my lungs, trying to yank myself out of the pit I've landed in. No use reliving what happened, but with Maddox showing up, demanding to see me, to take me home, I realize I need to tell Ryker everything. I splash water on my face, while Ryker continues to pound on the door. With a snarl on his lips and concern in his eyes, he busts in as I'm drying off.

"If I wanted you to help, I'd have asked," I state calmly.

"MacKenzie . . ." he warns, nostrils flaring.

"I'm hungry. Feed me." I plant my fists on my hips, but hit a sore spot and end up rubbing it instead.

"Fine, but then you're going to . . ."

"As much as I appreciate you letting me stay here, you're not going to boss me around, Ryker."

"Oh, yes I am. Ink is coming by in an hour, and you're going to let him look you over. If you're not going to take care of yourself, then I'll do it for you," he says, striding forward and scooping me up again.

"I can walk you know," I say, burrowing my head in the crook of his neck.

It's not often I have someone tall enough for me to do this with. Not that I have much opportunity to find out, even if they are. The fact I've been fantasizing about this exact scenario since I left Synd with Dante a couple weeks ago doesn't escape me.

"You'll take too long, and I'm starving."

Ryker takes the stairs almost sideways, careful not to jostle me, then sets me down on the couch. He's staring again, but I can't figure out what he's fixated on this time. He shakes his head and stomps from the room, muttering to himself.

"I can eat in the kitchen!" I yell.

I run my hand over the pillow next to me. It's like I've fallen into the past as I glance around, spotting the differences between then and now. Gone are the hideous curtains and off-white walls, replaced with bright blue fabric and light gray paint. The mantle above the fireplace used to hold random bullets from whatever bullshit Dain, Ryker's dad, thought needed remembering.

Now frames hold smiling people. It's cozy . . . and weird. When Dain ran the Reapers, he was so absorbed with the club he hardly paid attention to us kids, unless we got in his way. I don't know if it would have made a difference if our mothers stuck around or not. One day, my mother was here, effectively ignoring me, then she was gone. Dad never did tell us why, and we eventually stopped asking. Most of the others around here wanted nothing to do with us, either. We were too wild, too mischievous, and our fathers too high up in command to take the risk to discipline.

"Here." Ryker hands me a bowl, sitting in the farthest seat from me in a chair. Expecting pasta or chicken, I blanch at the bowl of soup.

"Um, why did you give me soup?"

I am not a soup person. The last thing I want or need is to slurp down this watery broth and be hungry in an hour.

"It's good for you. You haven't eaten, and I'm not going to clean up your puke when you upchuck all over my rug," he says before devouring his fried chicken.

The deep aroma fills the room, and my stomach gurgles. I swear I can taste the spices in the air, making my mouth water. I'm caught between demanding some and crying. I try not to, but I can't help the whimper. Ryker whips his head up and scowls when he notices I'm staring at his food.

"For fuck's sake, Kenz, don't give me that look. Just eat your damn soup." He turns his body slightly, trying to hide the chicken from view, but he's glancing at me out of the corner of his eye.

"Please?"

He tips his head back, like he's praying for patience to deal with my whiny ass before setting his half-eaten plate on the coffee table and stomping back to the kitchen. I'm tempted to sneak a few bites from his plate, but I'm not agile enough right now to get away with it. Sniffing the broth, I almost gag. Rosemary. I hate rosemary. Why anyone puts it in food is beyond me. It's a worthless herb. Its scent is overpowering, and it's crunchy, no matter how it's cooked. It makes all the other flavors taste like a fucking flower. Gross.

"Give me that." He snatches the bowl back, soup splashing on his hands, before setting it down and plopping a new plate on my lap.

"Thank you." I smile, grabbing a leg and debating on whether I could stick the whole thing in my mouth and just spit the bones out when I'm done, but his hand circles my wrist lightly, stopping me.

"Do not put the whole thing in your mouth. If you insist on eating it, fine, but you'll make yourself sick if you don't take it slow," he grumbles, waiting for me to nod before letting go.

Nibbling at the fried goodness, I force back the moan when the taste hits my tongue. I can't help my eyes falling closed or the sigh that follows. I stuff a fry into my mouth before I look up and find Ryker's eyes on me, his chicken laying forgotten on his lap.

"What?"

"Don't do that" is all he says before going back to eating.

I have no idea what he's talking about. We eat in silence, me pacing myself, Ryker pulling out his phone every two minutes. I'm too absorbed with the chicken to ask, though. He won't tell me who it is if I *did* ask. I'm licking my fingers when he gathers our plates and walks out again. I lay back, sucking in a breath when my muscles pull and twist. I barely ate anything, but, of course, Ryker was right.

My stomach is cramping, and I close my eyes, hoping the nausea will pass. The last thing I need is to puke all over the lovely blue rug—or god forbid—the couch. It's suede. Lord knows he'll never get the stain out. Then again, perhaps the constant reminder of my visit would be good for him. Ryker seemed content to ignore me for years, so who knows how long he'll go when I leave this time.

"I told you not to eat the damn chicken," he grumbles, his shadow falling over me, blocking the shallow light through my closed lids.

I refuse to open them. He'll want to talk. He'll badger me to tell him what happened. He'll scold me for being stupid, for getting myself in to this. Fucking Maddox.

"Go away. I'm sleeping," I mutter.

I can practically hear his eyes rolling.

"You can't avoid this conversation forever, MacKenzie."

"Why don't you ever call me Mac?"

I've always wondered but never had the nerve to ask. Ever since we were young, while everyone else called me Mac, he always called me Kenz or Kenzie, unless he was mad at me—that's when my full name would come out. Laying here, eyes shut tight, it's like I'm having a conversation with a dream instead of the real man.

"Mac is a stupid name," he grunts.

"You never were a good liar, Ryker. You should work on that." I smile.

He sighs, arms sliding under my knees and shoulders. This should feel weird. Me, cocooned in his embrace, should be a strange event, but for the first time in a long time, I feel safe. Back up the stairs, down the hall, and eventually in his room, I hide behind my lids the whole time, not wanting to burst this bubble of safety. It'll pop soon enough. Maddox won't be gone long, or he'll tell them . . . My eyes fly open, body locking up. The need to run, to hide, to flee as far away as possible floods my mind, overriding any previous feelings of contentment.

"Kenz? What is it? Where does it hurt?"

Instead of putting me on the bed, he turns and sinks down with me on his lap. The tremors come back to my hands, and I stare at them. I can't feel my hands. I didn't know they were shaking. I try to turn my head, but it's stuck, ticking like a broken clock on my neck. Ryker's hands run up my arms, and I flinch, not from pain but because they conjure the sensation of fire. His fingers ghost down my back, leaving licks of flames in their wake. Is this a panic attack? I don't know, and I'm sent into another spiral, worrying about the tightness in my chest, my rapidly beating heart, the lightheaded feeling invading in my brain. Pulling in a gasp, I close my eyes, but it doesn't help. Ryker's frantic voice filters through, but it's like he's in a tunnel, too far away. A pillow of softness envelops me. Usually, I would love the feeling of floating on a cloud, but I jerk, knowing I'm falling. I can't go back. I can't stay. I can't . . .

"Kenzie!" Ryker howls, his hands closing in on my face.

The biting pain of his grip on my bruises snaps me back, and my eyes fly open, flitting everywhere, until he leans in, and he's all I can see. The darkness hovers in the corners of my eyes, threatening to pull me back into its embrace. Refusing to acknowledge it, I focus on the deep pits of blue before me. I'd be content to swim in those depths forever. They're almost sapphire, with flecks of green speckled throughout. I'll survive if I concentrate on his unblinking eyes, no matter if they're filled with fire and sarcasm or concern and guilt. My breathing calms the further I fall into his eyes. It's broken when he blinks, dark lashes fanning across his cheekbones. He fixes his gaze on me again, and I see it finally. My lip ticks up, and my body loses the last of tension. My shoulders relax, I suck in a full breath, and my chest brushes his.

"Hi," I say sheepishly, unwilling to break our connection.

"Hi," he whispers back. "Are you"—he clears his throat—"are you okay?"

"Sorry. I kind of freaked out for a minute."

"Is that what happened last night?" His brows pull down, and two divots appear. My finger traces them, trying to smooth them out.

"I don't know," I answer when he sucks in a breath.

"Kenzie . . ."

A knock at the door has him flinching back. My hand falls to my side, the moment broken. I swear I'm going crazy. The constant push and pull between a full-on freak out and tranquility and hiding behind sarcasm is taking its toll on me. I can't keep up with it much longer before I shatter, with no hope of being put back together.

Ryker is at the door, talking to someone through a crack. I'm not even curious who it is anymore. I'm losing parts of myself I don't know if I'll ever find again. The decision to stay or go has to be made now. I ran to Ryker for a reason; I need to trust the scared woman who fled in the first place. She decided he was the safest option, and I have to trust her. She knew what I needed when I didn't.

"Ryker," I croak as he murmurs through the door. "Ryker."

"Hold on," he says to whoever is there before striding back. "What do you need? What's wrong?"

"I need to tell you . . ." I suck in a gasp, and a tear slips out, gathering in my hair.

"Okay, Kenz. I got you," he murmurs, resting his forehead on mine.

I never know which version of him I'll find when I open my eyes, but I'm always hoping for this one.

"Maddox."

Ryker rears back, studying my face, jaw clenching. "He did this?"

"No. Yes. Sort of. Dante was gone. Maddox took over. He . . . he . . ." I gasp again, trying to fight the fear and shadows.

Images flash behind my lids, blood and fists and threats.

"I'll kill him," he declares, lethal venom threading his words.

"He gave me away."

Calloused hands scraping my scalp, burrowing into my hair. An insane giggle bubbles up my throat when I think about how greasy my hair must be, matted and snarled. I swallow the bubble back at the last second, and it burns its way back down, then settles into my stomach like a rock.

"I don't know what that means," he says, resting his lips on my forehead. "Tell me what you mean."

"Another MC moved in last year. They're . . . wild, vicious. Dante's been trying to force them out, but they're like a cancer, infiltrating a new area as soon as we oust them from one. They want our territory. Dante refused. Maddox, though, he doesn't have the wits to fight them; doesn't think we should. He proposed a truce as soon as Dante left. When he didn't come back, Maddox settled with them, said they should pick something else, anything else."

I hold the air in my lungs until it burns, my brain screaming for breath, but still, I wait, knowing what comes next.

"They picked me."

The tears fall in earnest. I couldn't stop them if I wanted to. My heart shatters as my hands tremble again, but I tuck them under my arms, ignoring the ache in my chest.

Ryker lets out a string of curses. "He gave you away? You mean he sold you, for a truce that will never last. And after?"

"Maddox grabbed me from my room, dumped me in an alley, and they picked me up. It was . . . brutal. I can't . . ."

"Fuck, Kenz. I don't want to ask, but the more I know, the better I can protect you."

"At first, it wasn't that bad," I whisper, the scenes still playing in my head.

"You've got to be fucking kidding me."

Meeting his tormented gaze, I shake my head. "I was in the basement for a while. There's a room down there. It's wet and dark, but no one touched me. I don't know how long, but my eyes about seared out of my skull when they let me out."

"And then?" He grimaces, the tightness around his eyes giving away how hard this is for him.

I swipe at the wetness gathering on my chin. "There was a lot of pain."

I don't want to give him more details. His face has already darkened, giving away how close to the edge he is. I won't tell him about the shackles they snapped around my ankles and wrists or the metal collar that dug into my neck. I won't tell him how they threatened to brand me, waving a red-hot rod in my face. I can't tell him how they egged each other on when they would beat me, but never enough so I couldn't function. They didn't want me broken beyond repair but just bruised enough to be forced to stay. I didn't even see him until the last night I was there.

"I should have paid more attention. I could have learned more about their plans."

"Stop. Kenzie, just . . . don't. How long?"

"I think a week." I wait until he no longer looks like he's going to punch something. He paces across the floor, fists clenching, before he settles in front of me again. "I didn't see their president until the night I ran. I don't know where he was."

Sucking in a shuddering breath, I'm not sure what else to tell him. I don't want to relive the memories, the pain. My nerves are already frayed with the little I've told him.

"I don't want to ask this, Kenz, but I need to know how much they need to suffer."

I stare blankly at the wall. I know what he's asking, but I don't know how to explain it all. There's only so much I can handle before I shatter.

"They talked about"—I tip my head back, wishing the words would appear on the ceiling—"taking me. They were . . . handsy. But they were waiting for *him*. When he showed up, he told them they could fight over the scraps."

His entire body seems to be vibrating, and I lean away. "Did he?"

"He left before he could," I whisper. He falls to his knees, pressing his lips to my forehead. "He got a call. Something went down, but I think I passed out. When I woke up, most of the room had cleared. They didn't chain me back up, and I didn't think I'd get another chance . . ."

"So, you ran." Ryker finishes when I can't. I nod, and he doesn't meet my eyes, leaving the imprint of his lips on my skin as he pulls back.

He paces away, and a spike of anxiety shoots through me. He's contemplating the implications of what my story has on his own MC. He's wondering if I'm telling the truth. He's pissed I came to him. Each thought pierces me, but I fight against them all. He isn't Maddox. He isn't my father. He's Ryker, and he always believed me. I can't fall prey to my own self-doubt. Struggling back, I lean against the headboard and watch the muscles in his back bunch and roll. Ryker shakes out his hands, curling them into fists, and I catch the tremble in them before they flex again.

"What do you want me to do, Kenz?"

His question catches me off guard, and I thump my head against the wood. I don't know how to answer. I don't know what he wants from me. I needed a safe space, but I never expected more. Hell, I didn't even know if I'd find safety here. I'm still struggling to form a sentence, to force any words out, when he swings back. The intensity on his face is almost feral. I don't know this man before me. Ryker is always collected, in control of his emotions. It's the only way he was able to survive taking over the Reapers at nineteen.

"I don't know," I whisper.

"Well, you're going to have to figure it out because, if you don't, I'm liable to burn them all to the ground."

SEVEN

Ryker

"Where is she?" Hawk asks as soon as he steps in the kitchen the next morning. I don't bother looking up. After the bomb Kenzie dropped on me, I can't think straight. I knew whatever happened was bad, but this is too much to process, even for me.

"Upstairs with Ink. She's refusing to go to the hospital. Hopefully, he can talk some sense into her," I say, shoving another mug under the machine and starting it.

"Think she had a run-in with some dirty cops? They're rampant in Rima."

"No, she didn't," I grunt, still avoiding his eyes.

"Shit, she tell you what happened?"

Hawk's questions are making my skin itch. Kenzie told me I could share her story, but she was hesitant with anyone other than him. I don't know if it's because she doesn't expect to be here long or she's embarrassed. She has nothing to be ashamed of, but it'll be awhile before she believes me.

"Yeah. She told me." I fix my eyes on the coffee streaming into the cup.

"Is she okay?" he murmurs, glancing up the stairs.

"What have you heard about the Night Slayers?"

"Who the fuck are they?"

"They're the ones who beat the shit out of her," I bite out, not trusting my voice to be steady.

"What a shitty name. Is it another MC? Retaliation?"

I tip my head back. "Rival in Rima, apparently. It wasn't retaliation. She was a truce gift."

"I didn't know clubs were doing that still."

My eyes snap back to him. "Fuck. Do other clubs do this shit?"

"Oh, yeah. I ran into a couple of them before I came here. They trade the women back and forth, usually based on who won the latest territory war. It's like they keep score with how many women they've gathered. Obviously, they do it without consent. It's disgusting. I thought most did away with the practice, but I'm sure they're still out there," Hawk murmurs.

I never asked him about his life before coming to Synd, and he never offered, but I gather it wasn't a fun time. When I asked him to be VP, he disappeared for two days, holing up in his house. I thought he'd turn the position down when he emerged, but when he came to the next meeting, he accepted. I never mentioned his disappearance, and neither did he.

"Did they"—he clears his throat—"you know."

With rage bleeding through me, I shake my head. "No, but they planned on it."

"Some of them would bid on the virgins." He flushes. "Not that she'd be in . . . uh . . . that kind of situation."

"Oh, are we talking about my deflowering?" Kenzie's voice floats in from the bottom of the stairs. Hawk winces, hanging his head. I can't stop the smirk pulling at my lips. He's clearly terrified of her.

"'Course not. Hawk would never be so crude, would you?"

He glares at me before shuffling around and muttering an apology to her. He tries to sneak around her to bolt out the door, but she blocks his way.

"You should stay for this. I promise I won't make you blush again." She smiles, and his cheeks redden.

"I don't fucking blush," he grumbles.

"Sure you don't." She pats his shoulder as she sweeps in the room. She's moving easier at least, but her movements are still jerky. I wave to Ink as he slips out the front door.

"What'd Ink say?" I ask, scanning her body again, trying to assess if she's okay.

I'm no fucking doctor, but I swear a couple of ribs are broken. She's favoring her left side more.

"Why do you call him Ink instead of Doc? And why the hell is Doc called Doc? It makes no sense. Or is that the point?" Kenzie grabs the mug right out of my hand and takes it to the table.

Sighing, I grab the other coffee, still sitting by the machine, to start another for Hawk. We won't get through this conversation without a shit ton of caffeine and possibly food. I move to the fridge and take out the leftover chicken to heat up. The last thing I need is for her to starve to death or get hangry with me.

"Ink has a lot of tattoos," Hawk says, filling the seat across from her.

She rolls her eyes. "This is a motorcycle club. Everyone has a lot of tattoos."

"Yeah, well, he's got more than most, I guess. Doc was a therapist before he joined, but whoever he was working for let him go."

"But he's so nice!" Kenzie cries, then winces, pressing on her side.

Eyeing her, I wait, but she wraps her hand back around her mug. I slide the plate in front of her, and her eyes bug out, glancing from me to the plate.

"Thanks," she whispers.

Nodding, I gather mine and Hawk's. "Not our story to tell, Kenz."

"So, why they call you Hawk, then? Were you a bird in another life?" She grins around a mouthful of chicken.

Hawk ducks, shoveling food in his mouth to avoid answering.

"Eat, MacKenzie," I snap, and her eyes track from me to him and back again.

"Oh-kay," she mutters. As the minutes pass she sneaks glances at Hawk, opening and closing her mouth every once in a while, but always returning to her food. "So, I figured out the answer to your question, Ryker."

"And?" I grunt.

"Obviously, I need a place to hide out until I'm healed a little more. I was also hoping you could help access my money."

Watching her, I can't tell where the hell she's going with this. There's no reason she'd need money here. So, what's her plan? Then it hits me, and my nostrils flare.

"No."

After snatching the plate from her, I stack it on my own and swipe Hawk's as well, despite his protest. I toss the bones and then rinse the plates before loading the dishwasher. I need something with clear steps—an end goal—to stop myself from losing my shit. Cleaning the kitchen is the only thing I can think of doing while still keeping an eye on her.

"What do you mean 'no'? It's my money. I can't get it. I need it, so help me pull it out."

"No."

Hawk raises his hand, like we're in fucking school. I'm half expecting Kenzie to call on him, but she glares instead.

"You wanted to know what I needed. This is what I need."

"No."

"Uh, why do you need money, Mac? We can get whatever you need," Hawk states.

"Because she's going to run again. Only, this time, she won't be running to us," I explain, glowering.

"You mean the Reapers can buy me shit. Then I'll owe them more than I already do." She turns to me. "And how the hell do you think this is going to go, huh? You think I came here, and the Slayers will just forget I exist? Maddox was here, trying to round me up and deliver me back. At what point do you think they'll stop? I'm not bringing the Reapers into this. It's not fair to them or you."

Hawk gapes and then swings his gaze to me, but I'm fixated on Kenzie. A decade apart, and it's like no time passed at all. She's still stubborn, trying to solve all her problems alone. Ten. Fucking. Years. And she's still the only one who can get under my skin, make me lose my goddamn mind, and send me over the edge with only a few words. I thought time would have changed us so I wouldn't understand her anymore. I wouldn't look at her and know exactly what she's thinking. I don't know what to do with Kenzie. I never knew what to do with her. I can't help but wonder what would have happened if Raymond wouldn't have dragged his kids to Rima, leaving me to deal with this bullshit alone.

"Kenz," I murmur, waiting until she looks at me, "there's nowhere you can run. There's no place far enough, especially in your condition. It doesn't matter if you wait a day or a week or a month. They'll still find you. You'll be in the exact same place, only I won't be there to save you."

MacKenzie's eyes well up with tears, and she tips her head back, trying to stop them, but they fall anyway. Hawk is silent, staring at the table. Ren's voice echoes in my head, telling me not to push her, to give her the space she needs. My stomach rolls, and I cross my arms, if only to stop the tremor in my hands. Patience never was my strong suit, but for her . . . for her, I'll do anything.

"Okay," she whispers, staring at the ceiling.

"MacKenzie."

"I know. I won't, but if shit goes sideways, remember this moment, Ryker. Remember I tried to keep you out of my problems as much as I could," she spits out, hazel eyes burning with accusation when her gaze meets mine.

Hawk clears his throat. "So, what are we going to do?"

"I don't know yet, but your number one job, Hawk, is keeping that piece of shit out of our area. Did you call Mason?" I ask.

"Yeah, he said he'll do what he can. He's got a lot of bullshit to clean up from Victor taking over and being in a coma for so long. You okay with me giving him the short version, Mac? It'll be better to have allies if they do come here."

She nods, eyes unfocused but no longer wet. She looks exhausted and still battered as hell.

"Go to bed, Kenzie. We'll figure some shit out while you sleep," I say.

"You'll tell me, right?"

The vulnerability in her tone almost breaks me. My Kenzie is fire, confidence, no nonsense. What these fuckers did was more than break down her body. They broke her spirit, made her question who she is, what she's capable of. I hope she can find herself again, before she's lost for good. I hope I can find a way to bring back the spitfire she's always been.

"Of course. It's your life. We're going to have to talk about what to do with Maddox soon. Dante . . . we'll have to figure out what to do about him, too." I sigh.

Nodding, she shuffles toward the stairs and pauses when she reaches the archway. I jolt, intent on carrying her up to bed if need be when her head swings to the side.

"Thanks."

Before I can respond, she walks away, and I look to Hawk, his concerned gaze tracking her up the stairs.

"Spread the word. I don't want anyone getting ambushed because we kept this to ourselves."

"How much you want me to tell them? Members are asking questions, even more after you put Maddox Raines into a wall and then threw his ass out. I've shot down rumors of a spurned lover and put my fist into three stomachs. I don't want to spend a bunch of time chasing down rumors, but I'm not going to overstep and spout off what happened."

"Tell them we're returning a favor. It's not like they've forgotten what happened two months ago. If anyone has a problem with it, send them my way."

"We should call a meeting. We need to loop Doc in, too. He'll need more than the others, so he can help shut shit down."

I nod. "Do that first. Ink clearly knows, but he'll keep his mouth shut. Then, call Mason and set up a time for a meeting. I'm calling the Kings."

"You think she'd be better off there?" he asks, making me scowl.

"Fuck that. She stays here. Don't even fucking put that shit out there. I'm not getting in a fight with Samantha Byrns over MacKenzie. She came here, we'll take care of her. I'm not going to pass her off like an unruly puppy," I spit out.

He grins. "Good."

Fucker set me up, and I walked right into it. I walk away, saying over my shoulder, "Get the fuck out."

EIGHT

MacKenzie

When I wake up this time, the fuzziness is gone from my brain, and I burrow further under the covers. In the middle of stretching, I freeze when my skin pulls, leaving an ache behind. I'm on my side, facing the still empty chair. I didn't realize how much I hoped Ryker would be here when I woke until the disappointment crashes through me, sucking the breath from my lungs. Wiggling back, I duck under the comforter, but I bump against something behind me. I glance over my shoulder, thinking I'll find a rogue pillow and find Ryker, who is spread out on top of the covers, one arm tucked behind his head, the other cupping his crotch, of course, fast asleep. Swallowing a laugh, I try not to wake him. Even deep in slumber, his cheekbones are severe, brows pulled low, like his dreams are as distressing as his waking life has been lately.

I wait for the panic, the regret, the pain to overwhelm me, but it doesn't come. Revealing all I did earlier locked up the fear I'd been carrying all the way from Rima. I didn't anticipate feeling relief once I told him. The fact I ever doubted whether he'd help me or not makes me want to brain myself in the head. Ryker was always that way. Somehow, he sees every angle, all the pitfalls and the solutions. He did it when we were kids. Apparently, he hasn't changed much.

I expected things to be different. For some reason, it's more jarring we fell right back in to the easy rhythm between us. Staring at him now, seeing his rugged face that's changed but hasn't all at the same time, I feel seventeen again. I woke alone then. Light wasn't streaming through the curtains, ruffling in the slight breeze. He slipped out then, leaving me to deal with the aftermath of my decisions alone. I thought our relationship wouldn't change after, but it did—he changed. Everything is new yet not, and I don't know how to reconcile the Ryker I knew and the man lying next to me.

Shimmying off the bed, I'm careful not to jostle him. I just need a little time alone to come to terms with my life falling apart around me. Maddox's hatred for me was such a gradual process I didn't notice the rift until it was too late. I miss the smiling, freckled seven-year-old he used to be. We used to be inseparable, which is to be expected with him, only being three months older than me. I wish I knew the point where he went left and I went right. I wonder what the fork in the road was that he thought was so monumental I needed to be despised. I shake my head when I make it to the bathroom. No use trying to find something that might not be there in the first place. I'll probably never get the answers I want. I can't ask Maddox why he hates me so much to sell me. There's no justification he could hand me that would warrant his actions and grant him my forgiveness.

The shower is calling my name. The dirt covering my body coating me like a second layer. Now that I'm aware of it, my skin itches. Splashing my face with water is all well and good, but it doesn't replace a full shower. I'm digging in the vanity, trying to find towels, when Ryker bellows from the bedroom and then bursts in.

"Well, it's a good thing I wasn't on the toilet, huh?" I say and smirk over my shoulder before going back to my search.

"What the hell are you doing?" he demands, breathing hard.

"Looking for a towel that will actually cover my body," I say, holding one up and spinning to him. "Seriously? What is this for? It's too big to be a hand towel and way too freaking small for a bath towel. Explain."

He runs his fingers through his dark hair, mussing it up more. He looks me up and down before sighing. "I may have had an issue with the washing machine at some point. I wasn't about to throw out a perfectly good towel because it's a little weird."

"An issue?" I raise an eyebrow at him. "As in, you shrunk it?"

"I didn't shrink it; the washing machine did." He glares at the fabric dangling from my fingertips.

"Oh, sure, the washing machine did it. And what did you do with the washer after this incident?"

"I bought a new one, obviously. The old one was defective." A blush stains his cheeks, and he glances away.

"Of course you did. It couldn't be that you messed up and did something wrong. The washer must have been defective," I choke out, trying to hold in my laughter.

"Shut up," he mutters, stepping around me to grab a normal one, then shoves it in my arms. He opens another cupboard and steps back, revealing a range of shampoos, conditioners, and a women's razor still in the package.

"What's all this?"

"You wanted shit. I got you shit," he says gruffly before stomping out the door.

Mouth hanging open, I stand there as he stomps back in. He yanks open the vanity under the sink and grabs a package. I expect him to run away again, like the hounds of hell are on him, but he pulls open the shower door. He drops to his knees and starts messing with something. I blanch when he stands up after installing flower grips on the tiles.

"Did you buy those so I wouldn't slip in the shower?" I whisper, not trusting my voice.

"Last thing you need is more bruises, Kenzie. I'll be in the bedroom if . . . I'll be there." He points to the door.

I swear it takes me ten minutes to finally move. I don't know what to do with all the emotions he's dredged up, so I shove them aside, concentrating on not falling on my ass, even with the grips securely in place. When the water hits me, though, I yelp, then curse. The last thing I need is Ryker busting in again.

"I'm fine! Water was just hot!" I yell. Peeking at the door, I stare at the knob as it gradually spins back.

All the wounds covering my body prevent me from taking a normal shower. The water is lukewarm at best, but it still stings when the spray hits my skin. I brush a finger across the cut on my hip. Ink said I didn't need stitches, but the wound sends prickles of pain down my leg. I wash it the best I can. Since I'm not a doctor, I have no idea if it's healing well or not.

Tipping my head back, I let the water soak my head, but as soon as my fingers brush my scalp, pain radiates through my skull. Tears fill my eyes, and I let the water wash them away, along with the burning ache in my chest. At some point, it has to get better. I contemplate if I can get away with not washing my hair. Looking at the brown water flow down the drain, I realize that's not an option. I'll feel better if I can wash away the memories of his hands gripping my hair, dragging me across the floor by the strands. The bruises will fade, my head will heal, but I won't ever forget the terror.

It takes me three times as long as it usually does, and I sit under the spray when I'm done. I could hide in here, pretend my problems aren't waiting on the other side of the door—no people coming after me, no brother who hates me. The door bursts open, cutting my pity party short, but it's not Ryker standing there.

"We have the same fucking parts, Helms. She's not going to give two shits if I crash her shower party," Sam yells over her shoulder and kicks the door shut behind her, clicking the lock while he pounds on the wood.

"Hey, Mac." She grins as she leans against the door. She opens her mouth, but there's more bellowing from the other side, and she slams her foot back, making the door rattle.

I can't help but smirk, shouting, "Knock it off. Ryker! You're going to break the door like you broke the washer!" The pounding stops, and he grunts and stomps away.

"He broke the washing machine?"

Before reaching for a towel, I turn off the water. It'll hurt too much to dry my hair, so I pat it dry. Goosebumps erupt on my skin when I step out.

"He thought he did, but it was user error."

"Oh my god, tell me he just went out and bought a new one instead of admitting it was his fault." Sam's eyes twinkle.

"Of course. Although, with him, it was a toss-up between that or breaking the whole thing down because he could 'fix it himself,'" I say, picking up the pants I've been wearing for almost a week. Unable to stomach putting my underwear back on, I don't bother with them.

"Oh! Hold on, I got you shit," she exclaims, slipping out the door and back in before I can protest. She brings in a shit ton of bags, plopping them on the floor. Digging through them, she mutters to herself.

"Sam, I appreciate this, but none of your clothes are going to fit me."

It was funny when Hawk gave me her clothes, since he wouldn't know any better, but the embarrassment of explaining to Sam is somehow worse.

"Duh, you're fucking goddess height. Plus, you have tits and an ass. These are definitely not my clothes," she mutters.

"Not a goddess, but thanks. Wait, please don't tell me you went out and bought me clothes," I moan. I press my hands to my flushed cheeks gently.

"Uh, no. I don't buy my own clothes nowadays. I leave the shopping to Ren. He bought you this shit," she explains before cawing out in triumph, waving a fistful of thongs in the air.

I recoil from the fabric dangling from her fingers. "Ren bought me those?"

"Oh, don't worry, he won't imagine you in them or anything." She grins. "Ren barely registers other people. Half the time, I think he forgets about Shane and Alex until they're bugging him. Thankfully, I don't count as other people."

"Well, tell him thank you. Let me know how much it is, and I'll . . ."

I'm not sure how to finish. I don't have any money and no way of accessing what I do have. I wouldn't be surprised if Maddox somehow found a way in and took it all.

"Seriously, Mac, don't worry about it. You helped us, now we help you. That's how this whole friend thing works. I would tell you I hope they fit, but Ren's crazy accurate with this type of shit."

I expect her to leave, but instead, she hops on the counter, pulling out her phone from the black hoodie that's at least two sizes too large for her. I'm mostly dry, so I slip on the underwear, trying to keep the towel around me. I wouldn't care other than the fact I look like I got hit by a bus. Once they're on, I dig in the other bags, and the towel slowly slips. I peek at Sam, but she's absorbed in her phone, so I take a chance and shed everything, pawing through the fancy bags. Each one reveals a new outfit, and by the end, I'm gaping. I haven't picked anything to wear. I'm so overwhelmed. What the fuck.

"You going to put something on, or are we having a naked party? I'm cool either way, but it might freak Helms out, so maybe not. On second thought, let's totally have a naked party." She grins, but it falls from her face, and she tilts her head. "What's wrong?"

"This is too much. Where the hell did he get this shit? This is the only one with a tag still on it, and it's $1200! For a fucking dress!" I shake the skimpy strip of cloth, wondering if I could even squeeze into it.

Sam purses her lips and waves away my words. "I told you, Ren's got a thing. I told him you needed clothes, he said okay. Alex said he grabbed some of my shit, but go easy on him. His heart was in the right place. He clearly didn't even notice you're like a foot taller than me."

"But . . . but twelve hundred dollars! Sam! That's fucking insane," I cry, staring at the pile of designer clothes surrounding me in every color of the rainbow.

She winces. "Sorry. I think I'm the reason he went a little wild. I really only wear black, and I think it hurts his soul on a deeply personal level. Don't make him take them back. He wouldn't say anything, but it would hurt his feelings."

Head bobbing, I still gape at the clothes. I grab the least offensive thing, a blue shirt and some leggings. Shuddering, I ignore the bag of bras, imagining trying to put one on with all the bruises covering my body. Like the shower, it takes me much longer to pull the clothes on than normal. By the time I'm done, I'm sweating, which has me scowling at the deodorant and toothbrush in the cupboard. How Ryker knew what products I use is beyond me. I'm so annoyed by the whole thing, I'll never ask. Sam scoots over when I brush my teeth, who's still glued to her phone, but her head tips, a look of concern plastered on her face.

"You okay there? You're brushing . . . aggressively."

"I'm fine," I mumble around the brush.

"Great. Since I've got you here, I'm going to ask you this once very nicely because I promised Ryker I would and then we don't have to ever speak of it again, m'kay?" Sam smiles, the cheery voice at odds with the mania in her eyes. She waits until I nod.

"Awesome. Would you like to go see an actual doctor who wears a stethoscope and not a leather jacket?"

"I'd rather not," I say after I've rinsed and wiped my mouth.

"Okie dokie. You hungry? I figured we could go to this diner. They serve a fan-fucking-tastic breakfast. Hawk told me about it."

"Breakfast?" I ask, confusion flooding me.

It's the afternoon. I'm sure of it.

"Uhh, yeah. It's like nine in the morning," she says. She tips her phone, and it flashes 9:07 a.m.

Head spinning, I close my eyes, trying to stop the rolling in my stomach. I hold my breath and let it out gradually before my nerves settle.

"I'm fine. I didn't realize I slept all afternoon and night," I say, meeting her concerned gaze.

"I know I said I'd only ask you once, but are you sure you don't want to go to the hospital?"

"No. Other than feeling like I was in a tornado, I'm fine. There's a slice on my hip, but Ink said it should be fine. You look tired. Everything okay?"

"Oh, fine. Just normal shit. Plus, I was out late last night with Shane," she mumbles.

"Uh, I'm guessing it's not for spicy good times, then?"

"Unfortunately not. One of the warehouses in the south caught on fire. Probably electrical or something, but we were dealing with that until like five in the morning. Plus, the commissioner is pissing us all off. I'm sure it's nothing."

"You don't think someone did it on purpose?" I ask.

Her head pops up, eyes finding mine. She opens her mouth, worry lining her eyes when the pounding is back—Ryker telling us to hurry the fuck up. Swinging the door open, I meet his scowl with one of my own. His eyes scan the bathroom, taking in the destruction I made. His lips press into a thin line as he nods.

"Breakfast is ready," he says before marching away.

Sam slides next to me, and we watch him retreat. "We can still go to the diner. I swear their hash browns are to die for," she mutters from the corner of her mouth.

I sigh. "Ryker's a good cook. He used to make us breakfast when we were kids. Took him awhile to figure out bacon, but by the time he was fifteen, he'd perfected it. You'll like it. Promise."

After linking her arm with mine, we head to the kitchen. She stops me at the top of the stairs, clearing her throat before ducking.

"Helms told us what happened. I hope you don't mind, but if they come here, he wanted us to know what was going on. I know what you went through isn't the same as me, but the panic attacks get better. And the nightmares. At least, they have for me. Helps to have my guys there, but Ryker will help. I wanted you to know if you need me, I'm a phone call away or a text—or hell, just show up like the other night. We don't have to talk. You don't have to explain. As long as you understand you're not alone."

Breathing in deep to keep the tears at bay, I nod. I only have one friend who isn't even in the MC back home, which is isolating, especially with Maddox's constant digs. Sam doesn't understand how much her words mean to me. She tugs me down the stairs, and I follow, feeling better than I have in a long time.

NINE

Ryker

"**G**et the fuck out of my house, Alex. I'm not going bowling with you," I grumble, pushing him off me.

"Come on, Helmsy! It'll be fun!" He laughs as Shane snatches the back of his neck and hauls him toward the door.

"Just call. Don't worry about the time, 'kay?" Sam whispers to Kenzie, who nods.

It's only been a couple of hours since she woke up, but exhaustion is heavy in her eyes. The dark rings under them are more pronounced today, though she slept half the day, and all night. Hawk is sitting at the table, reading something on his laptop. As MacKenzie walks Sam to the front door, I slip in the seat next to him.

"Where'd the computer come from?" I ask, then stuff cold bacon in my mouth.

"Ren gave it to me. Said I'd be able to access the cameras on the perimeter of our territory. Might help if I can figure out how to set up an alert," he answers, eyes fixed on the screen.

"You can understand this stuff?" I glance over his shoulder, but the screen is a mess of code I don't understand.

"Yeah, this shit is a little much, but I think I can work with it."

"I didn't know you knew anything about this kind of thing."

He looks up at my tone, scowling. "I did do other shit before I came here. I learned some coding along the way. Obviously, it's been awhile since, though."

"Whatever," I mutter, pulling out my phone.

"What are you actually upset about? 'Cause I'm sure it's not my ability to code or the fact I had another life before the Reapers."

"I don't give two shits what you did before the Reapers," I say.

His gaze pierces me, but I refuse to meet it. He can sit there all fucking day for all I care.

"He's pissed because you had a life that has nothing to do with the club, but he never did. In short, he's jealous," MacKenzie says from behind me, and I scowl.

"Is that so?" Hawk's eyebrow twitches up.

"No, it's not. Now, get the fuck out," I snap, pushing myself up to grab the dirty dishes. I glare at MacKenzie when she tries to help and nudge her toward a chair.

"I can help. I'm not a complete invalid."

"Sit down. Hawk can help," I state, kicking his chair to get his ass moving. He smirks at Kenzie before getting the rest of the plates.

"I got the meeting scheduled. Gonna happen tomorrow—regular time. You want prospects there?" he asks as he fills the dishwasher.

"No, not for this."

"Didn't think so. I told Doc we'd let him know if you changed your mind. Anything else you need me to do beforehand?"

"Just meet with Mason."

Hawk glances at the clock and curses. "I gotta get going. I'm meeting him in twenty."

"Tell him to call me if he's got questions. Go easy on him."

He waves to MacKenzie on his way out before he slams the front door behind him, leaving me alone with her. My eyes are drawn back to her over and over while I keep cleaning the kitchen. The bruises have started to fade, but it only makes them more pronounced. I swear I can pick out the outline of knuckles, the imprints of fingers, the shadow of boot heels, and my breath catches.

The light blue shirt she's wearing doesn't help. The color makes her wounds stand out more, and the V-neck highlights the cuts on her chest. I don't want to ask how they got there. Unable to handle hearing the specifics, I force my gaze away again. Only one of us needs to be a mess right now.

Rinsing off another plate, I stare at my trembling hand in the water. Fury and guilt roll through my body, screaming for me to hunt them down and end them. I could do it. I could put her to bed, have Doc come and sit with her. I could ride all the way to Rima and kill them. I'd be back before she realizes I'm gone. I can't, though, because the sliver of a chance they'd take me out is too much. Kenzie would lose it completely if I died trying to avenge her. She'd bring me back from the dead just to ream my ass out for pulling a stunt like that.

"I think the plate is clean," she calls, and I snap back to the present, smacking the handle to turn the water off.

"You should go take a nap," I say, without turning around.

"I'm not tired."

I snort. "Sure you're not. Except you were falling asleep in your eggs not five minutes ago. But you're not tired."

"I want to know what you're planning."

"Who says I'm planning anything?" I peek over my shoulder, and she rolls her eyes.

"'Cause I'm not an idiot. You haven't changed *that* much, Ryker. You have something up your sleeve, some grand plan, and you don't want me involved, just like every other scheme you've cooked up over the years. So, how about we skip the bullshit, and you include me from the beginning for once?"

"Don't worry about it. I'll take care of things," I say, snapping the dishwasher closed and starting it. Unfortunately, the kitchen is clean, so I have nothing else to distract me.

"For fuck's sake, Ryker! Is it really that hard to tell me? To let me decide what happens?"

I walk right the fuck out of the room, straight up the stairs, and into the bathroom. It's a disaster from Sam's little shopping spree. I grab fistfuls of fabric and shove them back in the bags. They're fancy clothes, everything from a little black dress to a bright red bikini. I shake my head. What the hell was Sam thinking? MacKenzie doesn't wear this type of shit. She wears jeans and a T-shirt most of the time, not . . . I drop the thong. Fuck.

"Seriously, asshole? You think walking away is going to make this conversation magically go away?" she snarls at the threshold.

My retort dies in my throat as my eyes travel up her body, from her bare feet to her legs wrapped in leggings. My eyes fix on the curve of her hip, where her fists are planted, arms jutting out. Her shirt is hugging her tits, pushing them up, drawing my eye to her cleavage and then the sweep of her neck. I'm on my knees, and it hits me what a fucking goddess she is, fire spitting from her eyes as she glares. Somehow, I forgot how stunning she is, even with her hair a mess, no makeup on her face, covered in bruises. I'm lying, though. I didn't forget. I shoved it aside, pushed it deep down to focus on the immediate problems in front of us. It's smacking me in the face now, conjuring up memories of her I should leave in the past.

"What the hell are you staring at?" she demands, my eyes snapping back to her face. Shit.

"Nothing. Listen, MacKenzie, we don't have a plan yet. So, I don't have anything for you. You can keep screeching about it, but it's not going to change anything," I say, going back to stuffing clothes in the bags.

There's got to be thousands of dollars worth of clothes here.

"I do not screech. I'll call Sam, then. She'll tell me whatever the plan is."

"Do whatever you want. It's your life," I grumble.

"What the hell is your problem? I get it. You're a grouch, but all morning, you've been nasty to everyone around you, including me."

Huffing, I gather all the bags, then stand up. I glance around, trying to decide where the hell to put all this shit, but I don't have any room in here, so I drop them again. I need a break, a little time away from the last few days of constant anxiety dogging me. Last night was more terrifying than she realizes. When she didn't come down after two hours, I checked on her and found her fast asleep. I left, but after five hours, I freaked the fuck out and called Ink. Apparently, I was overreacting, but I ended up next to her, counting her breaths long into the night.

"I'm not a grouch. Probably wouldn't be so tired if I could sleep in my own fucking bed," I mumble.

Kenzie jerks back, then winces at the movement, and I instantly regret the words. I want to take them back, but she's nodding before I can.

"Sorry, I got the shit beat out of me. Clearly, I wasn't in my right mind when I came to you for help. You're the one who put me in your bed, though. I didn't ask you to give up your space for me. I could have taken a spare room. I could have stayed at headquarters. Hell, I can . . ." She stares over my shoulder.

"Kenz, I didn't . . ." She holds her hand up.

Hell, I don't even know how I was going to apologize.

"It's fine. I get it. This whole situation is over-the-top crazy for everyone. If you'll excuse me," she whispers, still not meeting my eyes. She practically runs from the room, then down the stairs. I wait for the slam of the front door, but it never comes.

Hesitating, I stare at the bags at my feet before scanning the bathroom, remnants of her filling the space. She's right. I didn't have to keep her here, in my room. I could have chosen anywhere else, but the thought of her not being close, not knowing if she was safe, would send me into a tailspin. If she's not here, I can't protect her. I don't examine why I need to protect her so fiercely, but the need is too great for me to fight against. I dash after her, frantically searching the living room and kitchen, but they're empty. A low murmur leaks out from under the laundry room door, and I burst inside. She's tucked between the wall and washer, phone pressed to her ear, sheets of dark hair falling on her knees, hiding her face.

"Kenz," I breathe. Her head pops up, whispering in the phone. Then she hangs up.

"Ryker, at what point are you going to figure out you shouldn't bust into every fucking room like you're the goddamn Kool-Aid man?"

"I didn't mean it." She snorts, glancing away. "I'm serious. You need to stay here. I don't care if you take over the whole damn house, but you need to stay here."

"Why?" she whispers, tears shining in her hazel eyes.

"Because this is the safest place for you."

"Why?"

I sigh. "You came here for a reason, MacKenzie."

"That's not an answer. Tell me why, Ryker," she demands, her a tear-soaked face turning toward me.

"Because I can't protect you if you're not here!" My heart cracks.

She blinks, searching my face. My shoulders bunch when she pushes herself up, coming to stand in front of me. She tilts her head, lifting a finger and pressing on my forehead. Even if I wanted to, I can't pull my gaze away. I'm caught in her eyes.

"Did you know you have a vein that pops out when you get worked up?" she mumbles, eyes tracing the vein along with her finger.

A shudder runs through me. "I didn't know that."

"I used to see how far I could push you before it would make an appearance."

"Is that why you'd always grin when you pissed me off?"

She laughs lightly, meeting my eyes. "Yeah. I missed that. I missed you."

Closing my eyes, I suck in a breath and tip my head back, forcing her to drop her hand. All the reasons I pushed her away before rush through my mind, but none of them make sense anymore. We were too young. I didn't have time after the coup. I couldn't keep her. She needed to live her life without me. I was to blame. Guilt licks at my insides, still present after all this time. She sighs, but when she steps away, I grab her hand before pulling her closer. Tipping my head down, I rest my forehead on hers, closing my eyes again.

"I missed you, too."

TEN

MacKenzie

It's dark when I open my eyes. I spy Ryker's sleeping shadow next to me. After our interlude in the laundry room, I expected . . . I don't know what I expected, but it wasn't for him to pull me out of the room and tuck me into bed, commanding me to nap. I didn't think I would fall asleep but also didn't think he'd lay down next to me, closing his eyes, then scolding me when I spent the time staring at him instead. I did sleep, though.

"Ryker," I whisper into the dark.

His soft breaths fill the room. I lean to grab the phone Ren gave me off the nightstand but yelp, then collapse back, breathing through the pain. Ryker grunts, shuffling to his side to wrap an arm around my waist. I yelp again, and he rears back. His face hovers over me, concern lining his eyes.

"What hurts?"

"Nothing, I'm fine. You just hit the scrape on my hip," I say in a gravelly voice.

"I'll call Ink," he states as he pushes up, but I grab his arm.

"I'm fine. Stop freaking out," I say.

He huffs and lies back down, turning his head toward me.

"Are you sure you're okay?"

"Never better." I smirk, and he rolls his eyes, turning to stare at the ceiling.

"This is why you're staying here. I think my heart is going to beat out of my chest. I'm not letting you out of my sight until I stop freaking the fuck out every time something happens to you." He rubs his chest, groaning.

"I'm sorry," I mumble, wanting to bite back, but I stop the words from pouring out.

He turns, pressing a kiss to my hair, whispering, "Not your fault. Just let me take care of you."

"I don't know how to do that."

My head falls to the side—our lips a hairsbreadth away as we stare at each other. A twitch, and we'd tumble into a whole other situation I'm not sure I'm ready for. He doesn't want to be in the one I've dragged to his doorstep, much less the precipice we're standing at the edge of now. Too many things are standing in the way, blocking our path. I wish I was good enough, strong enough, just . . . enough to fight for something more. Unable to answer the questions swimming in his eyes, I close mine. I could throw caution to the wind and pray for the best, but the last time I did that with him . . . I don't know if I could survive his rejection a second time. The ghost of a sigh whispers across my lips, and I peek at him from under my lashes. He's still studying me, eyes roving over my face.

"What are you . . ."

Pounding on the front door cuts me off, and I flinch back while Ryker bounds up, leaps over me, and thunders down the stairs. I'm frozen, heart trying to force its way out of my chest, and my lungs seize. I can't pull in a full breath, spots dancing in my vision. The panic attacks I thought I'd conquered when I unloaded to Ryker were hiding behind a wall in my mind.

Hawk's bellowing from below has my head snapping to the door, and my muscles unlock, one by one. Sliding off the bed, I scan the space. There's still no way I'd be able to make it through the window, but the bathroom is too obvious, with no corners to hide in. The sudden silence filtering through the air is scarier than the yelling from before, and I bolt to the closet. It's not large, like the ones at the King estate. Their closets would be the perfect place to hide, with so many built-in nooks and crannies. Calling Ryker's a walk-in would be generous, but it's stuffed full of random shit where shirts would usually be hung. Wedging myself behind a box, I shove aside a set of saddlebags and pull a blanket over my head. Once I'm no longer moving, the trembling starts. A voice in my head is screaming at me to be rational. There's no reason to think anyone is after me, but the fear is deafening, drowning out any common sense.

Footsteps rattle the stairs and creaking bedroom door makes me suck in a breath. It could be Ryker or Hawk, but what if it's Maddox? Or *him*? What if Ryker is lying dead downstairs, and I'm here, stuck in a fucking closet, while he bleeds out? Guilt mingles with my terror, and I squeeze my eyes shut, tears leaking from under my lids. The constant anxiety I've been under threatens to pull me back down into the dark, but I fight it. The closet door swings open, the hinges squeaking, and my eyes fly open. Holding my breath again, I hope the trembling from my body doesn't give away where I'm hiding.

"Kenzie?" Ryker's voice floats through the space. I let out a strangled sob, burying my face in my hands.

Random items fly off me, and he pulls me into his lap, holding me close. I try to tell him I'm okay around the lump of my throat and the sobs wracking my body. He shushes me, pressing my head into the crook of his neck as he pets my hair.

"She okay?" Hawk asks from the doorway, and Ryker murmurs something back before Hawk's footsteps retreat.

"I'm sorry. It'll be okay. We'll get through this, Kenz. I promise."

Tension flows out of me as my tears subside, leaving exhaustion in its wake.

"I don't know how to do this," I cry.

His chest moves as he sighs, and I'm suddenly aware he's not wearing a shirt. Heat floods my body, from embarrassment or something else. I wiggle to scramble off his lap, but he grips me tighter. At some point, we're going to have to address the elephant in the room but not tonight.

"Do you think you can sleep? Or do you want to come downstairs with me?" He pulls back slightly, scanning my blotchy face.

I clear my throat. "Downstairs, please."

He slides me off his lap and stands. As I push myself up, my muscles protest. I wait for him to lead the way, but he stares before shaking his head and heading out the door. Hawk paces back and forth in the kitchen, but he freezes when he spots me. I wave with a small smile. Peeking at Ryker, I see him glaring at his friend, before turning to me.

"You should go put some clothes on," he says gruffly.

"Uhh, I have clothes on. These are pajamas." I gesture to my body.

"They're . . . short," he says before grabbing a bottle of water from the fridge and passing it to me.

"Sorry my choice of nightwear doesn't fit your description of appropriate clothing."

I'm used to him being a borderline asshat, but after he's helped me the last few days, I thought he'd ease off. Instead, he swings between holding me while I sob to scolding me for what I'm wearing. Ready to ignore them both, I roll my eyes and plop myself into the chair. I open the bottle, and the cold liquid soothes my sore throat. I shiver, both from the water, and remembering the fear rolling through me in the closet. Exhaustion licks at the edges of my vision.

"So, what do you want me to do about them?" Hawk asks.

His question pulls me from my thoughts.

"Who?"

"Couple of strangers went to Trigger's, asking questions. Don't worry about it. Maybe you should go back to bed," Ryker grunts, arms crossed over his naked, tattooed chest.

"Maybe you should go put on a shirt, Ryker. You're a little underdressed, wouldn't you say?" I say sweetly before taking another drink and turning to Hawk. "Who were the strangers?"

"Uhh . . ." His wide gaze bounces between us.

"They're strangers, MacKenzie. Obviously, we don't know who they are," Ryker snaps.

"Well, what type of questions were they asking?"

Ryker throws up his hands before stomping to the fridge and pulling out his own water bottle. I turn to Hawk, questioning him with my eyes, but he avoids my gaze.

"They were asking about new people in town, wondering who was running this territory, shit like that. Again, we'll deal with it," Ryker says.

I freeze, sucking in a breath, before slowly releasing it, trying to slow my heart. I whisper, "Were they another MC?"

"Yeah."

My stomach flips. "What's the patch?" Every MC has a patch. It's a clear way to identify them to others. Riding around without one is asking for trouble, both from their clubs and others.

Hawk slides his phone in front of me, and I almost throw up all the water as I scan the familiar patch. I stared at it while lying in a bloody heap on a cold concrete floor. I fixated on it, memorized it, while their fists and boots and chains left bruises on my body. Fighting a wave of panic, I push back the urge to run as far as possible. Ryker and

Hawk aren't paying me any attention, murmuring amongst themselves. When the screen fades to black, I shove it away, but the image is seared in my brain. Fucking Maddox.

"We need to find out their name, see if they're who's after Kenz." Ryker's voice filters through the haze.

"Night Slayers," I choke out.

"Are you sure?" Hawk asks, concern in his eyes, but I give him a withering look, still fighting the need to bolt out the back door.

"Fucking Maddox," Ryker grunts, pulling out his phone as he stalks in to the living room.

Afraid he'll start yelling again, I watch him.

"Hawk, what happened before?"

"I'm sorry, Mac. I wasn't sure what else to do, and Helms wasn't answering his phone. I may have overreacted," he mutters, a blush creeping up his cheeks.

"I'm sure you didn't expect me to lose it. I haven't exactly been in my right mind lately. Do you have a picture of who was at the bar?"

"No. Trigger doesn't want cameras inside, and the ones outside didn't catch their faces. Ryker called Ren to see if we could find out where they went. We'll find them."

"No, we won't," Ryker states from the threshold. "They're already gone. I don't want to go back into lockdown, but we might not have a choice."

"Guys won't be happy," Hawk says, eyes shooting to me, then skittering away again.

"I should . . ."

"You're not going anywhere, MacKenzie. Stop bringing that shit up. The guys will deal. I'm not ready to do it now, anyway, but it's a possibility, so everyone needs to brace themselves."

Hawk shakes his head and claps Ryker on the shoulder as he passes him. The door shutting behind him echoes through the house.

"You know, it would be a lot easier to include me in these things if you wouldn't bite my head off every time I open my mouth." I tip the bottle, watching the water slosh inside.

"You know, it would be a lot easier if you'd just let me take care of things instead of thinking I can't protect you," he growls.

My head snaps up. "What? I know you can protect me. For fuck's sake, I ran to you when I was barely able to keep a coherent thought in my head. When did I ever say you couldn't protect me?"

He crosses his arms and leans against the counter, glaring. "How about when you refused to tell me what happened? Or when you tried to run away—multiple times. Or it could have been when you bit my head off when I said I wasn't going to access your money or . . ."

I swipe my hand through the air, cutting off his tirade. "I didn't tell you what happened because I didn't want to bring my problems to your doorstep, especially since we hadn't seen each other in god knows how long. I tried to run because I was out of my mind, and you were freaking me the fuck out by threatening to call Maddox. I wanted money so I wouldn't be a burden. None of those things had anything to do with how safe I felt."

His mouth fell open at some point during my outburst. The fire in his eyes extinguishes, and his eyebrows pull low. I'm not about to give in, though. I didn't do anything wrong. There's no reason he needs to be putting all this on me.

I didn't ask to be sold. I didn't ask to be beaten. I didn't even ask for him to save me. He chose to do it. He *insisted* on being the one to save me, and I let him. I let him in and told him all the horrible shit that happened. I trusted him. I still trust him.

It feels like a repeat of our past. I trusted him then, too, and he pushed me away, breaking my heart a little more every time he wouldn't meet my eyes. I can't go through that again. It was hard enough at seventeen, when I didn't understand the world. Now, it would be a whole new heartbreak I don't know if I could crawl out of.

"Kenzie," he breathes out, arms falling to his sides, as if he doesn't know what to do with them anymore.

"Don't. Don't call me that. You don't get to come in and boss me around like we're kids. We're not teenagers anymore, Ryker. I'm all grown up, and I won't let you make me feel less than just because you grew up, and took over and did something with your life, and I didn't." I swallow the sob that's choking me, begging to be let out.

I want to scream, cry, pound my fists into him to get him to see reason, but I can't. I never could. He didn't want to listen to me then, and it seems as if nothing has changed. With as much dignity as my battered body will allow, I stand, determined to make it upstairs without breaking down, but he doesn't even have the decency to give me that. He grabs my hand. I expect more commands, snark, anything, but he stills, clinging to my hand like he'll never let go.

ELEVEN

Ryker

I can't see Kenzie's shadowed face, but her hand is trembling. I saw the sheen in her eyes before she turned away and now I can't unsee it. My thumb moves of its own accord, back and forth over her skin. This goes beyond the past few days, the past few weeks. It's been building for years, an unfinished in our lives, waiting for the opportunity to rear its head and demand we deal with the feelings we tried to bury.

"Ke—MacKenzie," I whisper.

My heart cracks when a muffled cry escapes her. She presses the back of her hand to her lips, as if she can shove the tears down. I clear my throat, squeezing her hand, and peer at her. "We can't keep doing this."

She's so still for so long, I wonder if she heard me when she murmurs, "I know, but I don't know how to fix this . . . fix me."

I squeeze her hand until she meets my eyes. "Baby, you're not broken. There's nothing to fix."

She collapses into me, body shaking with the force of her tears. I swear she's cried more in the last week than she cried the entire time we were growing up. I have to admit, I'm the reason for a lot of these tears. I don't know how to help her, other than protecting her, keeping her safe, fighting her demons when she can't.

"We have to stop meeting like this," she says with a shaky laugh.

I chuckle, kissing the top of her head. "As long as we can keep meeting, I think that can be arranged."

"Are you sure you're okay taking all this on?"

She pulls away, wiping her face with the bottom of her shirt. My eyes fall to her stomach, and I look at the pattern of black and blue dancing along her ribs. She yanks it down, a flush covering her neck and cheeks, as she stares into the dark.

"Don't," I whisper, grasping the hem and tugging it up again.

I brush my fingers along a bruise, yellowing around the edges. Goosebumps skitter across her skin. I trace what appears to be the heel of a boot, rage making my fingers tremble. Kenzie didn't give me specifics, but the evidence is stamped on her body, and I fight to control the urge to kill Maddox, the Night Slayers, anyone who stands in my way at extracting justice.

"Ryker?"

"Hmm." I trace her side, ghosting my fingers to her hip, drawing along her shorts and then back up her ribs.

"What are you doing?" she whispers. Her eyes watch my fingers paint across her skin. I don't have an answer.

"I'm checking your injuries," I murmur.

"Bullshit," she mutters as a shiver overtakes her when I brush her stomach.

I wasn't willing to admit it before, but when I got the message she was here, under the anger, buried deep was the rush of desire. Finding her hurt, I buried the lust even deeper. The craving is back in full force now, sending all the blood straight to my cock. This is terrible timing. I should pull back, send her to bed, take care of shit myself, and stay far away from her body. All those plans fly out of my head when my eyes meet hers.

"Kenz . . ." I warn, seeing desire flooding her eyes, making them brighter than usual.

Having seen this look on her face before, I know exactly where it'll lead, but the voice of reason is drowned out by her tongue, darting out to lick her lips.

"Ry . . ." she breathes.

Wrapping my arm around her side, I dragged her closer, eliminating the space between us. Her skin meeting mine sends a shiver of longing through me, and I groan, tipping my head back. I swear this woman is going to make me lose my fucking mind.

I slide my other hand behind her neck, holding her in place for my lips to graze hers. Of course she can't just let me take things slow. She has to take control, grabbing my neck, fusing us together. It was stupid to think enough time has passed to forget the taste of her—the feel of her—against me. Time can't erase the memories living in my skin.

I back us up until she's flush with the wall, wresting back control, and I swipe my tongue along her lips, begging her to open. Kenzie meets me, fingers digging into my neck, her soft moans egging me on. Her leg slides up my thigh, and I hook a hand behind her knee, grinding my cock against her. My hand drifts up her leg, and her soft skin almost undoes me as I glide under her cotton shorts, gripping her ample ass. I yank my mouth from hers, our gasping breaths mingling before I duck, and latch on to her earlobe. As I bite, she squirms against me, making my cock twitch. I suck the lobe in my mouth, letting it go with a pop.

"I'm not fucking you against the wall, Kenz," I breathe in her ear, before tracing my nose along her jaw.

"Why the fuck not?" she bursts out, body rubbing against me, creating more friction.

"You're still hurt. I'm not going to add to your injuries. I won't be gentle when I take that sweet pussy again."

Her breath stutters at my words, and I lower her leg but keep my hips pressed against her. She whimpers when I bury my head in her neck, fingers gliding under her shirt to brush my finger over her nipple. It pebbles, turning harder when I pinch it, and her hips jerk in response.

"Ryker, please," she moans, twisting her fingers in my hair.

"Oh, baby, there's plenty I can do without fucking you."

Dragging her tank top strap down her arm with my teeth, I scrape my way to the nipple I've exposed. I stop and stare before she thrusts her tit toward my face, and I suck the bud, swirling as needy pleas fall from her lips.

I knead the other while I revel in the intensity of having her in my arms again. It wasn't enough before, and I have a feeling it won't be enough now. I'll always crave her, her sass, her body, every fucking inch of her. I tug her shorts over her hips, pushing a knee between her legs to open her up for me. I drop a hand, cupping her, as she jolts into my palm, begging me without words.

"This where you want me, baby? Tell me what you want." I grunt when she grabs me through my pants, squeezing my cock.

"I want you to fuck me," she hisses, tightening her grip, leaning forward to sink her teeth into my neck.

I groan, throwing my head back and thrust into her hand. "Not going to happen, Kenz." I gasp as she strokes me.

"You sure about that?"

It's the cockiness in her voice that has me pressing into her again, our hands trapped between us, and I growl, eyes burrowing into hers. The need in hers is clear, but she'll never back down. Kenzie never could.

"Listen to me, Kenzie Raines. I will fuck you, but you'll have to be a good girl and wait until you're healed. Doesn't mean I can't make you scream my name as you come."

I circle my fingers around her wrist, tugging her hand away from my cock. It's harder than I imagined. She throws her head back, a needy moan falling from her. I ease back, hand stealing into her shorts and working my fingers into her folds. I groan again when I find how wet she is. My forehead falls to her shoulder as I delve inside to stroke her pussy as she clenches around me. Sinking my teeth into her skin, I swipe my tongue along her flesh as she rides my fingers. Her panting sounds in my ear and her legs begin to shake. I slide an arm between her back and the wall to hold her up. Her cries for relief echo throughout the room, and my thumb circles her clit, sparking her climax. She moans my name, shuddering through waves of pleasure.

Watching her come all over my fingers almost sends me over the edge myself. I pull my fingers out and set her clothes right. Keeping hold of her waist, I guide her up the stairs. Her eyes are still glazed, and she blinks up at me when she settles on the pillow, holding her hand out to me, but I smirk, shaking my head.

"You didn't honestly think I was done, did you, baby?"

Her eyes widen as I peel off her shorts and drag her down until her ass is practically hanging off the end of the bed. Kenzie gasps when I spread her knees. With one last wicked grin I bury my face between her legs, lapping at the remnants of her orgasm. A growl escapes me when her taste hits my tongue and my cock jerks, remembering. Her hips kick up, and I pull away, eyes meeting hers.

"I can't hold you down and devour you like I want, so you're going to have to control yourself, Kenz," I breathe.

I dart my tongue out, circling her clit as she squirms, obviously trying to keep still. Slowing my movements, I lazily circle her entrance. Breathing her in, I reacquaint myself with her scent, her taste, her whimpers, everything.

"Ryker," she whines, desperation filling her voice. She sighs as I drive my tongue in and out, traveling up to suck her clit between my lips. My fingers sink into her wetness, coating them. She writhes on the bed, her fingers finding my hair, yanking. A delicious pain shoots straight to my cock. I could happily spend the rest of my life right here, feasting on her. Her thick thighs clamp tight around my head as she seizes, sailing over the edge again. I stroke inside her as she floats back to earth, pulling back to watch her face.

"Fuck, you're intoxicating. A goddamn goddess," I murmur, nipping at her thigh, when her legs fall open. Her pussy squeezes, trying to suck my fingers back in, and I can't hold back the chuckle as I pull them away. I lick them clean, humming at the explosion of her in my mouth. She rolls to her side, eyes drifting shut. I crawl next to her and nuzzle her neck as she purrs, a satisfied smile plastered on her face. I stare, my heart clenching, and I rub my chest, trying to relieve whatever emotion is coursing through my body. My cock is rock-hard still. I push off the bed and go into the bathroom to start a bath. When I come back, she's fast asleep.

"Baby, you gotta get up." I brush the hair away from her neck, sweeping it up to press a swift kiss behind her ear.

She groans, stretching her neck, and I catch the wince. Dammit. I tried to take it easy on her, but with so many muscles tensing, she's in pain. I gather her up, protests halfheartedly falling from her lips, and walk us into the bathroom.

"I started a bath for you. The water will help," I say when her eyes are still shut.

"I don't want a bath," she whines, burrowing into my chest.

"You will once you get in, promise." She sways when I set her on her feet, but I steady her before stripping her top off.

"Wait, I have to pee." I turn to go, but she stops me. "Find another towel, not the one you shrunk." She yawns.

I dig in the cupboard, and she flushes, the splash of water reaching me. I spin, thinking I'll have to save her when she slips in the fucking tub, but she's drying her hands, smiling at me in the mirror. Stalking toward her, I throw the towel on the counter and sweep her in my arms again to lower her in to the warm water. She sighs as the water flows over her body. Now that I'm not drunk with desire, I see the bruises covering her, distorted under the water lapping her skin. I shuck off my pants and underwear. When I glance up, her eyes meet mine, a small smile playing on her lips.

"Don't get any thoughts, MacKenzie Raines." I nudge her forward to slip in behind.

The tub isn't the most comfortable. I should get some sort of cushion, but I barely use the thing, so it always seemed a waste. At least I had enough sense to buy a huge fucking tub, so we both fit. Her hair tickles my cheek when she leans back against my chest.

"Thank you," she whispers, the lapping water echoing through the room.

"For the orgasms? You're more than welcome." Her elbow jabs back, and I wheeze, snickering.

"For taking care of me, jackass."

"Well, you know what they say, 'an orgasm a day.'"

"I'm trying to be nice."

"Stop it. It's freaking me out." I rub my rib, making the water slosh more.

"So . . . what do we do now?" she asks.

Not wanting to have this conversation now, I suck in a breath. Not when she's tired and I'm horny and things are up in the air.

"We'll dry off, go to bed, and you'll get some sleep. Tomorrow, I'm making waffles."

"You know that's not what I meant but okay. Are you going to be there in the morning, though?" Her voice is small, laced with doubt.

"Why wouldn't I be here in the morning?"

"You weren't the last time."

Sighing, I remember the night I slipped away from my warm bed, staring at her sleeping face in the moonlight, wondering if I made a mistake in taking what I did from her, regardless of whether she wanted me to. I left, knowing it would hurt her, but it was better than the alternative. I was halfway in love with her already. I would have been lost completely if I had stayed.

"I promise I'll be there."

TWELVE

MacKenzie

Insistent beeping invades my sleep the next morning, and I want to smash whatever it is with a ball-peen hammer. A groan rolls from me as I swing to my back, and my hand smacks into something soft and fleshy. My eyes fly open, finding a glaring Ryker staring back.

"Whoops." I grin, tucking my hands under the covers.

"Turn the damn alarm off," he grunts, even as he flips to his back to grab his phone off the nightstand. He jabs the screen, but the noise continues until I yank it from his grip and turn off the alarm.

"Why do you have an alarm for Saturday? Don't you sleep in?"

A giddiness sweeps through me. I feel better than I have in a long time.

"I *do* work, Kenzie. I don't have the luxury of staying in bed all day." He throws an arm over his face.

"Is that a dig because I've slept more than I've been awake while I've been here?"

"Good god, woman, not everything I say is an insult toward you. I don't remember you being so damn sensitive."

"I don't remember you being such an ass, either . . . Oh, wait, you always were. Never mind." I smile sweetly when he peeks an eye out.

He studies my face, and I drop the dopey grin. Ryker somehow became grouchier since we were kids. I didn't think it was possible, but the evidence is right in front of me. His face darkens, and he puffs out a sigh, cutting off my view with his arm again.

"You look better," he says.

"Gee, you sure are a charmer, Ryker. Bet all the girlies fall at your feet with lines like those tumbling from your luscious lips."

"Seemed to work on you," he mumbles, and I catch the edge of a smirk. "I meant your bruises. They're fading—at least from your face. The ones on your neck are almost gone, too. I'll have to check the other ones, though, make sure they're getting better."

"Oh, *you'll* have to check, huh? I'm not trusted to do that myself?" When he turns his head toward me, I raise an eyebrow.

"Definitely not. You're not qualified to assess your own health appropriately." I can't tell if he's flirting with me or if he's dead serious. The intensity in his eyes as the blue darkens could be concern or lust.

"Uhh, I . . ." My mind goes blank. My eyes skip down his body before settling back on his face.

He raises an eyebrow. "Did you forget how to word?"

"You"—I clear my throat. *What the fuck is wrong with me?*—"I . . . well, see, I can take care of myself." Before I can get the words out, he chuckles, and I huff, going back to staring at the ceiling.

"Aww, Kenz, sure you can."

He cuddles my side, looping an arm around me, propping his head in his hand. One finger swipes the strip of skin my top isn't covering, sending a shiver through me. Not wanting to admit he might be right, I realize I might not be the greatest at doing what's best for myself. My mind hasn't been the most reliable place to be lately.

"So, what do you need to do today?" I pick at fuzz on my top, avoiding his gaze.

"Other than you?" He laughs when my eyes shoot to his face. "I've got the meeting today. Plus, I want to talk to Trigger."

"What should I do, then?" I'll do whatever I want, regardless, but this new, giggly Ryker has me wondering how much he thinks he can boss me around.

"Well, first, you're going to get up and take a shower. You'll need to drain the bath, since you didn't do it last night." He levels me with a look. "Then breakfast. Some laundry needs to be thrown in the machine, and there's a basket down there that needs folding. Oh, and the front porch needs to be swept."

Falling to his back, he stretches his arms over his head and yawns. I glare at him, though he doesn't notice. I open my mouth to tell him off, but he shoots up, scrubbing his hands over his scruff.

His eyes light up when he turns to me. "You know what? The back porch needs to be painted. Hasn't rained in a day, so you could get going on those things."

I push up on my elbows. "You think you're so damn funny."

"What? You said you wanted to be included in things."

"Yeah, like knowing what the hell was going on, dumbass. I'm not painting your back porch." He's fucking with me, but for some reason, it still pisses me off.

Confusion floods his face. "Don't you want to earn your keep?"

My mouth falls open, and I throw back the covers, intent on getting as far away from him as this house will allow. Ryker grabs my wrist, though, and pulls me back as he busts out laughing. My face is smooshed to his chest, heaving under the strain of his amusement. I pinch his side, but he laughs harder.

"It's not funny." I pinch him again, and he yelps.

"Oh, I think it's fucking hilarious." He chuckles, skimming a hand down my back.

"I'm pretty fucking capable," I grumble, my voice muffled.

"Oh, yeah? You figure out how to not burn eggs, then?"

"Oh, fuck off," I mutter, pushing away to scoot off the bed.

When I slam the bathroom door, he only laughs louder. Sure enough, the tub is filled with water. That was Ryker's fault, though, not mine. He's the one who said to leave it for later. Part of me wanted to protest when he scooped me up yet again to carry me back to bed, but it feels nice to be pampered. My height alone makes it a challenge, not to mention I'm not tiny like Sam. Not like many men line up for the privilege of carting my ass around. I stare at the tub, remembering his face going up and down the stairs, me in his arms, no strain or effort. I pull the plug, the water gurgling as it flows down the drain.

"You don't have to do that, Kenz," Ryker murmurs. Lost in my thoughts, I didn't hear him come in. I think about asking him why he insists on hefting me around, but I don't. I'm content to live in the fantasy that he enjoys it rather than he thinks I'm too weak to walk on my own.

"I'm hungry. Feed me." I turn, planting my hands on my hips and sticking out my lip.

He laughs again. "Yeah, okay. Call Sam before she comes stomping in here, thinking I'm holding you hostage or something."

The bathroom door clicks shut, and his footsteps fade away. I should call Sam, but after last night and this morning, I'm tired. I don't know if I can handle a conversation with another adult. Showering is a much better idea. Once I undress, though, I examine my wounds in the mirror.

The cut on my hip is a thin red line, but it doesn't hurt as much when I press a finger to the gash. The bruises on my ribs are splotchy, a mix of greens and yellows, except where *he* stomped his heel in. That one is still splattered with broken blood vessels, surrounded by angry blues. Ryker was right, though. The ones on my neck are almost gone. I can barely see where he wrapped his fingers around my throat. The swelling on my face is gone, too. Thank god. Two black eyes still stare back at me, but I might be able to cover it with makeup. I wonder if Ren is as good at buying makeup as he is at buying clothes, even if the shit he bought was really freaking fancy.

The shower is easier than yesterday. I've never been this excited for hot water, and my muscles relax one by one under the spray. I stay a long time until Hawk knocks, calling out about food being almost ready. I'm drying off when Ryker starts pounding, telling me to get my ass downstairs, or he's eating my food.

Five minutes later, I tromp down the stairs, following the delicious smell of bacon and find Hawk already seated and devouring a plate of waffles. Mouthwatering, I plopped down next to him. The one thing that didn't leave me through this whole ordeal was my appetite. *Go figure.* Ryker sets a plate loaded with food in front of me, kissing my head before settling in the chair next to me. I catch Hawk's raised eyebrow out of the corner of my eye but focus on my food.

"So, most of the members will be there tonight," Hawk says around a mouthful.

"Who's not coming?" Ryker growls, and I stuff bacon in my mouth.

"Trigger. He's going to keep the bar open, in case those guys come back. Tank won't be there, either. Shipment coming in."

"All right, he taking anyone with him?"

"Just some prospects. Should be an easy run."

Keeping silent, I don't want Ryker to shut me out again. I scoop a bite of waffle in my mouth, moaning as the fluffy, buttery goodness explodes in my mouth as my eyes fall shut. Ryker's waffles always were the best. He never would tell me what he put in them to make them so damn delicious. Bastard. I open my eyes, finding both men staring at me, Ryker's fork halfway to his mouth.

"What?" I ask as I chew.

Hawk's eyes fall to his plate, and he heaps more hash browns on his fork.

"Glad you like the food." Ryker smirks, continuing to eat. "We know who runs the Night Slayers yet?"

"No. Other than the Vipers, we don't have many connections in Rima, so getting info on them isn't easy."

"I know," I murmur, fixating on the waffles and cutting them into small pieces.

Their eyes are on me, waiting, but I pick up another piece of bacon and nibble on it. Saying his name out loud will make it real, and I don't know what to do with that. I can't tell if I'm surprised Ryker didn't ask me what I knew or not. Other than when I told him, he hasn't asked me anything.

"Kenz?" Ryker prompts.

"He goes by Panther." I suck in a breath. "But his name is Kane Riley." My stomach rolls, threatening to expel the waffles, but I doubt they'll taste as good coming up as they were going down.

"Stupid fucking name, but I'm on it." Hawk's voice is distant, like I'm in a tunnel, and a ringing in my ears drowns them out.

I grab the glass Ryker left for me and sip the orange juice before downing the whole thing. My insides bunch, stomach cramping when the liquid hits, but I push the feeling down. I can't keep reacting like this every time someone slams a door or mentions *them* or yells. I don't know how to stop it.

It's clearly not healthy. I need to channel my emotions into something productive, like revenge or rage. Those things aren't healthy, but in my world, it's the way of things. My chair spins, and I find Ryker kneeling in front of me. He cups my face, pulling me down and kissing me gently. I rest my forehead on his, still trying to reel my emotions in.

"You don't have to be strong all the time."

"I'm hardly ever strong," I huff.

"What are you talking about? You're always strong, confident, independent, sexy. I could go on, but I don't want your head to get too big."

"You ever heard of fake it 'til you make it?"

"Baby, you are all those things, regardless if you feel like you're faking it. You always have been. What happened doesn't change that."

"But our world . . ."

"Fuck the world. I'll be strong for you."

THIRTEEN

Ryker

"No, MacKenzie. You can't come with." I slide on my leathers and then run my fingers through my hair.

"Come on, Ryker. It's not like I haven't been to a meeting before. We used to play under the fucking tables at these things."

"Yeah, when we were nine. I have to run the damn thing now. Are you going to hide under the table while I'm talking?" I shoot a glare over my shoulder, but instead of attitude, a sassy smirk is playing on her lips. "For fuck's sake."

"I mean, if you really want me there, I suppose I could . . ." She slips her arms around my waist, pressing against my back and meeting my eyes in the mirror.

"You're not making this any easier, you know. Meetings are for members. You're not a member. This isn't your first time at the rodeo, Kenzie."

She throws her arms up and rolls her eyes. "But I'm the reason you're having it. And if I have to spend one more fucking second in this house, I'm going to lose my mind. Let me come. Please, please, please."

The begging crumbles my walls. I sigh, tucking my head to my chest. This woman is making me soft, and she hasn't even been here a week. The longer she stays, the harder it'll be when she leaves.

"Fine, but I'm leaving in two minutes—with or without you. Once the doors close, I'm locking them." Leaving her squealing behind me, I stomp out. Five minutes later, she's finally coming down the stairs, and I groan, seeing she's snagged one of my leathers from my closet.

"I'm ready!" she chirps, as if she isn't late.

"You're three minutes late and wearing my shit." I cross my arms, blocking the front door.

"You're still here, and Ren didn't get me any leather. It's all lace and booty shorts, so I made do."

"What do you mean *Ren* didn't get you any leather? I thought Sam bought all that shit?" I grind out between clenched teeth. She raises an eyebrow, crossing her own arms.

"Sam brought them. She didn't buy them. Apparently, she's not a shopper. Ren buys all her clothes, so she told him to get me some things. Don't worry, he wasn't imagining me in them," she says, another smirk on her lips.

Swinging around, I ignore the burning in my chest. Revving engines fill the night as members pile in the parking lot a block down. Kenzie's skipping steps crunch on the gravel, and she loops her arm with mine, bouncing as we walk.

"Would you settle down? It's a meeting, not a shindig," I grumble over the racket.

"Shindig? What are you, eighty? No one calls a party a shindig. I'm just excited. Am I not allowed to be excited? Should I be somber and grumpy like you? We could be a matching pair of scowls." Her mouth pulls down, and I frown.

"Don't make a scene. There's a few of them that'll make a racket you're here in the first place."

"Yes, sir." She salutes, skipping along again.

"Prez!" Tiny, our treasurer calls out, lumbering up to us.

"What's up, Tiny?" I yank Kenzie to a stop when she tries to prance away.

"They seriously call you Tiny?" Kenzie asks, tipping her head back to see his face.

He ducks his chin to his chest. I nudge her. I feel her tense under my arm. My head whips to her, and she shakes her head subtly. There's no way I hit a bruise, since I've memorized where they are, but if it's something internal, I'd have to take her to the hospital.

"Uh, yeah, they do," Tiny says, cheeks flushing.

"Like Little John from Robin Hood?"

"I guess so." Tiny shoves his hands in his pocket.

"That's cool. I don't have an amazing nickname. This one"—she pops her thumb at me—"just shortens my actual name, so it's not very creative." She laughs, rolling her eyes.

"Don't most people call you Mac? That's a cool name."

I'm hesitant to break up the conversation, but the meeting is going to start soon. Members try to catch my eye, and I turn away from them. Hawk walks closer and waves me over, eyes widening when he takes in Tiny and Kenzie chatting back and forth like they're old friends. I slip her arm out of mine and meet Hawk half way.

"What's up with that?" he asks, still watching the pair.

"Kenzie being Kenzie. She can talk to anyone. Seems to know how to be with them before they open their mouth." I follow his gaze. Kenzie is waving her hands in the air.

"So, you like it when she's snarky with you? That what you're saying?"

"Fuck you. Is everything set? I don't want to be here all night dealing with bullshit not on the agenda."

"Rooster might give you some trouble. He's been crowing about something for the last couple days, but whenever I ask him, he clams up, tells me it's nothing. I have a feeling his problem is right there." He nods toward Kenzie.

"Good thing I don't give a fuck what he thinks, then, huh?" He chuckles as I walk away to pry Kenzie away from her new bestie. She waves as I pull her along, a big smile plastered on her face.

"He's so nice! You know he said his favorite thing to do was learn something new on a spreadsheet. Isn't that crazy? I don't even know how to make the boxes bigger. He said he could teach me if I ever need one, but I told him he'll just need to do it for me."

"Shit, spreadsheets," I curse, spinning to find Tiny again.

"Whoa there, why are we going back?" She stumbles, but I catch her elbow.

"Tiny didn't tell me what he wanted, since you decided to talk his ear off."

"Oh, he said there was a discrepancy in the books. A shipment came in last week but was off. He's looking into it, but wanted you to know so you didn't think he was skimming off the top," she says. I yank her to a stop, mouth hanging open.

"He told you all that?" I narrow my eyes.

"Uh, yeah, but who am I going to tell?"

"I don't care that he told *you*. I care that he's telling anyone before me."

I swing us around to march back toward headquarters. I snarl at Rooster, who tries to stop me, brushing past and through the door, leaving his complaints in our wake. Most of the members are inside, the remnants of dinner strewn across the tables. Kenzie tries to swipe a bun off Hawk's plate, but I tug her away.

"Hey, I'm hungry," she whines, reaching her hand back to snatch it but misses.

"I fed you before we got here."

I don't want to leave her to her own devices in this sea of bikers, many of whom are eyeing her. At least they're trying to be subtle about it. I spot Doc at the front and weave my way toward him. Something hits my back when we're halfway, and I swing around, dropping Kenzie's hand. I spy a bun, sitting innocently at my feet. Hawk's head is ducked, avoiding my eyes. Kenzie swoops down to grab the bread, hiding it behind her back, as if I'm going to miraculously forget about it.

"MacKenzie, why would you have him throw it? You're terrible at catching anything." Instead of answering, she shoves it in her mouth, and I cringe.

"I don't know what you're talking about," she mumbles, her mouth full, grinning.

The tension in my shoulders loosens. I didn't notice the strain until it flows out of me. Last week was terrible for my stress levels. Seeing her grinning and laughing, messing around with Hawk, striking up a conversation with Tiny, fighting with me instead of crying in my arms, eases the ball of guilt sitting in my stomach. The relief wells up, and her grin fades.

"Are you okay?" she whispers, stepping closer.

I clear my throat. "I'm good. Don't eat that, though. It's probably got shit on it."

I grab another bun off Tiny's plate and shove it at her, stalking away to talk to Doc. Her footsteps follow close behind. I expected her to stay with Tiny, but I notice she's trailing me all the way to the front. I nod to Doc, glare at Blue, our secretary, until he slinks away, throwing a half-hearted wave over his shoulder.

"Doc, anything else?" He blinks, then turns his gaze to MacKenzie.

"Hello, dear. How are you feeling?" he asks. I roll my eyes, but neither of them notice.

"A lot better today. You?"

Nodding, he studies her face. I can practically see the gears turning in his mind. Most people miss the calculating going on in his head. They're too distracted by his size, his soft voice, his tats, the leathers, anything to distract them from his therapist brain picking them apart, analyzing their movements, figuring out how they tick. It's the reason he runs most of our interrogations, not that there's many of those happening here.

"I'm annoyed," he murmurs.

"You're an honest one, huh?" she snickers.

"I find it helps. The problem is when we lie to ourselves more often than not." He turns to me. "Rooster is going to try to take over the meeting. Don't be surprised. Let me know if you'd like me to remove him."

"Is he always like that?" Kenzie asks, eyes tracking his movements through the crowd.

"Yup. What you see is what you get when it comes to Doc." I settle in a chair, pointing at the one next to me for Kenzie.

"Oh, I'm pretty sure you're wrong but whatever." She drops on the chair, munching on the bun.

"What do you mean?"

"He says he's honest, but then talks about lying to ourselves? Yeah, he wasn't talking about me or you, or people in general. He was talking about himself. Have you ever talked to him about what's going on with him?" She's scanning the area, waving to Hawk who waves back. I have no idea when they became friends, but I'm glad she has someone else to turn to when I'm busy.

"Why the hell would I bring old shit up? This is a biker gang, Kenzie, in case you forgot, not a therapy camp. We're not here to work through our emotions and deal with our problems."

"Oh my god. You haven't noticed the kinds of people in your MC, have you? They're all misfits, seeking refuge in a group, reminding them of themselves—where they feel safe. I swear, you're so blind sometimes." She huffs out a laugh.

"We're not fucking misfits," I grumble, but now that she says it, she might be right.

Hawk has a past he's not willing to talk about. Doc was a therapist, but he's never said why he left and did a one-eighty to join the Reapers. Tiny is a gentle giant and a berserker all rolled into one. Hell, even Blue is a twitchy guy, running from an abusive past. We're the dredges of society, the ones no one wanted. The world threw us away because we are too hard to deal with. I'm probably the most stable person in this room, and I grew up in this shit, knowing I'd take over for my dad one day, but never knowing it would happen when I was nineteen. I didn't realize I'd have to cobble our group together and build us back up after the coup. Somehow I did, though. We reinvented who we are as the Reapers, not leading on fear like my father but respect.

She sighs. "It's not a bad thing. It's actually nice. Gives you hope, ya know?"

I swing my head to her. "We'll figure this shit out, Kenz, even if we are a bunch of misfits."

She smiles. "I know. I trust you."

Fuck.

FOURTEEN

MacKenzie

Ryker stands, and I contemplate whether I should crawl under the table just to fuck with him, but that wouldn't be a good look. Plus, I might not be able to get back up again. My body may feel better than it has in a long time, but I'm losing steam. An ache seeps into my bones, slowing me down. I'm trying to keep the smile on my face, but it's not like anyone is paying attention to me. Hawk sidles up next to my chair, gesturing to follow him to another one off to the side. I glance back at Ryker, but he's deep in conversation with who I'm assuming is Blue, whose hands are twitching while he waves them about.

"Sorry, I figured you didn't want to be right in front, having everyone stare at you," Hawk mutters, pulling out a chair for me.

I slide into the seat. "I don't think anyone was paying attention to me, but it's fine. Be a little weird to have me up there."

He chuckles. "Mac, everyone noticed you."

Scanning the room, I see at least a dozen guys openly staring, some glaring, others merely watching. My skin itches, and I rub my arms, a tremor running through my body when I hit a bruise that isn't quite healed. I thought I'd be more aware of my wounds by now and would stop doing this shit, but I keep forgetting my body is beaten down.

"Maybe I should leave," I whisper, wondering if I can slip out the back and make it to Ryker's house before he can stop me. He'd insist on someone staying with me. Hawk shoots me a look, but I glance at Ryker, trying to catch his eye. Of course he starts the meeting right then.

"Anybody got any shit to say before we get to the reason we're here? Anyone other than Rooster?"

"What the fuck, Prez? I got shit to say!" A ruddy man who looks like he's run into more than a couple fists in his day is on his feet.

"Now ain't the time. You can bring it up at the actual meeting. Which is exactly what Hawk told you. And Doc told you, but you ignored them, so fuck off. Anyone else?"

"What's the old lady doing here?" someone in the back calls.

It's been a long time since I've spent time in Reaper territory. I don't recognize anyone. To step into this place and see the same flags hanging on the wall is jarring, the same set up I grew up around, but there's no one left I recognize. Ryker peers at me, and I can see the indecision in his eyes. He didn't want to bring me in the first place, and now I'm learning why, when it's too late to hide away.

"That's Mac. Some of you remember her from a couple months ago. You'll respect her, or you'll lose your colors."

He states it so matter-of-factly it takes a minute to process what he said. He's moved on, explaining the situation with Maddox. I peek at Hawk, who doesn't look surprised by the news.

"Hawk." I nudge him. "He's not serious, right?" He smirks, nodding. "He can't do that."

He leans in. "He's the Prez. He can do whatever he wants."

Ryker's droning on about security measures. There's more than a couple sneaking glances at me, each more hostile than the last. I may have wanted to come to the meeting, but I didn't want Ryker to make it all about me. He's screwed up any chance I have at winning them over. I'm sure he'll argue he wasn't putting me before the club, but based on the nasty looks I'm getting, I'm not the only one pissed about it. I'm not a part of this club. I'm not patched. Technically, I shouldn't have even come to Synd. There are rules in place for a reason, and I broke every one of them. They should be pissed. I don't blame them. I *can* take my frustration out on him, though.

Ryker talks about the shit the Night Slayers have done so far. The small incidences are piling up, some I've heard about, others I haven't. The more he talks, the more I realize how much he's been keeping from me, and a wave of fury washes over me.

Hawk leans over, whispering in my ear, "We're pretty sure the Slayers aren't to blame for the shipments going missing. The Kings and Byrns have been having the same problems. Tank's dealing with it."

Groans, grumbles, and scraping chairs reverberate through the room as everyone files out. No questions were asked, no debates on what they should do—this was the head of the Reapers handing down commands. I don't know how meetings go here now, but when we were kids, they were silent. Fear coated everyone in the room. Now there's a layer of respect. Rooster is still trying to waylay Ryker, but Doc intercepts him and pulls the man away, baring his teeth when Rooster objects.

"Went better than I expected," Ryker says, watching Doc and Rooster over his shoulder.

"Surprised there wasn't a revolt, honestly," Hawk responds.

"Ready, Kenz? Sam wants you to call her tonight. Something about ice cream." He finally glances at me, and his eyebrows shoot up as he notices I'm still glaring. I push myself up and march past him, taking the back door. The last thing I want to do is run into any of them. There's plenty of ways men can insult a woman no one thinks is disrespectful. Embarrassment flooding through me, making my cheeks flush with heat, I slam out the door.

"Kenzie!" he yells, footsteps pounding after me. "MacKenzie!"

"I can't believe you," I grind out when he reaches my side.

"What the hell are you talking about?"

"You fucking asshole."

"Would you stop?" He grabs my arm loosely, pulling me to a stop. "Seriously, what are you so angry about?"

I yank my wrist out of his grasp before crossing my arms. "You made me a fucking target. Lose their colors? Are you for fucking real? You can't kick people out of the Reapers if they're not nice to me. That's insane!"

"I was establishing boundaries. I'm not going to have you walking around getting confronted or hit on by every fucking member you come across."

My eyes widen, and I throw my hands up. "They're not going to hit on me! What fantasy world do you live in? You put a target on my back, and I have to deal with the fallout from your fuck-up."

"No, I protected you," he growls.

"From who? The Reapers? I'm not in danger from them. I have scarier villains than your MC out there."

"I'll protect you from them, too. Stop fighting me on this, MacKenzie." He stomps away, then spins when I don't follow. "Are you coming?"

Flipping him off, I stomp after him. He's never going to see the damage he's done until the consequences pile up. The Vipers are filled with men who think they can say and do whatever they want, simply because they're men. My father brought men in who thought women were property. I'm not going to lower my guard because Ryker thinks his men are upstanding oddballs. He clearly missed the rage in some of their eyes tonight.

The uncertainty and guilt I harbored before rushes back. I shouldn't have come here. Bringing my problems to Ryker was a mistake. I should have dealt with the consequences myself. At least then, I'd be the only one to get hurt, the one to shoulder the responsibility of keeping myself alive. Instead, I selfishly heaped it on to Ryker.

I cared about the cost, but not enough to stand my ground when he kept insisting on being told what happened. Kane's face flashes in my mind, his soulless, almost-black eyes reflecting his shriveled soul, staring down at me as I lay battered on the floor. His callous voice, laughing about using my body for whatever sadistic games he wanted to play echoes through my head, and I shiver. Whipping my head around, I scan the tree line. It's shadowed and eerie, the branches casting beams of moonlight to scatter across the forest floor. I hurry to Ryker's side, not wanting to be left alone, searching the trees for phantoms that don't exist.

"Why can't you just accept my help?" he grumbles, eyes fixed ahead.

"You shouldn't have to save me. It's not your job." I wrap my arms around my waist. The anger seeped out of me when the Night Slayers intruded my thoughts. Fear and guilt are all that's left.

"Don't you think I should decide what I want to do instead of assuming?"

"You'd help me even if you didn't want to. You've always been like that," I murmur.

"Not with you. Never with you, Kenz. I helped you because I wanted to, every time. I don't know why you're still questioning me. You never thought you deserved it, but you did—you still do. You're worth it."

I don't know what to say when he says things like that. I don't understand why he believes in me when I can't even believe in myself. My life has been one struggle after another, trying to fit in, find a place in the MC as a girl, fighting for a spot in the boys' group, wanting to be heard by my father, Dante—hell, and even Ryker. I adopted a persona I thought would make others notice me, but instead I'm labeled as too much.

"I don't want to be a burden," I admit. I push past him, barreling through the back door but freeze just inside the threshold.

"Kenzie . . ." Ryker wraps his fingers around my arm, drawing me behind him. I huddle close, glancing behind at the trees, silently standing vigil over the dark yard. Ryker slips his phone to me, eyes still trained on the quiet kitchen.

"Text Hawk, tell him to bring Doc and Tank if he's back," he mutters. I wake it up, and am met with a password screen. Peeking at his back, I punch in a guess, and it unlocks. Well, that's something we'll be talking about later. I shoot off a text, and push the phone down my shirt, tucking it into my bra.

"Are we going in?" I peer over his shoulder, taking in the destruction of the room.

Plates are smashed, cutlery littering the floor, and the fridge is hanging open, the contents spilling out. Whoever did this even smashed the bulb inside, leaving the space dark and ominous. I can't imagine what the rest of the house looks like.

Heaviness settles in my bones, and I wonder again if I should have run anywhere but Synd. I knew it was a risk, but for some reason, I assumed they couldn't touch me here. They've infiltrated my bubble of safety and tainted it. Ryker reaches back, and I grip his hand tightly, crowding into his leathers, burying my face between his shoulder blades. His smell, a mixture of leather and cinnamon, eases the tension in my muscles. Breathing him in, I don't feel so conflicted anymore.

We stay like that until a commotion at the front sends Ryker into action. Still gripping my hand, he leads the way through the destruction while glass crunches under his boots. The living room is a mess with pillows and cushions with fluff scattered around as if they were stabbed. A frame skitters across the hardwood when my shoe clips the edge, eventually disappearing under the couch. I suck in a deep breath as my heart pounds in my chest. I shake my head at the wreckage around us, trying to keep my shit together.

Ryker swings the door open to usher the Doc inside, followed closely by Hawk. Without a word, they sweep the house. Ryker crowds me into a corner by the door, and I'm stuck staring at the patch in front of my face. Tracing it with a finger, I focus on the swoops and the feel of threads under my touch instead of worrying about what the others will find.

"At least I'm not freaking out," I whisper, my breath flowing past his ear. He shivers, making me grin.

"Well, I am, so stop distracting me," he mutters.

"What am I distracting you from? You're not doing anything." Another exhale, another shiver, and I grin again.

"I'm keeping you safe, dummy. You're making it hard to listen. They could still be in the house, waiting for us. You think about that?" He glances over his shoulder, and I kiss the corner of his mouth.

"Nope. Your guys would have found them by now. Besides, messing with you is helping me not have a panic attack. You don't want that, do you?"

He sighs as my fingers dance under his jacket, then his shirt and along his warm skin, making him jolt.

"Kenzie."

"Hmm?" I follow the curve of his hip bone, stopping when I hit his zipper. I walk my fingers up his abs, trying to count as I go, but lose track when he pushes me farther into the corner. His hand snakes back, grabbing my thigh.

"Ouch," I whine, but he chuckles.

"Oh, did that hurt? You realize I've seen you naked, right? I remember precisely where each and every bruise is on your body." His words send a shudder through me, and heat gathers in my cheeks and flows straight between my legs. His fingers caress my thigh, drifting closer to my clit with each pass.

"It's not polite to remind someone you've seen them naked."

He snorts, squeezing my thigh again. I brush my fingers higher, his shirt riding up with the path my hand is taking. Footsteps upstairs has him tensing, and he pushes back more.

"Knock it off, Kenz, unless you want an audience when I turn around and fuck you against the wall," he grunts.

I pinch his nipple, and he jolts. "Fine, party pooper."

Dropping my hand from his body as he eases forward, I tuck it in his back pocket, trying to squeeze his ass, but it's as hard as his abs. I can't imagine going on a ride with an ass like his.

"Does your butt hurt after you ride?"

"What? Get your hand out of there. I swear to god, MacKenzie, you're driving me up a wall," he grumbles, letting go of me.

Tugging my hand out and tucking them both behind my back, I try to put more distance between us. He might not be entirely serious, but the tone he's using is the same one he used when we were kids. Clearly, my ability to annoy him hasn't diminished over the years.

Tipping my head back, I stare at the swirls on the ceiling. I rack my brain, trying to remember how I snapped him out of his bad moods back then, but I don't think I ever found a way. At some point, I stopped trying and would walk away, hiding in the woods, or my room until I figured he wouldn't snap at me anymore.

Huffing, I bounce from foot to foot. I swear it's been an hour since Hawk and Doc disappeared upstairs. Letting out a muffled giggle, I rhyme their names in my head. Ryker's head dips, so I stop. Finally, the two tromp down the stairs, Doc heading straight out the door without a word.

"Well?" Ryker demands.

"Nothing up there. Seems it's just the main floor. Don't know if they even went up there. Nothing looked out of place, but you'll be able to notice more shit than I can. Swept the place, and there's nothing. I'll check down here, but it'll take a bit." Hawk leans over and catches my eye. "You okay, Mac?"

"Yeah, I'm good." I poke Ryker between the shoulder blades to get him moving, but my finger crumples instead of getting him going.

"Other than driving me batshit crazy, she's fine. Go upstairs, MacKenzie," he orders, stepping away, and they head to the kitchen. I'm not a naughty child who needs to be sent to their room.

Narrowing my eyes, I purse my lips, before I dash up the stairs, shutting myself in the bathroom. I'm dialing Sam's number before I click the lock, not wanting Ryker to barge in on me. Dickhead.

"MacKenzie Jean Raines. I have been worried sick, young lady. Is it really that hard to call and check in?" Sam scolds, then starts laughing.

"Sorry, Mom," I say, sarcasm dripping from my voice.

"I'm working on my authority voice to use on Emma. How'd that sound?" The door shuts on her end of the line.

"I feel immensely guilty and properly chastised. Might want to add in a long, drawn-out sigh, too. Oh, and a little more passive aggressiveness. Dante used that on me a lot when I was younger."

"Noted. How are things over there? Helms is ignoring my texts. Okay, he's not ignoring them, but he won't answer more than one word at a time, and it's driving me bonkers."

Unsure of how much I wanna reveal, I sigh, but with Willow still in Rima and not having any other friends, I need to vent. I'll go bonkers if I have to keep everything inside anymore. Besides, I want to brag about keeping my cool, and Sam will understand.

"Well, Ryker painted a target on my back. The entire lower half of the house is trashed, which might send Ryker into a tailspin. I'm hanging on to my sanity by a thread. Oh, and he snapped at me and is being an asshole." Now that I don't have anything to focus on anymore, I'm slowly unraveling.

"All right, let's start from the beginning. We'll talk until you no longer feel like you're drowning."

I sigh. "Thanks, Sam."

FIFTEEN

Ryker

"We going to talk about that?" Hawk bends down, picking up a plate cracked down the middle.

I kick shattered glass aside to grab a broom from the laundry room.

"You have any idea who broke into my house and destroyed it? If not, then I don't know what we'd discuss."

Closing the fridge, I curse the fact all the food most likely went bad when we were mere blocks away. Whoever did this knew we wouldn't be home. It doesn't make sense, though. Did they leave the upstairs untouched on purpose? Did we interrupt them? And if they heard us coming, how did they get away without us catching them? They stole in and out of our territory with us none the wiser, and that's more fucked up than anything. If I can't see them coming, how do I keep everyone safe?

"So, we're going to ignore how you essentially ordered Mac around?" He scrapes food off the table into the garbage.

"I don't have the mental capacity to deal with this shit and the shit going on with her, too. I can only focus on one problem at a time." I sigh, sweeping the broom under the table. There's no way I'll get all the glass. I should get a prospect in here to deal with it, but I hate having people in my house, especially little shits like the prospects. They always snoop, but the mess will send me into a tailspin if I leave it.

Hawk clears his throat, and I glance up, following his eyes over my shoulder. MacKenzie stands in the doorway, looking casual, arms crossed, leaning against the frame, but the tightness around her eyes gives away she heard me, and she's not fucking happy. I hang my head, moving a chair out of the way, and pull the broom across the hardwood.

"I was going to ask if you need any help, but I'm guessing you'll turn me down. So, I'm going to bed," she says.

I wait, and after a minute, her footsteps fade up the stairs. I expect the slam of a door, but the house is quiet.

"What the fuck is going on between you two? I thought you were good?"

"It's complicated." I concentrate on putting my house back in order. I don't have a plan for any of the problems weighing on my mind, so I'll focus on what's in front of me. It's the only way I'll keep my shit together.

"Pretty clear to me," he mutters, grabbing another broom.

"What the hell does that mean?"

"Ryker, you're in love with her. You have been for fucking years. I mean, you'll have to figure out how to love who she is now, but she's right there. Mac came to you. When she needed help, she ran to you. That's gotta tell you something. You're fucking it up by being a dickhead at the drop of a hat. You're going to have to pick a lane, because if you keep pushing her away, you won't get another chance."

"When did you become a relationship expert?"

"Oh, we're calling it a relationship now? I thought you'd say it was just a fling or something," he chuckles.

"MacKenzie has enough to deal with without me coming in and making it more complicated."

"Maybe you should have said that instead of calling her a problem. I'll get some prospects in here to clean this shit up. Don't feed me some bullshit about not wanting anyone in your house, either." He drops the broom, then walks about the back door without another word.

I fall into a chair, something squishing under my boot. The buzz of my phone has me pulling it out, and I scowl.

"Ren, what can I do for you?"

"For one, you can stop making your girl cry. She cries, calls my girl, and suddenly, I'm pulled in to your relationship problems. Second, I got you the footage of those bikers at Trigger's, but you're not going to like it. They went north and disappeared. Third, I heard you had a break-in."

I skip straight to the things I can fix, which currently isn't my feelings about Kenzie. I wasn't lying when I told Hawk I didn't have the mental capacity to keep up with all the issues being thrown at us. I shouldn't have taken things so far yesterday. I should have stuck to keeping her safe, fighting her battles, nothing more. Like an idiot, I crossed the line again, not thinking far enough ahead about how many obstacles would be hurled in our path in the process.

"Did you get a good look at their faces? We know where they came from, but I need to know if they come back, preferably before they walk back into Trigger's and set the fucker on fire or something."

"Nothing. They knew there would be cameras and reacted accordingly. Who broke in?"

"Don't know. I'm leaning toward someone inside my club. Only the lower level was hit. It wouldn't make sense if it was the Night Slayers." I gaze around at the muted room.

"Have Hawk call me. He should have received an alert if someone was there. I put in extra measures so something like this wouldn't happen." Keys tap in the background, and something beeps. I never understood how he learned all this stuff, but he's helped me a lot lately. Except putting shit in without my approval makes my stomach twist.

"Extra measures?"

"Nothing serious, just extra alerts on the specific cameras outside your major places, like your house. I'll come tomorrow and sit down with him, make sure he understands how it works."

"I'll tell him. Anything else?" I'm itching to get off the phone and find Kenzie.

I need to dig myself out of the hole I created, maybe set up some boundaries. The last thing I should do is sleep next to her tonight, so I'll need to move my shit to the spare room. My stomach twists again, wondering if I'm just piling mistakes upon mistakes.

"Alex would like to speak to you, but I told him no. He wants to yell at you. However, Shane would also like to speak with you, and I'm more inclined to let him," he mutters.

I huff. "Fine, let's get this over with." Alex's yelling fills the line, and I gather he's pissed, but his shouts fade.

"Helms. What the fuck is going on over there?"

"The same shit that's been going on for the past week. What do you need, Shane?"

Exhaustion floods my body, and my eyes fall closed. Being on high alert has taken its toll on my body. Last night was the first night I slept well, all because of Kenzie.

"I need for you to stop fucking shit up with Mac. Your issues are seeping into our house, and as much as I love that Sam has a new friend, I want them to be able to have a movie night rather than a sob fest." I snort, imagining Sam sitting down for a cozy movie night.

"We're working through some shit. I'll tell her to knock off bugging Sam."

"The fuck you will. Stop being an asshole and life goes much smoother," he barks.

"You would know," I mutter, remembering the shit he put Sam through.

"Yeah, well, learn from my mistakes. You don't want a mad dash across town to save her from a psychopath to be the thing that tells you your true feelings for her. Save yourself the heartache. Figure your shit out."

He hangs up before I can respond. I never thought I'd be in the position to be receiving relationship advice from Shane fucking King. An itching in my back, a tingle in my fingers, keeps telling me to get up, clean up this mess, find whoever thought it was a good idea to fuck with my shit, and to hit back at the Night Slayers and the bastard leading them, but I shake out my hands instead. I push myself to stand and face the music.

My room is dark when I push open the door. I scan the muted light, but Kenzie isn't in the bed. The bathroom is open and dark, so I stride to the closet, but that's empty, too. Even when I dig in the back where I found her before, I don't find her. I'm at a loss.

Did I miss her sneaking out the door? She wouldn't go out the window. I stalk back to the hallway, freeze next to the spare room, and push it open. It's dark, too, but I see a lump in the bed. Her back is to me, soft breaths filling the quiet room. I shuffle to the window, making sure it's locked before turning around and taking in her sleeping face. Her cheeks are still blotchy from crying, and a pang hits my chest.

I should have come earlier. I should have thought about what I was saying, how it would affect her. I should have done a lot of things differently, but now I'm stuck dealing with damage control. No, not damage control—groveling. I may have my doubts about where we should go from here, but hurting her, dismissing her, was a shit move. The last thing she needs is me piling on.

I want to wake her up, but I don't know what to say. I don't know how to fix this. Instead, I go back to my room, intent on taking a shower. Kenzie's things are still scattered throughout the bathroom, filling up the counter and taking up space on my shelves. Organizing it, I throw clothes in the hamper, and find places for her bottles in the shower.

It doesn't help the anxiety welling up in my chest. The feeling is still there when I step under the spray. The uneasiness dogs me while I wash my hair, dry my body, and shave. My heart is pounding when I yank the comforter off my bed and bring it back to the spare bedroom. Flexing my fingers, I try to banish the pins and needles as I spread the blankets on the floor, then snag a pillow off the bed next to her. I settle down between the door and bed, exhaustion overcoming me.

A pillow to my face wakes me. Jolting upright, I reach for my gun. The room is still dark, no sounds or shadows coming from the dark corners of the room. I don't want to flip on the light, but I might have to if I can't find whoever is in here with us.

"What the hell are you doing?" Kenzie's voice pierces the silence.

Whipping around, I find her sitting up, annoyed and glaring. I bring my finger to my lips.

"Stay here. I'm going to check the house."

"Oh my god, Ryker. I threw the pillow at you. No one is in the house. Why are you sleeping on the floor?" She gestures to the pile of blankets.

"You're in here," I mumble.

The last thing I'm going to do is leave her to sleep alone. Knowing my luck, someone would come for her the minute I do.

"Uh, yeah. I moved rooms. Didn't mean you had to follow me," she bristles.

"Well, I wasn't going to leave you all alone."

"Why didn't you just get in the damn bed, then?"

I open my mouth, then snap it shut. This isn't the time to have this conversation. Plus, I never did work out what I should say to her. Usually, I ignore whatever is bothering me until it goes away, at least when it comes to her. I don't think that will work now. I duck, taking a deep breath, trying to form the words, but it's still blank.

"You're not a problem," I say, staring at my feet.

"I know I'm not."

My head snaps up, taking in her raised eyebrow and snarky tone. "I was stressed before."

"I know."

"But you were crying."

"How did you know I was crying? Wait, never mind. I know how you found out. I wasn't crying because of you. I knew you were anxious. I don't blame you. I'm not mad at you, at least for that." Kenzie tucks her hands under the covers, pulling them up to cover her arms while she cocks an eyebrow.

"Then why were you crying?"

"Oh, the whole break-in hit me, that's all. I had a freak out. I talked to Sam. She got me through it, and I'm okay now. Still pissed at you," she mutters.

I'm not sure if I buy her excuse, but it's plausible.

"Why didn't you just come to me? And why are you sleeping in here if you're not mad?" I cross my arms, pinning her in place with my stare.

She rolls hers in response, puffing out a breath. "Because you were dealing with your own shit. It's fine. I came in here because of what you said, but I'm not mad. I get it. You've already done a lot for me. Adding another layer isn't smart. So, I thought I'd make it easier for both of us and sleep in here from now on."

I nod, but the ache in my chest is back. The itching between my shoulder blades makes my head twitch, and there's a quivering in my stomach. I fucking hate this. Rationally, I should agree with her, but the riot in my body says we're making another huge mistake. I didn't lose her before, I actively shoved her from my life. It's the only regret I've carried. Making those mistakes again would only send me into another spiral I don't know I'd survive.

"No," I say.

"Um, no? What do you mean 'no'?"

"I mean no. You're going to go back to my bed, where you belong."

"Ryker, this week has been a shit show. You can't just make those decisions."

Stepping over the mess on the floor, I brace my hands on either side of her and lean in.

"Watch me."

SIXTEEN

MacKenzie

We're in a stand-off—Ryker demanding I follow his asinine rules and me sick of being pushed around. These last couple of weeks have taken their toll on my sanity, but they've also buried who I am, or who I thought I was, under layers of anxiety and doubt. I thought I was confident, strong, and independent, just like Ryker said. But the minute something went wrong, I ran straight to a man. Not any man—one I have history with. A man who has always pushed and prodded me every step of the way. One who can't seem to figure out what the hell he wants.

"What are you going to do? Throw me over your shoulder and tie me to your bed?"

The second the words slip out, I wish I could stuff them back in. His eyes darken, and a seductive smirk overtakes his mouth, sending heat straight to my pussy. Fuck.

"That can definitely be arranged," he growls, leaning in and running his nose along my jaw.

"This isn't . . ." I clear my throat. "We are not going down this road again."

"What do you mean?" he murmurs, sucking my earlobe between his teeth. Before registering what I'm doing, I tip my head.

"You and me. We can't." I swallow my groan when he latches on to the spot behind my ear. "You're being very wishy-washy."

"Hmm." He moves to my neck, nipping and sucking his way down and back up to my ear. My eyes fall closed, but I snap them open and jerk back to see his startled face.

"Ryker, stop."

His eyes flash, hurt building in them before they shutter, and he stands. I want to explain, to talk about it, but he bends, scooping up the bedding, and stalks from the room. Stunned, I stare at the closed door. I almost face plant when I scramble off the bed. I fling the door open, expecting to chase him to his own room, but I fall. His arms wrap around me, swinging me up, then plants my feet.

"What the hell are you doing, MacKenzie?" he barks, stepping away. His bedding is arranged outside my door now.

"I thought you were going to your room," I babble, eyes fixed on the blankets.

"So, you thought you'd what? Run off again? You're not even wearing pants."

He's right. I'm not. I'm not even wearing shorts. The underwear isn't sexy or fun, but they're comfortable, and they're all I wanted when I crawled into bed. I try to pull the tank top down, but it crawls back up. His words filter through my brain, and I glare.

"I wasn't going to run off. You did, though. I mean, you clearly didn't go far, but seriously? Who does that?" I grab the hem of my shirt, holding it down. It's hard to have a conversation when my clothes have a mind of their own.

"You said stop, I stopped. Not much else to say." Ryker bends, straightening the pillow.

"What the fuck are we doing? This is ridiculous. Why can't we ever have a normal conversation?" It's something we've never achieved, a simple conversation without sarcasm or bickering.

"Because we both like to fight." He says it so quietly, I don't think I was meant to hear. But I did, and it makes sense.

"Speak for yourself. I am a model of composure until *you* come around."

He snorts. "Sure you are. Except you start half the fights we have."

"This can't be healthy." Blowing out a breath, I tip my head back.

"Maybe because it's fun? Kenz, you frustrate me more than anyone else in this goddamn world, but fuck if it isn't fun."

As I meet his eyes, something inside me clicks. I can't pinpoint where or why, but it's there, a shift inside my body and mind.

"I need to know what you want," I say, planting my hands on my hips.

I may feel differently, or maybe I'm just acknowledging it now, but I need Ryker on board. I'll deal with the fallout if he's not after, but if I never force the conversation, we'll keep having these mini blowups. We'll never get off this rollercoaster.

"I've been clear with what I want." He mirrors my stance but avoids my eyes.

"No, you haven't. One minute you're spouting how I'm safe, and you'll protect me. The next you're shoving me against the wall and doin"—I pause—"things to my body. Then the next minute, you're telling me I'm a distraction and a problem. I can't be all those things. Well, I mean, I can be, because I can be whatever the hell I want to be, but not once have you said what you want."

"I told you I wanted you. I thought I was clear when I was doing 'things' to your body."

"The air quotes are a little much," I hiss, narrowing my eyes.

"Your mouth is a little much." He smirks, as if he's won something.

"Clever. Now, what did you mean?" Pretending his answer won't make or break me, I purse my lips.

"You want to know what I mean?" He steps around the blankets, slowly advancing on me, crowding me against the wall. He's not even touching me, but my body quivers, like his nearness is enough to wake all my nerve endings and crave his touch.

"Yes, I do," my voice wavers, but I straighten my spine as he plants his hands on either side of my head, boxing me in.

"I admit, I've been torn between wanting you and wanting what's best for you."

"Shouldn't I make the decision of what's best for me?"

"You did when you told me to stop," he snaps and ducks his head. His hair brushes my cheek, sending another shiver through me.

"I didn't tell you to leave. I can't keep guessing at what you want."

"I want you—just you. Fuck, Kenz. Do you know how hard it was to let you go the first time? To let you walk away and know it wasn't right? Nothing was right then. I couldn't keep you safe. I couldn't protect you. But we're not kids anymore. I want your fears. I want your dreams. I want your desires. I want to lock you in this damn house. I want to tie you to the goddamn bed. I want your everything." His eyes meet mine, burning with emotion.

"Oh." That's all I can get out.

For as much as we fight, he's always been the one better at expressing himself. He keeps them locked up, but when the flood gates open, he knows precisely what to say. My brain, however, short-circuits, refusing to form words, much less sentences.

Leaning into my neck, he breathes into my skin. "I want to keep you."

"Are you sure?"

I have to ask. The doubts in myself force the question out. I pretend I'm okay with who I am, but I've never felt comfortable in my own skin. I don't have it in me to blindly believe him when he says these things. I want to, but something holds me back every time.

"Fuck, Kenz. It's the only thing I'm sure about."

My hands latch on to his sides, pulling him closer, and his hand ducks under my hair, holding my neck while his head stays buried. We hold each other until I'm squirming against him, wanting his body pressed to mine. He wants my everything, but so do I. I've waited long enough. Burying my hands under his shirt's hem, I scrape my nails across his skin, making him tremble and grip me tighter. I tilt my head forward, biting his collarbone, and he jerks into me.

"Why are you still wearing clothes?" I tug at his shirt, and he rips it off, one-handed.

He reaches for me again, but I bring my hands up, tracing the whorls and patterns of the ink tattooed into his skin.

"Kenzie, I'm not"—he coughs when I pinch his nipple— "I'm not fucking you against the wall."

"You told me before, and I still don't agree with that decision." Smirking, I pinch the other nipple, loving when he sucks in a breath.

"You're still sore. I'm not going to hurt you merely because I want to fuck you." He groans, his head falling back when my fingers brush lower, teasing the waistband of his boxer briefs.

"I'm not all that sore. I think I'm all better now. So . . ."

"Still not fucking you against a wall," he growls.

He bends, curling an arm under my ass, then picks me up. I lock my arms around his neck as he strides for his room. I expect him to toss me on the bed, but he lowers me gently, covering my body with his. He fuses his mouth to mine. I catch his lower lip between my teeth, and his tongue plunges in, forcing me to release his lip. Whimpering, I push my hips up, begging for his weight. He tears his mouth from mine, traveling down my neck. His fingers brush my arm.

"Kenz, tell me you have protection."

It takes me a minute to process his words with what his mouth is doing to my neck.

"We're good." I gasp as his hips jerk, his cock hitting my clit through my underwear.

He pulls back. "How are we good?"

"I'm not trying to trap you with a pregnancy. I have an IUD."

He dives back to my neck, cupping my breast. "Wouldn't be a trap, baby."

I swear I heard him wrong, but I'm not going to have *that* conversation now. Later, when he's not setting my body on fire, sending lightning bolts through me, I'll bring it up. I skim my fingers into his hair, gripping tight and then yanking him back to my mouth. He devours me as he rocks his hips. Hooking a leg around his, I try to create more friction. His hand skims down, settling on my hip, squeezing as he thrusts his tongue in my mouth. Meeting him, I grip his arm and leave half-moon imprints on his bicep.

He tugs back, eyes shut tight. "Kenz, tell me you want this." His forehead falls to my chest. "Tell me I'm not just a distraction for you."

My brain switches, heart stuttering, and I swear he can hear it, feel it, when he twitches, waiting for my answer. It never occurred to me he'd worry about something like that.

"I'm not good at the declarations," I whisper into his hair. "But you are anything but a distraction."

"Thank fuck," he huffs. His lips fuse to my skin, and he pushes my tank top further up my body.

I fling my hands over my head, arching my back so he can peel it off. As soon as it's gone, I tuck my arms against my sides, trying to stop my tits from spilling over into my armpits. It's awkward, but the alternative is having two half-deflated boobs flopping around, not sure if they want to suffocate me or go in two different directions. He tosses the fabric over the side of the bed, then glances down at me, grinning.

"Whatcha doin' there?" He's fixated on my chest—no, not my chest, my arms.

"Nothing. Why are you looking at me like that?" I peer down, but all I see is cleavage. They look halfway decent from my viewpoint, most of the bruises fading, leaving only a slight discoloration here and there.

"Are you holding them up with your arms?" He tilts his head this way and that, looking from every angle, and it's starting to piss me off.

"I thought we were in the middle of something?"

"Oh, we most definitely are, but I'd rather your hands on me, instead of trying to contain these," he states before sliding his hands up, grabbing both of my tits and burying his face in them. He blazes a trail with his lips toward my stomach, but I wiggle, trying to pull him back to my mouth.

"Ryker," I whine when he doesn't respond, and he nips at my ribs.

"Woman, are you trying to stop me from seducing you?" he growls, peering from under his lashes at me. Eyes widening I shake my head. "Then what's the problem?"

"Come back here."

"No." He folds his arms over my stomach.

Waiting, I clench when he rests his chin on his hands. "Fine." I huff, reaching for the bedside lamp, but his hand shoots out, capturing mine before pulling it back in gently.

"What are you doing?"

He raises an eyebrow. "The question is what are *you* doing? I made you come against the wall with the lights on. I made you come again with my head buried in your pussy with the lights on. I'd like to fuck you with the lights on."

"That was different," I mutter, staring at the ceiling.

"How? Because you'll be naked now?" He smirks.

"Exactly. I like having the lights off."

"Do you really?"

"Of course. I wouldn't do it otherwise." I purse my lips.

He pushes up, covering my body with his, framing my face and forcing me to look at him. "Kenz, what are you worried about?"

"I want to be sexy."

"You are sexy."

"No, not like, sexy, but *sexy*."

Widening my eyes, I try to infuse my tone with whatever I'm feeling. I can't find the words. He rolls, grabbing my hand. He tugs me to the bathroom, flipping on the light, then shutting the door behind us. He swings me around, my back flush with his chest, facing the mirror on the door.

"What do you see?" he whispers in my ear, gripping my hips so I can't escape.

"I don't know." I shut my eyes. "I just want to get laid."

He chuckles. "Liar. Open your eyes and tell me."

"I see"—I suck in a breath—"long legs." He presses a kiss to my neck. "Wide hips." Another kiss. "Stomach, big tits, and my face."

"And what's wrong with those things?"

"Nothing. I just don't think those things are sexy. I don't understand how you see those things and think they are. If I saw that—"

He covers my lips with his finger. "You think they're flaws."

"Of course they're flaws! It's fine. I like my body, but I don't understand how you can look at me and think it's sexy," I cry, throwing my hands up, but he keeps me where I am, planted in front of this damn mirror.

"Baby, I don't see those things when I look at you. I only see you—all of you. And you're beautiful. That's what I want. So, if you'll stop insulting my taste, I'd like to get back to worshipping this body."

Melting against him, I can't stop the welling tears. It hits me that he isn't saying it for me. He isn't telling me I'm beautiful to get laid. Ryker truly believes it. He wants this, the extra skin, the heavy, drooping mounds I call boobs, thighs that could suffocate him in a matter of minutes. He wants it all, whether I see it or not. I like my body, but it's rare to find someone else who does, too.

Letting him lead me to the bed again, I wrap my arms around him, burrowing into his chest. Tears fall, dripping on his chest and rolling down his stomach. He folds his arms around me, cradling me as he kisses the top of my head.

"Kenz?" he whispers after several minutes. "Let's go to sleep."

Climbing under the sheets, I nod and cuddle close to his side, swinging my leg between his. The room is shrouded in darkness as he flips off the light.

"You think we're ever going to get this right?" I murmur, breaking the silence.

"Probably not. But any other way seems fucking boring, if you ask me."

"I meant actually having sex. We've been this close"—I hold my fingers to his face—"like twenty-seven times."

"Twenty-seven? What the hell are you talking about?"

"Well, I've been close to jumping you at least that many times. I've imagined it another fifty times at least. If you include when I was here a couple months ago—well, I don't even think I could count that high." Ryker pokes my side, making me squeal.

"So, you're saying we have some time to make up for, then."

"I'd say so. You've been slacking."

Breathing deeply, he kisses my head, and his body relaxes when he exhales, clutching me tighter.

"We'll get there, Kenz. I promise."

SEVENTEEN

Ryker

Waking up with a raging hard-on, I groan before I register Kenzie tucked up tight against my side. Blinking at the ceiling, I try to remember the dream I was having, but it floats away until all that's left are the sensations skimming at the outskirts of my consciousness. Something brushes against my cock, and I jolt, choking back another groan. Again, something skims over me, and I glance down in time to see movement under the covers. A hand grips me through my underwear, and I don't hold back the noise this time.

"Kenz, you'd better be ready to take care of that." I rumble, and her body shakes with suppressed laughter.

She sucks in a gasp when I reach around to grasp her tit, pinching her nipple. Goosebumps erupt across her skin as

I skim my hand down her side, using her ass to tuck her closer. Her finger dips under my waistband, and I hold my breath, wondering how far she'll take this little adventure. I was ready and willing last night, but after everything she confessed, it didn't feel like the right time. Hooking my fingers in the crease and holding on to her supple ass, I knead her flesh.

She might not see herself like I do, but hopefully she'll believe me when I worship every inch of her body. Her hand inches under my waistband, a knuckle grazing my shaft before she wraps her fingers around me, making me moan. I don't know what I expected, but it wasn't for her to latch on, working her hand up and down. I make it five pumps before I'm gripping her wrist to stop her movements. Her chin tips up, hooded gaze finding mine.

"Baby, you gotta stop, or I'm going to explode all over your hand," I say between gritted teeth.

She grins. "Kind of the point."

"I'm not cumming all over your hand. Down your throat, okay. When I'm deep inside that pretty pussy of yours, even better. But not on your hand, and especially not before you come."

She shudders, and her hand contracts, forcing a hiss from me.

"Are you ever going to let me take control?" She smirks, assuming she already knows the answer.

Tugging her wrist until she lets go, I slide her hand out of my boxers. I push them down and kick them and the covers off. I reach for hers, but she bats my hands away, wiggling them over her hips. She's already topless, and I can't drag my eyes from her tits, watching a gorgeous flush travel toward her face. Leaning over her, I bury my face in the juncture of her neck, breathing in her delicious scent.

"You want to be in charge?" I breathe into her skin, feeling her nod. Then I bite down, sucking on her flesh until she's trembling beneath me. "Do your worst, baby."

Laying back, I tuck my arms behind my head to wait. My cock is throbbing, but I force the thoughts of sinking into her from my mind. Allowing her to take charge will feel just as good, and she needs this. I need her to see herself like I do.

Kenzie crawls over me, planting her hands on my chest and hovering over my stomach. My hands itch to touch her, but I dig my fingers into my hair to keep them off her.

"Ryker?" She shimmies back, tits swinging as she settles above my hips.

"Hmm?"

She wraps a hand around the base of my cock, and I can't help but thrust into her fist. My eyes are fixed on her hand, twisting around as I twitch in her grasp.

"Are you sure you want me to be in charge?" My gaze snaps to her hazel eyes gleaming with desire.

I swallow, forcing the words from my throat. "You can have me any way you want, baby."

A hiss leaves me when she sinks down on my cock, enveloping me in her soaked pussy. My hips kick up without a thought, and I push further into her, slamming my eyes shut. I'll explode if I watch her ride me. I won't be able to stop myself. She digs her nails into my stomach, and the bite of pain centers me. Cracking open my eyes, I watch her. I don't know if I've ever seen a more perfect sight. Head thrown back, dark hair cascading down her back, tits squeezed between her arms. She looks like a fucking goddess.

"Move, baby. Take what you need. Take everything," I groan as she rocks back and forth.

Although I hold back, letting her set the pace, I'm itching to touch her, grab her, flip her over, and drive into her. Slowly, she rises, plunging back down, and I groan, her pussy contracting around me. She shudders, her burning green eyes find mine.

"Ryker, touch me."

My hands fly from behind my head, grabbing her hips, and I surge deeper into her. I guide her up, slamming her back down, her hips fusing with mine. I settle my hands on her calves, kneading the muscles, letting her take control again. She moans, riding my cock, and I think I'm seeing her for who she truly is for the first time. Even the first time we were together, it was dark, with her hiding under the covers, refusing to let any light in. We were kids who didn't know how to navigate the new areas our relationship went. We weren't together; weren't anything more than friends.

Shaking the memories away, I focus on the here and now, reveling in the feeling of being inside of her, seeing her lose herself to the pleasure washing over her. Her body is flushed, and her head falls forward. The scent of her shampoo along with us mingles together, creating an intoxicating scent.

She stops suddenly, panting. "I can't . . . I want you to take over."

I search her face, unsure of what I'm looking for. Maybe regret or shame. When she lifts her head, eyes meeting mine, I see it. I sit up, wrapping my arms around her waist, still deep inside her.

"Are you tired, baby?" I whisper in her ear, and she nods. She might look a lot better than when she first arrived, but her body isn't fully healed, and I'm kicking myself for not remembering. "Do you want to stop?"

"God, no. If you stop, I'll have to finish myself off, and lord knows that won't be nearly as fun or satisfying." She smiles into my shoulder.

I lay back, taking her with me, who's still folded against my body and roll to the side, careful to not spill us right off the bed. She squirms under me, but I take my time, nipping and sucking along her neck, circling my hips just enough to tease her. She might not be willing to admit it, but she'll be sore if I take her hard and fast like I want to, and it won't be the delicious kind of sore I want her in.

"Ryker," she whimpers, pulling her knees up, forcing me further inside her.

I chuckle. "Greedy little thing, aren't you?" I bite her nipple, and she clenches around me again. She gasps when I thrust harder, then go back to circling around.

"For fuck's sake, Ry, stop teasing me!"

"Forgot your manners, didn't you, Kenzie?" I nip at her ribs, skimming a hand across her stomach, her muscles jumping under my palm.

It takes another minute of slow torture, but she finally breaks.

"Please," she gasps, digging her nails into my biceps.

"Gladly."

I surge to my knees and grip her hips, thrusting into her hard, pulling back to bury my cock into her over and over.

Her hands find the slats on my headboard and latch on, knuckles turning white. The moans falling from her lips drive me on, the perfect symphony. The tingling starts, but I hold back, knowing she's close to exploding. I'll be damned if I go before she does.

"Baby, play with your clit. Show me how you like it," I grunt, slamming into her.

Her hand snakes down, finding the small bud. I can't pull my eyes away from her fingers touching herself without abandon, driving her pleasure to higher heights. My eyes fly to her face, ecstasy overtaking her, and I feel a flood between us as her pussy pulses around me. Stuttering, I grunt as she squeezes me tighter before spasming, and it sends me over the edge. My entire body freezes as I empty inside her, my eyes falling closed. Her pussy clenches again, and I fall. I catch myself on my forearms, still trying to catch my breath, pressing kisses across her chest. I roll my hips to draw out her pleasure as long as possible. With a tremor shivering through her body, she wheezes. I want to live here, buried in her for as long as she'll let me.

"You need to move," she pants, pushing against my shoulders.

"Two times isn't enough for you?" I grin into her flushed skin, driving my hips forward.

"I only went once, but you're suffocating me."

"Shit." Scrambling back, I pull out of her, and she squeals. "Shit. Sorry."

I kneel between her legs as she struggles to catch her breath. I tip my head back and a chuckle escapes me. I try to hold it in, but my stomach contracts and another slips out. Snickering under my breath, I brace myself on my legs, but before long, I'm full-on cackling.

"What the hell is wrong with you?" she demands, propping herself up on her elbows to scowl at me.

I open my mouth, but all that comes out is another burst of laughter. I can't even form words at this point. The thought of her trapped under me as I recover from the sweet agony of finally fucking her is too much. It shouldn't be funny. In fact, nothing about this situation is funny, but this is exactly how our entire relationship has been thus far.

"It isn't funny, Ryker," she snaps, as she struggles to sit up.

Grabbing her arm, hauling her to me, I bury my hand in her hair. My body still shakes as I swallow down another chuckle. She mumbles something, but her face is squashed into my chest, and I'm not letting her go until I'm ready. I grip the riot of hair, tugging her head back and fuse my lips to hers. The jolt of arousal stops the giddiness as desire shoots straight to my cock, hardening it again.

I retreat, resting my forehead against hers. "Baby, there's no way you only went once. You forget I could feel every pulse of that sweet pussy of yours clinging to my cock. You definitely went more than once."

She scoffs but doesn't deny it. "I have to pee."

Laughing again, I untangle her hair from my fist. She scrambles off the bed, heading for the bathroom. It clicks shut, and I notice the mess we made. The sheets are twisted, evidence of our morning romp staining them. I grin, grabbing the corner and yanking them off. I'm throwing them in the hamper when she emerges. I freeze, taking in the lines of her body. She stops, planting her hands on the arch of her hip and narrowing her eyes.

"Got something to say?"

"Oh, there's a lot of things I'd like to say, preferably with my cock, but I just stripped the bed," I say, dropping the pillow case in the hamper before stalking toward her.

My hand settles on her ass, grabbing a handful and pressing a kiss to the curve of her neck. Her arms wind around my neck, clutching tighter.

"So, what now?" she whispers, nuzzling into me.

"Now I feed you. Get dressed," I tell her, stepping back.

When she bends to grab her clothes, I smack her ass. She yelps, and I chuckle. I pull on my underwear and sweatpants, leaving her to finish.

I make it to the kitchen before I remember my kitchen is trashed. It's worse in the light of day, piles of broken plates and dried food everywhere. I twist my neck, hoping to relieve the tension gathering in my muscles. A pound on the door snaps me out of whatever spiral I was headed down, and I swing open the door.

"Good, you're awake. I got guys coming in ten minutes, so put a fucking shirt on," Hawk says, pushing past me. "Hey, Mac, you're looking better."

"Come right on in. Not like we were doing anything," I mutter, closing the door behind him.

"Hey, Hawk. Still a little sore, but I'm doing okay." I glance over my shoulder, watching her smile at him.

"If you need Ink to come by, just let me know," he says on his way to survey the damage in the living room from whoever broke in.

I glare at his back, but Kenzie's giggle has me looking at her. She shakes her head, smirking. I flip her off, if only to prevent myself from devouring her on the stairs in front of my best friend.

"We're going out. Go put some actual clothes on."

"What's wrong with this?" She gestures at the black leggings and some sort of athletic tank she's currently wearing.

"We're not going to work out. You look like you're ready for the gym, not breakfast."

Hawk spins around, taking her in before chiming, "It's actually closer to lunch. Figured you two would want to sleep in."

His snicker is what puts me over the edge. I snatch the back of his leathers, pulling him toward the door, then shoving him out while he laughs and waves to Mac while she squawks behind us. I slam the door again, flicking the lock behind him.

EIGHTEEN

MacKenzie

"What the hell, Ryker? Why did you kick him out?" I try to sneak around him, but he blocks the way, crossing his arms, then leans against the door.

"He was pissing me off. Go get dressed." I expect him to walk off, but he stays put, blue eyes fixed on me.

Throwing my hands up, I start up the stairs again. I make it half way before I realize what I'm doing. I spin, marching back down. He's still planted in front of the door, and I poke his chest.

"What I'm wearing is fine. You don't get to tell me what clothes I put on my own fucking body." Crossing my arms and pulling myself up to my full height, I mirror his stance, not quite able to look him directly in the eye, but it's close enough.

"Is that so?" He lifts an eyebrow, and I can't tell if he's playing with me.

"I'm right, and you know it. Just because we slept together doesn't mean you get to boss me around."

He studies me, and my stomach flutters, waiting for whatever asinine thing he'll come up with next.

"Glad you're back to your feisty self." He flings open the door, sweeping his arm for me to exit.

"Ryker, you're not wearing a shirt or shoes or actual pants."

He laughs, slamming the door shut again.

"Seemed like a good way to end the conversation," he calls as he walks upstairs.

I can hear him stomping around before the shower starts. I want to take one, too, but forgot the kitchen was a mess. I'll have to brush my hair if we're going out. Standing in the doorway to the kitchen, I sigh. I don't think this is because of me or at least it wasn't the Night Slayers. They would have burned the place to the ground instead. This seems personal. The mess might still be my fault, though.

Closing my eyes, I see faces from last night's meeting flash behind my lids, all the men who didn't appreciate my presence in Reaper territory. I doubt Ryker noticed them, who's so intent on dealing with the logistics of keeping his area secure. At some point, he'll have to face the truth. Quite a few people resent my being here. I'm still pissed he put a target on my back, but shit is piling up faster than I can deal with emotionally.

I'm glad I went to him. Hell, I'm grateful I had someone to run to in the first place. I've known more than a few women who didn't have the option. Growing up in an MC as a woman doesn't have a lot of perks. It's better than it was, but the old ways dug their claws deep into the foundation of motorcycle clubs. Ryker's dad wasn't much better than my own dad, both of them too set in their ways to see that girls were good for something other than fucking or breeding or using. Dante told me Ryker wanted to change things, wanted it to be different. They wanted the same things.

I can't figure out if Maddox took after our father or if he merely hates me more than anyone else. My heart squeezes, remembering sitting in this very kitchen when we were kids, eating pancakes Ryker had only half-burnt, flinging whipped cream at Maddox when he wasn't looking. I can almost hear his giggles echoing through the air when I hit Dante in the back of the head, and he didn't notice. We were left to run wild. We used to be inseparable. We used to have each other's backs. He used to love me. I don't know when he stopped, but it feels like something I should have noticed. I can't help but wonder, *If I'd caught it then, would I be here now?*

Ryker's hand grazes my arm, startling me. Heart pounding, I turn, plastering on a smile to hide the panic. He gives me a look. I'm not convincing him, but he doesn't say anything. Another knock at the door, and I slip my shoes on, ready to be anywhere but here, staring at the mess I'm sure I'd inadvertently caused. The prospects file in, nervously glancing around and avoiding my eye. Doc nods to me as Ryker guides me out the door.

"You going to be good to ride? I can call Blue instead," he says, handing me a helmet.

"I'll be fine. Not like we're going far," I say, slipping it over my head.

When my hair bunches around my face, I remember I forgot to brush it, but I'm not going back now. Instead, I try to tuck it back, but it's a lost cause. Pieces catch on my lips. I scrub at them, and my skin starts to itch.

"What the hell are you doing?"

"My hair is touching my face." I rip the helmet off, trying to use one hand to shove the strands back, but now they're staticky and clinging to my eyelashes. Ryker laughs, stepping close to brush it back gently. He pulls a ponytail holder from god knows where and hands it to me, taking the helmet while I tie it back.

"Better?"

At my nod, he slips the cover over my head, tapping the top before swinging a leg over his bike. My muscles scream when I follow suit. Maybe I should have told him to borrow Blue's car. I grit my teeth, wrapping my arms around his waist to grab on to his belt, and he tenses.

"Don't get any ideas, Kenz," he says before kicking it into gear.

We fly down the street. I close my eyes, forgetting the ache of my body, both those from the beating and from our escapades this morning. Even with the helmet, I can feel the wind on my cheeks, and I lean back, reveling in the feeling. I haven't been on a bike since Dante took his unexpected vacation, and I didn't realize how much I missed it until now. I almost miss when we fly by the diner. I watch it pass, but he doesn't slow in the slightest.

Businesses flash past, falling away to the residential area. I don't recognize any of the streets until we slow, the houses growing larger, the lots taking up more and more space. Everything looks different in the day, and it takes me a lot longer to recognize where we're headed.

When the Kings' mansion comes into view, a sigh of relief leaves me. I'm not ready for Ryker to take me some place new. I wasn't worried about being within Reaper territory, even with the break-in, but anywhere else, and I might have freaked out. The exposure of a new place in the city might have sent me over the edge. Synd might be the city I grew up in, but I've been gone so long, it feels like a foreign place now.

Ryker nods to the guard at the end of the driveway, and I wave. I think his name is Titus. He grins, lifting a hand as we pass. The front door opens as we round the fountain, and Shane King fills the doorway. He intimidated me when we first met, but the more time that passes, the less I see the mask he plasters on for everyone else. He's scowling now, though.

"Ryker," I whisper when he kills the engine, "did you tell him we were coming?"

He chuckles, helping me off the back. Shane is still glaring, but he's shoved aside as Sam squeals, bounding down the steps. She skids to a stop in front of me, jumping up and down instead of barreling into me like she wants. I grip her hands, jumping with her, ignoring the twinge in my back when I do. Ryker walks past us, and Sam squeals again.

"I didn't know you were coming! Why didn't you call?"

"I didn't know, either. Do you know anything about the break-in? I figured we were going to The Flaming Skillet, but Ryker drove here instead. I'm sorry. He should have called."

She waves away my concerns. "It's fine. Hawk called Ren about all the shit going down. They'll figure out what's going on. Doesn't seem like it's got anything to do with you, so don't worry about it."

Squeezing past the two men glaring at each other, Sam pulls me inside. I wonder if Shane will kick us out.

"Are you sure it's okay we're here? Shane doesn't look very happy."

"Ryker's been doing this for a couple months now. Just randomly shows up at mealtime and expects to be fed. Sometimes, he brings food, but I'm guessing you two have been busy with other things. It's a little weird, but we figured he was lonely."

"I mean, he has Hawk and the other guys in the MC. I wonder if it's easier being around you guys, though," I say as she pulls me in the kitchen.

Ren is posted on a stool, buried in his tablet. Sam tugs me toward the open patio doors.

"What do you mean?" She plops down, snatching at a half-full coffee mug.

"Oh, I would think it's hard, leading things, and all." I smile at Ren when he puts a mug in front of me, who retreats back to the kitchen. "Everyone needs something from him, including me. So, maybe he comes here because you guys don't need anything from him. Must be a nice break from the responsibility."

Gazing at the trees, she nods. "Could be. He keeps making comments about how things used to be. None of us remember it, but apparently, the major families worked together. Ren said something the other day about meeting me when we were little, but I don't remember it."

"Oh! I know this!"

Sam whips her head around. "Wait, you do?"

"Of course. I grew up here. Well, in Reaper territory. There was this old guy, Salt. He had salt and pepper hair. He used to tell stories about Synd and how it started. He said before the Reapers, there was just a couple families who lived up north, kept to themselves mostly, but when the Byrns and the Kings came to town, they worked to grow it into a city, with them leading things. I think the illicit shit was part of some elaborate plan, but I can't remember what."

"Because, if they controlled the underbelly, they could decide what came into the city and affected the people living here. We can't stop crime, but we can control it. So, that's what they did. Put people in charge they could play like puppets, so they could deal with shit as they saw fit," Ryker says, leaning against the door frame, arms crossed.

"So, we're not getting kicked out?" I raise an eyebrow.

"'Course not. They love me. Don't you, Sam?" He smirks at her as she rolls her eyes.

My gaze bounces between them, wondering what type of secrets they hold. I don't think it's jealousy burning in my chest, but maybe it is. I'm hurt that I'm on the outside, wondering if I'll break into their circle. My breath catches when it hits me. I felt this exact same way when I was young, chasing the boys around, waiting for them to accept me into their group. Ryker was the only one who paid me any attention, but he left me behind, too.

"I wouldn't go that far, Helms. Keep showing up unannounced and Shane's liable to nick you with a bullet. Accidentally, of course." She stands, snatching my hand to pull me up. "We'll be going. Call us when lunch is ready." She sticks her tongue out at him.

He laughs, turning back to join the others in the kitchen. Sam rushes me past Alex and Shane, yelping when Alex smacks her ass, and we leave his laughter behind.

We make it to the main hallway before Sam stops and pushes me against the wall, peeking around the banister of the huge staircase. A second later, a teenager scurries down the stairs, glancing left and right before making her way to the front door. Sam clears her throat as the girl reaches for the handle, making her jump and spin around.

"Sam! Hey," she yelps.

This must be Emma. She's the spitting image of Shane, with the same blue eyes and strong jaw. She was fast asleep when I ran to the Kings before and long gone before I woke up the next morning, so I haven't officially met her.

"Going somewhere?"

"Oh, I was, uhh, going to . . . shit." Emma hangs her head. "I wasn't prepared to lie."

"No, you weren't. Next time, have an excuse ready. You'll get caught every time when you don't have a reason. Now, where are you really going?"

She blushes. "I was going to bring these to the guard house." She holds out a bag filled with what looks like cookies.

"You realize you're too young, right? And it's totally okay to crush on him, but don't get mad when he doesn't do anything about it, okay?"

Emma nods and whispers, "I know."

"Then, off you go. Have fun. Don't let Shane catch you, or he'll ground your ass." Sam bounds up the stairs as Emma grins, and I wave.

"I'm Mac. Boys are dumb." I smile back.

"For sure." She slips out the front door, so I follow Sam, who's half way down the hall by the time I reach the landing, panting. I might feel a lot better, but my body is still mad.

"I swear, that girl went from being completely clueless to only slightly clueless after the few months she spent training. I don't know if I was ever as naive as her, though. We grew up knowing shit. I want to stab Shane every time she does something stupid." She hangs a hard right, leading me into a bedroom. It doesn't look like it's ever been used, but piles of random things litter the floor.

"Are you training her?" I sit on the bed as she flits from the closet to the bathroom.

"Fuck no. She'd hate me then." Her head pops around the corner, eyeing me. "You don't know anything about shit around here, do you?"

Looking around the room, I flush. "Not really."

"Shit, I didn't mean it like that. I figured Helms would have told you, is all."

"Told me what?" I lean to see into the bathroom.

"I'm the Wraith."

I feel like this should be a lot more climactic than it is for me. I have no idea what she's talking about. I've been away from Synd for so long, and when I was here a couple months ago, no one mentioned the Wraith. I struggle to come up with a suitable response, but nothing comes to me.

"That's great."

She comes back in, crossing her arms, pursing her lips. "That all you got?"

"Thanks for telling me?"

She bursts out laughing, doubling over and clutching her stomach. I don't know what's so funny, but I force a laugh out, the burning ache in my chest coming back.

"Sorry," she wheezes, bracing her hands on her knees, "you had the complete opposite reaction than when the guys found out. You're amazing, Mac."

"Thanks?"

I'm so beyond confused and embarrassed.

"Seriously. I don't know if I've ever had to explain this, so bear with me. So, when I was about Emma's age, the coup happened, real shitshow. I'm sure you remember. Mason freaked out and sent me to some mountain retreat to train—you know, to take out nefarious men in creative ways. I spent every summer there for six years. When I was done, I started taking jobs for my brother, fixing problems no one wanted to deal with, if you catch my drift." She wiggles her eyebrows. "Well, it started out for him, but the more I did, the more people kind of hired me to do their dirty work. So, that's what I do now. I'm like a silent assassin, I guess you could say. Only a few people know who the Wraith is, but Helms is one of them. I figured he'd tell you since we've been talking and all."

"Wow, that's . . . a lot. He didn't tell me, but not surprising." She hands me a brush, and I flush again, moving to the mirror to run it through my hair.

"Not surprising?"

"Nope. He's good at keeping secrets. Always has been. He figures it's not anyone's business what people share with him." I hit a snarl and wince when the brush yanks a few strands out.

"Got any juicy secrets only he has knowledge of?" she chuckles.

"Well, he never told anyone I begged him to take my v-card, so I think your secret is safe with him." I spin, eyes wide, meeting her shocked expression. "I shouldn't have said that."

She recovers, waving away my concern. "Oh, but you did. We're good. It's fine. I mean, that's fucking amazing."

"What's amazing?" An emptiness swirls in the pit of my stomach.

"Well, you guys were together back then, and you're here now and you'll stay and everything will be perfect." She sighs, falling back on the bed, spread eagle.

"Oh, we weren't together back then. I just talked him into it somehow. I don't know how long I'll be here either. I mean, I don't even know if Ryker would want me to stay." I chew on my bottom lip, turning back to the mirror.

The reflection shows her propping up on her elbows, glowering at me. "Do not make the mistakes I did. Ask him now, before you get too far in."

"I'm not in." I roll my eyes. "Besides, you have three guys to deal with. I only have Ryker. We've got enough going on without defining whatever is going on between us."

"Just don't wait too long. Don't be a dumbass, or you'll end up a blubbering mess in your childhood bedroom, wondering when the hell your life went to shit."

"I feel like that's more of a *you* problem." I slide a sly grin in her direction.

Her phone buzzes, and she waves it at me. "Let's go eat before they freak out, thinking we're planning something nefarious up here."

The ache in my chest loosens just a bit as I follow her out the door.

NINETEEN

Ryker

"New people have been filtering into town. Your kind of people," Ren mutters. I give him a sideways glance.

"You want to elaborate on what that's supposed to mean?" I raise an eyebrow, but he's focused on his tablet.

"Bikers. I thought that was obvious."

Grunting, I try to figure out if he's insinuating more than he's saying, but with Ren, it's hard to tell. Kenzie's laugh has me spinning toward the kitchen door, scanning her from head to toe. She's moving easier than before, but with the activities this morning, I'm worried she'll keel over any minute from a muscle cramp or something.

"How many? Is it enough to worry about, or can we deal with them easily?" I ask, eyes still on Kenzie.

"Not many, but they're causing some issues in the Barrens. Folks there aren't very happy with them. They might take care of the problem for you. These guys might give up soon."

"I doubt that."

I drop my phone in front of him with a message already pulled up. Maddox hasn't stopped texting me since I threw his ass out of Reaper territory. At first, he boasted what a mistake I was making, then moved on to mild threats, and now he's demanding I return MacKenzie, like she's a toy I stole from him. I knew he'd changed, but it's still jarring. The older we got, the more he pulled away from Kenzie, seeking out Dante. When he wasn't successful at breaking us apart, he clung to Raymond, who never cared to pay attention to him.

"Well, he seems like a peach," Alex murmurs, leaning over Ren's shoulder.

"Do you have a plan to deal with this?" Shane asks, glancing at Sam and Kenzie across the room, who are still deep in conversation.

"I don't want to wait around for them to show up, but there's no way I'm bringing Kenzie back to Rima until this Kane guy is dealt with. Leaving her here is"—I pause, watching her—"unsettling."

"She can stay here," Shane says, but the look in his eyes is wary.

I don't want to rely on them too much, but I might not have a choice.

"We'll see."

Kenzie will flip shit if I make a decision without her. Plus, if I leave her here, expecting them to keep her safe,

I'll be worrying about her instead of concentrating on dealing with Kane and his Night Slayers.

My phone lights up, and I snatch it from the table before walking out the back door.

"Hawk, what's up?"

"We got a problem, Prez."

"For fuck's sake. What's wrong now?"

I don't know how many more issues I can handle without losing my fucking mind.

"Trigger's is gone," he says, sirens echoing in the background.

"What the hell do you mean?" I pace into the yard. It's massive, so I have plenty of room to freak the fuck out.

"Pretty obvious someone burned the bar down." He yells something I can't make out. "We're trying to figure out what happened."

"Are you fucking kidding me? Anyone hurt?" A small hand on my arm has me swinging around. Kenzie takes a step back when she sees my face, but I don't have time to reassure her.

"No. Trigger wasn't there. Thankfully, it happened when it was closed. The bakery next door got some damage but nothing bad. The police showed up before I could stop them. They want to do an investigation," he grumbles.

"I'll deal with it. I'm coming back. Don't fucking talk to them," I snarl, hanging up.

Kenzie retreated back to the patio, wide eyes following me as I stomp across the grass away from her. Not wanting to answer any questions, I turn back to the trees. This whole situation is getting more complicated by the day. I convinced myself if she was here, away from Rima, that they wouldn't follow. I'd have to deal with the backlash from Maddox, but the Night Slayers would let her go—forget she existed.

I can't help but wonder what the hell they want with her. It has to be more than an exchange or owning her. I stalk back to her, intent on getting to the bottom of things, when Sam steps outside, raising an eyebrow. I'm not stupid enough to tangle with her, especially when she's so set on MacKenzie being her friend. Loyalty in our world comes slowly—but break it and the retaliation is swift and brutal. The last thing I'm going to do is piss her off. Instead of the tirade I planned, I don't say anything, brushing past her to head straight back into another mess. The Kings are crowded around Ren's screen, mostly likely watching the footage he's pulled up on the bar going up in flames.

"You need anything from us?" Shane glances up before fixing his eyes on the screen again.

"No."

I walk out, Alex's snort following me. I'm hustling down the front stairs when MacKenzie's voice reaches me, telling me to stop. I contemplate ignoring her, but I doubt she'll let me. She'll poke and prod until she gets her way, like every other time I try to leave her out. I'm not used to having to bring someone else into my thought process. It grates on my nerves, going against everything I've ever done.

"Ryker! What the hell is going on?" she yells as I swing my leg over my bike.

"Gotta go back, deal with this shit."

I'm assuming she knows what's going on. It's not hard to understand that I can't sit around eating breakfast when there's a crisis in my territory.

"Okay. Were you going to just leave me here?" Glaring, she plants her hands on her hips. I hang my head, trying to settle the rapid beating of my heart, but it's no use.

"I have to go, MacKenzie. Go hang out with Sam or something. I'll call you later." I tuck her helmet in the saddlebag hanging from the side.

"Seriously?" It's the hurt lacing her words that has me peering up. Her arms are wrapped around her stomach. My fingers itch to smooth out the furrow in her brow, but I clench them into fists instead.

"I can't keep track of you and deal with Trigger's burning down. I'll have to talk to everyone, see if anyone saw anything . . . I don't want to worry about you, too."

Looking away and biting her lip, she nods. "Fine. Guess I'll see you later, then."

She turns, shuffling back to the front door still hanging open. I'm arguing with myself, wanting to call out to her yet wanting to let her walk away.

"Kenzie," I call out, not sure what to say, when she glances over her shoulder. "I'm sorry."

"No, you're not."

The sheen in her eyes glints before she's bounding up the stairs, the click of the door echoing across the empty space. Starting the bike, I sigh before I talk myself into chasing after her.

The streets are busier than our ride here, and it takes longer than I want. I finally pull in front of a blackened shell that used to be Trigger's. It's been here since I was a kid, since before I was born, really. Now it's gone.

This has to be arson. The building wouldn't have burned so quickly without help. MacKenzie and I might have even spotted the men responsible, but I was too distracted by her to notice. The men sniffing around before should have put me on alert, but I convinced myself nothing would happen. I'm more pissed at myself than anyone else. I'm surveying the damage, watching the firemen spraying down the last few smoking areas, when Hawk walks up.

"Where's Mac?"

I suck in a breath, guilt warring with the anger. "I left her at the Kings. What do we have?"

"Nothing really. No one saw anything. The camera we have over there"—he points across the street—"doesn't point in the right direction to pick up anything. It could be an accident."

"It burned down in a matter of an hour. No way this was an accident. How did no one fucking see anything?"

"No idea. I got everyone gathered at headquarters. Figured you'd want to talk to them. Rooster is throwing a fit. He's riling some of the members up."

"What the fuck is his problem now?" I grunt, striding back to my bike.

"He's not too keen on Mac being here. Thinks she's bringing trouble we can't afford after all the shit with the Guild."

We turn, eyeing the police cruisers pulling from the lot. They're avoiding our stares. The police chief peeks at us but spins away, phone pressed to his ear. I pull my own phone out when it vibrates. I show Hawk Alex's text saying not to worry about the police.

"King took care of them." I nod at the fading taillights. "I'm thinking I might keep MacKenzie there for now. Maybe things will settle down if she's not around."

Hawk snorts. "Sure, we'll say that's the reason. You're fucking this up but whatever. It's your life."

"I don't recall asking your opinion."

"'Course you didn't. You think you can deal with everything on your own, without input from anyone else, even me. If you think shoving Mac off on the Kings is going to change how you feel about her, you're in for a surprise." He smirks.

"I'm not shoving her off. I'm keeping her safe." He snorts again, shaking his head. "This shit is complicated enough without you sticking your nose in our business. Let me worry about MacKenzie, and you worry about who the hell is coming into our territory without us spotting them."

My rumbling bike drowns whatever asinine thing he's spouting back. The prospects file out of my house when I ride by. One waves, but the guy behind him smacks him in the back of the head. These kids are getting dumber every year. I try to be fair, keeping shit in line without starting a revolt. My father ruling with fear was what triggered his death years ago. He'd never listen when I told him members were getting restless. Dain Helms ruled with an iron fist, never thinking his empire would fall. To an extent, he was right. A Helms still runs the Reapers, but we're different than we were. MacKenzie wasn't wrong when she said we're misfits finding each other. We're still criminals, but we're not assholes taking out innocent bystanders and shit. Not like when Dad was in charge.

Pulling into headquarters, I find the lot packed. Members milling about outside nod to me when I push through the doors. Half of them shout into their phones, talking to their partners, trying to reassure them we're not under attack. One of them glances at me as I pass, worry lining his eyes as he tells his wife it'll be okay.

The best thing I ever did was do away with the women being property. It never sat well with me how they were treated when Dad was in charge. The problem is, old habits die hard. Rooster is a prime example. He's standing at the front, booming at a group of older guys nodding along, all of whom are remnants of my father's legacy. They can have it; I never wanted it. I lean against the wall, listening to the bullshit he's spouting.

"If Helms isn't going to do anything about it, then maybe we need to," he spits out.

"Watch yourself, Rooster. All that cawing you're doing is going to get you stripped or shot," Tank, our road captain, calls from a nearby table, absently reading a magazine.

It takes a lot to rile Tank up, but once he is, there's little we can do to stop him from bulldozing everything in his path. With his broad shoulders and short stature, we should have named him Bulldozer.

"What are you going to do about it?" he sneers.

A few of the others glance around nervously. They're pissed but not enough to defy me as president.

"Oh, I won't have to do anything. Our Prez might have something to say about it, though," he says, nodding at me.

Rooster's eyes find mine, and he blanches. Apparently, he's not as confident when faced with the consequences, either.

"Rooster." I nod, and he flinches.

"Prez, got something for you to check out." Tank waves me over, and the other members slink away.

Most of them were the same guys glaring at Kenzie at our last meeting. I add another mental note to my list of shit to deal with.

"So, we've got some issues with the shipments. I don't know if Tiny talked to you yet, but someone is skimming off the top, thinking we won't notice. I brought some prospects with me last time. The young kid, who came from Harris, said he's seen this before." He slides a paper covered in numbers across the table. "See here? This one's supposed to be coming from Harris, but it's not. Someone is redirecting it through another city. Then, when it gets here—well, whatever we're getting isn't right." He sits back and crosses his arms.

"Where are they going through?" Knowing the answer, I hold my breath, but I need a confirmation.

"Rima."

"Fuck. You think the Night Slayers are catching our shit?" I study the reports, trying to find dates.

"That's exactly what the kid thinks. He said it happened in Harris before. Night Slayers were there before they moved to Rima. Don't know what happened to make them move along, though. Might be in league with someone bigger, or it could be a coincidence." Tank grumbles, shaking his head.

"When did this start? There're no dates on this." I toss the sheet down and clench my fists to stop the rage coursing through me.

"About two weeks ago." He clears his throat and lowers his voice. "This isn't just about keeping her safe anymore. It's affecting club business."

"Keep this to yourself. I'll figure out what to do."

"Helms." My eyes snap to his—he rarely calls me anything other than Prez. "You can't do this all on your own. That's what we're here for. It's our home, too. You keep relying on yourself, you'll fuck it up and wish you would've asked for help."

"Talk to these guys about Trigger's. See if anyone saw anything. I'll deal with Rooster."

He nods, opening his mouth and snapping it shut again, before shaking his head. "Might be best to trim the fat. Let me know if you want me to make him disappear."

I nod, then stride away to throw myself into fixing the problems piling up at our doorstep.

TWENTY

MacKenzie

I stare out the window of Sam's bedroom. She went to take a shower in Alex's room a half hour ago, so I'm sure she was distracted by him on the way. Wrapping my arms around myself, I sigh, wishing I could see all the way to Reaper territory. Instead, I'm stuck staring at the driveway. If I could manifest Ryker, I would. It's been four hours since he left me here, and I'm slowly losing it. I like Sam, but I didn't want to be left behind. Every time I feel like we're making progress, something comes along and knocks us back. Usually, it's Ryker and his stupid teetering between helping me and pushing me away. I wish I had my phone, but in the rush this morning, I forgot it in Ryker's bedroom. I don't know who I'd call, anyway.

"Come in," I call at the soft knock on her door. Glancing over my shoulder, I find Shane in the door frame, but he doesn't come in.

"Mac." He nods. "Think we could talk?"

"Sure." I turn, swallowing down the nausea.

Shane King is one of the most intimidating people I've ever met, and with the way I grew up, that's saying something. I can't put my finger on it, but it's something in the way he carries himself. I feel like I'm one wrong word away from pissing him off. I'm sure Sam would have a heyday if she knew.

He crosses his arms, leaning against the frame. "I wanted you to know, if you need to stay here, you can."

I rear back. "Why would I need to stay here?"

The look of pity crossing his face almost undoes me.

"Things might get intense up there. I just wanted you to know it's an option."

Jutting my chin out, I let out a rueful chuckle. Of course, it's not really an option. This isn't my decision. The more shit goes down, the more I'm convinced I did the wrong thing in coming to Synd. I never should have expected Ryker to solve my problems. I thought I'd moved past everything, accepted he'd be able to help, that his offer of protection was genuine instead of an obligation, but every time, he pulls away or pushes me to the side . . .

I might have to face the reality that Ryker's words are only words and not intentions. Sure, he wanted to fuck me again. He's said things I needed to hear and wanted to believe. But maybe he said them, so I would stop freaking out. I *could* be nothing more than an obligation. I can't blame him. I was a mess when I first got here. I still am. At some point, I have to take responsibility for the position I put him in.

"Thank you. I appreciate that."

Elaborating what I'm feeling to Shane is pointless. He wouldn't care. He doesn't want me staying here, but here I am, another obligation to someone who never asked for the responsibility of taking care of me.

Shane nods, walking away before I can make a fool of myself by asking him if he's sure. I go back to staring out the window, wondering what the fuck I'm supposed to do now. Another knock on the door has me huffing. Living with this many people must be exhausting for Sam, although, they love her, so she probably doesn't even notice.

"Mac? You got a minute?" Alex's voice floats across the space, but this time, I don't turn around.

"Why not? Not like I have anything else to do," I mutter.

"Ahh. We'll circle back to that little tidbit, but Ren was wondering if you needed another phone. Sam mentioned you weren't answering her texts. Sent me up to find you."

"No. I left it at Ryker's. I didn't realize she was done with showering. I'll go find her," I say, turning.

He holds up a hand. "You know you can explore the house, right? You don't have to stay in what ever room she sticks you in."

"I didn't think about it. This isn't my house. I'm not going to go snooping around because I'm bored," I huff, flutters erupting in my stomach again.

"Just a quick check-in—are you pissed at us or at Helms?" He raises an eyebrow, smirking.

"I'm not pissed," I say, even though my hands curl into fists.

"Sure you're not. Listen, just don't make any rash decisions, okay?" Alex straightens, and I almost let him walk away.

I almost keep my mouth shut, but I'm so sick of people telling me what to do under the guise of safety.

"Fuck you," I seethe. His eyebrows shoot up, and he freezes.

"Uh, what?"

"You fucking heard me. I'm so sick of everyone expecting me to fuck shit up. As if I can't take care of myself. As if I'm a helpless girl who doesn't know how to deal with my own shit. Rash decisions? I haven't made a rash decision since I was eleven.

"I learned a long time ago to pick my poisons, yet every fucking time, someone comes in and says I'm doing it wrong. I didn't ask for Maddox to fuck me over. I didn't ask to be sold off like fucking chattel. And I certainly didn't ask to get beaten senseless. The only thing I have ever asked for was a place to stay.

"I tried to not pull anyone else into the shitshow my life has become. I tried so hard, but no one cared what I wanted. He didn't care I was trying to protect him. No, because it doesn't fucking matter, as long as he gets to be in control and make all the decisions. Who fucking cares about my intentions because, now we're so far in, there's no way out. No one gives a damn what I want. No one wants to clue me in on what the fuck is going on. No one will remember I tried to stop it. It'll be my fucking fault when the world burns. But who fucking cares? I should just sit down and shut the fuck up, right?"

Tears streaming down my face, I'm shouting by the end. I can't stop the words from pouring. It's not Alex's fault. He didn't mean anything by it, but if I don't scream at someone, I'm going to explode.

His mouth hangs open, concern lining his bright green eyes. I suck in a deep breath, shaking out my hands before rubbing them against my leggings, trying not to spiral into the mess I was before. I thought I had my emotions under control. I thought I'd moved past feeling like I was drowning at any moment. One fucking question is all it took to set me off again. Alex steps toward me, but Ren pushes past him and shuts the door in his face.

"MacKenzie, sit down," he commands.

I can't fill my lungs with enough oxygen, and spots dance in my vision. I sink onto the bed. His hand latches on the back of my neck, pushing my head between my knees, and I jerk in his grasp until he lets go.

"I-I'm sorry." I gasp, digging my nails into my thighs.

"Stop. You're going to think of one thing you can control—one small thing—and you're going to focus on that. When your vision clears, you'll tell me what you can control." His feet crowd between my own, and I focus on them. The light from the window gleams off the top, the loops from his laces symmetrical.

My brain clicks over, filtering through his command. One thing I can control. There are so many things I can't control that focusing on one I *can* is harder than it should be. My breaths are still short, a crushing weight on my chest not allowing my lungs to expand. I panic again until it hits me.

"Words," I wheeze.

"Yes, you can control your words. What you say to other people, how you shape them in your mouth, and how you react to other people's words. Now, take a deeper breath."

His command clicks, and the band around me loosens the tiniest bit. I suck in a little more air. The spots clear, but my fingers feel like a million pins are jabbing into the tips. I feel like I'm on fire, but goosebumps burst across my arms, making me shiver.

"I'm fine," I gasp, throwing a hand out to push him away. My arm hits his leg, but he doesn't move.

"We're not going to start lying to ourselves. You're going to listen to me, and you're going to keep breathing. Understood?"

I give him a thumbs up, since I have nothing else at this point. My stomach cramps. Everything stacked together has created a dark pit within me, and I'm balancing on the edge, barely holding on to my sanity. This shouldn't be happening again, but at least I haven't blacked out yet. It's the only bright spot in this mess.

"The first time I saw Sam as an adult we were at a gala. She was wearing this plum dress with slits everywhere. Shane and Alex kept track of her through the years, but I never cared enough to notice. I wish I would have now. So many years were lost, but we wouldn't be where we are if we had. That's how life works, I suppose. I didn't even speak to her, just watched. She thought she was fooling everyone, chatting away, but in the silences, she seemed"— he pauses—"lonely. Like she was searching for something, but didn't know it yet. I like to think it was us. She needed us like we needed her."

As he spoke, I closed my eyes, listening to him paint the picture of the start of their relationship. Sam glossed over a lot of their beginning. We haven't known each other long, but I didn't expect it to be so deep for someone like Ren. He almost never opens his mouth when I'm around. When he drove me back to Ryker's, he said maybe ten words to me.

"How did you know for sure?" My muscles unclench, one by one.

"I knew long before I was willing to admit it. Do you want to talk about Helms?"

The words seem like they're being ripped from him, like he knows he should ask, but he doesn't want to understand. I sit up slowly, wobbling to the side, but catch myself. The pain is gone from my hands, but I'm still chilled.

"We don't have to talk about it. I think I'm okay now. Does this happen to you?"

My lids droop. All I want to do is curl up on the bed and sleep. I don't want to lose the rest of my day, though. I'll be awake all night and be left with all the feelings I've been hiding from.

He tilts his head, gray eyes narrowing at me. "Not like yours, but I've learned what to do when it happens. Before your kidnapping were they a problem for you?"

"No. I mean, seems like a good reason to start having a ridiculous reaction to things," I say bitterly.

"It's common, not ridiculous. Mostly brought on by trauma. I'll tell Helms how to help you deal with them, so he doesn't grab you again when you're spiraling." He steps back, tucking his hands in his pockets.

"Don't. I can handle them on my own now. Thanks for helping me."

Now that I'm removed from the episode, my cheeks burn, realizing he witnessed something I never wanted another person to see.

He rocks back, sucking his bottom lip between his teeth before answering. "Okay, but I think that's a mistake. He might be making some decisions now, but I do believe he cares about you, MacKenzie."

I snort. "Oh, he does, which is the issue."

"What do you mean?"

Curling inward, I tuck my arms in and hunch my shoulders, both wishing I could escape this conversation and desperately wanting to have it. Inhaling, I remind myself I control my words. I don't have to share if I don't want to. I need to let something out, or I'll have another freak-out like I did on Alex, who I now have to apologize to.

"Ryker is so caught up in protecting me. He always had this push-and-pull reaction to me. He wanted me around, but he didn't. He feels responsible for me, and that's not what I want. It's not what I need. He pushes until he gets his way, regardless of how I feel. I don't know. I'm not making any sense." I shake my head, trying to rein in my chaotic thoughts.

Ren hums, looking out the window.

I'm holding my breath, waiting for his response.

"It's funny, the perception we have of how others see us. Most of the time, we're completely off base. We think we're a burden or annoying or selfish, but in actuality, we're just us. We want someone to accept us for who we are, but we're afraid to show them our reality." He meets my eyes. "I think you're getting in your own way, but my words aren't going to change your perception. Helms's words won't, either. You have to believe what he's saying to you, judge whether his actions align with them, and decide from there what you want and need."

"You're kind of smart, huh?"

"Emotions aren't my forte, but being with Sam helps. Are you ready to go?"

Standing, I shake out my limbs, praying my muscles will loosen. I'm sure they'll ache tomorrow no matter what I do.

"Yeah, I heard Sam was trying to get a hold of me. Do you know where she is?" I stumble for the door, glancing back when he doesn't follow.

"I mean go back to Reaper territory. Shane said you could stay, but we both know you don't want to be here."

I stumble to a stop, swinging my head forward to avoid his eyes boring into me. Ryker doesn't want me there right now, but maybe it's exactly where I need to be.

"Can you give me a ride?"

TWENTY-ONE

Ryker

It's after nine when I trudge up my front steps, lights burning from the kitchen window. I silently curse the prospects for leaving it on. Most of the lights are on, and I wonder what the hell they were doing going through my fucking house. I've had a shit day. The last thing I need is to go off on the ones trying to join up, but my fucking god, they're pissing me off.

I swing the door open, praying Hawk had enough sense to stock my fridge. I never did get lunch, and I'm starving. I freeze when something sizzles in the kitchen. The washing machine is going, and music echoes across the house. I don't bother to take off my boots, stomping down the hall. I stop short in the doorway to the newly cleaned kitchen. I can't even tell someone trashed the place less than twenty-four hours ago.

Kenzie is standing at the stove, hair in a ponytail swinging back and forth in time with her hips. She's swaying to the music, singing under her breath while steak sizzles on the stove. I'm caught, unable to pull my eyes away. I don't know why I keep pushing her aside, fighting the way I feel. When she's gazing at me with those hazel eyes or in my arms, every inch pressed against me, it feels right. Something in me loosens and slots into place, making me whole. When the rest of the world seeps in, though, I question what I'm thinking. My worries and responsibilities intrude and muddy up everything else until I'm convinced it shouldn't be this way. *We* shouldn't be this way.

She spins to the beat, jolting when she sees me standing here. "Oh, hi."

"How'd you get here?" I press my lips together, cursing myself.

Of course the first words out of my mouth are accusatory. We never could get this right. I could never get this right.

"Ren drove me. You weren't home, so I made food." She flushes, spinning back and grabbing a potholder. Her movements are jerky as she stuffs the pan in the oven, setting the timer. "Those should be done in a couple minutes along with the potatoes. There's broccoli. I think it all turned out okay."

She skirts the island and goes to the laundry room. I catch glimpses of her moving the wet things to the dryer and then starting it. When I spy the table, though, it's set for one, not two.

"MacKenzie, did you only make enough for one?" I don't know whether to be pissed that she only made food for herself or that she's playing it off she made it for me.

"Yeah, it's all set up for you," she calls.

"Did you eat?" I don't move. I can't wrap my head around what the hell is going on.

"I'm not hungry," she answers, coming back in the room.

She won't meet my eyes; she hasn't looked at me since I walked in, other than when I startled her.

Crossing my arms, I snort. "You're always hungry. What happened at the Kings? They kick you out?" I'm half joking, but at the sharp intake of breath, I narrow my eyes. "They kicked you out? What the fuck."

"They didn't kick me out. I asked for a ride. Sam is going to come get me in a little bit."

"Why is she coming if you asked for a ride?"

Tucking her arms around her waist, she sighs, gripping her sides so hard her knuckles turn white.

"I needed to get my things."

Her whispered words hit me like a punch to the gut, forcing the air from my lungs. I might have considered having her stay with the Kings while I dealt with the threats, but I never thought about the aftermath. Emptiness seeps into my pores, numbness sweeping over my body.

"So, that's it?"

She's quiet for so long I wonder if she'll answer. Her bare foot taps against the linoleum, eyes fixed on some far off point only she can see. I'm tempted to shake her, force her to tell me what the hell is going on. It didn't work last time, and it won't this time, either. Chest tightening a little more with each passing minute, I wait.

"I had another panic attack," she whispers so quietly I almost don't catch her words. "I screamed at Alex and lost it completely. Ren talked me through it." I open my mouth to say something but snap it shut. "When he offered to teach you how to help me, I told him not to. I didn't want to be a burden any more than I already am."

"You're not a burden," I say with as much conviction as I can infuse in my voice.

"I'm not. Rationally, I realize I'm not, but convincing myself is something else entirely. Ryker, your words aren't matching your actions. You say you want to help, that I'm not a burden. You want my everything, but at the first sign of trouble, you leave me behind. You push me off on someone else to take care of, like I'm a child who needs looking after. *I* understand asking for help is not the same as being incapable of taking care of myself. Do you?"

"This isn't easy, Kenzie. None of this is easy. It's been ten fucking years since we've spent any amount of time together. And then you show up at my door, bloody and bruised, refusing to tell me what happened, expecting me to be okay. When you finally do break down, I'm supposed to be able to help. I'm supposed to have a solution. I'm supposed to be able to protect you, but I don't know how to do that and keep my club safe at the same time. It's a lot to deal with."

"I know, which is why I'm getting my things. I never wanted to bring my problems to the Reapers. My leaving might not stop them, but at least they'll see I'm no longer here, hopefully. Then, maybe they'll back off."

"For fuck's sake, woman, that's not going to change anything," I explode. "The only thing it will do is make me lose my goddamn mind."

The fight in her eyes burns, begging to be unleashed, but she's holding back. I want her to let go and throw everything she's got at me. It's the only way we know how to be. The calm and careful speech she spouted isn't her. It's her holding back, and I never want her to do that. The glint in her eyes tells me I've tipped her beyond reason, and she flushes such a pretty pink I want to forgo all the yelling and get to the make-up sex.

"You want to talk about what's not easy? You want to compare notes?"

Her voice is low, almost guttural. *Have I pushed too far?*

"This isn't a pissing contest. You want my actions to match my words, but I can't figure out what the hell to do with you."

"You don't *do* anything with me. I'm not a fucking object. Stop trying to shove me into your box of ridiculousness."

Confusion replaces the anger pouring out of me as I shake my head. "What the fuck did you just say?"

Her nostrils flare as her mouth opens and shuts once, twice, but nothing comes out.

"You have no idea what you meant, do you? You lost whatever you were pissed about." I smirk.

She squawks, throws her hands up, and spins, only to twirl back. She stomps toward me and jabs her finger into my chest.

"Fuck you. You think you're always right. You think you can pick me up and put me down whenever it suits your mood. I'm sick of hearing you spout how much you want me here and then turn around to drop me off on someone else. So, fuck you, Ryker Helms."

"I can't help it!" I bellow, all traces of humor fleeing. "I can't help you and want you at the same time. You wormed your way under my skin years ago, and there's no digging you out, but I never wanted to. When you came waltzing back in, expecting us to be okay, and then you fucked off again, only to show up two months later without an explanation . . . I should have . . ." I hang my head, all the fight going out of me.

"Should have what?" she whispers.

We stare at each other, daring the other to break. I fold first, marching to the door to tell whoever is here to fuck off. The timer goes off as I rip it open, my words dying in my throat when I come face-to-face with Sam. I scowl, wondering how long she's been standing here listening to Kenzie and I shout at each other before she interrupted.

"Go away. She's staying here." I swing the door shut, but her hand shoots out, raising an eyebrow at me.

"Let her in, Ryker," Kenzie calls from the kitchen.

Stepping back, I catch Alex's concerned gaze from his spot in the car parked in front of my house before I slam the door. I stare at the wood, listening to Sam's greeting and Kenzie banging around behind me. My lungs seize, my hand falling from the knob. I leave them, walking up the stairs to my bedroom. The pit in my stomach grows with each step that takes me farther from her.

I'm not continuing our discussion, fight, whatever it was, with Sam standing witness. I can't stop Kenzie if she wants to leave. I won't stop her. The fucked up thing is, as soon as she said she wanted to leave, that was the moment

I knew I didn't want to ever let her go. She was right—I wanted to keep her. I told her I did, but I never acted on it. I was always afraid something else would take her away from me again. First, it was Raymond, then it was distance. Mostly, it was my own stupidity. I don't have any more fight in me.

I close the bathroom door softly. I grab one of the bags she left in the corner from the clothes Ren bought her and start filling it with everything she'll need. I didn't bother to tell her I paid him back. He tried to refuse, but no one was going to take care of her but me. The irony of them housing her, caring for her, isn't lost on me.

"Ryker?" The door muffles her hesitant tone.

I finish throwing the last of the bottles from the shower in and open the door. I hold out the bag. She's ringing her hands, not even bothering to look at it. I give the bag a shake, not trusting myself to speak. I don't know what will come out if I do. I'll either yell or spout excuses again or do something dumb, like not saying anything, and haul her into my arms instead.

"I don't want it."

I drop the bag next to the door. I look around to see if I missed anything. Less than a month, and her things have taken over my space. They'll join the rest of her stuff I have tucked away in my closet. I'll have to get a bigger box, since it's crammed full at the moment. My leather jacket she wore to the meeting is crumpled in the corner. I snatch it up and hold it out to her. She doesn't take that either, just stares at me as tears gather in her eyes. I open my mouth, but still, nothing comes out. Dropping the leather at her feet, I press my lips together. I step back, ready to shut the door in her face, if only to stop the ache gathering in my chest, when she stutters forward a step.

"Should have what?" she whispers.

"I never should have let you go. I should have told you I didn't want you to leave. I should have fought for you."

"You could fight for me now. It wouldn't be much of a fight, though." The corner of her mouth tips up, drawing my eyes to her lips. Her tongue darts out, wetting them.

"I don't even know who I'm fighting anymore," I confess.

Her father is long dead. Dante is gone, but if he were here, he wouldn't stop us. Maddox doesn't get a fucking say.

"Well, I wouldn't fight you. I might fight *with* you, but not on this. I think you're going to have to fight yourself. I asked you what you wanted, but when it came down to it, you weren't ready to have my everything. Are you ready now? Don't you think we deserve a happy ending?" Hope shines from her face, begging me to accept her.

"You do. You deserve that, Kenz."

"Ryker, don't you get it? *You're* my happy ending. You always were."

Something in me breaks, slicing into me, shattering me apart and putting me back together.

"Okay." I nod, swallowing hard. "Okay."

TWENTY-TWO

MacKenzie

"That all you got?" My stomach flutters, threatening to upend everything all over his feet.

"Yeah, that's all I got."

His blue eyes shine, and it takes me a second to see they're sparkling with unshed tears. I don't know if I've ever seen Ryker shed a tear. Even after his dad was killed, he was so overwhelmed taking over the Reapers he shoved the grief down—or maybe it wasn't there at all.

"Okay. You'll stop fighting yourself. And you'll include me on shit that's going on because you understand I can help. And you'll stop threatening everyone around me. And you'll—"

He pulls me into his chest. "I'll do whatever the hell I want"—I squeak, but he smothers my face in his neck, whispering in my ear—"but I'll stop fighting."

I snort as I wind my arms around his waist. "I don't think that'll ever happen but okay."

"Are you going, then?" His voice cracks the tiniest bit, and an ache splits my heart.

"I sent Sam home. I didn't plan on staying there forever, just for a few days until things"—I clear my throat—"cooled off."

He sighs, his body relaxing into me. I wonder how many times we're going to have to go through something like this. We've spent so long trying to find our way back to each other without even knowing it. I don't know how much more heartache I can take.

I tip my face up, when his phone blares, making him groan. Grabbing the back of my neck, he slams his mouth to mine and releases me just as quickly.

"What?" he growls as he answers his phone, stepping around me.

I bend to pick up the leathers he dropped, and he slaps my ass, grinning when I glare at him. Watching him from the corner of my eye, I hang the jacket on the hook. He's still smiling, but his face morphs into horror. I swear fear flashes in his eyes before he walks away. My heart cracks again. We talked about this five minutes ago, and the first opportunity he has to prove he's not going to shut me out, he's hiding shit again. I don't know whether to be pissed off or resigned. I'm debating going after him when he steps back in the room, no longer on the phone.

"Baby, we have to go," he says gently, grabbing the jacket I just hung up, gesturing for me to slip it on.

Fear radiates from his eyes.

"Where are we going? Who was on the phone?"

He shakes the leathers again, and I tuck my arms in, letting him help me, though I don't need it.

Ryker grabs my hand before tugging me toward the stairs. I snatch my phone off the dresser as we pass and tuck it in my pocket. I don't want to be caught without it again. He still hasn't said anything when we make it downstairs. He grabs my boots and pushes me down on the bench next to the front door. I expect him to hand them over, but he drops to his knees, slipping the stiff leather over my foot before lacing it up, then lacing the other.

"Ryker, you're scaring me. What happened?"

It's not so much a question as a demand. The knot in my stomach swells, threatening to travel up my throat and choke me if he doesn't start talking. He rests his hands on my knees, either borrowing or stealing strength, I'm not sure.

"Kenz, Alex, and Sam were in a car accident. They're at the hospital. We're going down there now."

The knot disappears, leaving numbness in its wake. I can't process his words. He must have been mistaken. I just saw her. I sent her back home. I *told* her to go home. She has to be at home. I rip my phone from my pocket and pull up her contact. I notice my trembling fingers when I connect the call. It rings over and over, and when I think it'll click to voice mail, it connects.

"Sam?" Someone is breathing on the other end. "Sam!"

A low chuckle, nothing like Sam's contagious laugh, fills the line, and ice flows into my veins.

"Do I have your attention now?"

Blackness floods my vision. My body's tipping, and I'm no longer in control. Strong arms catch me, but the pull of darkness is too strong, and I'm gone.

"I don't know. Whoever was on the other end hung up before I could hear them."

Ryker's words are muffled, swimming through my head. My stomach twists, and I feel like I've forgotten something important. The memories come rushing back, and my eyes fly open, the bright light flooding my vision, forcing tears from my eyes. I roll to the side, but hands catch me before I fall off the couch. I gag, my stomach threatening empty all over Ryker's feet, but I swallow it down, bile burning my throat.

"Kenzie, breathe. I've got you," he murmurs, gently pushing me back.

"No, we have to . . ." I swallow again. "Go to the hospital."

"We will, but you passed out. Ink is on his way."

I yank my arm out of his hold before shoving my body up. "No! We have to go now."

Horror sweeps over me, and I turn to him. Hawk is hiding in the corner, concern etched in every line of his face. The Reapers, the Kings, Mason, everyone is in danger.

"What's wrong, Kenz?"

The words almost won't come out, but I suck in a shaky breath. "Tell Ink not to come. Where's Ren and Shane? The accident wasn't an accident. Ryker, you need to lock things down. Now."

"Slow down, baby. He's already on his way. He's not far. The Kings are at the hospital. Who was on the phone?"

A sob escapes me, and I shove my fist in my mouth, biting down hard enough to draw blood. I shake my head, curling my shoulders in. I can't tell him. He'll fly into a rage. He'll hunt him down. He'll blame me. He'll be split again on who to protect—his club or me. And Ren and Shane . . . I suck in another shuddering sob, and nausea turns my stomach. Ren will kill me. Shane will kill me. I don't blame them. *If she dies* . . . my heart shatters with the thought. It swirls inside my head, pounding into my ears and threatening to pull me under again. Ryker falls to his knees in front of me, hands sweeping over me, pushing back my hair as he whispers words I can't hear.

Ren's words come back to me, reminding me to breathe, to find the things I can control. I can't control his reaction. I can't control what the Kings will do. I can't control others' decisions. I can control what *I* do, though. I can stop this whole thing. I don't want to. I'm not strong enough to go back, and I won't survive. I don't know if it will be worth it. I could go back, let them use me, beat me, kill me, and they could still come here. They could still hurt the people I've come to care for. They could still hurt Ryker. A spasm shoots through my chest at the thought. It wouldn't be a good one to make, but I *can* control the choice and ask for help. I've wanted Ryker to let me in, to include me in his plans and his own decisions. I need to give him the same.

"Panther. Kane Riley caused the accident. Lock it down. Please," I plead, tears streaming down my face.

He grips my arms tight enough to make me gasp, the bite of pain shocking my system enough for my muscles to relax the smallest bit. I pull in a deeper breath, our eyes locking. He's gone in a blink of an eye, striding across the room. Grabbing my phone, he smashes it on the ground and grinds it under his boot.

"Call it in, Hawk. We're going to the hospital," Ryker says, grabbing my elbow, then hauling me to my feet.

I wobble, the protest dying on my tongue, knowing I'll never convince him to hide out in the house. He'll never shy away from a threat.

"C-Call the Kings," I stammer out, tripping over my feet. He stops my descent and pulls me upright again before marching me out the door. "Ryker, call Shane and Ren. They need to know. Tell them I'm sorry."

Ryker jerks to a stop. He spins to grab my arms, leaning in and glaring at me. His eyes are an electric blue, glowing in the porch light and stabbing into my soul.

"MacKenzie, you're going to listen to me, and you're going to listen good. None of this was your fault. You are not to fucking blame for them getting hurt. You are not to blame for Trigger's burning down. You are not to blame for any of this. That lies with the Night Slayers and Maddox. At any point, he could have made different decisions, and he chose not to. You did not start this, but I'm going to end it. Do you understand me?"

He waits, eyes boring into me until I nod. He nods back, then drags me to his bike parked next to Hawk's. I wonder where he came from, why Hawk was at Ryker's in the first place. It can't be a coincidence. Ryker swings a leg over before handing me the helmet and waiting for me to scramble on the back before starting it. I latch on to him just in time before we take off down the street toward whatever consequences I've visited upon my friend.

TWENTY-THREE

Ryker

The plastic chairs in the hospital waiting room are the most uncomfortable seats on the planet. I swear this is hell: bland coffee, chairs I can't stop squirming in, the constant pressure in the too-thin air, and, of course, the ever-present nerves jumping in my stomach. Insistent, beeping machines echo through my skull, sending my temples throbbing. Kenzie is tucked next to me, snoring lightly. My arm fell asleep an hour ago, but I hardly feel the pins and needles in my fingers anymore. I wonder if I'll be able to use my hand when she wakes up.

We've been here for four hours, waiting for news. We haven't seen the Kings, but I'm sure Shane and Ren are here, bullying whatever doctor and nurses are taking care of Alex and Sam. I tried to let MacKenzie deal with the head nurse, but when the lady refused to give any information, I had to step in, using my reputation to intimidate her into telling us Sam was stable and that Alex was in surgery.

I slide my phone from my pocket as it buzzes, trying not to wake Kenzie. Glancing around before I answer, I make sure the waiting room is still empty. It cleared out soon after Mason Byrns stalked through the double doors. A woman tried to flirt with him, but I don't think he even noticed. A flushed security guard escorted her out within seconds, hauling her by the arm. She squawked all the way out the door when no one gave her the attention she thought she deserved.

"What is it, Tank?" I murmur.

"We got another problem, Prez," he huffs.

It sounds like he's running, and the shouts of others in the background ebbs away.

My shoulders tense, making Kenzie shift, and I force my muscles to relax, curling my hands into fists instead. The last thing we need is more shit piled on top of us. I glance at Mason again, whose head is tipped back, eyes closed. I assume he's sleeping, but I don't know how. Between these chairs and the memories this place must dreg up in him, I doubt he wants to be here. He wouldn't be if it was anyone other than his sister, I'm sure.

"Fine. Tell me what happened."

"Someone fucked up the bikes. About half a dozen of them were parked at headquarters. They're trashed, and members are pissed."

The calmness in his voice is a lie. Tank is one of those guys who gets quieter the more pissed he gets. I just hope none of the prospects are around when he finally blows.

Someone will end up in the river before dawn if they do. I grit my teeth, wondering what the fuck is happening. I can't ask the Kings to look into this, and based on how shit has been going down with Byrns lately, I doubt he'll be willing to help.

"Who the fuck did it?"

Not many people are willing to fuck with us, so my gut turns, waiting for his response.

"Not a goddamn clue. Hawk is bitching about some shit with the cameras. Guys are pissed, and we don't know where they went. Doc sent some guys down to the border; another couple into the woods, but they ain't gonna find anything."

More shouts echo out behind him.

"I'll figure it out." I have no idea how the hell I'm going to do that, but the last thing I'm going to do is admit it to Tank.

"Prez, we need to deal with this shit. It's affecting the club, and it'll only get worse if we keep this up. We need to either hit them or let her go," he says, and I can't stop the growl that leaves me. "Shut the fuck up, you fucking neanderthal. I'm not suggesting you send Mac on her merry way. You gotta have a response for the club when they bring it up, though. So, figure your shit out and stop trying to do everything yourself, or we'll be facing another shit show like we did when you took over."

"You think I don't know that?" I hiss, fixing my eyes on the doors over Mason's shoulder.

"Oh, I know you do. Fuck, Ryker. I remember how Dain was. He was a fucking asshole when I came through before. The only reason I came back after was because of you. We were little shits and dumb as fuck, but at least we built something different. Don't let it fall apart now."

He hangs up before I can answer, but I don't know what I would have said anyway. It's rare I think about my father these days, other than to curse him when some shit rule he enacted crops up. Rooster is usually the one to bring shit up, and I've been close to stripping him more times than I can count. I fought against my father's legacy for so long that, when I was finally able to take over, I almost didn't know what to do. Pressing a kiss to Kenzie's head, I breathe in her scent that's lived in my pores for years. Dealing with the fallout and trying to reinvent the Reapers was the reason I never went after Kenz. My chest tightens, and I breathe her in again to calm the stab of pain.

I glance up, leaning to the side to see the doors. I wanted to burst through them, but Kenzie told me we would wait out here. Mason, who's seated across from me, meets my gaze. He's blank, a stark contrast to his frantic behavior when we got here. Somehow, Kenzie convinced him to sit with us, talking him through two panic attacks. I was no help, but seeing him this way convinces me we need to do more. Clearly, he's not dealing with the events from a couple of months ago. We can't afford to have him going off the rails. The Night Slayers' shit aside, the east side needs to have someone in control. With Mason not having a second anymore, there's no one to pull him back from the edge of oblivion. I haven't heard much chatter from the Byrns' side, but I'd put money on Victor sniffing around and trying to weasel his way into the position.

"Mason," I mutter, his eyes focused on me. "You good?"

It's the best I can do in the present situation. I kick myself. His sister is in the hospital, the same hospital he was in only a couple of months ago. Of course he's not fine.

"Don't fucking look at me like that," he snarls, but there's little bite behind his words.

"Like what?" Trying to relieve the numbness in my shoulder, I shift.

Kenzie sighs in her sleep, and Mason's eyes shoot to her, some emotion invading them, but I can't figure out what.

He swings his gaze back to me. "Like you pity me. I'm fine. Worry about your own territory. Why are you even fucking here?"

"Kenzie wanted to come. They're friends."

He nods, confusion plastered on his face. "When did that happen?"

"Since MacKenzie came, really. Hard being a woman with only men around them."

"They can't be friends," he growls, running hot and cold, emotions bouncing across his face in rapid succession.

"I don't think either one of us has a say in that," I say ruefully.

I don't care if they're friends. Kenzie could use some more people in her life. I won't deny her what she wants.

Looking away, he snorts. "And look where it landed Sam. In the hospital."

Kenzie stiffens, and I glance down. Her eyes are still closed, but there's a tightness around them that wasn't there before. Her hands, resting in her lap, curl into fists, nails digging into her palms. I told her the accident wasn't her fault, but Mason's words are undoing all the work I put in convincing her. My own hands curl into fists, and I fight against the need to punch Mason Byrns in the fucking face. He might be hurting, but I won't allow him to put her down.

"You want someone to blame? Search no further than Maddox Raines. You want revenge? You want to retaliate?" I ask, his brown eyes finding mine. "Then, help me burn the Night Slayers to the ground."

Tension drains from him as quickly as it came. He nods as he rests his elbows on his knees before burying his face in his hands. I can't figure out where his head is at, but I'm not going to worry about it. We have enough on our plates without dealing with his insecurities. The doors I've been watching swing open, and Shane strides through. At first, I don't recognize him he's so disheveled. Kenzie tenses even more and sits up. I shake out my arm as the ache sets in.

"Mason," he calls.

The Byrns' leader shoots up, almost upsetting the table next to him.

"Is she okay?"

Desperation cracks his voice, and I notice the nurse behind the desk eyeing him.

I stomp past them and reach over the desk before Shane has a chance to answer. I rip the phone from her grasp, glaring. She shrinks back, holding her hands up. My lip curls when I spy the video mode pulled up. Fucking hell. I feel Shane at my back peering over my shoulder, and he growls. The nurse cowers beneath his stare. Another woman comes around the corner, green-streaked black hair pulled back in a ponytail stops short as she takes in the scene. The nurse is trembling, mouth flapping, but no words are coming out.

"Cynthia. Go," the new woman hisses.

The nurse shoots up, chair tipping over in her haste to scramble away from us. She hesitates, eyeing her phone.

Shane snatches it from my grasp before dropping it to the floor to stomp on it once, twice, then the screen shatters. He calmly picks it up to slip it in his pocket, most likely for Ren to wipe clean later. A whimper escapes her as the other woman grabs her arm.

"Don't bother coming back. In fact, I suggest you take yourself to a new city." She waits until the nurse nods with a sob and rushes away. "I'm sorry. She was new, didn't know how things work around here."

"Thank you," Shane mutters.

Kenzie is right where I left her, staring down the hall as if she can see all the way to Sam. She flinches when I touch her shoulder. I raise an eyebrow, trying to gauge whether she's okay, and she sniffs, glancing away.

"So? What's going on?" Mason asks.

Shane runs his fingers through his hair before dropping his hand to his side. He clenches it over and over, like he doesn't know how to explain.

"Sam is okay. More pissed than anything. She keeps trying to get out of bed to go kick someone's ass. I haven't told her what happened yet."

"And Alex?" I ask.

"He just got out of surgery. They said it went well. As long as an infection doesn't set in, he should make a full recovery." Exhaustion pulls his eyes down, making him seem older than he is.

"I'm going to Sam," Mason says before marching away, glaring at the woman behind the desk. She rolls her eyes after he passes.

Her eyes widen when she sees me watching, and she scrambles away.

"Shane," Kenzie whispers. She stands, twisting her fingers together before wrapping her arms around her waist.

"Mac, I can't . . . I just can't. I'll tell her you were here but go home. I don't want . . ." He sighs, tipping his head back. "I don't want anyone following you here. I'm sorry, but you need to leave."

Kenzie sucks in a shuddering breath, but nods before turning away. Tears are streaming down her face, but she doesn't seem surprised. I wait until she's almost to the door before glaring at him.

"She feels guilty enough as it is. It's not her fault."

I'm fighting a losing battle with everyone.

He presses his lips together, crossing his arms before saying, "She might not be, but the fact still stands—if she hadn't come here, Sam and Alex wouldn't be in the hospital. Alex wouldn't be fighting for his life. We wouldn't have to worry about any of this shit. I don't blame her, but I can't have her around Sam. I have to protect my family, Helms."

He disappears through the doors, back to Sam and his brother. I shake my head, wondering what he'll tell Sam. If he doesn't say anything, Sam will surely try to call Kenzie, not that she has a working phone anymore. I snag Kenzie's elbow as I pass to pull her out to the stairs and through the side entrance. The warm summer air swamps us as soon as the doors shut, but Kenzie still shudders, goosebumps erupting along her arms, and she tries to rub them away.

"Do you think she hates me?" she murmurs, staring at the stars, muted by the nearby lamps lighting up the hospital.

"No, I don't. Shane needs to concentrate on them, though. I'm sure they'll call us when Sam can have visitors."

It's a lie, but I won't pile on her now.

"No, he won't. I heard what he said, Ryker. I know you said it wasn't my fault, but we both know he's right. This never would have happened if I ran somewhere else or never ran in the first place."

Swinging her around and crowding her back to the door, I growl, my body pressing into hers. She still has her arms tight around her middle as her head dips. I cup her face, forcing her chin up with my thumb until she's staring at me, tears filling her eyes again. I study the colors, amplified with her grief. The green in them is bright, but the browns shooting through are muted, subtle, the outer ring a bright copper. I press my body into hers, my fingers caressing her neck until I feel her pulse.

"I will never accept that. I will never accept you sacrificing yourself. I need you to know how vital you are to me. I will not allow you to throw away your life, thinking you aren't important enough. If I lose you"—I swallow the emotions threatening to overwhelm me—"I won't survive."

Concern lines her eyes, and I drop my hand from her face to her hip. She unravels her arms, cupping my face, and I turn into her hand, kissing her palm. A single tear travels down her cheek, and I lean in, kissing it away. We stand, me silently begging her to stay, her struggling to find a reason.

TWENTY-FOUR

MacKenzie

Days pass, and with each one, the knot in my stomach grows. Ryker disappears more and more to meetings I'm not allowed to attend. It took me a couple days to notice, but when I did, it was obvious—someone is always watching me. The first time I saw Tiny tinkering with his bike outside my old childhood home, I didn't think anything of it. I waved, dusting off the rug in my hands, and went back inside. Then it was Tank loitering in the backyard, mumbling something about a fence. Afterward, a parade of members would eye me when they thought I wasn't looking, always there, scanning the streets. No one ever came to say hello or ask where Ryker was. Hawk is the only one who ever comes in the house, but he isn't around much, following Ryker off on some mysterious mission or another.

Sitting on the front porch, I sip coffee and wait on Ryker to get back. Doc is across the street, pretending to inspect the abandoned house. A lot of people left or died in the coup, leaving this street almost deserted. Every so often, Doc peeks at me, and I wave cheerily. He pretends not to notice. I hate they have to be here, watching me, keeping me safe. I hate that I've disrupted their lives with my problems. Ryker is under enough stress trying to track down Maddox, finding the Night Slayers, and whatever else he's dealing with, without me piling my own insecurities on as well. He falls into bed each night, long after I've fallen asleep, and wraps his arm around me. He's asleep before I fully wake up. He slips out of the bed long before the sun rises.

The rumble of a bike echoes through the afternoon air. Usually, they're everywhere, floating up between the houses, drowning out the shrieks of children on summer break, but those are missing as well these days. Ryker didn't lock things down like I wanted—pleaded for—but he did tell the families to keep their kids inside or leave the city. Many women in the MC did just that, packing up their kids and kissing their men goodbye.

Thinking about the damage I've caused, I stop myself, reworking the words in my brain. I didn't cause this . . . I was merely an instrument in their destruction. My phone buzzes, flashing Ren's name. I couldn't find any comforting words when he dropped off my new phone, so I didn't say anything.

"Hi," I say, praying he's not calling with more bad news. Alex is still in the hospital, and every day he doesn't go home is another punch to the gut.

"Stop it, Mac," he grumbles.

Adjusting my voice, I try to make myself not seem so guilty, so pathetic. "Sorry. What did you need, Ren?"

"I need you to answer the damn phone."

"Uh, I did. I'm literally talking to you right now." I pull it away, staring at the screen in confusion.

"Not my call, dumbass. Sam's. She thinks you're mad at her. Why the hell haven't you called? I'm sick of hearing about it. She's been asking me every day to drive her over there. She's about to climb out the window and find her own way." A door slams, and Emma shouts on the other end.

"Oh," I murmur, not sure how to answer him.

I wasn't told to not call her, but Shane made it pretty clear Sam and I shouldn't be friends. I have to respect his decision, even if it's not really his to make. After what happened to Sam the last time I was here, I understand the need to protect his family. I can't be the reason they go through that kind of pain again.

"Yeah, oh. So, are you going to answer her call, or do I have to drive her over?"

"Ryker locked down most of the routes in and out. You won't be able to get through," I say, biting my lip.

His low chuckle fills the line. "You think he wouldn't let us through? Or we couldn't find a way in, regardless?"

Bracing myself, I sigh. "I don't think it's a good idea for her to come. It's safer there."

"Shane told you not to talk to her, didn't he?" Ren's voice turns amused.

"No, but he's not entirely happy with me." I bite my lip again and rush to add, "But I don't blame him. A little space might be a good thing."

"How long did it take you to come up with that bullshit?"

"What? It's not bullshit, Ren. Sam got hurt because of me. Alex is still in the hospital because of me. The last thing I want is someone else getting hurt because I don't learn my lessons," I huff.

"Wow, yeah, okay."

Silence seeps in, and I pull the phone away again. His name disappears, and I snort, seeing he's hung up on me. I want to be mad or annoyed—anything other than devastated—but the pit in my stomach opens again, swallowing more of my sanity, more of my resolve. Ryker told me to trust him, and I do, but it's hard not knowing where the next hit is coming from. I glance across the street, watching Doc spin away, like he wasn't listening in on my conversation. I'm sure he'll report back to Ryker that I was getting phone calls. He always seems to have the information before I have a chance to tell him. Tattletales.

Another rumble of a bike bounces off the building, but this time, it pulls onto our street. Doc is halfway to me before I realize he's moved. He's shooing me with his hands, but I stand, eyes focused on where the bike is coming from. Ryker lifts a hand, the chrome on his bike glinting off the setting sun. Doc scowls, stomping back to his own bike as Ryker pulls in, killing the engine. I don't know where he was today, but his eyes are lined with exhaustion as he gives me a tired smile.

"Hi," he whispers before pulling me in his arms and kissing my cheek. "You okay?"

"I'm fine. Are you in for the night?"

I don't have it in me to ask any questions. I can't handle any more information, even though I insisted on being informed. I'm emotionally tapped out.

"No." he sighs, releasing me. "I have to go out again in about an hour. Thought I'd grab something to eat."

I trail behind him, clutching my now cold coffee. I stop as he rifles through the fridge. I don't say anything as he unwraps a sandwich, grabs a banana, then shoves half of it in his mouth before setting it down on the island. He isn't bothering with the table, which tells me more than anything else he's not staying long. He gestures to me with the sandwich.

"Someone call you?" He raises an eyebrow before shoveling the rest of the banana in.

"Ren. He was just checking in," I say, avoiding his eyes.

"Bullshit. He called me, too. Why aren't you talking to Sam, Kenz? Is it because of what King said?" He scowls, barely chewing as he scarfs down his food.

"It wasn't because of Shane. I mean, he got me thinking about things, but I made the decision. If I can lessen the damage my coming here has caused, I think I should."

"So, what's next, then? You going to leave me behind, too? Maybe move in to your old house, try to lessen the damage?" The bitterness in his tone takes me off guard.

"What are you talking about? That's ridiculous. *You're* ridiculous. I'm not having this conversation with you if you're going to be like this." I plant my hands on my hips, ready to fight.

I've been left in this house, without any outlet for the emotions swirling inside me. My thoughts do nothing but spiral down.

"Oh, you're not going to have this conversation? Well, then, better not have it, then!" He grabs the plate and tosses it roughly into the sink.

I flinch, expecting to hear a crack, but he turns on the water to rinse it off. He won't leave it for later, too caught up in his own mind.

"What the hell do you want from me?"

"At some point, you're going to have to talk about shit, MacKenzie. You can't keep hiding from everything and everyone," he grumbles. He swings around, planting his hands on the counter top. I toss my hands in the air.

"I haven't been hiding! Where the hell am I supposed to go? How the hell am I supposed to get there? You fuck off to god knows where and leave me here. I don't know what grand reveal you think is coming from me, but I have nothing but anxiety and guilt rolling around. You already knew, so why would I keep bringing it up? You didn't want to talk about it, so I stopped trying."

I'm panting by the time I'm done. I wasn't angry before, but now I'm spitting mad.

"You could call Sam. You could talk to her. I trust them to keep you safe, regardless of what happened the last time they were in a car. And I asked if you wanted to come. You said no. So, don't get pissed at me because you're regretting your choices."

I rear back. "What are you talking about? You never asked me to come along."

"Yes, I did. You said no one would want to see you." What he's talking about clicks, and I roll my eyes.

"You asked me to go talk to Rooster. The man who actively hates me. Of course I wasn't going to go meet with him. You never asked again."

Someone clears their throat behind me, and I whirl around to find Doc standing awkwardly in the open doorway. I glare at him for interrupting and flush. The front door has been hanging wide open the entire time we've been yelling at each other. Anyone who walked by— hell, people at headquarters—probably heard us.

"What do you want?" Ryker grunts, and I glare over my shoulder.

He can be pissed at me all he wants, but he shouldn't take it out on his men.

"Sorry, Doc. We didn't realize the door was open. Did you need something?" I ask, my heart still racing. Doc's eyes bounce between us, settling on mine.

"I thought you'd like to know Ren and Sam crossed the line. They'll be here in a couple minutes, so you two might want to finish pecking at each other before they do," Doc says.

"We weren't pecking at each other," Ryker grumbles.

"You're picking fights because there's too much built up, and you don't know how to deal with the stress. Try talking about what you're actually upset about instead of picking off the low-hanging fruit." He spins and lopes off to his bike.

"Is that what we're doing?" I ask, my eyes following Doc as he rides away.

Ryker's breath tickles the hairs on the back of my neck. I didn't hear him move, but I can feel him at my back. His fingers brush my skin, sweeping my ponytail over my shoulder and pressing his lips there. His hand slips down my side, settling on my hip, then tugging me against him. He rests his chin on my shoulder, nuzzling into my neck. He's ghosting his lips along my shoulder, to my jaw.

I turn, if only to see what he'll do, and he fuses our mouths together. It's not a proper kiss with the weird angle. He's not moving, not really. His tongue isn't darting out, he isn't demanding me for more. It's a rest together, a reminder he's here. I sigh against him, and my body relaxes more. Tension I've been carrying flows out. Worries I didn't realize I was bottling up disappear in a puff of smoke and shadow. He pulls back, eyes flicking over my features, scrutinizing every dip and valley.

"I'm worried," I whisper as his forehead falls to rest against mine.

"Me too."

TWENTY-FIVE

Ryker

I slam the door behind Ren and Sam before breathing out a sigh of relief. I don't know what the hell Sam and Kenzie were yelling about, but it took everything in me to not burst in the room and throw Sam's ass out.

Ren kept giving me a look, posted up at my kitchen table with his laptop, tablet, and at least four cellphones. I don't know what he was doing, but I left him alone after he snapped at me. He didn't have to help us out at all. I can't figure out if he hates me, so I try not to piss him off.

I stalk back into the kitchen, where Kenzie is eating ice cream and staring off. I stare from the doorway, drinking her in. I have so little time to watch her, to admire the little things I love about her. My phone buzzes, reminding me of the meeting I'm supposed to be at, but I want to wait a little longer. She turns, and I huff out a breath, knowing I won't get more time.

"You and Sam good, then?" I round the island, rinsing the cloth to wipe the counters again.

I've done it twice, but I need to keep my hands busy, or they'll be on her, and I won't get to my meeting at all.

"We're fine. We feel a bit differently about the situation and how it should be handled, but we're fine. Don't you have to leave?" She tilts her head, sticking a spoonful of ice cream in her mouth before pulling it out slowly. Her tongue darts out to catch a dollop left on her lip, making my cock harden. Dropping my gaze, I scrub harder at a spot I'm pretty sure is a part of the design.

"I think she really needs a friend, you know, one she's not in love with," I say.

"Who says she's not in love with me?" I peek at her from under my lashes, spying the smirk.

"Pretty sure she has enough partners without adding you to the mix. Besides, you're pretty . . ." I freeze, every muscle tensing.

"Pretty? Pretty what?"

Clearing my throat, I resume running the rag over the pristine counter. My mind is still blank, but there's no way I'm finishing my thought. At some point, she'll give up. I glance up—maybe not.

"You're pretty. She only goes for those rugged guys."

It's the best I can come up with.

"I'm pretty? You think she wouldn't fall in love with me because I'm pretty?" She raises an eyebrow, spoon hanging in the air, a drop of ice cream splatting on the table.

When she swipes her finger across the wood and sticks it in her mouth, I cringe. Thank god the island is high enough to cover my lower half. Now is not the time to get horny and fuck her on the table. I have a meeting. Maybe if I remind myself enough, she'll stop looking like a fucking dessert I want to devour.

I nod vigorously before putting my back to her and attacking the oven. Like the counter, the stove top is clean, but I need something to keep my hands busy. Otherwise, I'll be sanitizing the island after I bend her over . . . I stop the line of thought before it can fully form. Tonight isn't any different from any other night, but for some reason, I can't look at her without wanting her.

"Ryker. I'm pretty what?"

The clang of her bowl hitting the marble rings out behind me. I force myself to keep working. The cupboards over the oven have spots, so I run the washcloth over it, trying to eliminate them.

"Kenz, I can't even remember what we were talking about." I toss the rag in the sink but grab it as soon as it splats to ring it out. I turn to bring it to the laundry room. When I do, though, Kenzie is right there, inches away from me.

"Bullshit. What were you going to say?"

I roll my eyes, sighing. "Pretty wild. I was going to say you're pretty wild. She couldn't handle you." I brace myself, but she laughs, joy dancing in her eyes.

"Well, it's a good thing you can, huh?" She smirks, and I'm lost. I'm lost in her eyes, lost in her smile, lost in her curves.

The cloth squishes under my boot as I step forward and haul her in my arms. I swallow her gasp, covering her mouth with my own. She moans when my hand skims up her side, brushing the side of her tit. My own echoes through the room when I find she's not wearing a bra. I can't believe I didn't notice before. No way am I doing anything other than worshipping these tonight. I tug her shirt up, exposing the pair, and rip my mouth from hers, then bury my face between them. Nipping the insides of each before latching on to a nipple. I pinch and roll the other as she moans.

My phone buzzes. Fuck the meeting. Fuck everyone else other than her and these beautiful tits. Kenzie gasps out my name. I fucking love them. I bite down on the underside, and she yelps. A low chuckle escapes me. My tongue laps at the marks I've left. I could die happy, being smothered by these glorious, amazing, supple . . .

"Hello?" Kenzie's breathless voice cuts through my worship, and I glance up.

She fucking answered the phone. Her hazel eyes are bright, brimming with desire, but she widens them, gesturing to the phone. I grin before latching on to the other sorely neglected nipple. A shudder travels through her as she mumbles at whoever is on the other end.

I let it go with a pop, scraping my nails across her nipple. She glares, even as her body shivers with desire.

"Take this, now," she mouths, shaking the phone all while trying to listen to the person on the other end.

I smirk, falling to my knees before yanking at her waistband. Her free hand grabs a fistful of my hair, pushing me away, then pulling me back in. I get her pants past her hips when she lets go. She gathers the material, stopping me from peeling them off her body. I reach around, digging my fingers into her plump ass, and I bury my nose in her crease, just barely visible over her waistband. Breathing deeply, taking in the scent of her arousal, I moan, knowing I'll win whatever game we're playing. She's wet—sopping, no doubt—so ready for me. There's no way she'll fight me for long.

"I know he has a meeting. He's just a little busy."

Flicking my eyes up to hers, I chuckle again, and I'm met with heavy lids. She's sagging in my grasp.

"Hang up," I mouth against her hip bone. I suck the skin at the juncture into my mouth, then pull back, admiring the mark I've left. I'd cover her in them if I thought she'd let me. I nuzzle back in, taking advantage of her slackened hand to yank the leggings over her ass. They're around her knees now. I push her feet apart so I can see her pretty pussy.

"I'm sorry," I whisper.

"Are you talking to my vagina?" she demands, incredulously, making my head pop up.

"Thought you were on the phone?" I crook an eyebrow, fixing my eyes on hers as I lean in.

My tongue darts out, diving into her slit. She grabs the counter, knuckles white. Her eyes fall closed when I reach her clit, swirling around lightly.

"You have a meeting," she murmurs with a sob, grabbing my hair to shove my face more firmly on her.

I hum, knowing it drives her wild, making her hips buck forward. The phone buzzes again, forgotten on the island, dancing across the marble, pausing, then rumbling again.

"You're right," I say, leaping to my feet. I snatch the phone up, trying to contain my smirk at her shriek of protest.

"Yes?" Her gaze flicks down when I lick my lips, the taste of her exploding across my taste buds.

Her mouth falls open, and her gasps fill the air. Her leggings and underwear are still around her knees, shirt pushed up over those magnificent tits, hanging like two ripe pieces of fruit, begging me to take a bite. I sway toward her, but Hawk yelling my name shocks me out of my trance.

"What?" I snap.

"Seriously, are you fucking or something? I swear to god, if you answered the phone when you were in the middle of . . . You know what—never mind. I'll take care of shit here. I can see you're not coming."

"Not yet." I laugh at his noise of disgust, hanging up on him before he can say anything else.

"It's okay. You go. I'll see you when you get back," Kenzie says.

The dejection in her voice cracks my heart. She reaches for her pants, but I drop to my knees again. I rip the fabric from her grasp, shoving them to her ankles.

"Did I say you could put those on? You don't listen very well, baby. I'm going to need you to follow directions if you want to come." Her mouth falls open, but she snaps it shut when I lick her slit, swallowing another groan when I find her wetter than before.

"Ryker, the windows are open," she mutters, her head falling back. She's back to gripping the counter for dear life.

Her knees buckle on the next pass, so I wrap my arm under her ass, hoisting her with me as I stand. I plant her on the island. Her hands slap the cool stone, and she squeals, lifting herself up.

"Shit, that's cold."

"Stop wigglin'," I growl, bringing an arm down across her lap.

I'm about to drop to my knees when I notice the height. She's way too high for me to enjoy her coming on my face.

"What's wrong?"

"I can't. This isn't going to work." I stare at the counter before searching the area for one that'll work better when she sighs, trying to push my arm off. My head shoots up, leaning into her to prevent her from slipping off the edge.

"It's okay. You can go. I'm not stopping you." Annoyance weaves into her tone.

"What the hell are you talking about? And why do you keep trying to get me to leave?"

She throws her hands out, giving me a look, but I have no idea what she's talking about. I give her the same look back, hoping she'll finally talk.

"You keep saying you have to go. I'm trying to give you an out," she cries.

"Why the fuck would I want an out? For fuck's sake, Kenz. I'm trying to fuck you here, not get out of it. Where the hell did you get the idea I wanted to leave?"

Her hand goes to her throat, petting the flush traveling to her cheeks. She shakes her head, a thoughtful gaze crossing her face, before she focuses back on me.

"You're right. I did it again," she murmurs. "Shit, and now I broke the mood. I'm sorry." She buries her face in her hands.

Watching her hide while her pants are around her ankles is ridiculous. I snicker, but it quickly turns into a cackle when she peeks out from between her fingers.

"What are you laughing at? This isn't funny!"

Stepping between her legs, I wrap my arms around her and drop my mouth to her neck. I have to bite down to stop the laughter from spilling out, but my shaking shoulders gives me away.

"Kenz-z," I say between gasps of air.

"Would you cut it out? It's not fucking funny." She smacks my side, but I've trapped her, and she can't get much momentum.

"You're something else. Irresistible, I swear."

Scooping my hands under her ass, I lift her up before she can hit me again, and her arms loop around my neck. I carry her to the table and drop her onto it. It's the perfect height. Shoving the chair aside and I drop to my knees, finally able to reach where I want. I yank her to the edge, her ass almost hanging off, then tear the fabric from her ankles. She props herself on her elbows, opening her mouth to make some sassy comment, but a gasp comes out when I suck her clit into my mouth. She drops back, head banging on the wood, and I chuckle against her flesh.

Kissing my way across to her leg, I pause when I reach her inner thigh before I sink my teeth into her tender flesh. She curses, legs jerking. I run my lips over her clit, then past as I latch on to her other thigh, reveling in the whimpers falling from her lips. Her hips pop up, so I snake my arm over her waist, gently holding her still. She's cursing me under her breath, but I'm enjoying myself. I'll be damned if I'm going to rush this. Her legs snap shut, thighs crushing my head, when I suck her clit into my mouth again.

"Baby, you're not going to rush me," I hum against her skin.

"Stop fucking teasing me," she snaps, squeezing her legs together.

Grabbing her ankles, I roll her body on to her stomach. One tug, and she's exactly where I want her. She's struggling, trying to pull out of my grasp, but her shrieks turn to moans when my mouth finds her clit again. I add a finger, then another, as her pussy clenches around them. One stroke of my teeth scraping against the sensitive bud, and she's thrashing and shuddering through her orgasm. I lap her up one last time, standing to find her fingers wrapped around the edge of the table, knuckles white. Gripping her hips, I tug until her feet slap against the hardwood. Her legs try to collapse, but I grip harder, holding her up.

"Ryker," she whispers. "I can't. Oh my god."

I trail my hand up her back as I lean over her. I brush her hair to the side. Her eyes are closed, lips still parted as her body quakes every few seconds.

"You can take more," I murmur in her ear, then nip the lobe while I push my pants down just enough to free my cock. Bracing a hand next to her, I use my free hand to guide myself to her wet core.

"You can take everything," I grunt, driving my cock to the hilt.

A groan leaves me when I bottom out inside her. Kenzie's back arches up, her ass pushing back, trying to take more of me. I pause, basking in the flames licking at the corners of my consciousness.

"Ryker," she whines, wiggling back and forth. I straighten, my fingers finding her hips. I want to remember this feeling of being so deep I don't know where she ends and where I begin.

"I got you, baby," I grunt when I can't take it anymore. With each passing second, her pussy is clenching tighter, like she's purposefully driving me insane.

I pull out gradually, and when there's only the tip left, I lunge back in. The table scrapes across the floor, leaving scratches, but fuck if I care. I repeat the move over and over until she's back to panting and cursing me.

"Tell me what you want, what you need." I thrust forward, lingering, and pulling out again. "Do you want to beg?" Thrust again. "Do you want me to ruin you for anyone else?" Thrust again.

"Never anyone else," she gasps, and I shudder, her words flowing over me and settling in my mind. "Never beg."

I chuckle, snaking a hand under her and pulling her up, so she's braced on her hands, and I have access to her tits.

"I love fucking you like this, but fuck I wish I could bury my face in these while doing it." I pinch her nipples, making her jerk.

She flies to her toes, then falls back down when I punch into her again. It's harder this way to get as deep as I want, but I can't release her tits, not when they make her pussy clamp down on my cock every time I roll the buds between my fingers.

"Please," she moans.

"See? That wasn't so hard, was it? But you can do better."

I straighten, mourning the loss of her tits in my hands. I latch on to her hips and surge into her harder, finding a rhythm. It's not fast or hard enough to send her into ecstasy, but it takes the edge off. I run one hand up her spine to grip her neck and guide her head lower until her forehead is touching the wood, and she's forced on to her elbows.

"Fuck, Ryker. Please," she whimpers.

"Beg me for what you want, Kenz." I keep my hand on her neck, slowing my pace. I'll never get used to the feel of her pussy wrapped around my cock.

"You fucking bastard," she gasps.

Buried deep, I stop, balls settling against her ass. I have to grit my teeth when she clenches again, trying to force me to continue.

"Try again, baby."

"Goddammit, make me fucking come. Please, oh god, please. I can't . . . I need you to make me come."

She's practically sobbing, as I lean over her, whispering in her ear, "Good girl."

I drag my cock out and slam back in again and again and again. She's choking out "please" with every thrust. Leaning in again, I wrap my hand around her throat, pulling her up and fusing our bodies together, pushing into her, harder, deeper. I freeze, waiting for her to stop me or panic. Instead, she wraps a hand around my wrist, holding me there.

"Play with your clit, baby. Let me hear you scream while you come around my cock," I grunt.

I won't last much longer. I'm surprised I haven't exploded with how amazing she feels.

When her hand drops from my wrist, I loosen my grip, but her hand flies back and forces my fingers to wrap around the delicate flesh again. A low moan leaves me. I can tell the moment she touches herself, though my eyes are closed, head thrown back. One circle on her clit, and she's folding in, detonating around my cock. My arm around her waist is all that's keeping her upright as she convulses with the pleasure rolling through her. I push in one last time and explode, jerking as the waves of tremors surge through my body. We collapse on the table, but I catch myself at the last second. Fuck, it's the hardest thing I've ever had to do.

"Oh my god," she wheezes, pussy still quivering around me, making me grunt.

"You can call me Ryker."

TWENTY-SIX

MacKenzie

I stare at the shower wall, running the loofah over my body, replaying the sensations Ryker put me through last night, when a blast of cold air shoots past my ass, making me jump.

"What the hell, Ryker? Close the door!" I squeal, retreating under the hot spray.

He chuckles, moving to join me, but launches out of the water. He plops down on the bench. My mind flashes back to me straddling him on it while he told me how he installed it with me in mind five years ago. I rode him, lust dripping from his gaze before he buried his face between my breasts, mumbling to them. I thought he was talking to me, but he told me to stop interrupting their conversation.

"Why the hell is the water so damn hot? Fuck. Is this why I've been taking cold showers all week?" He reaches out a hand, then yanks it back when it hits the spray.

I grin. "I like hot showers."

"That's not hot. It's fucking lava. I'm turning down the hot water heater." He stands, as if he's going to do it now, and I move to block the door.

"Don't you dare. This is the first time I've been able to have a shower as hot as I want. You will not ruin this for me, Ryker." I poke his chest, and he peers down before tilting his head, eyes finding mine.

"What do you mean you've never had a shower as hot as you'd like?" All laughter has fled from his face, replaced with concern.

I huff, not wanting to reveal another part of my life that fell apart, but knowing he won't leave it alone until I do.

"Maddox found out I like hot showers, convinced Dad I was the reason we never had enough hot water, and Dad turned down the temp. When we moved—well, we were living at headquarters for a while, so nothing was great. Once we got in a house, Dad turned it down again." I move back under the spray, letting the warmth seep in my bones. Sighing, I peek at him from under my lashes.

"Why didn't you say something after Ray died?"

I wave away his words. "Wasn't worth it. Maddox would just turn it down again. Then he went to live at headquarters, but I guess I only remembered when I was in the shower. I forgot once I got out. Maybe I got used to it. I don't know."

"Well, you can have it as hot as you want here." He shudders as the water hits his skin, but he wraps an arm around me. "Why didn't you ever move out?"

Not knowing how to answer, I sigh. There's a million reasons I never left Dante's house. It wasn't where I grew up, like the one next door. It wasn't a place I loved, like Ryker's place. It wasn't even all that amazing, as it was empty most the time. Dante always had to put out one fire after another. Maddox was at headquarters, sowing dissension and hate.

"I don't know," I murmur.

"Yes, you do. You just don't have one answer. Give me all the answers."

He reaches past me to grab my shampoo, but I snatch it back. I hand him the conditioner instead. A new favorite thing of his is to wash my hair. No idea why, but I had to teach him, so he wouldn't snarl it. His fascination with taking care of everything from washing to brushing to braiding the strands is weird, but it's one less task I have to worry about. My muscles relax more as his fingers massage my scalp, and I heave out a sigh.

"I didn't know where to go. I don't have any skills other than what I learned in the MC, and let's be honest, that's not exactly something you can put on a resume. I was scared to leave. If I left, it meant trying something new. If I tried something new, and it didn't work out, well . . ." He guides my head back to the spray, rinsing the strands before grabbing the loofah. I'm not going to complain if he wants to wash me again.

"What else?"

"Where would I go? I never wanted to live anywhere other than here. When Dad said we were leaving—well, you weren't the only reason I threw a fit over it. I love this city. I love being here. I haven't seen much else, obviously, but I never had the urge to go anywhere. Dante did. He always wanted to travel, just hop on his bike and ride away, see where he ended up. But not me. I always wanted to come home at the end of the day."

I've never revealed my reasons to anyone. Dad didn't care. He just called me a spoiled brat. Dante was too shocked by everything, traumatized by the attempted coup and his best friend taking over. Maddox—well, Maddox didn't matter. He was an asshole then, too. By that point, he was a snake, whispering in Dad's ear, poisoning him against me more. I can admit our father wasn't a good man, even by club standards. Honestly, I'm surprised I wasn't given away a long time ago. Mostly, I was ignored. I was too wild, too outspoken, too much. Maddox said no one would ever want to be saddled with me. I thought I didn't care, but for some reason, his words wormed their way into my brain, settling there and resurfacing at my darkest moments.

Suds run down my body with each pass of the loofah. Ryker's movements are unhurried, like he's giving me enough time to process what I want to say. I lean back against his chest as his arm envelops me, holding me close. I've spent so many days—even after I got here—living in constant near-panic I forgot what it felt like to be safe. Knowing he'll catch me if I fall is more settling than any drug or reassurance uttered. Certainly, more than anything, I can provide for myself. I'm strong, but having him at my back makes me feel invincible. I haven't felt strong in a long time. I lost myself when I ran. I left the core of who I am behind in Rima, bleeding out on the floor of the Night Slayers' clubhouse.

"Any other reasons?"

His voice pulls me from my thoughts. We sway, the loofah forgotten on the tiles. It's almost dancing, and I shut my eyes, drinking in the silence. These moments are few and far between, and I cherish them. I don't know what will happen, how we'll free ourselves from this hell I've thrust us into. I don't know if we'll get out alive, but I push the thought from my mind, grasping at the peace from seconds before.

"I think I was waiting," I whisper into the steam, half hoping he won't hear my confession.

His lips brush the shell of my ear. "Waiting for what?"

I swallow, forcing the admission out. "You."

He doesn't respond, squeezing me closer. The water cuts off, and I want to protest, not wanting to leave our bubble. When we step out, the real world will intrude, filled with demented half brothers, psychotic bikers, mafia leaders we have to bring into our circle, and members we have to explain things to. He shushes my protest, picking me up, then setting my feet on the rug before grabbing the towel to dry me off. I'm too relaxed or whiny—I'm not sure—to tell him he doesn't have to. He gets another towel, squeezing the water from my hair and wrapping it up like I taught him. Resigning myself to starting the day, I huff, but when I reach for my clothes, he grabs my hand, pulling me to the bedroom. He scoops me up before laying me down on the comforter.

Staring into his vibrant eyes, I'm caught in his gaze. We're both still naked, and I expect his eyes to roam. He seems obsessed with my breasts, but his serious gaze holds mine, like he's deciding something. Smiling softly, he nods in response. I don't know what I expected him to do, but crawling next to me, turning my body to face him, wasn't it. His hand skims up my side, enough for goosebumps to erupt on my damp skin.

"What were you waiting for me to do?" he asks, searching my face.

I tense. "I don't know."

"Liar," he whispers.

Huffing, I roll my eyes to escape his gaze. His fingers guide my chin down, forcing me to look at him.

"Waiting for you to change your mind. Waiting for you to want me. Waiting for you to admit you were wrong, that you made a mistake, and you needed me. I was waiting for you to save me."

Tears fill my eyes, remembering how hard it was when he told me to leave. We stood in this very room, my knee scuffed up from climbing through his window, the night before I was whisked away from everything I had ever known. I remember how hard it was to be vulnerable, to admit I wanted to stay with him. I wanted to help. It was the hardest thing I'd ever done. My cheeks flush when I recall the embarrassment I felt when he stood there, still and silent as I poured my seventeen-year-old heart out. I begged him to let me stay, to keep me, but he shook his head and refused to meet my eyes. When I screamed at him to look at me, his eyes were blank and cold. I knew right then what he would say, what he would do. I knew I wasn't enough to fight for.

"I'm sorry, Kenz. I couldn't save you before. You had to save yourself. I've regretted turning you down every day, but we never would have survived then. We were too young, too impulsive, too . . . something. But I can help you now. I won't save you, Kenzie, but I can help you save yourself."

"Why? Why did I have to come to you? Why didn't you come after? Later? Sometime in the last ten fucking years?"

He sighs, tucking a knee between my legs to pull me closer and resting his forehead on mine. "I wanted to. A couple years later, I was finally starting to get somewhere in building things back. It wasn't nearly as organized or efficient as before the coup, but I had a couple guys I felt like I could trust. I waited, though, knowing I wasn't stable enough. Things were still up in the air, and I couldn't protect you. I heard about your dad dying, and I thought I could do it. We were older, the club wasn't on the verge of collapse. I thought I could . . . I don't know. I rode all the way to Rima, rode straight into Viper territory. I didn't even call Dante. I didn't tell anyone I was coming. I don't know what I thought would happen, but I didn't expect to see you, laughing with some bikers. You looked"—he sucks in a breath—"happy."

A sob catches in my throat when I think about how close he was, and I never knew. I expected him to forget or remember me as the annoying girl who followed them around. The one who begged him to take her virginity and then lost it on him later when he wouldn't acknowledge what we'd done. Tears fall, and he catches them with his finger to brush them away. I wish he could brush away the ache in my heart as easily.

"I wasn't." I hiccup, trying to pull myself together. "I wasn't happy. I was faking it, hoping some day it would feel real."

"Oh, Kenz, we're pretty fucking stupid, aren't we?" He chuckles, then kisses my nose.

"Not so stupid anymore, right?" I'm sure my face is flushed. We've talked about this so much, but every time, it digs a little deeper and settles a little more into my soul.

"Not stupid enough to not tell you how much you mean to me, that's for fucking sure."

"Well, I'm glad we're on the same page, then." I snort, trying to roll away from him, but he snatches me back. I squeal as he pulls me on top until I'm straddling him.

Short of breath from laughing, I settle my hands on his bare chest. His hard cock bounces against my ass as he pulls his knees up. He runs his hands up and down my thighs. When my gaze collides with his, it's like the whole world pauses, holding its breath with me, sucking in the emotions between us.

His fingers scrape my skin, skirting the sides of my breasts. He caresses the tops before sweeping down, grazing my nipples. I shift, chasing his touch, and he skims his thumbs along the juncture of my legs. Focusing on where he's touching me, I tip my head back. He focuses on my thighs, circles my ankles, scrapes the arches of my feet, then up to my shoulders, across my collarbone and then along the column of my throat. I shudder when he grips my hips and tries to pick me up, but from this angle, he can't. I push up on my knees, and he fits himself at my core. I sink down gradually, stretching to accommodate him.

I don't want to be in charge right now. I can't handle the spark I'd need to finish, so I sink down, laying on his chest, my face fitting in the crook of his neck. We lay still, him deep inside, hands skating across my skin as he presses a kiss to my hair. He tightens his arms and rolls us. I've never been more thankful for a king-size bed than right now.

Ryker braces himself on his forearms, and I open my eyes, gazing into his as he moves. This isn't the frantic fucking we had last night. It's not the rushed coupling against the wall. This is the gentle, steady, unhurried pace of a man who has all the time in the world to build my body up, coaxing it toward a climax. My core coils tighter, and I lift my leg, fitting it around his hips.

"Kenzie," he breathes, lips brushing over my neck, shoulders, chest.

I expect him to say something else, but he seals his mouth over mine, like my name was a prayer falling from his lips. His kiss is just as unhurried as his thrusts, his tongue exploring mine. Lifting my other knee, I plant my foot next to his hip, taking him deeper. I swallow his groan, drinking in each sound.

His painstakingly slow pace falters, and he jerks, his cock twitching within me as he rips his mouth from mine. He thrusts harder, one of his hands tangling with mine. I don't know if I can peak like this, but he must sense it, eyes piercing me.

"Touch yourself, baby," he grunts through gritted teeth, holding himself together with will alone.

Moving my hand between us, I scrape my nails down his side and across his stomach, and he shudders. Then I find my clit, already wet from our exploits. I slide my fingers on either side.

"Don't play. Come for me," he growls, ducking to capture my nipple between his teeth.

I press down, circling my clit harder, faster. Ryker's knee slides, and he surges deeper, making my breath stall in my lungs. My orgasm barrels into me, stealing the feeling in my fingers. Stars burst behind my lids, and my ears ring. I can barely make out Ryker hissing, which gives way to a guttural groan so deep I feel it in my bones, and sparks erupt again, cascading over my body.

Ryker's hair tickling my chest brings me back to my body. He's gasping. No, that's me, gasping for breath. I inhale deeply, my tongue swiping across my lips, the salty taste on my upper lip invading my taste buds. Our fingers are still intertwined, and when he loosens his grip they tingle, the sensation racing down my arm. I fling my arm out, knocking the arm holding him up, and he falls on me. He curses, but I hold him there, the delicious weight of his body pressing me into the mattress.

He shifts, pulling out, and I can feel both of us running down my thighs. Knowing I'll hate it as soon as I get up, I shift, but I'm too content to worry. He settles his hips on me, hands brushing through my hair over and over, like he can't stand to not touch me. Bliss exploding through my pores, I smile.

This is what I was waiting for.

TWENTY-SEVEN

Ryker

"Mason, I don't know what to tell you. I understand they're coming through your side of the city, but it's not like I can stop them. Not yet," I say. Finally, I secured a meeting with him, but he would only do it if I met him at the Byrns' estate. I don't blame him. It didn't end up well for him last time we met up.

"What's your plan to deal with the Night Slayers, Helms?" he grumbles.

I eye him, noting the exhaustion lining his gaunt, wrung out, defeated face.

"I don't know yet. We're having a hard time getting any concrete information on the layout of their territory, how many members they have, allies they have in their pocket. They're elusive. People are either scared of them or fronting for them. I don't have any contacts in Rima other than the Vipers, and with Maddox at the top of my to-kill list, I can't exactly call him up and ask him for favors," I say ruefully, glancing out the window.

I've never been in this room. In fact, I don't think I've been inside the Byrns estate since I was nineteen, freshly minted President of the Reapers to meet with Mason. He was the brand-new leader of the Byrns mafia, and I worried I would have to fight him for my territory. I was scared shitless, which I thought I was hiding well, but looking back, I doubt it. Mason's face told me I wasn't the only one terrified out of my mind. Neither of us knew what we were doing, but none of us had the energy to reach for more than what we already had.

I imagined the mansion would be cold and lifeless, which, I guess it is, compared to my house, but at least it looks like people live here instead of being a showroom for rich bitches. The hallways are weird, turning in places that don't make sense. Once we made it to his office, everything softened. Pictures line the bookshelves behind him. Most of them are of Sam when she was younger.

"What's with the globe?" I point to the corner.

"What?" He glances around. "Oh, it's got whiskey in it. Got it at some stupid silent auction."

"Why'd you bid on it if you didn't like it?" He's staring off into space again. He's doing it more the longer our meeting has gone on.

"Um, I was . . ." He sucks in a breath. "Sammy and Colin used to do this thing at galas. It doesn't matter."

He scowls, but I'm sure he's pissed at himself. I make a mental note to text Sam and tell her to pull her head out of whoever's ass she's currently buried in and check on her fucking brother. I can't imagine going through what he has, but he is not okay. Seeing him at the hospital was one thing. It was a stressful situation all around, but now? Mason Byrns is falling apart, and we can't afford to deal with the fallout.

"Mason, what the fuck are you doing?" His face whips up, but I narrow my eyes until he sighs.

"Your guess is as good as mine, Helms. Listen, I'll do what I can, but I have enough to deal with trying to fix shit Victor fucked up when I was under."

"Get your shit together. People are starting to talk," I snarl.

The world we live in doesn't afford us the luxury of dealing with our shit privately. We bury our problems six feet under or someone will take advantage. In Mason's case, Victor fucking Smith must be waiting in the wings for him to fuck it up.

"Fuck you. Worry about your own territory. How the hell would you know people are talking? You're holed up north in no-man's land."

"That's how you know it's bad. If I've heard about it, it's clearly got around."

"No, it means you've been talking to the fucking Kings. Or Sam," he grumbles, pulling his phone out. He gazes at the black screen before slipping it back in his pocket.

"Either way, you need to choose a second. I swear to fuck all if you don't rein your uncle in, Shane's going to float him."

Mason rolls his eyes, and his face transforms, losing the cloudiness in his eyes. Leaning back, he crosses his arms and taps a finger on his lips. It's the most aware, the most like his old self I've seen since the night we were ambushed. Wondering what the fuck he's going to drop on me now, I wait.

"Victor used to live in Rima. He might be able to help."

I shake my head. "I worked with the asshat before, and I almost shot the bastard. I don't know how you haven't floated him yourself. He's fucking boring, never says a damn thing, and thinks he's ten times smarter than he is. Oh, and he's creepy."

"Well, shitty information from a shitty person is better than going in blind. Are you going to go in guns blazing? Or are we looking at a systematic take down?" He leans his elbows on the desk, picking up a pen and twirling it between his fingers.

The change in him is throwing me off.

"I don't know. We have some issues with shipments, much like we had when the Guild rolled in, but I'm not sure if they're related. I'm afraid if we go and wipe them out, we'll miss something. If it's something bigger than just the Slayers, we might have to deal with retaliation," I say.

"They won't hit back. They don't care about the people they're working with. They don't have allies. They have minions they've convinced are indispensable, when, in reality, they'll do whatever it takes to line their pockets. The lies they spew make those working for them feel like they have a say, or they can control the narrative, but it's a smoke show. I'd tell you to use the Guild to take out the Night Slayers, if I thought you could get away with it, but I wouldn't know how to start or finish something like that." He splays his hands out, shrugging.

"Yeah. Well, if you have any ideas, let me know," I say, planting my hands to stand, but he holds up a hand, and I settle back in my seat.

"Why did you come here?" he asks. I raise an eyebrow. "We've never worked together before. Obviously, you reached out when the Guild was rearing its head, but even then, you weren't as . . . open. So, why are you making connections now?"

"You remember anything from when we were little kids? Before we were trained or really understood the kind of life our families led?"

"Not really, why?"

"Our families used to get together. Parties and backyard shit. I think one time it was Shane's birthday." I shake my head, trying to remember details from a lifetime ago. "We weren't always so closed off. Hell, I think one time you and I set a fire in one of these rooms."

I glance to the rug, though the chances of it being the same one or even the same room would be crazy. Mason's phone buzzes, but he's lost in memories my words have dredged up. He shakes his head when it keeps going.

"I don't remember that. Seems like I should, though. The Kings remember this shit?"

"No idea. I haven't mentioned it. Our families used to work together. The Byrns and Kings built this city together, turning it from a speck on the map to what it is today. Somewhere along the way, Synd was split by the river. My family moved in and carved out a portion no one bothered with. Then something happened. Some event brought the families back together, but I can't find anything on it. My father wasn't into record-keeping," I snort, remembering my father, who was angry and distant most of my life.

He nods. "Why tell me?"

"Thought you might be able to figure out what happened. What made them split, what brought them back together, and maybe why we never saw each other after we were kids. Seems like it's something we would remember. Might be good to get back to that." I sigh, pushing to my feet.

I've been gone all day, leaving Kenzie home alone, though I hate it. Even if it isn't at my side, she's safe where she is.

"Tell me what I can do to help with your Night Slayer issue when you come up with a plan. I'll keep tracking them through the train station if I can. Oh, and I have the commissioner stacking up more on the north side—help mitigate a larger group getting through. Make sure your guys wear their colors, though."

I scoff. "As if we'd do anything else."

Mason doesn't follow, trusting me to find my own way. Spying Victor slipping out of the front room, I pause at the top of the main staircase. He closes and locks the door behind him before striding away into the bowels of the house. Fucking creep. I make my way out the front door, hefting it closed behind me. Peering at the monstrosity looming over me, I swing my leg over my bike. I never could wrap my head around growing up in a place like this.

I round the fountain, pointing my bike toward home. Usually, I'd take the long way to make sure I'm not being followed, but I can't be bothered. I don't want to assume the Night Slayers—or Maddox, for that matter—have given up getting to Kenzie, but the more days that pass make me think they've lost interest. It will pave the way if they have. Ambushing them will make protecting her easier than if they're just lying low.

Crossing the line into Reaper territory, I breathe a sigh of relief. The charred remains of Trigger's greets me, no longer smoldering, but the echoes of the smoke floats through the air. We'll rebuild soon, whenever I have time to get to it. Everything else has stacked up, taking precedent. Trigger isn't complaining, but choosing Kenzie over the club makes me feel like I'm letting them down.

I nod to a few members gearing up for the shipment tonight. We don't get as many these days. I've pulled out of a lot of the deals my father set up back then. We don't touch the drugs, leaving them to the Kings and Byrns. More than anything, we're a conduit in and out of Synd. Most members have businesses in our territory or work under the agreement with the other leaders, but after the Guild swept through, our businesses were hit harder than most. Going into lockdown will hurt. I warned them, but I also promised I wouldn't do it again unless we had to. It's why I didn't lock shit down when Kenzie asked me. Our businesses wouldn't survive, at least not without a lot of help from the club. Tiny informed me we wouldn't be able to help them all if we did.

The clubhouse is buzzing, and I slow. My chest grows tight as I pass headquarters. I should stop. Telling myself I'll check in later, I ride on, but I'm lying. The only thing I want to do is lose myself in her body. After the stress of meeting with Mason, the lack of anything happening, and the tension settling in the air, I need a night, a day, a weekend, just some time to do nothing more than be with her. Fighting her demons won't matter if I don't have her in the end, so I kill the engine outside my house, and go in search of Kenzie.

TWENTY-EIGHT

MacKenzie

"Fuck!"

Ryker's voice follows a thump, and I scramble for the light. I knock it over instead of turning it on, and I curse. I leap from the bed, dashing for the switch, and the room floods with light. My heart is racing as I scan the room for whatever threat woke him up, but all I find is him kneeling naked in the bed and rubbing the back of his head.

"What the hell, Ryker?"

"My phone buzzed, but it was in my head and then I moved and . . . fuck that hurt." He reaches for his phone.

"It buzzed in your head?" Hands down, the worst way to wake up.

"In my dream. I was dreaming, I think. My phone went off and then . . . never mind. Sorry," he mutters, staring at his screen.

I can't imagine who would be texting him at three in the morning. I set the lamp back on the nightstand, then flip it on before turning out the overhead light. Crawling between the covers, I hum contentedly when the blanket settles over me again.

"Holy fuck," he mumbles. I roll over, watching his face drain of color.

"What is it? What happened?" I spring upright, leaning to see what he's looking at, but he angles it away. "Ryker, tell me what's going on. Is it Sam? Alex? Did you hear from Dante?" Fear seeps into my stomach, and I almost double over from the pain.

"No, I have to"—he stares at me then, finally registering my presence—"everyone is fine. I have to go. I'll be back."

"What? That's it?" I scramble after him as he practically runs for the bathroom, grabbing his pants along the way.

"Everyone's fine. Kenz. I don't have time. I have to go. I'll talk to you when I get back, promise," he says over his shoulder as he steps up to the toilet.

Not ready to be intimate enough to pee in front of each other, I spin. That's not a step I'm ready for. I cross my arms, staring at the rumpled sheets strewn about the bed.

"Ryker, you're not leaving until you tell me what's going on, or I'm going to lose it," I say as the water runs behind me. I can feel my chest starting to tighten, my breaths coming shorter and shorter. I force myself to breathe, control my words, control how I react. I can control this.

"Shit, Kenz." He pulls me back to his chest. "Okay, we'll talk about it now, but I have to get dressed."

I inhale, letting it out gradually before nodding, then stepping away. "Talk while you put clothes on."

He rushes into his closet, and I snatch the pants he dropped. I stand in the doorway, holding them out. He reaches for them, but I yank them back, looking at his cock swinging around and widen my eyes. He scoffs, grabbing underwear.

"That was Tank. There's been some shit going down with our supplies. Tiny thought someone was skimming, but it didn't add up. We did some digging, and our shit's being routed through another city before it gets to us." He rips open drawers and slams them shut. I have no idea what he's searching for. "Can you guess which city?"

"Don't tell me . . ."

"Yeah, it's Rima. We weren't sure who was behind it, though, so Tank set a trap of sorts. Looks like we actually caught something." He pulls a shirt over his head, then slips his arms through his leather vest covered in patches, showing everyone he's the leader of the Reapers.

"What or who did you catch?" My eyes bug out when he opens one last drawer and tucks a pistol in a holster I didn't notice before.

"I don't know. I didn't think it would work. I kind of just let Tank do whatever he wanted. So, I gotta go down there, figure out what's going on." He scans the closet one last time before stalking out. Snagging my hand as he passes, he drags me along behind him down the stairs. He lets go when he sinks onto the bench to shove his feet into his boots.

"What am I supposed to do while you're off catching ghosts?" I raise my eyebrow, dropping to my knees to lace his other boot.

"You look good on your knees, baby."

I roll my eyes. "Again, what am I supposed to do while you're gone?"

"Go back to sleep. I shouldn't be long. Scratch that—I have no idea how long I'll be."

"You're not going to call someone and have them babysit me?" The sarcasm drips from my tone enough that his head snaps up, but his eyes fall again, hiding from my accusation.

He mumbles, "I have no idea what you're talking about."

"Oh, you don't? So, Doc just happened to be looking at the house across the street? And Tiny needed to work on his bike right next door just because. Oh, and Trigger . . ."

"Okay, but I didn't tell them to do that shit. They fucking wanted to help, they wanted to make sure you were okay. I didn't say a fucking word. I mean, I told Hawk I was worried about leaving you alone, but they decided to show up all on their own."

My mouth falls open, and I shake my head, ready to deny what he's saying. The annoyance in his eyes softens as he takes my hands. He pulls me to stand between his legs.

"They care about you. Not hard to see why."

"I figured I was . . ." I shake my head, not willing to finish.

It's my insecurities answering, not reality.

"An annoyance?" he finishes, tugging me down in his lap.

Wondering if I'll squash his legs, I cringe, but he settles his arm around my waist. We're the same height now, not that he's much taller than me, but I'm able to look him directly in the eye.

"No, a liability. I understand what my coming here has brought on the club. I figured they would resent me for it."

"Well, turns out you were wrong. They've become protective of you." His hands hook around the backs of my thighs, pulling me around so I'm straddling him.

"Not everyone, but that's okay. So, is anyone coming?" I lean back.

I don't mind people watching me, especially knowing they're doing it on their own other than at Ryker's command, but I'd rather know. I don't want to freak out when someone pops up in the backyard randomly.

He lifts me off his lap, standing, too, and presses his lips to mine. I lose myself in the kiss. Breathing deeply, he rests his forehead on mine.

"No one is going to ambush you. Most are off dealing with this situation. The rest are either sleeping or dealing with the boundaries. I'm sure you'll be fine. There's another gun in the nightstand, just in case. Call me if you have issues. I don't know how long I'll be. Don't wait up."

And then he's gone, waving when he reaches his bike, but he doesn't look back again. I shut the door, and flip the lock, the thud reverberating through the empty house, sending a shiver through me. It's like he took all the life with him when he rode away. Too keyed up to go back to sleep, I spend my time checking each door and window, making sure no one will slip in without me realizing.

Dizziness invades my head, and the knot in my stomach returns. It feels like something is coming, and I can't explain it. My eyes jump around the room, trying to find something, anything, but the space looks normal, just like every other time I've been in here. I walk to the window again, double-checking the lock, then the door, then the kitchen. Scanning the room, I notice the pristine bare counters, the dining table that seats at least eight, the door to the dark laundry room. The more I check, the more frantic my pace is. By the time I'm back in Ryker's bedroom, unlocking and locking the window, my hands are shaking. Pulling in a deep breath, closing my eyes, trying to slow my racing heart.

"There's nothing here. I'm safe. There's no reason to think you aren't," I whisper, trying to get my brain and body on board.

"Are you sure about that, Kitzie?"

My breath stalls in my lungs as my feet refuse to turn. It doesn't matter. I don't need my eyes to confirm who is standing behind me. No one else ever called me Kitzie. I haven't heard him use it in years, but time hasn't dulled the memories the nickname conjures.

"What, aren't you happy to see me?" He's closer now, slightly to my left, and I squeeze my eyes tighter.

I need to remember how to breathe, how to react, how to not fall apart. Lifting my lids, I pivot. The black boots are the same, scuffed, but mostly clean, like every other piece of clothing he wears. He's wearing black jeans, which are ridiculous, and I want to scoff at them, but my voice has fled. His black shirt is covered by his leather jacket.

It's too hot for leather.

Ryker has been wearing his vest for the last two weeks, even at night. I don't know why it's so jarring to see Maddox's jacket covered in Viper patches, marking him as the VP, proudly displaying the club's colors and logos. I never liked what Dad came up with when he moved us and started a new MC. They're garish, a vomit-green with bile-colored lettering. I missed the patches from the Reapers. Maybe I just missed the Reapers.

Maddox grins, probably thinking he looks boyish and charming, but his eyes are teetering on the edge of insanity. The older we got, the less he hid his hatred of me, usually only pretending in front of Dante. I learned long ago that going to Dante for help was pointless. Maddox played the part so well of a doting brother in front of him, so anything I said came across as jealousy or whining. I stopped bringing my problems to my brother once I figured that out.

"Cat got your tongue?" He smirks, running his hand through his windblown blond hair.

The black strands fall over his forehead, the only thing we have in common. I'm surprised to see him so disheveled. Usually, he gels his hair to within an inch of its life.

"What do you want, Maddox?" I shift closer to the nightstand, Ryker's words ringing in my head. *Gun in the nightstand.*

My phone is across the room, no use to me, while Maddox blocks the door. I could go out the window, but he'd catch me. I doubt he's here to kill me. He's here to take me back.

"You already know the answer, Kitzie. It's time to come home."

I tilt my head, my mouth falling open, and I huff out a laugh. "Home? Or to the Night Slayers?" I shift again, closer to salvation.

"Well, seeing as how you belong to them now, clearly Night Slayer territory is your home now. I mean, for however long you have left."

Searching my mind for something else to ask him, I nod, but there's not much to say. I need to keep him talking, just long enough to reach the nightstand.

"Something I never understood, Maddox, is why you hate me so much. We used to be inseparable, two peas in a pod, so what happened to make you do something like this?"

I want to rage at him, but I can't. His presence only makes me mourn the years we lost.

"Does it matter? Won't change anything. You'll be gone, and I'll finally get what I deserve." He shrugs, as though things are decided, like there's no way he'll lose.

"What do you think you deserve?"

I try to keep the sneer from my voice, but it leaks through. A flush splashes across his face, and his hands curl into fists.

"I deserve everything. I'm done with you standing in the way of what should be mine."

Another shuffling step, and I'm almost there. If I lunge, I could reach the handle, but I keep my eyes on him.

"What should be yours?"

"I don't owe you shit. I'm taking you back to Panther. He'll have to deal with you instead of me, thank fuck. Let's go," he snaps, stepping forward and reaching a hand out to grab me.

I throw myself toward the nightstand and rip the drawer almost completely out and plunge my hand in. I'm met with nothing. No gun, no knife, no weapon to defend myself.

Only a book and a couple of batteries. Bracing myself, I expect Maddox to tackle me, but he laughs quietly. I glance over my shoulder, wondering if I can leap over the bed to check my side, but his cocky grin stops me.

"Looking for this?" he asks, pulling a pistol out of his jacket. "I didn't think Ryker was stupid enough to keep a gun in the nightstand, but here we are."

I blanch, wondering how long he was in the house before I realized it. I thought he broke in downstairs, intent on ambushing me once I was here, but if he had time to search the room, to find Ryker's gun, then he must have been here for much longer. *Did he watch Ryker ride away? Did he watch me check the house, knowing the threat was already inside?*

Maddox settles his hand more firmly on the weapon before pointing it at me. "Bang," he yells, cackling when I flinch. "All right, let's move. I'd rather not have to shoot Ryker while being in the heart of his territory."

He gestures with the gun toward the door, but I'm frozen, processing his words. If Ryker tries to save me, he'll kill him but not here, regardless of the consequences.

"Move, Kenz," he barks, stepping forward.

Hatred floods my veins when he calls me Kenz. My fingers tingle, and I'm no longer trembling from fear or anxiety but rage. He steps forward, not bothering to see the change in me. He's close enough to touch now, and I'm reminded of how short he is compared to Ryker. He's the same size as me in his boots. I plant my feet, sucking in a breath, waiting a beat more. It's like the world has slowed, giving me time to execute the hasty plan that's popped in my head. His hand reaches toward me, and I reach behind. I wrap my fingers around the lamp on the nightstand. It's not big or heavy, but I swing it with as much force as I can muster.

Time resets and speeds up when the bulb shatters against his head. As he rears back, I ram it toward his face. He roars, blood spurting from his nose. I drop the mess before throwing myself as far as possible across the bed and scramble the rest of the way. My bare feet slap against the wood, Maddox's cursing following me out the door. I slam it shut, my mind racing on where to go, what to do. I didn't think to snatch my phone on the way past the nightstand. I wouldn't have the time to call anyone. I wish I had those babysitters now.

I fly down the stairs and hardly touch the wood before slamming to the landing. I curse when my ankle rolls, but I don't stop, pushing the pain from my mind. The front door seems to warp, getting farther away the faster my legs churn.

Maddox roars behind me, his boots thundering down the stairs, and I push myself harder. My body slams into the door, and I fumble with the lock. I glance back as my hand wraps around the cool metal, and I watch as he trips, face morphing from rage to surprise. I stumble into the humid night and slam the door behind me.

Faltering at the bottom of the steps, I scan the darkness lit by the lamp up the street. I could run to the clubhouse, bang on the door, pray someone is awake, but I doubt I'd make it. I swing my gaze the other way and spy Maddox's car hidden in the shadows in our old driveway. A thump from behind jolts me into action, and I take off toward the vehicle. Fifty feet looms between Ryker's porch and the car, but I'm not fast enough to make it before a thud echoes into the quiet and Maddox is racing after me.

Every second, I expect him to snatch me, but his feet pound out a strange tempo into the dark. I skirt the trunk, praying he left it unlocked. A sob escapes me when my hand closes on the handle, and it gives. I wretch it open and throw myself inside before bashing on the lock just as he slams into the passenger window.

Maddox steps back, grinning again. A whimper escapes me when he holds up his keys, dangling them in front of the window. I'm on the edge of panic, but a thought needles through, whispering to me to remember. I wait until he walks toward the driver's side before reaching under the console, all while trying to keep him in my sight in the mirrors. He's leisurely lopping along, tapping on the windows as he goes. A manic laugh bubbles out when my hand connects with the box. I rip it off before sliding the lid open, and his spare key falls into my palm.

Jamming it in the ignition, I glance in the mirror. He's rounding the trunk, and I throw the car in reverse, then slam my bare foot on the pedal. Tires squeal, and there's a thud followed by a shout, and I slam on the brakes, my gasps the only sound now.

I yank the wheel, putting it in drive, then bump into Ryker's yard, praying some random sinkhole doesn't swallow me whole. Knowing my luck, I'd find it, if there is. Tears leak down my face as the tires jump and reach the pavement. I speed up. I can't go much further like this. At this point, I don't even know where to go. I can't call Ryker. The clubhouse isn't far enough away from Maddox, and I don't think I'll make it to Sam before I break down.

Headlights cut across my vision, and I slam on the brakes again, completely losing it. The bike's rumble sends a flurry of relief through me, followed closely by panic, until Ryker's face fills my vision, tugging on the handle. His mouth moves, shouting something, but the ringing in my ears is too loud. With shaky fingers, I reach out to unlock the door, then it's ripped away. Ryker paws at me, yanking me from the car and checking for blood, I'm sure, but I can't find the words to tell him I'm okay. I point toward the driveway, at the silhouette of Maddox's unmoving body.

I might have fucked up, but at least I'm still alive.

TWENTY-NINE

Ryker

I envelop Kenzie in my arms, and she sighs, the anxiety and tension draining from her body. The adrenaline that kept her going deserts her, and she sags, forcing me to hold her up.

"Kenzie, what happened? Are you hurt?"

She yelps when she steps down, gingerly leaning on her foot. "I'm okay," she gasps. "Just my ankle. It's not bad."

She pulls back to plop into the driver's seat again. I drop in front of her, lifting her ankle gently, as if I'll figured out what's wrong with it. She snorts, and I glare up at her.

"Move." Ink's gruff voice comes from the dark, but I bare my teeth at him. "Yeah, yeah, yeah, you're a protective prick, got it. Now, get the fuck out of the way and figure out what's going on over there while I see if it's broken."

Waiting for her to nod, I glance at Kenzie, and she gives me a small smile. I lean up, kissing her cheek, before stepping toward the other shadows milling around the body, which still hasn't moved. I stop at Ink's questions.

"Can you move it? Flex your foot?"

"Yeah, I just rolled it, then ran on it immediately after. I think it'll be fine in the morning."

"Were you running when you rolled it?"

"No, I jumped to the bottom of the stairs. Rolled it when I landed."

He nods, twisting it this way and that. A hiss leaves her when he hits a sore spot, but he puts her foot down.

"I think you're right. You'll be fine. Prez will try to keep you on bed rest or some shit, but don't let him. I'll grab you some shoes."

I open my mouth to demand her to rest but snap it shut and stalk back to her, Tank not far behind. Scanning Kenzie's face, body, down to her toes and back up, I look for any hint of pain or injury she didn't tell us about. Tank rolls his eyes, and he leans to the side to see her better.

"Why the fuck did you run over Maddox Raines with his own fucking car?" Tank barks.

The words have barely left his mouth when I slam him against the car, hand wrapped around his throat, growling in my road captain's face.

"I will fucking end you," I growl, fingers flexing while Tank tries to pull my hand away.

Rage rolls through my body. A voice in my head tells me to squeeze harder, force him to suffer for disrespecting her.

"Didn't . . . mean . . ." he sputters, struggling for breath.

"Ryker." Kenzie's voice floats over me, calm and soft, and my eyes swing to her as I bare my teeth. "Let go."

Flexing one last time before I step back, I suck in a breath, dropping my hand as Tank coughs and doubles over. Halfway to us, Hawk freezes. Kenzie shakes her head, shooing him away. Eyes wide, he pivots, going to deal with other issues we have.

"Tank, why don't you go help Hawk. You'll need to find a place to contain him. Careful, he has a gun, maybe some other weapons as well," Kenzie says.

He coughs, rubbing his throat and stumbling toward the other men. Pacing back and forth, I curse under my breath, trying to smother the flames raging inside me. It wasn't the words Tank used that set me off, it was his tone. The accusation rang clear in his voice. Not knowing what happened but knowing she was in danger because I left her alone . . . it's too close to how I felt when she first got here, covered in bruises and shuffling around.

"MacKenzie, tell me what happened," I growl.

"I was checking the doors and windows, making sure they were locked. I went to lock the one in the bedroom, and Maddox was behind me. Oh, you're going to need another bedside lamp. And there's broken glass on the carpet I'm sure. So, we'll have to deal with that . . ."

"Kenz, stop. Just tell me what happened." I shake out my hands, and her eyes track me as I stomp back and forth.

She clears her throat. "He wanted to bring me back. I went for the gun, but he already had it, so I smashed him with the lamp instead. I ran and saw his car, so I got in and locked the doors."

She skips everything but the essentials. I'll need to hear them later, but neither of us are in the right head space to relive things so soon.

"How did you get the keys? He didn't leave them in the ignition, did he?"

Imagining Kenzie grappling with him, getting his keys, fighting her way out . . . with no other injuries can't be how it went down.

She huffs, staring toward the other men. "He always kept a spare key in a magnetic box inside his car. So, I didn't need his key. Then I ran him over. I mean, I didn't run him over. I hit him with his car, but yeah."

She sucks her lip between her teeth, biting down hard. A giggle bubbles out, and she claps a hand over her mouth to stifle it. Her shoulders shake, and my stomach tightens. I press my lips together, and an image bursts in my mind of her laughing maniacally while throwing the car in reverse. The amusement chases away the last of the panic. A chuckle seeps out, and when our eyes meet, she loses it, doubling over. I swipe my hand across my mouth, trying to wipe away the grin. I pull her back into my arms as she trembles.

"I'm glad you're okay," I whisper in her hair when she's quieted.

Her arms reach around me, holding me closer, and I sigh, the rest of my anxiety leaving me.

"Did you figure out your trap?" she asks, voice muffled from being pressed to my chest.

"It was Rooster, but we don't think he's behind it. I think he was just being a little pissant and ended up getting caught being a dumbass. We'll deal with it later. Let me get you inside. I have to deal with Maddox."

Her arms fall away as she steps around me, avoiding my eyes. I grab her arm, forcing her to turn back, and she sighs. Her head swivels, evading my questioning look. I lift my hand, grasping her chin to force her to meet my gaze. Tears brim in her hazel eyes, and the pain in my chest returns.

"Sorry, I'm trying," she says shakily, but her words aren't explaining anything.

"What are you sorry for?" I ask, and her nostrils flare, and she tries to pull away, but I hold her there.

"I thought it might be over. I mean, not over, but not as urgent. You've been busy, trying to deal with all this shit, and I haven't helped at all. I feel like this is one more thing I'm dumping at your feet, expecting you to clean up," she huffs.

"I told you I don't care. I want to protect you."

She throws her hands up, wrenching her chin to the side. "But you shouldn't have to. And I know what you're going to say, so just don't. But it doesn't change the way I feel about it. It's hard to deal with is all."

A groan behind her has us both glancing over. Maddox is writhing on the ground, clutching his side. I can scarcely make out his face, but she hit him hard enough to break something, since he's caked in blood. Maybe it's from Kenzie hitting him with a lamp. I grin again, imagining how she took his ass out.

I snort. "Kenz, you took care of the problem all on your own. I'm only here to take out the trash."

Trying to hide her smile, she grumbles, but I catch it. I tuck my arm around her shoulder and tug her toward the porch as Maddox bellows into the night. No one is paying him much attention except for Ink, who's trying to examine him, but he's not being gentle.

"What are you going to do with him?" she mumbles, peering at the pathetic piece of shit.

"Whatever *you* want to do with him," I say when we reach the front door, which is still wide open from the chase.

I'm forced to let her go, and I expect to deposit her in our room, but she pivots to the couch, collapsing with a grunt before tipping her head against the arm. I take the other side, guiding her feet into my lap and rubbing her ankle.

"I don't know what to do with him. He's still my brother," she says, closing her eyes.

"Half brother. And we can always keep him locked up, wait for Dante to reappear and make him decide. Nothing wrong with shoving the judgment onto him. Technically, it should be Dante's choice, though."

"Like an extradition?"

Softening my touch when she flinches. "Exactly like an extradition. It'll be a bit complicated, but it's fine. We have the means to hold him."

She wraps her arms around herself. I run a finger up her arch, causing a shiver to run through her body. I smile, keeping my eyes on her face, waiting for her to open her own. I drag my nail to her toes, my touch turning featherlight and traveling up her calf.

"Whatcha doing there?" she asks, peeking from under her lashes.

"Whatever the hell I want." I smirk, palming the back of her calf and squeezing.

A knock at the door breaks our connection. I round the couch, hoping they took care of everything. Hawk pushes past me, swinging his head to the kitchen, then the living room, striding to Kenzie.

"Are you okay?" he demands, glaring.

"I'm fine."

"The shit he was spewing . . . was he always like that?" He crosses his arms, and I swing the door shut.

"I mean, he became worse the older we got. He kept it to himself when other people were around. I still can't make sense of why he hates me so much or why he thought *this* was a good idea. I mean, he wouldn't have gotten away with it if Dante was around, so it must have been impulsive, right?" She looks to me, pleading to explain Maddox's reasons.

Hawk settles next to her. "I think he took advantage of the situation. He saw an opportunity and seized it. Probably set us up tonight, too, making sure you'd be alone."

"You think Rooster is a mole?" I ask.

"I mean, it wouldn't be surprising. He's always been an asshole, but the way he's been talking lately . . . it's not right. I say strip him and get it over with. Take his bike, too. It's Reaper loot. Sack of shit doesn't deserve it."

"Ooh, that reminds me. Can I have Maddox's car?" Kenzie launches upright, pleading, eyes fixed on me.

"Sure, baby, you can keep the car but let me get the prospects to clean the blood off it first."

Hawk's laughter fills the room as her nose scrunches. He reaches out, squeezing her hand before marching out the door without another word. My gaze follows my men, stomping past with a howling Maddox. His demands to meet with me rattle the window, as he claims he has rights, being the leader of the Vipers. I roll my eyes, dismissing him but see Kenzie's eyes following him, too.

"Come on, baby. Let's go back to bed. I'm sure you'll be up early with Sam demanding to know what happened."

I guide her up the stairs as she calls over her shoulder, "I don't know if I'll be able to sleep."

"I'm sure I can find a way to tire you out."

THIRTY

MacKenzie

I can tell it's late when I wake, and I reach to Ryker's side of the bed, feeling it empty and cold. Most mornings, I wake up alone, a note left on his pillow, taped to the bathroom mirror, or stuck on the kitchen counter. It would be cute if they were love notes. They're all short, though, saying he'll be back later.

A week after my run-in with Maddox, he's back to multiple meetings a day. He's disappeared once or twice, but when I ask where he goes, he avoids my questions.

Sitting up, I snatch up the paper slipping off his pillow.

early meeting; won't be back until later.

His notes are getting shorter and shorter. Some nights, he slips into bed so late I barely register his arms sneaking around me. I'm trying not to be annoyed, but his lack of communication is starting to grate on me. My phone buzzes, and I answer it without looking.

"What?" I snarl into the phone.

"Well, hello to you, too, sunshine." Sam laughs.

I can hear her guys in the background, silverware clinking. A pang of jealousy hits me, and I suck in a breath before answering.

"Sorry, not a great morning. What's up?"

I force my voice to even out. It's not Sam's fault she has everything I want. Well, besides the multiple peen situation.

"Uh-oh. What's wrong?"

The sounds behind her fade, Alex, who came home a couple of days ago, shouting to her.

"Nothing. I mean, other than normal shit. This is just hard." I heave off the bed, intent on doing something productive today.

"Ha, you think I'm going to buy that? Nuh-uh, tell me what's really bothering you."

"I miss Ryker." I didn't mean to say anything, but it fell out without warning.

"Ahh, gotcha. What else?"

I snort. "Isn't that enough?"

She clears her throat, calling me on my bluff with one sound.

"Fine," I grumble. "I might wish I had what you have. I mean, not everything you have, because that seems like a lot of dick to juggle, but it must be nice to have them there, wanting you around, and not feeling like you're failing all the time or bringing a bunch of problems on them."

She's laughing by the time my rant is done. I wait, pressing my lips together, so I don't cuss her out or hang up.

"Mac, are you serious? I hate to break this to you, but shit is still hard. I mean, it's good they love me, but Ryker loves you, too. Our journey, or whatever the hell you want to call it, was a shitshow I wouldn't wish on anyone. Well, I might wish it on your brother but no one else. This shit is not normal, and it isn't easy. I still feel like I'm failing most the time. You have to figure out how to deal with your insecurities, though. I can't tell you they're not valid. Ryker can't either. You have to decide to believe him, that's all."

"You sound like Ren," I grumble, glancing at myself in the mirror.

The dark circles had almost faded but are back in full force. I wish we could skip the waiting part and get to the good part, but I don't know what my future looks like, even if it was here with him.

"Well, Ren's fucking smart. He says he's not good with emotions, but he just sees them differently than most. I think he's got a good handle on them. Sharing them, however, not so much. Mac, have you talked to Ryker about this stuff?"

I turn, not willing to face the woman staring back at me anymore. I lean against the counter. "I've barely seen him since I ran Maddox over with his car. I feel like he's keeping things from me, but then again, there hasn't been time to share shit. He's really stressed."

"Then, call him and tell him he needs to make time to talk. Make sure he knows it's talking and not a euphemism for fucking, like Shane thinks it is. Listen, I have to get back, but call me. We'll figure this out."

"Yeah, okay. See you later." I hang up, not waiting for her goodbye. I mull over her words, and making my decision, pull up Ryker's text thread.

Call me. We need to talk. I erase it.

When are you coming home? Too needy.

Will you be home for lunch? I blanch, wondering when I turned into a suburban housewife.

Get your head out of your ass and call me.

I smirk, pressing send, then dropping my phone on the counter. I'm finishing my business, drying my hands, when the screen lights up, showing he's calling.

"What the fuck, MacKenzie. I left you a goddamn note," he bellows.

"Oh, I got your note," I say sweetly, which only serves to rile him up more.

"Well, what the hell is with your text, then? Do not tell me you pulled me out of a fucking meeting just to fuck with me," he growls. His voice grows muffled as he shouts at someone, then heaves out a sigh.

"W-We need to talk," I stutter, trying to keep the nerves from my voice. Shit, I did not mean to say it like that.

"Kenz?" He draws out my name in warning.

"I didn't mean it like that. But you've been MIA for days. We haven't connected, and you promised we would a week ago, after the shit with Maddox. Yet, we still haven't." I walk from the bathroom to the bedroom and sink down on the crumpled sheets.

"I haven't had time, MacKenzie. There's a lot going on." Someone calls Ryker's name in the background, and I sniff, knowing what's coming, but I have to try one last time.

"I understand, but we need to make time, or I'm going to . . ."

"Going to what? Run away?" he asks, sarcasm dripping from his tone.

"Uncalled for. Keep being an asshole, and we'll never get anywhere." Forcing back the tirade I want to unleash on him, I bite my tongue.

"Don't know what you want from me, MacKenzie. I have to go."

And there it is. Every time I talk to him, text him, catch him coming or going this week, I get about five minutes before he has to go again. The amount of quickies we've engaged in has grown exponentially. I'm starting to feel like a fucktoy instead of whatever it is we are.

"Sure. Well, I won't be here whenever you get home." I brace for the blowout, smirking.

"For fuck's sake, MacKenzie. Seriously? I can't talk one time, and you're just going to take off? I don't know when I'm getting home. I'm doing all this shit for you. You realize that, right?"

"Ah, the guilt trip. I wondered when we'd get there. Listen very closely, Ryker. I've been patient. I've been understanding. In fact, I've been the perfect woman, watching you come and go and being available whenever you desire. I'm done being left out. I'm done begging you to include me. So, instead, I'll go to Sam's *for the day*, pick her guys' brains, and they'll tell me what's being planned. If you'd like to join us, feel free." I wait.

I want to hang up, but that's not good communication, and I've been trying to do better.

"Fine. Just . . . don't leave. I'll be there in twenty." He hangs up.

I pull the phone away, staring at it. Shit. I didn't mean to force him into anything. I mean, I wanted to be included in things, but I didn't mean to derail his entire day. I pull up his text thread, shooting out a message as quick as I can, trying to backtrack. I wait, then watch it flip to read. The more that time passes, though, the less I'm convinced he'll answer me.

"Well, this is just great," I mutter, starting the shower.

Twenty minutes later, I pull on my pants, hopping to get them up, when the front door opens. My pants are tight now that I've been eating regularly, and I'm not overcome with pain. I scurry into the bathroom, trying to put off the inevitable. He finds me, but I'm running a brush through my dark hair and avoiding his gaze.

"You wanna tell me what the hell is up with you?"

I grit my teeth, digging the bristles into my scalp, trying to use the pain to rein in my frustration. It doesn't work. My eyes dart to him before focusing back on my reflection. He's leaning against the door frame, arms crossed, eyebrows pulled low, as if he has any reason to be angry. I didn't tell him to leave his meeting. I didn't tell him he needed to put his entire day on hold. I'm not the one making this a huge fucking deal.

"Well?" he spits, exasperation running through his tone.

"Well what? I didn't tell you to come rushing ho"—I suck in a breath—"here." I close my eyes, centering myself again.

"Well, I'm fucking here, so what was so important you had to pull me away from a meeting with Mason Byrns?"

I spin, almost choking. "Byrns? Sam's brother? Why are you meeting with him?"

He raises an eyebrow. "That why you wanted to talk?"

"Obviously not, since I didn't even know you were meeting with him. Which is exactly the problem. We talked about this, Ryker. You told me you'd start including me, and now you're shutting me out again. Clearly, these meetings are about me, or at least the problems I brought in, so I'd like to be included or at least informed." I pop my hip out, planting a hand on it, and giving him a look.

"Before I didn't tell you because I was worried how you'd react. It's not like that now. I'm not purposefully keeping you out, MacKenzie."

"End result is the same, dickhead."

He throws up his hands, turning away only to spin back around, bellowing, "What the fuck do you want from me, MacKenzie? I'm fucking tired. I don't get any sleep. I'm in the middle of coming up with some plan to take care of the Night Slayers, all while trying to keep them out of Synd. I got the heads of two mafias breathing down my neck, asking me what the hell I plan to do. I can't tell them I have no fucking clue. All I want is to ride in to Rima and burn them to the fucking ground for you, but I can't. So, excuse me if telling you every single detail wasn't at the forefront of my mind."

"Why can't you?" I ask in a low voice, wrapping my arms around my middle.

"What?" he breathes, confusion mixing with defeat in his usually vibrant blue eyes. They're muted now, carrying the weight of everything I've placed at his feet.

"Why can't we burn them to the ground?"

He heaves out a breath, tipping his head back. His eyes find mine, burning now. "Do I need to remind you what happened the last time I left you alone?"

"I took care of him just fine on my own." I sniff.

"But you shouldn't have had to! I should have been there. Instead, I got complacent, and you're the one who suffered for it. I won't repeat my mistakes."

"Aren't you repeating the mistake of not talking to me?" This rollercoaster of emotions has my feelings ping-ponging back and forth. I can't settle on whether to be pissed at him or sympathetic to everything going on.

"I *am* talking to you. I've talked to you every fucking day."

"You're not saying anything, though," I cry, fighting back the tears.

Ever since coming back to Synd, I feel like all I've done is cry. I'm not that girl. I'm not the one who falls apart at the drop of a hat. I'm sarcastic and tough and independent. I take care of my own shit, and I don't apologize to anyone who doesn't like who I am. It's like as soon as I came face-to-face with Ryker again, I opened my mouth, and all my insecurities fell out.

Realization dawns on his face, and something must have clicked in his brain. I brace myself, not knowing if he'll fight me some more or admit he's fucking this up. He tilts his head, a predatory look entering his eyes, and I straighten, all senses alert. Ryker's eyes track my movements, up and down, and my breath stalls in my lungs. When they reach my face, he narrows them, and I step back on instinct.

"All right, Kenz."

He nods, taking a predatory step toward me. My feet shuffle back, my ass hitting the edge of the counter. His mouth ticks up, eyes darkening, and I swallow, trying to clear my throat, which is suddenly dry. My hands slap the porcelain as he reaches me, and his hands cover my own, keeping me in place, right where he wants me. He doesn't even have to bend to look me in the eye.

"Ryker?" My voice comes out strained, somewhere between a question and a warning.

"Kenz?"

There goes his eyebrow again.

"What are you doing?" I whisper, if only to hide the quaver in my tone.

"You want me to listen to you, so I'm going to make sure I hear every fucking sound that falls from those plump lips."

He leans in, and my eyes fall closed as I expect his mouth to reach mine, but his teeth graze my neck. My head tips back without a thought, and he ghosts his lips over the column of my throat. My knees weaken, and I grip the counter tighter. When his teeth scrape over my collarbone, a gasp leaves me, and I curse myself for being so distracted by him. I was angry— about what, I can't remember—but all it took was one look from him, and I'm lost.

"I didn't say you needed to listen. I said you needed to talk."

I choke when his finger hooks on to my shirt, pulling it lower, so he can reach the top of my breasts. His teeth sink in again, leaving a mark, but I'm beyond caring.

His breath puffs across my skin as he hums, "I'm going to unravel you slowly, leaving you right on the edge of ecstasy, begging me for more, and only when I truly think you can't take anymore, I'll give you what you need."

He releases my hand, and he yanks the material aside, taking my bra with it, and my breast spills into his waiting palm as he sighs. His callused thumb brushes over my nipple, back and forth until I'm panting, my eyes still squeezed shut.

"Not what I meant," I gasp.

"Oh, we'll talk about other things, too, but not when I'm about to be so deep inside your pussy you won't know where you end and I begin." His nose nuzzles the side of my breast, and he reaches over, freeing the other one, too. "Hello, I missed you."

My head snaps down, mouth falling open. "Are you talking to my breasts?"

"No, I'm talking to *my* tits. These things are mine now. Along with this." He sneaks a hand between my legs, cupping me roughly.

"The fuck it is."

He chuckles, hand leaving my pussy, which is already soaking my underwear. "Oh, baby, even she knows she's mine, which is why she gets so wet for me."

"What the fuck," I mutter.

We might need to discuss boundaries, but for some reason his words only make me wetter.

He returns his attention to my chest, cooing at them, as if they'll pop up and start responding. When he pinches my nipples, I tilt my head back. He twists just enough for a bite of pain to shoot through my body, then heads straight for my pussy. Then his mouth closes around one, and I think I'm done arguing. I'll demand to talk later, after he's apologized with his cock.

"Kenzie, my lovely, beautiful goddess. Do you know how much I'm going to ruin you? Do you know how much I'm going to worship your body? I don't think you have any idea how I'm going to make you scream for me. You're going to be hoarse by the time I'm done with you. You'll love every fucking second of it. And then we'll have a nice, long conversation about all the shit I've been doing for you. Only for you."

A moan leaves me, and his mouth descends on mine, swallowing the noise, as if it's only for him. He wraps his arm around my waist, the other tangling in my hair, then tugs my head back. Another tug, and my back arches over the sink. His mouth leaves mine, traveling down my neck. He isn't gentle this time. Ryker's mouth is demanding, biting, nipping, sucking every inch of skin he can reach. I don't think I can stretch any further, but he pulls harder, and my knee pops up, heel settling under his ass, and he buries his face in my breasts, giving them the same treatment my throat received.

"Look at yourself," he growls, and my eyes pop open.

I can hardly see in the mirror behind me, but he tilts my head, controlling my movements with his grip at the base of it, and I catch sight of us in the mirror on the back of the door. I didn't even notice he closed it when he was stalking me. I'm mesmerized by the scene unfolding in the reflection. I'm flushed. Tits, as he calls them, spill from my shirt, which is stretched to its breaking point. It's the curve of my spine, him leaning over me, face hidden from view. We look . . . sexy. Wanton. The picture is erotic, and I feel another gush between my legs as another moan spills from me.

"Now do you see?" he asks, turning his head to catch my eyes in our reflections. "Do you see how fucking delectable you are? How seductive and alluring you are?"

Unable to form words, I nod. He sucks my nipple into his mouth again before rolling his tongue around. He releases my hair to wrap his hand around my neck again and pulls me upright. He grabs my hand planted on the counter. My hands and his body are the only thing holding me up; otherwise, I'd be a puddle on the floor. I swear his words alone could make me come.

"Ryker, we should . . ."

He guides my hand down straight to his cock, which is still covered by layers of clothes, but he's practically ripping the seams he's so hard.

"Do you feel what you fucking do to me? Every goddamn time I see you, I get so fucking hard I can't walk. Every time you text, every time I hear your voice. Every. Fucking. Time." He pushes into my hand with each word. I squeeze, forcing a groan from him. His head falls back, exposing his throat. I swoop forward, sinking my teeth into the juncture of his neck and shoulder, lapping at it after.

"What are we going to do about it, then?" I smirk as I lean back, pulling my hand away.

Ryker's head snaps down, desire burning in his eyes. An evil glint enters them, and I realize I've said too much. The smirk blooming across his face is my only warning before his hands rest on my shoulders, and he's guiding me to my knees. I don't resist. What would be the point when we both want this? Doesn't mean I can't put up a little fight, though. He snaps off the button, then tugs the zipper down. He shoves both his pants and underwear down enough to free his cock. It bobs in front of me, leaking from the tip. My tongue darts out, licking my lips instead of his cock. His finger trails along my jaw, settling under my chin before tipping my head up to meet his eyes.

"Open up," he says, though his voice is strained. I give him a smug smile, then shake my head. His eyes harden. "Oh, baby, I wasn't asking. Open up, or we'll find out how long I can keep you on the edge before you lose your mind."

My eyes widen. "You wouldn't."

"I most certainly would. Now, be a good girl and open up like we both know you want to."

I debate for five more seconds, but when his fingers tighten the slightest bit, my mouth falls open, tongue darting out and lapping at the tip. The saltiness of his cum hits my taste buds, and I lean forward, sucking his head into my warm mouth. He's big, I always knew, but when his cock pushes further in, I realize how thick he is. Much thicker and longer than I'm able to accommodate. There's no fucking way I'll get it half in without gagging, so I wrap a hand around the base, hoping I can use it as a stopgap. My other hand lands on his thigh, and his moan fill the air. I suck, swirling my tongue around before pulling back, then pop him out of my mouth.

"You can take me deeper," he pants.

Ryker wraps his hand in my hair again, gripping at the roots, forcing his cock to slip through my lips. I intentionally scrape my teeth over the head, but he only snarls, forcing me to take more until I reach my fingers already at the edge of my throat. I hum, and he groans again, but when I try to push back, his grip on my hair stops me.

His hips slide back, and he's surges forward, repeating the move until I cough. His hand wraps around my wrist, yanking my hand away from the base, and he drives straight to the back of my throat. I gag, tears springing in my eyes. I expect to be pissed or hurt, but my nipples peak, pussy clenching around nothing. Fuck, I didn't think it would be hot for him to dominate me like this.

He pulls out abruptly, wrapping a hand around his cock and squeezing. The head turns purple before my eyes. I stare, trying to gauge what he'll do next. His eyes find mine, and I see how close to the edge he is.

"Bed. Now," he commands, but I stand before stripping out of my leggings.

Pulling my shirt off, I leave my bra still tucked under my tits. I plant my hands on the counter, hoisting myself up, and my ass hits the cold counter. I yelp, trying to slide off again, but his hands on my thighs stop my momentum. His mouth finds mine, tongue delving in immediately, and his hand skates up my thigh. His finger plunges in, and he rips his mouth from mine, head dropping to watch himself tunnel his fingers through my folds. I lean back, trying to watch, too, but between the rough pads of his fingers and the sounds of how wet I am sends bolts of pleasure through me, and my eyes fall closed.

I gasp when he pulls away, and my eyes fly open. "What . . ."

He lifts his fingers to his mouth, licking them clean. My breaths become short, and I don't know if I'll last through all the things he said he'll do to me. I might explode if he makes me wait. He grabs my hips, pulling me to the edge of the counter. He buries himself into me in one stroke. I gasp, hands flying to his shoulders and holding on.

"Fuck, I couldn't wait. I'll tease you later," he gasps into my shoulder.

"You can still ruin me," I remind him, rolling my hips.

He moans, sinking his teeth into my skin, thrusting into me hard, deep. I chant his name, feeling the build in my stomach, pulling me closer and closer to my orgasm. Neither of us will last long, not with the buildup we just went through. His cock twitches, and he stutters, leaning over me. His stomach hits my clit, rubbing it just right, and I explode, stars fireworking inside of me, my vision going spotty, and I close my eyes. Just like he said, I scream his name. I shudder as he follows, grunting as his fingers dig into my ass. A minute passes before he's covering my face in kisses.

"Fuck, it's good to be home."

THIRTY-ONE

Ryker

My body jolts awake, and for a second, I don't recognize where I am. I slam my eyes shut, digging my fingernails into my crossed arms, then opening them again, scanning the room. This is the fifth place I've been today, trying to gather info on the Night Slayers and Kane Riley. Like a ghost, he disappears every time I get close to figuring out where the fuck he came from. Why I'm now sitting in a room with Victor Smith is beyond me. He's droning on about Rima, but I've heard this all before.

I glance at Shane out of the corner of my eye to see if he's as bored as I am, but I'm met with Alex's laughing eyes. Like the psychotic prick he is, he grins. Of course he caught me sleeping. The fucker will hold it over my head for weeks. I can't really fault him; it's the first time he's been anywhere since the accident, so I'm not about to burst his bubble.

Shane cuts into the man's droning, exasperation clear in his voice. "Victor."

Victor keeps going, ignoring Shane's and Ren's glares. I let him go for another minute, seeing what Shane will do, but he just buries his head in his hands.

"Shut the fuck up, Victor. No one wanted you here in the first place," I say.

He keeps going, and I'm pissed.

"Seriously, Victor." Shane leans forward, but I heave to my feet.

Casually, I pull my gun out before placing it on the table, then plant my hands next to it, glaring.

"What do you think you're doing with that?" Victor sneers, and my muscles tense at the disrespect.

"I'm contemplating how much Mason would care if I put a bullet in your head," I reply, staring at the weapon.

Alex snorts, Shane curses, and Ren hums, but Victor is silent. I raise my head, meeting his eye and find him bleached of color. Before my eyes, he transforms, from afraid to livid. His face flushes, and his hands ball into fists. I pick up the gun, pointing it at him, and he deflates before my eyes. I always knew he was a little pissant, but I can't fathom why Mason thought it was a good idea to send him to this thing instead of coming himself.

"Why are you here, Victor? You've given us almost nothing, you haven't contributed new information, and you've droned on for the better part of thirty minutes," Ren asks, tilting his head.

"Well, I, uh . . . I lived in Rima when I was younger. Rightly so, Mason thought I could tell you what the city was like. It's different than Synd."

"A snapshot of Rima fifty fucking years ago does us little good now." Alex snorts, shaking his head.

"Besides, I already have that. So, again, why are you here, Victor?" Ren continues. I can practically hear the gears turning in his mind.

He smirks. "I know how the territories are most likely laid out."

"You couldn't possibly know, based on information from so long ago, what the current lines would look like."

"I've seen the lines, so you really are useless. Get the fuck out," I say, exhaustion settling in my bones again.

He sputters. "But . . . dammit . . . but this isn't your house!"

"No, it's mine. Get the fuck out," Shane states, gesturing to the man standing by the door, who immediately steps toward the older man. Victor's hands fly out, glaring at each of us before marching from the room, followed by the guard.

I collapse in my chair, running a hand over my face, scrubbing away every piece of anxiety battering at me. I close my eyes, and Kenzie's face flashes across my lids, as if her image is burned there. I suck in a deep breath, opening my eyes, and find the others are staring, waiting for me to get my shit together.

"So, would you like to tell us how you've seen the territory lines? And how recent this information is?" Ren asks.

The temperature in the room rises ten degrees, but I resign myself to dealing with the fallout.

"I went there. About three weeks ago and then again last week."

"Are you fucking insane?" Alex cries. "Why the hell wouldn't you take us with? What, you think we don't want to take some motherfuckers down, too?"

I chuckle, then I lose it. Once I've started, I can't stop. I hold my breath, hoping it will stop the insanity from bubbling out, but my shoulders shake, and I hiccup instead.

"Uh, what are you guys doing?" Sam's voice rings over our cackling.

"Aw, Bug, come here." Alex holds his hand out to her. She skips over and settles in his lap.

"I gotta go, but I'm not waiting until it's too late with this one. We did that with the Guild. I'm not about to put Kenzie's life in danger merely because I don't have all the pieces to the puzzle. And someone pick up the fucking hippo they dropped on my doorstep," I grumble, expecting someone to call me on my bullshit. I stride for the door.

"Tell Mac to call me," Sam calls over Alex's peals of laughter.

I flip them off before hustling through the labyrinth of hallways and doors until I'm out in the open, able to pull in a full breath. I used to enjoy riding, getting on my bike, just going, but as the years passed and more responsibilities piled up, I didn't make the time. The first time I felt free in a while was when Kenz was on the back a couple of weeks ago. It was like something slotted into place then, but it took me awhile to notice. I'm supposed to meet with a contact who has ties in Rima, but I turn toward home, needing the reassurance she's okay. Safe. Hell, I just need to see her, if only to soothe the jagged parts of my soul.

Regret and rage spins through me as I pass the charred mess that was once Trigger's. Trigger himself didn't seem too bothered by it, moving into an abandoned building and throwing some wood on top of a couple of kegs. He even moved that hideous statue to the new place. Still, I failed him. Looking back, I see what I should have done, the steps I should have taken, the decisions I should have made sooner. It makes it worse that he doesn't blame me.

Pulling into the drive, I can see the front door is wide open, and panic slices through me. I launch off my bike, barely turning it off before rushing inside. Bellowing Kenzie's name, I bound up the stairs and slam open doors, but she's not here. I blast into my bedroom. The window is thrown wide open, and her full-bellied laugh floats through it. Relief slams into me, almost bringing me to my knees. I stumble to the window, leaning on the sill.

There she is, tipping her head back, clutching a football to her chest. Where the hell they got a football is beyond me, but Doc, Blue, and Hawk are running around. Another piece settles in my chest, and I can't help but stare as her dark hair glitters, hints of purple shining in the sunlight, joy radiating from her. This was what I was missing without even knowing it. No, that's not true. I knew I was missing her, but I never thought I'd have her. I never believed she'd come back. I never thought I deserved her. I still don't know if I do. Even after we talked last night, finally getting on the same page and coming to an agreement on how to deal with all the shit coming at us, I worry. I might lose her, even if I do everything right. Last time was hard enough. I won't survive going through it again.

"Helms!" My eyes drift to Hawk, waving, and I lift a hand in response.

Somewhere between her collapsing in his arms and now, she's worked some change in him. Before, it was rare to see him smile. I've never seen him doing anything remotely fun. In fact, I've never seen any of them messing around like they are now. Most of us keep our heads down, do our jobs, and keep the business of the MC running.

I'm lost in thought when Kenzie's shout pulls me back. Bikes thunder through the neighborhood. Blue picks her up as she yells at him to put her down, but he hustles her into the house. Usually, the sound of bikes would be normal, an everyday occurrence, but lately, we've been skittish. I launch down the stairs, meeting them at the back door, and snatching Kenzie from Blue's arms.

"Ryker, I can walk. Go find out if there's a real problem or if you're all freaking out for no reason," she complains, squirming in my arms.

I pivot, dropping her to her feet in the laundry room and pulling the door closed. She's not happy, if her grumbling is any indication.

"Hawk, take the back. Blue, go keep an eye out from upstairs. Doc, you're with me," I bark.

"I should go. You take the back, Prez," Hawk says, stepping around me.

"It's not up for discussion."

"If it's the Night Slayers, they'll be gunning for you, not me. I mean, they'll try, but they'll be looking for you. Don't make yourself a target," he grunts.

I'm torn. The last thing I want to do is put my VP in danger, but he's right. They'll shoot first if they see me. There's a sliver of chance they'll hesitate if it's Hawk out there.

"Fine. Doc, go out back. Blue, upstairs. I'm going to make sure Kenz isn't freaking out," I say, throwing a thumb over my shoulder at the laundry door.

"You know I can hear you, right?" I can hear the eye roll in her voice.

"Excuse me for caring about you. Now, stay in the fucking room."

"Go." Hawk pushes me toward the door.

I step through, and Kenzie tries to slip past me, but I herd her back, slamming the door behind me. I crowd her back against the washer, searching her face for any signs of another panic attack. Two weeks ago, something like this would have sent her spiraling. I finally sucked it up and asked Ren how to help her, but I haven't had to use the strategies yet.

"Ryker, it's probably not even them."

Turning my head, I listen to roaring engines close in on us. The sound of the front door closing, followed by the slam of the back door has her jumping. I push my body into hers, planting my hands on the washer and boxing her in. Her head tips up, fire in her eyes, but a smile tipping her lips.

"MacKenzie. Please don't question me when I'm trying to keep you alive."

"Ryker. Please don't boss me around."

Tucking my head to my chest, I grin, and her arms wrap around my waist. Her body presses against mine as she inhales deeply, pushing her tits into me, and I shiver, remembering my face buried between them last night. My mind drifts over the memories as my hand skims over her back, dipping under the hem of her shirt. No, not her shirt, mine. Fuck. I suck in a breath and dip my head, nipping at her neck. She tilts her head to the side for me to nibble her earlobe. I suck it in my mouth as she shivers.

"We shouldn't fuck while there's a possible thing going on outside," she says breathlessly.

"If you think this is fucking, then I haven't been doing my job right," I mumble, scraping my teeth along her jaw before capturing her mouth with my own.

She tastes like beer and strawberries, and I groan, grinding my hardened cock into her. Her tongue pushes mine, fighting for dominance, just like every time we collide. I'll never get enough of this, of her. A thousand lifetimes would never be enough.

She rips her mouth from mine, panting. "We should stop, or this whole fucking room is going to smell like sex."

I grin. "We can say you needed a distraction." She reaches a hand between our bodies, squeezing my cock through my pants, making me grunt. My forehead lands on hers, and my eyes fall closed.

"I don't think I'm the one who needs the distraction," she whispers with a soft giggle. It's a sound I never heard from her before, that giggle. When we were younger, she was always trying to be the biggest badass on the block, trying to keep up with us. Knowing I'm the one who gets to hear it from her is a heady feeling I don't entirely know what to do with. The door bangs open behind us, and we jump away from each other.

"Well, at least they're not naked," Hawk says, a grin on his face. I turn away as I adjust my hard-on.

"Who was it?" I demand, hoping they'll drop it.

"They're still here, but it's not the Night Slayers. They want to see you." I resist the urge to ring his neck. I take one step before he's holding up his hand.

"Not you, her." Doc points at Kenzie. My eyes find hers, shock filling her face.

"Me? Who are they? I don't know anyone."

"They say they know you, just wanna talk, apparently. We relieved them of their weapons, but they want to meet you alone," Hawk says.

I shake my head, but Kenzie beats me to the refusal.

"Absolutely not. Tell them they can go, and we'll keep the guns." She glares at Hawk for even suggesting it.

"Oh, I told them you wouldn't go for that, but they're okay if I'm with you. I think they're afraid Ryker will shoot them if they so much as look at you," he laughs.

"I will," I mumble, looking to her, and she searches my face.

It's her decision. I won't stop her, no matter how much I want to throw her over my shoulder and lock her in my bedroom.

"Let's go, then." She sucks in a breath and squares her shoulders. I snake an arm around her waist, pulling her to me, then slam my mouth on hers. I pull back quickly, releasing her when my fingers itch to keep her here, where she's safe. I follow her out of the room, stopping inside the kitchen to track her as she looks back one last time before disappearing out the door.

THIRTY-TWO

MacKenzie

"Hawk, I don't know if this is a good idea," I mumble, running my hands up and down my arms. I'm cold, though it's hot and humid outside.

"Don't worry. I called in a bunch of others who *happen* to be at headquarters. I won't let anything happen to you, and not only because Helms would kill me, bring me back to life, and kill me again." He shoots me a grin.

"Oh, I'm sure he wouldn't kill you right away. He'd just torture you for weeks before ending your life. I mean, I could always ask him for leniency, but he's pretty set on protecting me, so I'm not sure my words would do much to help," I say, crinkling my nose.

He pushes open the double doors, and I step into the coolness. I blink, trying to erase the dark spots jumping in my eyes now that we're inside. When my vision clears, I freeze, and my mouth falls open. Hawk turns back, a questioning look on his face, but I can't concentrate on anything other than the five men sitting at the table. They're all shapes and sizes, but they're all my age. And I know every fucking one of them.

"Mac?" Blaze stands, twisting the ring on his middle finger.

"What the hell are you guys doing here?" They are the last people I thought I'd see in Reaper territory. Blaze glances at the others for help, but no one moves.

"Well, Mad's been gone for a while—not that he was doing much—but we wanted to make sure you were okay. Plus, with Dante still missing, we need to make some plans. I've been runnin' things best I can, but without a clear leader, we have some . . . dissension," he says in a rush. My gaze bounces between them.

Uncertainty flashes in each of their eyes.

"What the fuck am I supposed to do about any of those things?"

"You know what to do. We didn't want to step on your toes, if you were coming back." Blaze widens his eyes, trying to convey something I don't understand.

Step on their toes? I don't have a rank in the Vipers. Hell, I'm not even a member. Maddox always made such a fuss about it, and Dante never pushed the issue. I didn't care all that much. Maddox's been gunning to get rid of me for years. He was the only one who fought for me to stay in Synd after the coup. At the time, I thought it was because he was finally starting to fight for me, but I found out it was only a clever tactic to be rid of me.

"Blaze, I don't have a say, even if I was coming back. I don't know what you thought would happen, but you're lucky the Reapers didn't shoot first and ask questions later," I say, exasperated.

He glances around again, like someone is going to jump them. Maybe he's thinking someone else will speak up, but as Sergeant-at-Arms, he's the leading rank among them. Hell, Picker isn't technically a member yet. At least he wasn't when I was sold.

"Mac, do you know where Mad is?"

Five faces stare at me, brows pulled low, waiting for my answer. I suck in a breath, looking to Hawk for help, but his eyes jump between us.

"I do," I say hesitantly, not sure how much I should reveal.

"Is he alive?"

"Yes." My heart pounds.

"Fuck. I thought for sure Helms would take him out for us," he grumbles, shaking his head.

My mouth falls open. "What?"

"That's why we let him go. We knew he was up to no good. But we couldn't take him out ourselves."

"Wait, you knew he was coming, and you didn't warn me?"

Hawk steps forward, angling in front of me. I elbow him, stepping next to his side. While I appreciate the sentiment, I'm not afraid of them. They might have fucked up, but they didn't mean to hurt me. None of them were there when I was bustled into a car or dropped in an alley.

I doubt Maddox revealed his grand plan to do away with what he saw was a threat.

"We tried," Blip says, leaping to his feet and holding his hands out. "I texted, but you didn't talk back. Dante's office's locked up tight, so we flew Bean over. Part reason we rode, see if he got here." Blip's broken speech drains the anger and annoyance from me.

He rarely speaks in front of others, worried of their reaction.

"Okay, it's okay, Blip. Hawk, can you get us something to drink? Maybe some food?" I glance at him, but he shakes his head, never taking his eyes off the group. I sigh, stepping forward, but he yanks me back, keeping me next to him.

"Torture for weeks, Mac," he reminds me.

"All right, so Maddox is out of commission. He won't be back. Blaze, you're in charge until Dante comes back," I say, pointing at him. "Tell me what's happening with the Night Slayers."

Blaze's feet shuffle, and he won't meet my eye. "Well, see, that might be hard."

"You can't tell us about the Night Slayers?" I raise an eyebrow, crossing my arms, tapping a foot on the concrete.

"No, we can tell ya, but I doubt we can go back. Lots of the members were . . . well, they were happy when Mad took over. I don't know what happened with ya, Mac, but the Vipers are falling apart. They're working more and more with Panther. He's been coming around, ordering us to do shit . . ."

I stare at the Reapers milling around in the back, then scan the walls, covered in flags plastered with Reapers' patches and colors. Everywhere I look is another reminder I'm not in Rima anymore. I'm not with the Vipers. The problem is, I'm no longer a part of the Reapers. I wasn't when I was younger, either. I don't have the authority to give them anything—asylum, refuge, direction. I'm at a loss. I can't ask Ryker for more. He's already housing me, feeding me, protecting me. Half the members are still questioning his decisions, especially Rooster. They'll never accept these guys, divided loyalties or not.

"Sounds like you need a club," a voice from behind rings out.

Ryker steps behind me, wrapping an arm around my waist, pulling my back to his chest. Blaze's eyes bug out before he clears his throat.

"Umm, yeah. I mean, yes, sir." His voice cracks, and I smother a smirk behind my hand.

"You think it's funny he called me 'sir?'" Ryker's breath ghosts across the shell of my ear, sending a shiver through me, and his hands squeezes my hip.

"'Course not," I wheeze.

Hawk clears his throat, bringing me out of the bubble Ryker's pulled me into. The arm around my waist tightens, leading me toward the side hallway. It's awkward, shuffling my feet between his own. He reaches around me to swing his office door open before herding me inside.

"What the hell, Ryker?" I squawk, shoving away from him and rounding the desk to plop down in his seat. He eyes me before sitting across from me, and I hide another smirk.

"Why don't you tell me what's going on out there, hmm?" He crosses his legs, raising an eyebrow.

"Well, they told me they wanted to check on me and find where Maddox was—and something about who is supposed to be in charge of the Vipers, but I think they want you to take them in. I don't know why they thought I could help them, but here they are. I didn't call them."

Ryker tilts his head, eyes narrowing, and I glance around the space. It's bare, only a few things tucked here and there. I spin around, scan the titles stacked in the small bookcase, but there's nothing interesting. I spin back, still avoiding him, but even his desk is bare. The chair I'm in is cheap, squeaking every time I shift. I'm slightly terrified I'm going to end up on the floor if I move too much.

"Kenz, stop avoiding the situation. If you want them in, they'll be put up."

"I wouldn't ask for them to be admitted or put up," I mumble, heart breaking a little for the men sitting in the main room.

"Clearly. Why is it you're not going to speak up for them? They're your friends." There's an edge to his voice.

Biting my tongue, I savor the contentment flowing through me. I didn't know if he'd take our conversation yesterday seriously or brush me off again. For once, he didn't run off to another meeting or take a phone call, content to hold me and divulge his half-made plans. He may be taking it too far, expecting me to speak up on club business.

Propping my elbow on the desk, I lean my chin in my hand and try to organize my thoughts. Sometimes, I forget how striking his eyes are, an electric blue, but they're also shot through with gray, rimmed with steel. His lashes are long and thick, and my nose wrinkles in jealousy.

"What?"

"Do you think if we had . . ." I straighten, clamping my mouth shut.

"Kenz?" he says in warning, leaning forward.

"Nothing. Never mind. It's not my choice whether you put them up or not, but I have a feeling they'll never pass," I rush, back to avoiding his eyes.

He chuckles, leaning forward on the desk. "We'll revisit the thought that went through your mind a second ago, but I wouldn't put them up right now. This is an emergency situation. They'll be on the same level as prospects for now. Then later, you can put them up."

"I can't put them up. I'm not a member."

He waves away my words, leaning back and then crossing his arms. I don't know why we're having this conversation in the first place. It's not my decision what he does with them. He could have asked if I trusted them, but that's about all I have to offer. Leaving me in charge of their fate won't endear me to anyone in the Reapers, I'm sure, but he's intent on thrusting me into the conversation. More and more these days, he's nudging me into giving my opinion. I wanted to be involved, but I imagined it would be communication between us, not sitting in on discussions with his guys. Just this morning, he informed me about another meeting tonight, and I should be prepared to speak. He brushed me off when I asked why.

"Are they trustworthy? Or are they moles?" he asks.

"They're kids. I mean, most of them. Dante made Blaze his third, but no one else really wanted the job. Come to think of it, *he* didn't want the job, but Dante insisted. Picker isn't a full-member yet. He was going to be before Dante left, but the thing with the Guild happened, and everything got pushed back. The only reason they came to me is because I listen to them. They're used to not having anyone listen to them."

"So, they're weirdos." He grins, eyes twinkling.

"I mean, I suppose." I sniff, crossing my arms again.

"Let's go welcome them to our band, then." He pushes up before holding a hand out to me.

"Band?" I round the desk to slip my hand in his. He interlocks our fingers and pulls me out the door.

Looking over his shoulder, he grins again. "Our merry band of misfits."

I laugh, wondering where the hell the grumpy, overprotective Ryker went and how long I'll have this new, happy Ryker. The way my life has been going lately, I'm afraid something is coming that will rip the smile from his face too soon.

THIRTY-THREE

Ryker

"Shut the fuck up, Rooster. No one gives a shit," Hawk yells.

The meeting's been going on for an hour, and I've had a headache for forty minutes of it. Between Rooster butting in every five fucking minutes and others grumbling under their breath at every turn, I'm about to say fuck it and throw all their asses out in the rain.

Kenzie leans in, whispering, "Ryker, maybe I should go."

Refusing to even look at her, digging my nails into my biceps, I shake my head. A lot of clubs let their members run roughshod over their presidents. They have a say in shit, vote on things, but we're not like that here. Apparently, Rooster forgot. Still running his mouth, he tries to argue with Hawk. I don't usually have to pull rank. My guys know who's in charge. They remember I hold their fate in my hands. Their asses belong to the Reapers, and as I am the embodiment of the Reapers, they toe the line carefully. I count to ten, breathing in and out to calm my racing heart.

"So, we're supposed to house these fuckwads, along with this stupid-ass bitch?" Rooster booms.

I abandon my chair, pulling out my gun along the way. I press the barrel against his forehead before most realize I've moved. "Say it again," I growl, watching his face drain of color.

His mouth flaps like a fish, gasping for the sweet release of water. I press harder, digging the metal into his flesh, and his eyes widen. A hand ghosts along my arm, fingertips dancing. Kenzie wraps her hand around mine, gripping the gun in my fist. Almost lovingly, she caresses my finger that's resting on the trigger.

"Ryker." She doesn't continue but waits until the tension eases from my shoulders. She pushes my hand down, a circle impression in the center of his forehead, the only remnant of how close he was to death.

"Remember this, Rooster. The only reason you live is because of her."

Tucking Kenzie close to my side, I turn. I don't glance back when I hear his chair crashing to the ground in his haste to run. I meet Blue's eyes, and he follows Rooster. As much as I'd like to let Rooster go and be far away from the Reapers, I can't risk him running to the Night Slayers. Kenzie meets my eyes as I settle her back in her chair at the front. I don't know what I expected, but it wasn't the gleam of pride.

"Anyone else have something to say?" Most of them don't move, but a few shake their heads. "Good. Now, when we finally move out, I'll expect some to stay here. The last thing we need is to come home to more places burnt to the ground. Anyone who has a request to stay behind, see Tiny. Tank, let the prospects know they'll be staying here. They do their job, this'll be their final test."

Hawk clears his throat. "The new guys coming in are in limbo. Don't fuck with them, but they're not members. We find you're messing with them and my friend will fuck you up. And then Ryker will finish you off."

He smirks, nudging Kenzie, who's gaping at him. This meeting hasn't gone how I thought it would. I run a tight ship, but between Rooster insulting Kenzie and Hawk's announcement, I don't see things changing anytime soon.

"Dismissed. Veiled in shadows."

"Chased by death."

The rumble of their voices reverberates through my chest.

They shuffle out, some milling in the back, glancing at the small group of us left in front of the room. Tiny and Tank whisper, planning how to deal with the prospects. I trust them, so I leave them to it. They don't need me interfering and micromanaging them. I snag Kenzie's hand, lacing our fingers together, as she talks to Hawk, eyes dancing. The difference between the last meeting and this one is glaringly obvious. Before, she was pissed. Now she looks like she belongs, and I can't contain my grin.

"What the hell are you smiling at?" Kenzie demands, turning to me.

"Nothing. Let's go home." I tug her along, lifting a hand to the rest.

The back door is closer, and the heat floods over us, crickets drowning out the traffic from the city. There aren't many who live in our territory, who aren't a part of the club in some way, and other than bikes, most of them aren't out this late.

"Not as scary as before," she murmurs, peering into the woods.

"What's not?" I follow her eyes, and she pulls to a stop.

"Oh, I used to be scared of the forest. I'd see you boys slipping in between the trees. I tried to follow you once. I wanted . . . well, whatever. I didn't make it very far. Everything seemed to close in around me, and I couldn't see you anymore. Then there was the howling." She shivers, pulling her hand from mine and rubbing her arms, despite the humidity.

"Howling?"

"Yeah, Maddox said there were wolves. I mean, he was probably lying, but still freaked me out. I tried to find you, but I couldn't. I only ever went to that one spot where we play seven rounds. Whatever, doesn't matter, but they always scared me afterwards. Then there was the break-in." She shivers. "I don't know. Now, though, they don't seem so bad."

"I'll take you back there."

"What, now?" She turns with wide eyes and steps back, like I'll throw her over my shoulder and haul her off.

I laugh. "No, baby, not now. We'll wait until daylight, but I'll show you where we always went. It's nothing exciting. In fact, I'm not sure our shit is still there, but I'll take you."

Deja vu sends a shiver through my bones as we walk. I tug her closer. Swinging open the back door, I pause, scanning the hall and what little I can see of the kitchen, but it all looks the same as we left it hours ago. Kenzie's head peeks over my shoulder, dark hair swinging around me with the move.

"Do you think there are ghosts?" Her whispered words bounce through the air, and I snort. "I'm serious. I think the salt shaker was moved."

"Weren't this flippant when you thought a ghoul was living in your closet, were you?"

"I was seven! You and Dante kept crouching under my window and making moaning noises. What was I supposed to think?"

I crowd her back into the laundry room, fitting my fingers in the crease of her ass cheeks, then hoist her onto the washer while she laughs. She's a few inches taller than me now. Her head dips down, lips meeting mine with a smile. I drink in the scent of her soap that mingles with mine, and I wonder if she's been mixing them to drive me insane. My fingers dance along the hem of her shirt. My lips leave hers, trailing down her neck, nipping and licking a path to her collarbone.

"Don't think I've forgotten. I'm mad at you for eating all the ice cream." She gasps.

"I don't think you're mad at all." I breathe into her flesh, biting down on the top of her tit, making her jerk.

I suck the mark in my mouth, knowing it'll be there for days, and my chest swells, along with my cock.

"I'm furious with you." Her fingers dig into my hair, gripping the strands and trying to pull me back to her mouth, but I merely move to her other tit, leaving a matching bite on that one, too.

"I'll fuck the mad out of you," I growl, yanking her hips closer to the edge of the machine.

I capture her wrists, forcing her hands on to the cold metal before meeting her eyes. I curl my fingers around her waistband, waiting for her to hoist herself so I can strip her. I peel them off quickly and toss them behind, then spread her knees before I run my tongue between her slit, not able to resist tasting her again.

Her essence explodes across my taste buds, and I moan as she jerks forward and almost slips from the machine. I grab her again, kneading her flesh with my fingers and standing between her knees. Her hands fly to my belt, shoving my pants as far as she can, and I surge forward, thrusting half way before pulling back and thrusting again, until I'm fully seated inside her. She falls back on her hands, and one connects with the buttons. The machine beeps and then starts up.

My hands are trembling from the sensation of being inside her again, but Kenzie probably can't tell between the machine vibrating beneath her and the laughter coursing through her body. I pull out slightly, pounding back into her, yet the giggles escape her, though her breath ends on another moan.

"You think this is funny, Kenz?" I grit, trying not to let on how amazing it feels every time my balls vibrate when my cock is fully inside her.

"I mean," she says, her voice quivering, eyes focused on where we're connected, "it didn't even take a quarter."

I lean forward to rest my forehead on hers, slamming my eyes shut, when the shift pushes me deeper.

"Kenzie, I'm trying to fuck you, and you're talking about quarters and laughing your ass off. Doesn't really do much for my ego."

She winds her arms around my shoulders, pressing her lips to mine in a quick kiss. "Do your worst then, tiger."

I groan. "Tiger? Seriously?" I shift back, punching my hips forward, the washer scrapping back an inch. She lets out the giggle I love so much. I swear I could hear it every day for the rest of my life, and I'd never get sick of it.

I slide my hands down to the backs of her knees before pushing them up until her feet are planted on the edge of the washer. Her arms fall away from me, but she braces herself again. I roll my hips, gripping hers, then pull out slowly before slamming back in over and over, gradually building us both up, but never enough to send her over the edge. My mouth falls open when her head tips back, watching me from under her lashes as the humor is chased away by my measured thrusts.

Dropping my gaze, I'm mesmerized by the sight of her body drawing me in. Our bodies fit perfectly together. I'll never get used to this. I'm pretty sure she's ruined me. I lift my eyes, captivated by her mouth falling open, her eyes swimming with ecstasy, the flush in her cheeks as I push her closer and closer to climax.

"Never again," I say under my breath.

"What?" she squawks, scrambling to sit up, but I plant a hand on her chest, pinching her nipple through the fabric.

After slamming into her, I stop, leaning over her again until her furious eyes meet mine. "I said never again. You're never leaving again. I will drag your ass back every fucking time."

Her eyes grow wide, and a soft *oh* leaves her lips right before I capture them with mine, plunging my tongue deep, completely owning her body. I tug her hips closer to the edge until she's half way off before plunging in and out of her soaked pussy.

Her fingers scrape the metal as she scurries to find purchase, all while the machine vibrates under us. I won't last much longer. Being inside of her is enough to send me over the edge, but seeing her splayed out, wonder playing across her face, knowing I'm the one who gets to see her like this, is too much for me to last very long. My thrusts aren't as smooth as before, and I snatch her hand up in mine to guide her fingers to her clit. She whimpers when we make contact, as I use her fingers to send her hurtling into her release. Her hand falls away, but I'm not done yet.

Clenching around my cock, she shudders as I keep pounding into her, rubbing her clit still with one hand. With every circle, she cries out, and I grit my teeth. I want to watch her fall a part again. Kenzie's eyes crack open as she pants, and I reach my other hand up to her exposed nipple, rolling it between my fingers. Her eyes roll back in her head. I can't hold back anymore, exploding inside of her. I collapse on top of her, both of us out of breath, basking in the glow.

"All mine," I growl into her skin.

The washing machine is still rumbling underneath us, and I throw my hand up, stabbing my fingers down, trying to turn it off as Kenzie's body starts shaking again. I lift my head from her chest and find her fist stuffed in her mouth, tears in her eyes. One last punch, and I find the right button to power it off.

"Baby, what's wrong?" My stomach tightens, but she shakes her head, biting down on her knuckles harder.

A giggle escapes her as I'm about to drag myself off. I grunt, hoisting off her body, pushing her up more, so she doesn't fall on the floor. I doubt her legs can hold her up. She's still laughing, curling into herself, as I peel my shirt from my body and wipe myself off. I clean her off as best I can.

"I'm sorry," she wheezes, sounding anything but sorry. I grunt in response, gathering up my pants and pulling them back on.

She reaches toward me to snatch my hand as she sits up, then winds her legs around my waist, still shaking. I run my fingers through her hair. Not exactly the ending I thought we'd have.

"Good run, tiger," she giggles.

"I swear to fucking god, Kenz, if you call me tiger in front of anyone else, I'll make sure your ass is red from the punishment."

She dissolves into a fit of laughter. I am totally fucked for this woman.

THIRTY-FOUR

MacKenzie

"Are we going or not?" I demand, planting myself in front of the door. Ryker has been trying to put me off for at least twenty minutes, and it's starting to piss me off.

"I'm going. You're not. I can't keep an eye on you while trying to do recon," he snaps, stomping into his closet.

He reappears, leathers in place now. I sneak a glance at my phone, wondering if I have enough time to jump him before we have to leave, but we were supposed to be out the door five minutes ago.

"You won't have to keep an eye on me. I'm not a stray dog. I can take care of myself. As much as I appreciate you including me, I can help more. Like going on this little mission."

He scans me from head to toe. I glance down, wondering what he's looking at. I pulled out the jeans I made Sam pick up for me, but they're a little tight. Dressed to ride, I'm wearing boots and a shirt and Ryker's leather jacket. There's nothing wrong with how I'm dressed, so he can't possibly sideline me because of them.

"Kenzie, I'm going to be honest. If I have to ride a couple hours with your pussy pressed against my ass, we'll never make it." He smirks.

I narrow my eyes. He's trying to distract me from the actual conversation. I clench, and I'm glad I wore a padded bra. Otherwise, my nipples would be saluting him, and we'd never get out of here.

"Don't think you can distract me. I'm coming with, and you can't stop me. Either I'll be rubbing against you or against whoever else is willing to give me a ride." I smile sweetly.

"I *am* the president. I could just tell them to leave your sexy ass behind. Or I could make good on my promise and tie you to the bed. You'd probably get hungry, though."

I snort. "I can convince someone. Or I can call Sam. She'll come get me."

He crowds me against the door, trapping me while sliding his knee between my legs. My breath hitches, and I grab on to his shoulders to steady myself. His head dips, running his nose along my jaw, and I shudder. He's still trying to distract me, but I'm not complaining. After waiting for his stupid ass all these years, I'm going to enjoy every second I have with him. With the threat of the Night Slayers hanging over us, we don't know how long we'll have before shit goes down. I'll take the time I have and cherish it.

"You sure you want to do that?" he murmurs in my ear, but I've forgotten what I said.

His hands roving over my body and dipping under the hem of my shirt isn't helping me remember. He pulls my lobe between his teeth, then releases it before scraping them along my jaw.

I shift, riding his thigh, but I can't find the right angle, and a groan of frustration leaves me right before he captures my mouth with his. Ryker's hand shifts down, trying to sneak into my waistband, but these jeans are really fucking tight. He growls into my mouth, attacking the buttons and finally grabbing a fistful of my ass, helping me rub against him. Bracing his leg, he angles up more and hits exactly where I need it most. He swallows the sob falling from my lips, then pulls back, eyes capturing mine.

"One of these days, I'm going to fuck you with only my leathers on."

He states it like a promise, the same way he promised he'd tie me to the bed, the same way he demanded I let him protect me. All I can do is nod, biting my lip to keep from crying out again. His free hand snakes under my shirt, squeezing and twisting my nipple, and a tremor wracks my body, sending a flood of arousal straight to my pussy. By the end of this, we'll both have to change pants.

His head dips while he pinches my nipple again, whispering, "Be a good girl and come for me."

My body obeys, my climax taking me by surprise. I never thought I was into this shit, but every time Ryker demands something from my body, it blindly falls in line. I swear he could make me come with only his words. My oblivion is short-lived as I clench around nothing. All I want is to feel him inside me. With fumbling fingers, I reach for his belt, but he traps them before bringing them to his lips and kissing each knuckle.

"Ryker," I whine, shivering, as another bolt of pleasure shoots through me.

"Don't be greedy, Kenz." He gives me a quick kiss before stepping back, taking my support with him. I stumble on flat feet, huffing in annoyance.

"Dick," I mutter, fixing my pants.

"You want my dick, but you'll have to wait," he chuckles, gazing down at the wet spot on his leg. Instead of changing, he pulls me away from the door.

"Aren't you going to change?" I whisper frantically, trying to adjust my clothes, so it doesn't look like I dry humped Ryker's leg.

"Nope."

"Ryker, you're not leaving without me. Don't think you making me come wiped my brain of all thought," I yell, chasing him down the stairs.

I skid to a stop at the bottom, cheeks flushing when I spot everyone scattered through the main floor. Most have the decency to look away, but Hawk tries to smother a grin in the kitchen, and Doc is staring like he's trying to pry into my brain.

Ryker's arm snakes around my waist, as he mutters in my ear, "Good to know you're not embarrassed about staking your claim, Kenz, but none of them are interested in stealing me away."

I can hear the smile in his voice. I peek over his shoulder, but everyone has gone back to their conversations they were in before I announced to them all how sexually satisfied I am.

"Fucking-A, Ryker. You could have told me they were all down here waiting," I grumble.

"And deny myself the chance to watch you fall a part in my arms? No fucking way. If you're good while I'm gone, I'll make sure you get another one when I get back." He steps away, calling out to the others.

I wait until most of them have filed out the doors to snag Hawk's arm before he can slip out, too. He raises an eyebrow, but I shake my head. When the last person is gone, I peek out the still-open door, spotting Ryker laughing with some guy I don't recognize. They're all loading up, looking like a suburban wife's worst nightmare. Imagining them rolling through the quiet streets and being cussed out for rumbling through a bougie neighborhood, I snort.

"Mac? I have to get going. What did you need?" Hawk pulls me out of my vision, and I peek at Ryker one last time before pulling back.

"Yeah, I'm going to need to ride with you." I plaster a smile on my face, hoping he won't ask questions.

He snorts. "Yeah, no."

"What? Why not?"

"Other than the obvious reason? I'm not going to deal with his shit mood if he sees you riding on the back of my bike. I have the will to live."

I wave his concerns away. "Oh, he'll be fine. Not like he's going to shoot you for giving me a ride. He'll be distracted by everything else."

"Negative. He most definitely will shoot me. I wouldn't even blame him. I wouldn't want my woman riding with another guy, either."

I roll my eyes. "You don't have a woman."

His eyes darken, face stony, and I realize I've stepped too far. He turns, intent on striding out the door, but I grab his arm again.

"Sorry, I didn't mean it like that, but I shouldn't have said it, regardless."

He shrugs me off. "It's fine."

He whips around, and I step back. "It's not a choice to not have someone. You're fucking lucky, Mac. You have someone who wants you, who will have your back, who will fight for you. Don't be dumb. Don't throw that shit away. It's not as common as you'd think."

He takes off, jumping on his bike and riding away, not waiting for the others. Ryker's eyes find mine, confusion clouding his face. I still want to go, but guilt turns my stomach sour. Of course, Ryker is striding for me now. I'll have to confess: I was a bitch, whether I meant to be or not.

"What the hell was that?" he asks, staring down the street where Hawk disappeared.

"I was insensitive. I apologized, but I don't think he believed me," I mumble, eyes trained where Hawk disappeared.

"What'd you say?"

I have to tell him. Otherwise, he'll ask Hawk, which will be worse.

"I was trying to convince him to take me, since you're so set on leaving me behind. He said no—you'll be happy to know—but he mentioned if he saw his woman riding on the back of another guy's bike, he'd be pissed. I may have—"

Ryker groans. "Please tell me you didn't say he doesn't have a woman."

I heave in a deep breath, nodding as I meet his eyes.

"Fuck, Kenz. I mean, I know you didn't mean to, but he's a bit sensitive about not having someone." He scrubs his hands over his face, groaning again.

"I figured that out, thanks. Do you know why?"

"No, and I'm not about to ask. If you're really this hellbent on going, get on the goddamn bike. We're not going to Rima anymore."

Hustling down the stairs, I rush back up to shut the door, then fly to his bike before his words register.

"Wait, we're not going to Rima?" I swing to Ryker, who shoves a helmet over my head.

None of the others have one, but he keeps insisting I wear it. It's not worth it to argue with him over wearing something that might save my life, even though I went years without one.

"No, we're not. We're going to the southern border of Synd. See what we can find down there," he grumbles.

Tension pulses in his neck, the vein throbbing in his forehead. I reach up, pressing a finger into his skin.

"You still want to go to Rima, don't you?" I say, and his lips press in a thin line, eyeing me through the open visor.

"I'm not bringing you to Rima. It's too volatile."

I duck, staring at my feet, searching for an answer in the dirt. I won't be able to convince him we'll be safe—not where he wants to go, but maybe . . .

"We could go to my friend's house. She doesn't live anywhere near Viper or Night Slayer territory." I tip my head up, watching his face.

His head tilts, eyes narrowing. "What friend?"

It isn't even a question, like I couldn't have someone who isn't a part of an MC.

"We met at a coffee shop. She's . . . normal. I mean, she knows who I am and all, but she didn't grow up around any of this shit," I say, waving my hand to encompass everything the Reapers are.

Just when I think he'll give in, since he's silent so long, he shakes his head. Disappointment wells in me. It wasn't a good plan, but it would have been nice to see someone who knows me. I can't even call her, since I don't have my phone anymore, only the burner Ren gave me.

"Sorry, Kenz. When we deal with all this shit, she can come visit, but it's too dangerous right now. Let's go before Hawk gets too far ahead and does something stupid."

I climb up behind him, wrapping my arms around his waist. As the miles are eaten up under the tires, I let go of all the guilt, disappointment, apprehension, everything. I close my eyes, feeling lighter than I have in weeks.

THIRTY-FIVE

Ryker

"You realize we can't wait forever, right? No time is going to be perfect," Hawk murmurs, wiping grease off his hands on the rag hanging from his back pocket.

I should be working on my own bike, but I lean against the porch of the Raines' old house, watching Hawk. I glance to my own porch where Kenzie and Sam chat.

I never thought of Sam as someone who talked a lot, assuming she was too keyed up to just sit most of the time. I find her over here more and more. When she's not here, her and Kenzie text or are on the phone. Somehow, they've become the best of friends, much to Shane's dismay. I don't know why he's been so fucking grouchy about it, but I think it's something to do with Sam leaving him behind every time she comes here.

"I want to leave Kenzie here," I admit.

"She's not going to like that plan."

"Not much I like about the plan, either, but here we are," I grumble, crossing my arms and staring at the women.

"Wait, you haven't told her, have you?"

I stay silent. I already heard it from Doc and then Blue and then Ink. I don't need another person telling me I'm fucking this up.

"I'll get around to it. We have time."

"Uh, no the fuck we don't. Which is what I'm saying. We need to move sooner rather than later. The longer we wait, the longer they have to strike first."

"I'm wondering if they will. With Maddox out of the picture, maybe they've given up. We're still feeding him, right?"

"Yeah, but I doubt they've given up. They went through a lot of trouble to get her. Not to mention, they seem to have taken over the Vipers. Fuckers have more men, more resources, and more reason to fuck around and find out. We need to bring the fight to them, and you know it. I'm sure if you explain to Mac why you want her here, she'll listen."

I snort. "Oh, I'm sure she'll be just fine being left at home, like a good little woman. I'll tell her to have dinner ready when I get back."

He chuckles. "I said she'd listen, not that she'd agree. Are we going to ignore you just called the Reapers' home when referencing her?"

Shaking my head, I check on Kenzie and Sam again. I tried to convince myself I wasn't keeping tabs on her, but even I didn't believe myself. The need to make sure she's okay, safe, protected, is too much to handle some days. Apparently, I'm going to be sticking to her side today so I don't freak the fuck out.

"I've made it clear she's staying. I'm not giving her up without a fight, even if the fight is with her, so might as well call it what it is. This is home, Reapers are family, she stays."

Kenzie lifts a hand, her wide smile catching me off guard. It's so different from when she first got here, battered and bruised, not willing to burden me with her problems. The change in her is night and day, or maybe day to night to day. Now that the fear is gone from her eyes, I see the girl she was when we were growing up, the daredevil, complete with sarcastic quips, and absolutely no shits to give. In between, I glimpse a softer side, one I never really knew existed.

I thought I knew all the facets of her personality, but the closer we get and the longer she stays, the more I'm reminded we're not teenagers anymore. Hawk was right, as much as I hate to admit. I was in love with a version of her in my head, but I had to fall for the person she is now. Safe to say, it happened without me noticing, since I was halfway there in the first place.

Creeping past headquarters is a car at the end of the street, which pulls up to the curb in front of my house. Smirking, I shake my head as I catch Shane's wary eyes. Sam pops up, running down the porch and around the car to yank open his door. They argue, her tugging his arm and him refusing to leave the car.

"Shane Reginald King! Get out of the fucking car right now." Sam's voice cuts across the lawn.

Hawk and I lose it, doubling over. I stuff a fist in my mouth, trying to stifle the sound, but Hawk doesn't even try to mask his laughter.

"Shut the fuck up! Goddammit, Sam, I didn't tell you so you could blast it to every fucking person you happen across," Shane yells, stepping out.

Sam takes off, not for the porch, where Kenzie leans against the railing. No, she comes straight for us, as if we'll save her from one of her psychotic mafia boyfriends. She crouches behind Hawk's bike, wide eyes peeking over the seat, tracking Shane's progress across the yard.

"Leave her alone, Reginald!" Kenzie calls, laughter lacing her voice.

"You stay the hell out of this, Mac. I blame you, anyway." He points at her, still making his way to us.

"Hey! It's not my fault she outed you."

He rounds the bike, where Sam is still pretending she can hide. "Time to go, Princess."

I expect him to reach for her, but he plants his fists on his hips, glaring. Hawk backtracks, but the look he shoots his bike is one of distress. He seems torn between leaving his ride in danger and getting out of the crossfire.

"You heard the man, Sam. Get away from Hawk's bike before he has a heart attack." I chuckle, saving Hawk the trouble.

"I wouldn't hurt it. I mean, it's shiny. I like shiny things." She grins up at Shane, who turns red for some fucking reason. He adjusts himself, and I smother a grin behind my hand.

Shane reaches for her, tosses her over his shoulder as she squeals, and smacks her ass when she demands to be put down. I smirk, glancing at Hawk, but his eyes are fixed on his bike.

"You good?"

He startles, eyes bouncing from me to the still retreating pair and back again before saying, "Yeah, sure. Remember to talk to Mac, like tonight. I'm gonna head out."

"Take someone with ya," I say as he starts his bike, waving a hand in acknowledgment, and he spins before gunning it down the road away from headquarters.

I watch until he turns, and the rumble of his engine fades. A hand slips around my bicep, kneading the muscle. I swing back, finding Kenzie tucked next to me. We watch Shane and Sam bicker as he throws her in the car. Kenzie waves, not that they're paying attention.

"She's happy," she breathes, laying her head on my shoulder.

"Seems like it. What about you?"

"Of course I'm happy. I'm right where I always wanted to be. I mean, it could be better . . ." I glance down at her, and her hair tickles my nose.

"Could be better? Pray tell, what more could I possibly be doing to make my goddess happier?"

She huffs out a laugh. "More ice cream."

I pinch her side, and she jolts. "Oh, her highness requires more ice cream, does she? Was the pint I dripped over you . . ."

"Stop," she squeals, pulling from me, then racing for my porch.

I chase her, letting her stay a couple of steps ahead. She glances behind as she bounds up the stairs. Her hair swings from her ponytail, eyes dancing, a grin stretching her mouth wide. Time slows, the outside world intruding on our bubble, and dozens of motorcycles thunder through the streets. I whip my head toward headquarters, seeing members pause before rushing for their own bikes or back toward the building.

My feet are frozen, torn between rushing to the clubhouse and organizing everything or herding Kenzie to safety. Swinging my head back, I watch as her face drains of color, eyes fixed where engines roar from the east. Horror sweeps over me, leaving me halfway between panic and determination.

"Go," I bark. "MacKenzie, go."

Her eyes find mine on the edge of terror, and she jolts into action, swinging open the door before disappearing inside. I have to trust she'll do what we talked about. The house isn't safe if no one else is here. I have to trust that she'll get to the clubhouse before the Night Slayers appear. I curse myself as I take off for the parking lot. I lulled myself into a sense of security we weren't afforded. I knew they would show, but I dismissed my fears as nothing more than paranoia.

I'm thankful Kenzie and I came up with half a plan if something happened. I'm still pissed, though. I went from being overprotective, never wanting her out of my sight, to believing they forgot about her. Logically, there's no reason they would go to this much work for one woman. The rumble is getting louder, and I pull out my phone as

I run, trying to connect with Hawk, but he could be miles away.

I skid to a stop outside, and all eyes are on me. When Hawk doesn't answer, I call Shane. He might not want to get involved, wanting to keep Sam safe any way he can, but if the Night Slayers take over my territory, he'll have to deal with them.

The call rings out, and I curse, looking around at the members waiting for orders. None of them are in my inner circle. I need my guys around me, helping me orchestrate things. Most of these guys weren't a part of the planning. We had jobs and divisions, but everything went to shit because we thought they would come at night; we thought they wouldn't come at all. The truth is I let them all down. Guilt crashes into me, threatening to pull me under. Dialing Mason's number, I suck in a breath.

"Helms," he answers before the first ring stops beeping in my ear.

"Byrns. They're here. I don't have anyone."

Ignoring the glare from the surrounding men, I force the words from my throat. These guys might be my family, but they're not the same. Fighting another MC, one who doesn't care whether innocents get caught in the crossfire, is a fight my guys have never been in, unless you count the Guild, and I kept them outside the boundaries then. We run our little section of Synd with rarely any issues—until now.

"I'll do what I can." He hangs up.

The roaring gets louder, and I wonder if they're tormenting the other people who live here. Are they setting more fires? Burning down more of my people's livelihoods?

I can't pick up any gunshots, so at least they're not killing anyone *yet*.

I point to Snag. He's barely an adult but has been here for years. He rushes to me, pushing through the others.

"What do ya need, Prez?" His eager face peers at me, and I hate what I have to do.

"Clear headquarters. Then set up post on the west side. No one in, no one out, unless you know they're on our side. If there's even a hint they're corrupt, deny or shoot." He nods, running for his bike.

I send groups off, trying to divide them as best I can with so little time. The prospects are tasked with hustling people off the streets while the members are sent to secure the boundaries.

We could have a whole ass firefight in the middle of the fucking day, trying to pick each other off one-by-one, but it's too risky. Better to funnel them out, catch them as they leave. I'm banking on them pulling out if they can't find anyone. Hiding grates at me, but I'd rather live today to fight tomorrow.

I slip around the corner of the clubhouse, the last of the members disappearing as the east end of the street fills with shiny metal roaring out their arrival. There's no mistaking they're Night Slayers. I'd put my whole club up to say the one in front is Kane Riley. I can't make out more than his shaved head, but the insignia on his vest is garish. Bright, almost neon-yellow and blood-red, the laughing skull is hard to miss. I peer around the corner as they creep along. Clearly, they're searching for my people, but they won't find them here.

At least twenty guys roll up, most covered in Night Slayers' colors, but a half a dozen stick out like sore thumbs, the rearing black and green viper plastered on their leathers. Fuck, Kenzie's guys were right. The Night Slayers took full advantage of the loss of leadership within the ranks of the Raines' club and took over. These must be the members who welcomed them with open arms. My stomach tightens, wondering what they did with the rest. Will Dante even have a club to resurrect when he shows the fuck up?

I pull my head back, sneaking through the fence and following it along, then dash across the opening until I reach my back door. I flip all five locks I installed after Maddox tried to kidnap Kenzie. I watch through the curtain while I check the weapons I have stashed in every possible place I could think of.

The growling bikes creep closer, several peeling off into the parking lot, and I pray Snag remembered to lock the door behind him. Others take side streets, until there's only a few stopping in front of my house, but not Kane. The asshole streaks past, turning the same corner Shane and Hawk took.

I'm trying to keep my eye on everything at once, but it's impossible. A truly ugly man cuts his engine and swings his tree trunk of a leg over his seat. The rest stay, their bikes still running, and one calls out, but I can't hear what he says. The man rubs a hand over his shaved head, throwing his head back and laughing. This doesn't feel like an ambush, but then again, maybe they're so sure of their victory he doesn't care I could easily shoot him. He'd hit the ground before they could react. I grit my teeth, resisting the urge to do exactly that.

"Helms!" he bellows from the bottom of the porch steps, a sneering grin still on his mouth. I think about not answering, but they'd just break down the door.

"You're in Reaper territory. Best to move along before you regret it." My lip curls as a sour taste invades my mouth. I hate not lashing out.

He laughs, the others joining. "Is that so? Well, you have something that belongs to us. Hand her over, and we'll get out of your little shithole."

Rage courses through me, and my muscles bunch, the metal of the gun handle biting into my flesh. As if my Kenzie is an object, a misplaced toy to be retrieved. Wondering where the fuck my guys are at, where the Byrns and Kings are, and why the fuck no one is calling me back, I glance at my phone. The chances of these men riding away without Kenzie is slim, but I can't fight them all on my own. Then they'll have what they want, me dead and Kenzie stuffed in some hole, broken, a wisp of herself.

"Don't know who you're talkin' about. Not a lot of people passing through these days," I yell, watching his face redden.

"Then we'll just have to go looking for her ourselves, then, won't we?"

"I suggest you leave, or they'll be finding you in the river tomorrow."

He lifts a tattooed hand and scrubs at his head again, turning away. A phone appears in his hand. I switch windows, sending a text to my men, hoping they see it in time. He ends his call, yelling over his shoulder as he walks back to his bike.

"We'll be back, and we'll be collectin' what's ours. Be ready, Reapers."

The tension remains long after they've ridden away, the streets falling silent in their wake. I send out another text asking for updates, and they trickle in slowly. I slam the back door open. By the time I reach the clubhouse, I'm running, praying Kenzie stayed hidden. I don't know why they rode away. I don't know why they didn't come in, guns ready to take us all out. We aren't ready. If they come back with an army, we're fucked.

THIRTY-SIX

MacKenzie

The darkness is all-encompassing. I always thought taking away sight was supposed to make the other senses come alive, working overtime to compensate for the loss, but all that's enhanced is my nose. My nostrils twitch when I breathe too deep, catching the coppery scent of blood. I'm tucked in a room under the clubhouse behind three automatic locks.

Thoughts swirl in my brain, trying to send me into a panic, but I'm battling against them. I suck in another breath, the mustiness dancing in the back of my throat, immediately regretting my actions. I don't know if I can get out if something happens to the people who know I'm down here. Ryker never said either way, and I didn't think to ask. Seems like something we should have discussed.

When Ryker first showed me this room, I balked, refusing to enter. I almost lost it, memories of my time in another basement swamping my senses. Three false walls bury the stairs that lead to this room. No windows, concrete floors, and some mysterious liquid on the floor, the room felt like a tomb—a coffin to stuff me in to rot away for decades until some random company buys the structure and demolishes everything. I'm not surprised I didn't know it was here, especially when I was a kid. I would have run, screaming for the hills, had I known it existed. Ryker said no one else knew, either, just our dads. Thank god. Maddox would have shoved me down here for sure.

Steadying my heartbeat, I suck in a breath, which threatens to smash its way through my rib cage, but all the techniques Ren told me are failing. The darkness is debilitating. The lack of sound, other than my own harsh breaths, presses on my eardrums, and I swear they'll pop at any moment, leaving me without two of my senses. I close my eyes, hoping it helps, but all it does is send flashes of my time with the Night Slayers behind my lids.

Kane's leering face dances by. I only saw him three times, but his features are imprinted in my brain. Thin lips, soulless brown eyes, sharp ridges everywhere, and a jagged scar ripping down his face from temple to chin, pulling his right eye at the corner enough to be disconcerting. Even his hair, bleach blond and cut short on the sides, blunt across the top, is memorable. He radiates evil, and I don't think I've ever been more scared in my life. Not when Maddox tried to shoot me with a BB gun. Not when Dante dared me to swim across the river, when I almost drowned. Not when my father got too drunk and threw things, taking his anger out on anyone who didn't run fast enough. Those memories pale in comparison to Kane's face ogling my body as I lay beaten on the floor of his clubhouse. I refuse to sit, the floors being too similar to those at the Night Slayers' headquarters. The flashbacks would overwhelm me and then I won't be any use to anyone.

I wish I could hear someone coming. No one can get in without the code, so I'm not afraid of someone stumbling upon me, but knowing they're on the other side of the door would settle my nerves. The unknown eats away at my sanity. If I knew Ryker was there, close to freeing me from this self-imposed prison, maybe I could calm my ass down. Crossing my arms over my stomach, squeezing tightly, I hope the pressure will relieve the rolling in my stomach. To think that, just a little while ago, I was laughing, dashing away from Ryker's smiling face.

He might be dead, a voice in my head whispers. A sob rolls up my throat, but I choke it back, refusing to give in to the demons of my past. No longer able to stand, I crouch in the corner, pressing myself as far into the walls as I can.

"He's fine. He's coming. He promised he'd come. He'll always come. He'll come," I babble in a hushed tone. Over and over I try to convince myself he's on his way.

A beep from the door has my head snapping up. Though, rationally, I know it must be Ryker. The dread gripping me is unyielding. When the door swings open, the single light bulb from the hallway blinds me. I throw an arm over my face. Tears, whether from the sudden light or the relief, sting my eyes as panic courses through my body.

"Kenzie," Ryker breathes, and I feel his arms gather around me, but it's as if there's a layer of film between us.

I can feel him, but it's muted, like I'm in a bubble he can't penetrate.

His hand pulls my arm down, and he cups my cheeks with his hands. I still don't open my eyes, afraid of the light after so long in the darkness. His lips ghost across mine, and the spell is broken, the bubble gone. I throw my arms around his neck, sobbing into his shoulder. He shushes me until I quiet, and my eyes become slits, but the light no longer stabs at my brain.

"Are you okay? Is everyone okay? Is he . . ." I can't ask, but I need to know. The answer might break me, but not knowing will hurt more.

"Everyone's fine. The plan went exactly how we expected. He rode off, slipping out a section we weren't monitoring," he murmurs, tugging me to my feet.

"But everyone is okay?"

Ryker tucks an arm around my waist before leading me out of my temporary prison, waiting until we're on the main level before answering.

"Yes, not one bullet fired. Kenz, they'll be back, though. I'm sorry, baby, but you might have to go back down there. I'll get you a light and a chair, like we talked about."

I'm shaking my head before he finishes. He blames himself for my state, but he shouldn't put more on his shoulders. We didn't have enough time to fully execute this plan. Being a little uncomfortable for however long is better than being dead.

Men trickle back in, gathering in groups, their voices creating a low din, which flows over the space. I didn't realize there were so many Reapers. For some reason, them bunched up like they are, it seems like there's more of them than there were at the meeting. I spot Sam bolting through the front doors, followed by her brother and Shane.

"Mac! Are you okay?" Sam runs her hands over my arms before crouching and skimming her hands down my legs, checking for injuries. Ryker yanks me back, away from her questing hands, and a smile breaks free.

"I'm fine. Nothing happened," I say as she glares at Ryker.

"Then, why are you crying?" she demands.

"The room I was in isn't great for my anxiety. It's fine. We'll fix it." I send a soft smile to Ryker, hoping to reassure him, but doubt still dances in his eyes. I squeeze his hand, which still has my hip in a death grip.

"Why didn't you fix it before?" Sam swings toward Ryker, and I can't help the smile from blooming across my face.

At five and a half feet, Ryker towers over her, but his face flushes.

"Leave it, Sam. We didn't have time. It's not a big deal. I lasted a lot longer than I thought I would." I wave away her concern, as Shane and Mason join us.

Exhaustion pulls at the edges of my vision, and I lean into Ryker more. It's the middle of the day, but after the emotional rollercoaster, I need a nap.

Ryker's lips pull into a frown. He cuts off whatever Shane is saying, then leads me back home and tucks me into bed. I don't fight him, no matter how much I want to hear about what happened. His hand brushing my hair from my forehead is the sensation I fall asleep to, content regardless of the threats hanging over our heads.

Fireworks wake me, and I jolt upright. The bedroom is dark, and I throw back the comforter, cursing Ryker for letting me sleep so long. Now I'll be up half the night. Another round of pops crackle, followed by shouts, and my heart stills. Not fireworks. Those are bullets.

I scramble up to slip my feet into my sandals. They'll slow me down, but I don't have time to search for anything else. I snatch my phone off the nightstand, and the attached cord whips around, sending the lamp crashing to the ground. Great, now I've broken both of them.

My feet pound down the hall. I skid to a stop at the top of the stairs, straining to hear anything. I should go out the back, like before. I should be half way there, but if they've surrounded us, I'll put myself in more danger by going in the open. The fight is further away to the east, but with sounds reverberating off the buildings and houses, I can't tell how far. I creep down the stairs. Fingering the curtain to peer out, I catch an orange glow in the distance, and my breath stalls. They're back, setting fires. They're wreaking havoc on the Reapers, killing whoever they can find.

Ryker almost had me convinced it wouldn't come to this. I was on the verge of believing we could settle this whole thing in Rima. Then I could stay here, live in peace without threats hanging over my head, but my dream is evaporating before my eyes.

Purring bikes mix with the gunfire ricocheting around me. I slide away, letting the curtain flutter back into place. I shove the guilt deep. I don't have time to deal with it. I'll handle the consequences of my decisions later—if I live. My phone buzzes, and I answer as I hurry toward the back door.

"Ryker? Where are you?"

Stupid question. He doesn't have time for stupid questions.

"Get to the safe room. Run, Kenzie. Run."

His strained breathless voice rings down the line, along with the chaos of wherever he is. He's probably right in the thick of it, still calling me, always trying to protect me. A whimper slips out. I fling open the back door, not bothering to close it as I dash for the trees.

"I'm going. I'm almost there. I . . . I . . ." I swallow as the darkness of the trees envelops me. "I love you."

I pull the phone away to stare at the screen, but it's dark. Tears fill my eyes, but I brush them away in annoyance. I didn't want to tell him like that, anyway. He knows. He has to know. I've made it clear, even if I've never said it so plainly. I resolve to tell him when this is over. Adrenaline courses through me, keeping the panic at bay, and I can't afford to break down.

I thread my way through the trees, bouncing between shadows. There aren't any lights back here to guide me, but I don't need them. The way is the same as it's always been. I spent hours walking this line between my house and the clubhouse, trying to sneak into meetings or spy on what the boys were doing. I don't need the light, but it would have helped to see if anyone else will ambush me.

Listening to the crickets still chirping, I pause every five feet, despite the clash of fighting rolling closer. The night falls silent, and I freeze. Even the breeze rustling the leaves over my head ceases, and the hair on the back of my neck stands up. I scan the area in front of me, but there's nothing there. I'm barely twenty feet from the back door of headquarters and less than a minute from the safe room. I can make it if I sprint, which I'm never happy about, but I can make it. My muscles tense, and I peer around one last time.

A branch snapping behind has me stumbling forward a step. I spin, blood running cold when I spot Kane. He's hiding in the woods, watching me with a lascivious grin. His eyes are black in the moonlight like a demon, straight from the depths of hell. He wiggles his fingers, like we were on a merry little game of tag, and revulsion cramps my stomach. I gag when the humid summer air smothers my lungs.

The step he takes spurns me into action. I push off a tree to pivot and then sprint for safety. His laugh chases me, footsteps crashing through the brush, and I push my body harder.

I'm not built for this, I think as my hip scrapes the bark when I'm ten feet from the door. My brain and emotions disconnect, leaving my body to deal with the anxiety and panic, while my brain analyzes why I didn't pick up running when I was younger. They crash back together when Kane's harsh pants ghosts across the back of my neck. I lean forward, trying to keep my feet under me. The door warps, the space around it glistening, and the metal retreats further away. A sob escapes me, and I know—

I'm not going to make it.

THIRTY-SEVEN

Ryker

I wipe the sweat from my forehead, dirt and blood mixing, coating my sleeve. I've ducked around a corner of the bakery to reload, but I'm running out of bullets. We've tried to keep the Night Slayers as far from the center of our territory as possible, but men have been peeling off from the fight, trying to sneak through. I assume they're off to set more fires or find Kenzie. I shake my head, pushing her from my mind. I can't dwell on the what-ifs. I need to concentrate on the fight in front of me and trust she made it to the safe room in time. I never should have left her with only a prospect to watch the house. Fucker took off as soon as the first gunshot lit up the night. What should have been a simple errand turned into a firefight.

"Helms, heads up!" Hawk's voice rings out.

I shuffle into the shadows as a silver canister lands five feet from me, smoke already spewing from it. Fucking hell. I'll be happy if I never see another smoke bomb in my life. I kick the metal before it can cover too much of my sight. It sails back toward the opposite end of the street as Hawk appears behind me, who's just as dirty as I am.

"Where the fuck did they come from?" I grumble, though it's the least of our worries.

"We thought they'd hit the main road, but they rushed the east and hit 'em hard. I don't know if they were able to push them back. More likely our guys retreated over the bridge. Jumper got a text to me before he went silent—said there was at least forty of them," he pants, handing me another magazine as he peers over my shoulder.

"Well, we can't keep this up. Where the fuck are our reinforcements?" I bellow over the gunshots echoing off the buildings.

"Mason called, said he's got some guys on the way, but apparently, there's more Night Slayers blocking the streets. All our allies are on the outside fighting their way in. We lined the west bridge with shells, hoping the cars would block their bikes from getting across. We've got the prospects on the bridge, but there's not a lot going on down there."

"What about the north? No fires, right? The last thing we need is the forest burning around us." I gaze into the smoke-filled night, trying to distinguish who is who.

"Ryker, we can't hold the main roads for long. We need to hit them now, before they get further in, or we're going to lose the territory."

Tiny takes out a Viper, blood splattering on his face. Hawk is right, but I don't want to admit it. The last thing I want to do is tear up my territory. I can't imagine the aftermath I'll have to deal with, but it's preferable to being dead. Scanning the street, I shake my head. It's quieter than it was, the fight moving closer to the center, closer to Kenzie.

"Fine. We'll blow the fucker up."

Not wanting to discuss anything else, I stomp past him. He'll take care of his side, but I need to be inside the line before he does. I rush to my bike, tucked in the backyard of a now-vacant house. I kick it to life before spinning around to roar away, the noise being lost in the chaos lighting up the night. I don't want to run from the main fight, but Hawk can handle it. I'll lead the ones inside the demarcation line.

Blasting through yards and back alleys, I stay away from the main road. I slow when I reach the main street, a mere five blocks from headquarters. It's quieter here, the orange glow from the fires the Night Slayers set blazing across the sky in the distance. I can't see my house from here, but an itch in the back of my brain and a voice in my head whispers to find her.

The small concrete building is tucked far enough away from the road, barely visible from where I'm standing. Most people walk by it every day, ignorant of its existence. I remember the first time Dad brought me here, bitching on the bullshit the mafia leaders were doing and how this would protect us. He never said what they actually did. Shit went sideways, and he was dead. He fucked himself. Apparently, the Reapers weren't the only ones who had the bright idea to layer their territory with explosives. That certainly made the meetings I had with Shane and Mason after we took over more interesting. We've never used any of the systems in place, though we came close when the Guild came through.

Before I punch in the code on the keypad, I shoot off a text to Mason and Shane. Dad had a key he wore around his neck, firmly against technology, but I wasn't about to do that shit. I upgraded and expanded, looped in the other leaders and hoped I'd never have to use it. I duck inside, and the lights flicker on, blinding me. Before, this place was filled with tires and gasoline. Dad's grand plan was to drag them over the road and set the fuckers on fire. That was the first thing I got rid of.

Four computer screens line the back wall, each controlling a different part of the territory. I won't have to worry about the west side, since Tank and the prospects took care of it, and Hawk will deal with the east. I doubt I'll have to set the forest on fire, and that's only for things like a zombie apocalypse. I wasn't a fan of burning the woods down, but at least, if it ever goes down, I'll be dead.

The commands are a string of letters and numbers. I don't know what they mean, but I've memorized the steps. I still pull out the codes from a lock box sunken into the floor. The last thing I'd want to do is fuck it up and blow up my members on the bridge. Ren talked about streamlining our process, make it easier to operate, but we never got around to it. There's a lot of things I haven't gotten around to.

I type everything in, double-checking before I pause, finger hovering over the button. A boom echoes out from the west side, rumbling through the night, and my head whips up. Another explosion rings out, and I slam my finger down. The computer chimes, then starts beeping. We've tested the system, but I hold my breath, waiting for the long tone that's supposed to follow, but it never comes. It keeps beeping, faster and faster, then a message flashes on the screen, too fast for me to fully comprehend. The only word I catch is headquarters, and ice floods my veins.

"Fuck," I breathe as another message pops up, asking if I want to proceed. The whole screen goes black, though the beeping continues.

A low siren outside starts up, sounding out a slow pattern. The time between tones will shorten the more time passes, alerting the others to get inside the boundaries. Whatever I put into the computer, though, set headquarters to blow, and I can't turn it off from here. The checks and balances we put in place seemed like a good idea at the time, but I wonder how bad I fucked up. I wanted to ferret out anyone who slipped past our lines, not race for the clubhouse to stop it from exploding.

Abandoning my bike, I sprint for headquarters, gasping by the time it comes into view. I loop around the side to access a little-used door, then slip inside. No one comes down this hallway, since there's only one small room. The computer flashes to life once I'm inside, and I shut off the countdown, breathing a sigh of relief when it stops. Once I'm back outside, I'm torn between checking on Kenzie and rooting out anyone who got past me, plus finding the rest of my guys. An orange glow billows from the west where Hawk is, and a chill runs down my back. I fucking hope they didn't have to blow the bridge. The clean-up will be a bitch.

I start back toward where I left my bike, scanning the parking lot, when a scream rings out from behind me between the siren warnings still blaring into the night. I recognize her scream, laced with pain. I wobble, my legs almost giving out, and the world tilts. Rage courses through me, burning away the fear paralyzing me, and I sprint back to headquarters. I slow, and a shadow skips across the clubhouse's open door. I have no plan. I have no idea what I'm walking into, but I don't care. I don't have time to execute the rest of our plans. I'll have to trust the rest of the Reapers to deal with everything else.

I burst through the doors, surveying the space. The single light in the back casts shadows in the corners. I zero in on the middle of the room. Kane's nose is skewed and dripping blood into Kenzie's dark hair, one arm cinched around her waist. His hand is wrapped around her neck, pinching her airway. Rage explodes inside me, and my vision tunnels, leaving only Kenzie's frightened face front and center. Her tears leave tracks through the dirt smeared across her cheeks, but other than a small cut on her forehead, she appears uninjured. I meet her wide, hazel eyes, screaming silently at me to run, as if I would.

"Helms, how convenient," Kane sneers, the scar running down his face forcing his mouth lopsided.

I don't respond, the siren ringing out in the streets penetrating the roaring in my ears. The time between the tones is shortening, bit by bit. I meet Kenzie's eye again, begging her to hold on.

"Let's get down to business," he says, running his nose along her hairline, her body shuddering. Her arms are trapped under his, but her fingers wiggle, back and forth.

"The only business we have is me putting a bullet in your head."

He tips his head back, forcing Kenzie's body to lean with him, as he brays, the sound grating on my taunt nerves. I use the distraction to map the space between us. Most of the tables are pushed to the side, but a few block my way to her. I could vault over them, but it will slow me down. He doesn't have a weapon on her, but he's the type who likes to use his fists instead of a knife.

"Here's how this is going to go. You're going to give me your territory, and I'll let you have this plump morsel."

A strangled noise falls from her lips as he flexes his hand. Kane dips his head, tongue flicking, licking her from chin to temple. A gurgle of disgust falls from her mouth. I flex my hand, forcing it away from my gun. Kenzie mouths a 'no,' tears streaming down her face. A burst of pride swells in my chest. Gone is the mania from her eyes, holding on in the face of her tormentor.

"Deal." My words drop into the silence.

I'm not stupid. I won't get out alive. He'll kill me, but maybe I can give her a fighting chance. Rage flames through me as he shifts, gripping her breast hard as he kneads her flesh through her shirt.

"Too bad I didn't get to ride this bitch. Maybe later," he sneers.

Kenzie jerks, and Kane's knuckles whiten, cutting off her denial. I shake my head, hoping she'll understand my decisions. Every time I have the choice, I'll choose her. If there's a sliver of a chance she'll make it out, I'll give it to her. Her life is worth a thousand of mine.

"No fun. Here I thought you'd fight, but . . ." He shrugs, looking off to the side.

The siren is a constant tone resonating through the air. Kenzie's eyes grow wide, recognition dawning in them, and I nod subtly. Kane swings his eyes back to me, death swimming in their depths. He opens his mouth, but an explosion thunders through the air, rolling across the territory in a wave. The ground shakes, and my eyes are pulled from her to steady myself.

The glint of a blade flashes from the corner of my eye, and Kenzie's hand swings down. The knife disappears into Kane's leg. He roars over the explosions still echoing through the night, releasing her, and she stumbles toward me. Shoving her behind me, I launch myself at Kane. I tackle him to the ground. A thud reverberates when his head bashes onto the tiles, but his hands still reach for me. I expect him to go for the handle sticking from his leg, but his fist cracks across my face.

Pain explodes from my cheek, radiating down. I barely feel it over the adrenaline coursing through me as I pound into him. He blocks my blows. Kenzie's shouts, distracting me enough to push off him and turn to her. Eyes wide, she drops the phone in her hand, soundlessly screaming as a gunshot rings out. I'm falling at her feet, darkness invading my mind.

THIRTY-EIGHT

MacKenzie

When Ryker's body falls, something in me breaks, and I fall to my knees. All my fears, my worst nightmares, are becoming reality, but the pain is so much worse than I thought. Kane's battered face is almost unrecognizable, but his psychotic grin, teeth streaked with blood, hasn't changed. He coughs out a laugh, causing more blood to splatter across the floor, mingling with the pool of red growing from under Ryker's prone body. Kane is still lying on the floor, blade sticking from his leg, but he's propped himself up on an elbow, the barrel of his gun pointed straight at me.

Tears fall, momentarily blinding me, and the crack in my chest widens. What's the point if Ryker is gone? Why fight when there's nothing left to fight for? I wasted all that time waiting and fighting. I can't live a lifetime without him, not after I found him again. He'd tell me to run. He'd tell me to fight. He'd tell me to not give up, but his voice is a fading echo in my head, bleeding out like his body.

"Guess it's just you and me, baby," Kane laughs, more blood trickling from the corner of his lips. The pain in my chest snaps, and rage fills my veins, boiling away the heartache.

"Fuck you," I spit, eyes narrowing. I struggle to my feet, eyes trained on the gun, which wavers in his grasp. I don't know what Ryker did to him, how bad he beat him. Between me stabbing him and Kane hitting his head, he isn't doing very well.

He tips his head back, cackling. He must be deranged with how much he laughs. He has nothing in his life to be joyful about. Kane thrives on pain, feeding off other's sorrows, until they're a husk of themselves. He laughs while he's inflicting whatever tortures he employs. I skid around Ryker, fold my fingers around Kane's wrist, and force the gun up. The shot drowns out his shouting, and I swear the bullet grazes my face. Kane struggles to push himself up, the blood loss hitting him. I grab the knife handle and yank it out. I expect to get hit with a spray of blood, but it seeps out, soaking his jeans and dying them red.

Kane's hand is suddenly around the blade, squeezing until more blood escapes from between his fingers. He tugs me closer, bearing his bloodstained teeth. I try to force the gun from his grip, but he's holding on too tight. He's too strong, even in his weakened state, and a wave of cold flows over me.

At least I won't have to live without Ryker.

Kane's eyes turn glassy, and he shakes his head violently.

I yell as I drag the knife down, giving up on the gun. It slides through his hand easily now, the blade sliding through his flesh like butter. My elbow snaps back, and I drive the blade forward, sinking the blade into his chest, just below his ribs. The strangest noise leaves him, a cross between the howl of a wolf and the shriek of a hawk, as he falls on his arm. I stab down again, and he lifts his hand, but his feeble attempt to stop me isn't enough. I shove his hand, holding the gun to the side, falling more on top of him.

His mouth forms an O when I wretch my blood-soaked wrist from his grasp. I stab him in the throat. The gurgling reminds me of the fountain at the Kings' house. A bubble of crazed laughter escapes me, followed closely by a sob, as I scramble off his blood-soaked body. I can't pull my eyes away as Kane's head bobs, fingers frantically curling around the dark slash I've made. Another laugh finds its way up my throat, but it's drowned out by the ringing in my ears as I brace my hands on the tiles.

All at once, everything stops. For ten seconds, I'm frozen in shock, then everything rushes back in. My breaths panting in and out of me, a siren wailing from miles away, the smell of carnage and death, a coppery taste filling my mouth, a stickiness coating my fingers, my vision clearing, colors bursting across the space. Everything was muted before, but now the bright ruby pool oozes across the white tiles, the flecks being absorbed as it spreads. The adrenaline I felt winks out, and exhaustion aches in my bones.

I crawl to Ryker, no longer trusting my legs to hold me. They've gone numb, tingling in a way I'm not sure is normal. I'm crying again, but I wipe them away, needing to see him clearly. I shouldn't move him. Hell, I don't know if I could, especially in my current state. My phone is crackling, someone yelling my name on the other end. I can't focus on anything other than Ryker.

I prop my shoulder under his arm before pushing, but he doesn't move. I heave into him one more time, gritting my teeth, then his body rolls, arm thudding next to him. I sit back, wetness seeping into my jeans. I fix my eyes on his chest, silently begging for movement, though I'm already convinced he's gone. His wound is hidden, but judging by the amount of blood and the fact he dropped almost immediately . . .

I reach out but yank it away, scrubbing the blood from my palm. When I slide it back, I notice the tremble in my limbs. In fact, my entire body is shaking as I lay my hand on his chest, willing breath into his lungs.

I should do chest compressions. I should stop the bleeding. I should call someone. I'm frozen, my hand fused to his body, begging the universe to give him back. My throat burns as I swallow the bile trying to force its way out. Closing my eyes, I press my ear to his chest, holding my breath. The roar in my head is too loud to hear his heartbeat, though.

I don't know how long I stay, kneeling beside him, but at some point, I think I black out. Arms gripping me, dragging me backward, jolts me back to reality. Someone is screaming. No, I'm screaming, sobbing his name over and over. His shirt is soaked with blood and tears, and I clamp my mouth shut. Ink and Hawk hover over Ryker, shouting to each other. They roll his body, searching for his wound.

His shirt, ripped up the back, gives them access, and I turn away. My stomach rolls and bile fills my mouth, making me gag. I brace my hands on the chilled tiles, and my mouth waters. The vomit travels upward, and I can't hold it back anymore. A warm hand clamps around the back of my neck, another rubbing circles, which would be soothing in any other instance, but now it only serves to make me heave again.

"He's not dead, Mac. Breathe. He's not dead. He needs to hear you. Pull yourself together." Doc's soft voice fills my head, his breath wisps past my ear.

His words filter through the anguish. I suck in a lungful of tainted air, holding it deep inside until the nausea subsides. I crawl toward Ryker again, but Hawk is in my way. I tug at his hand, trying to shove him aside, but he doesn't move. I scratch at his arm, shrieking at him, but he only shifts slightly, and I latch on to Ryker's hand lying limp by his side.

Doc picks me up as if I weigh nothing, and dizziness invades my head. I buck, and he settles me close to Ryker's pale, lifeless face. He's turned toward me, so I lean in. Resting my lips on his cheek, I jerk, finding his skin warm, and hope swells in my chest. I whisper in his ear, not registering my words, but knowing Doc is right. Ryker needs to hear my voice. He needs to know I'm here. I need him to hear me, to come back, to fight for us like I did.

I lay down, fitting my head next to his, murmuring to him, my chest tightening, and I wonder if Doc lied. Did he tell me Ryker lived so I wouldn't lose it again while they tried to yank him from death's arms? My ray of hope is dimming, leaving a bleak wasteland inside me, but I keep talking. I scoot closer, speaking against his lips, his name a prayer on mine.

A twitch against my mouth has me gasping. My eyes fly open, watching his lids as they flutter the slightest bit.

"Ryker," I breathe.

His lids crack open, the blue muted and dull, staring into mine. "Kenz." His voice is barely there, and his body jerks.

"Don't talk. Just . . . just . . . stay," I cry softly, blinking the tears from my eyes, but they fall anyway.

"Kenz," he sighs, eyes falling closed.

"No, Ryker, no. Open your eyes. I need you to stay with me. You promised."

His eyes creep open again at my demanding tone, and the corner of his mouth twitches. "Do . . . what . . . I . . . want."

"You stupid fucking man. I swear to everything on this earth if you die, I'm going to kill you."

"Love . . . you . . . too."

THIRTY-NINE

Ryker

Every fucking part of my body hurts. Between the fight with the Night Slayers and Kane shooting me, I don't think I've ever felt this fucking terrible. Every time I've woken in the past four days, someone is whispering outside the door. Blinding light filters through the curtains. Turning my head away, I groan. The door swings open and crashes against the wall, and I crack my eyelids, hoping it's Kenzie's face, but it's Hawk, crouching by my head.

"Hey, Prez, gotta pee?" he grins.

"What"—I clear my dry throat—"the fuck."

Shoving an arm under me to lift me up enough to drink the water he's holding in front of my face, he laughs. I glare at the straw but concede. I'll drown if I don't use it.

I fall back, groaning again, when my muscles protest. I don't know how Kenzie dealt with this. If she felt anywhere near as terrible as I do, she's officially my hero. I'm going to worship at her feet for the rest of my days. I'd do that regardless, but now I'll do it with more enthusiasm.

"Seriously, though, do you need to pee? 'Cause I don't fancy changing your sheets again with you in the bed. That shit's hard," he says, looming over me.

"Are you saying I peed the bed?" I don't have the energy to be embarrassed.

"Only twice. Don't worry, I let Mac dress you." He winks, and I shut my eyes again, grumbling under my breath.

"Where is she?" I croak, watching him frown from under my lashes.

"Uh, she's around." He's hedging. My VP isn't good at lying, and my heart jumps.

"Where the fuck is she?" I try to push up on my elbows, but I collapse, my back screaming in protest.

"She's fine. Don't hurt yourself again. She's just not right here at the moment. She's going to be pissed you woke up. Honestly, she's a bit scary." Hawk glances to the hallway, as if she'll appear and start yelling at him.

"Where?" is the only word I can get out.

The tension drains, but I need to see her. The memory of her face inches from mine, whispering words I couldn't make out, flits across my mind. I can't separate reality from dreams at this point. Exhaustion folds over me, like a warm blanket, but I fight against it, needing him to answer.

"She's running an errand. Go back to sleep. I bet she'll be here when you wake up next." He walks away to tug the curtains, and the sunlight is cut off, casting the room in muted shadows. I want to ask more questions, but the darkness reaches up, pulling me under again.

When I open my eyes next, nothing changes, and for a second, I freak out, thinking I've gone blind. Then I spot the thin line of light from under the bathroom door. I blink again, rolling my head around, but no one is here. Slowly shifting each of my muscles, I squeeze my hands into fists. When they ease, I reach for the glass next to me, propping up on an elbow and almost spilling myself on the floor in the process. The glass falls, bouncing across the hardwood instead of making it back on the nightstand, and I sigh.

The bathroom door flies open, and there she is, hair a riot around her head, in nothing but a tank top and thong, dashing toward me. The frantic look on her face has me smiling. Unable to hold myself up anymore, I collapse back on to the pillows as something burns in my back at the motion. She falls to her knees next to the bed before flipping back the covers to run her hands down my body, sending tingles through me. I doubt I have the energy to do much, but my cock didn't get the memo, and it twitches when she brushes against it. She scowls, finally meeting my eyes and flinging the comforter over me again.

"Can't help it," I rasp, grinning.

"This is hardly the time, Ryker," she scolds, but my smile grows.

"It's not me, it's you." I chuckle, but it turns to a cough, and I groan, curling in on myself.

"Serves you right for making such a terrible joke." Her hands flutter over the sheets, and I catch her trembling hand in mine.

"Where were you?" It's not what I wanted to say, but the words slip out before I can stop them.

She squeezes my hand, smoothing the hair back from my forehead before answering. "I'm not going to tell you until I'm sure you won't hurt yourself more. I'm not going to ask if you can handle yourself because we both know you can't. So, you'll have to wait. We'll talk about it when you won't rip your stitches leaping from the bed in a fit."

"Kane."

"He's dead. I"—she meets my eyes—"I killed him. And I don't regret it."

Pride swells in my chest, and my eyes fall closed, a smile blooming across my lips. Of course she did. I'd expect nothing else from my girl.

"Don't fall asleep yet. You need to take some meds." I open my eyes as she cups my face. "Here."

I swallow them dry, making her gag. On the edge of oblivion, I feel her wrap her hand around my arm, and I slip my hand on her thigh, gripping her tight as I float away into sleep.

I'm still hanging on to her when I wake hours later. She's fast asleep next to me, face serene, but the dark circles under her eyes give away how much she's been giving up for me. I squeeze, needing to feel her soft skin beneath my touch, to reassure myself she's here, safe. The door opens and Hawk pokes his head in. When he sees I'm awake, he strides in, followed closely by Ink, who's holding a backpack. I cringe, anticipating being poked and prodded. I still don't have the full story, but I shouldn't have turned my back on Kane. A bullet hole is worth it if it kept Kenzie safe, though.

"I need to check your stitches. You still got pants on?" Ink glares as I lift the blanket, seeing the world's smallest boxers covering me, and grins.

"Yeah, we're good."

"Don't trust him. Last time he was wearing tightie-whities." Hawk shudders, turning away.

Kenzie stretches, her leg sliding away, and my hand chases after her skin. Blinking, she spots Ink and Hawk hovering by the bed. She snatches the covers closer to her chest, sending me into a fit of laughter, which ends in a groan.

"Stop laughing," Ink commands, still scowling. "Mac, you might wanna go get dressed. We're getting him up today."

She scrambles from the bed, taking the comforter with her, while she races for the closet, dark hair streaming after her. The choking noise coming from Ink has me focusing on him once again. His face is etched in horror, staring at my underwear.

"What the fuck are those?" He tips his head up, gagging.

I chuckle. "I have no idea. You'd have to ask Kenz. I didn't even know I owned something like this."

"Sam and I went shopping. They were all I could find at the time," Kenzie's muffled shout comes from behind the closet door.

"Let's make this quick so I don't have to stare at your dick longer than necessary. Hawk, go get him some actual clothes."

"Do not come in here!" she shouts.

Hawk pivots, dropping into the chair next to the window, flushing. Ink has me roll over, the pulling from my wound excruciating. I wish I could grit my teeth and pretend pain doesn't exist, but this is the worst agony I've ever been in. Fuck Ink if he thinks I'm going to sit up, much less walk. He can go straight to hell. This shit is too hard. I'm gasping into the pillow. I don't have the energy to turn my head, though I'll suffocate this way. I'm not sure I care.

Kenzie's hands run through my hair, gently turning me to the side, and her face fills my vision. The bed dips as she settles next to me. This is the moment it would be great to be some meathead who doesn't feel anything, so she'd know how strong I am, but when Ink prods my back, a guttural scream leaves me, cutting off when I lose my breath.

"Just a little bit longer," she whispers. I latch on to her leg, trying not to squeeze too hard.

"This sucks."

"I'm sorry."

"Not your fault, baby. Besides, you took him . . ."

My sentence ends on a hiss, and she wraps a hand around the back of my neck, threading her fingers in my hair and tugging. The twinge doesn't come close to the rolling waves of anguish radiating across my body. I can't tell where I was hit. I open my mouth to ask, but a yelp comes out instead.

"Talk to me," I rasp, locking eyes with Kenzie.

"Okay, well, I stabbed Kane twice. Whatever you did to him"—her eyes turn glassy—"it helped."

My back spasms, and I grit my teeth, slamming my eyes shut. I don't know why they didn't just take me to the hospital. They have the good drugs there. My ass could be dead asleep instead.

Kenzie's frantic voice pulls me back. "I went to Rima."

My eyes fly open, the pain fading into the background of her words.

"What the fuck did you do?"

"I went to Rima. The Vipers needed someone to tell them what was going on," she babbles.

"Are you fucking kidding me, MacKenzie? Who the hell went with you? How did you even get there?" I brace an arm under myself, intent on pushing myself up, but dizziness invades my head, and someone shoves me back.

"Settle down or you'll rip your stitches," she scolds, eyes blazing.

I didn't realize I had stitches. Hot knives sear into my back. I have no idea what the hell he's doing, but I'm about to lose it on him if he doesn't stop.

"Tell me what happened," I grunt, the fight going out of me.

She sucks in a breath. "I went to the Vipers. Most didn't know what happened. Some were locked in rooms we haven't used in years. I sent the boys back. Blaze is going to take over until Dante is found."

"What else." It's not a question. I can see in her eyes she's holding something back. I brace myself for her confession.

"I may have ridden past Night Slayer headquarters," she whispers, leaning back, indecision written all over her face.

Closing my eyes, I turn my head away from her. The need to rage filters in, prodding me, but I wait for it to subside. I can't look at her right now. The fact she went to Rima at all, most likely alone, given the guilt in her eyes, is bad enough. Going into Night Slayer territory was an unnecessary risk. And Hawk let her. Betrayal coats the back of my throat, and I swallow down the bitterness. I press my lips together to halt the sensation of wanting to puke and to stop myself from saying something I'll regret.

"Ryker?"

The tape Ink is pressing on my flesh pulls, and I crack my eyes open. He steps back, surveying his work. Meeting my eyes, pity in his own, he nods. Hawk is hovering by the door, but I close my eyes again when he looks my way. They file out, Ink gathering his things, Hawk murmuring to MacKenzie. Weariness surges through my veins, and I groan.

"Ryker, I was only doing what you couldn't," she says. "I'm not going to apologize for this. I'm capable of taking care of shit."

My heart thuds. I don't want to shut her out, but I don't trust myself to deal with this right now. I don't care how capable she is. I don't care how much she's able to deal with shit. I don't care if she was trying to do what was right. I'm supposed to protect her. I made a promise to be there, to take care of her problems, but I can't fulfill my promise if she keeps throwing herself into situations that could get her killed. Next, she's going to tell me she went and had a chit-chat with Maddox. Ten minutes pass when the mattress shifts. Her hair brushes against my cheek as she leans in.

"I'm sorry."

And then she's gone, leaving an emptiness where she once lay.

FORTY

MacKenzie

Ryker's soft breathing fills the room as I stare at his back. Rationally, I understand he won't stop if I look away, but the panic seizing me when I do is too much to bear. My body protests when I shift in the chair. This monstrosity was meant for sitting, not sleeping. I'm not getting a lot of sleep, regardless.

I'm sure Ryker thinks I'm here instead of in the bed because of our fight, but it's because Ink told me to give him space. I think he's afraid I'll move in my sleep and hurt Ryker, but barely close my eyes during the night. I didn't bother arguing with Ink. I don't have the energy.

Ryker shifts, grunting, and I shoot up before skidding to his side. Laying a hand on his forehead, I check for a fever. I contemplate calling Ink, but I don't want to wake him in the middle of the night, especially if it's nothing. I pull my lip between my teeth, worrying the flesh. The door creaks open, and Sam pokes her head in.

"Everyone decent?" she whispers, looking from me to Ryker. She skips inside, pushing the door closed behind her. Ryker's face smooths out, and I exhale, waving her toward the bathroom.

"It's late. Is everything okay?"

My heart is pounding in my chest. I'm always waiting for the other shoe to drop, regardless of what I saw in Rima.

"Oh, yeah, we're good. I'm coming back from a job, thought I'd check on you. I was banking on you being awake, even though you should be sleeping," she scolds, hauling herself up on the counter, then tucking her legs under her.

Sometimes, I forget how short she is.

"I was, but Ryker was grunting in his sleep, so . . ." I glance out the cracked door and spy him still fast asleep. The tension in my shoulders relaxes.

"No, you weren't, but I don't blame you. Shane made me come home when Alex was in the hospital. Otherwise, I would have been there every second. None of them were happy when I started camping in his room after he came home."

"I'm sorry," I mutter.

"Not your fault. Things have been kind of dull after the whole Guild-trying-to-take-over-the-city thing. I mean, I wasn't asking for a full-on car accident, but it shook things up a little at least. Now, tell me what happened in Rima."

I huff. I should have known she was trying to ambush me into telling her what happened. I didn't tell anyone except

Hawk, and that was only because he caught me pushing Ryker's bike out of the driveway. Sam's been badgering me ever since. I still don't know how she found out, but I suspect Ren had something to do with it.

"I went to fix shit with the Vipers. Most of the guys who joined up with the Night Slayers are dead or ran. I knew there were others left at headquarters. Some of them were locked away. There were a few men from the Night Slayers who stayed behind, but by the time I showed up, they were gone, which hopefully means they're dead. I sent Blaze back to take over. The current road captain isn't a good leader. Good guy, bad at giving orders."

"Okay, and then you went into Night Slayers' lair. I heard Helms wasn't entirely happy about you going rogue," she says, pursing her lips.

"Who told you that?"

"Oh, don't get all pissy. Hawk mentioned you two weren't talking, and I got it out of him." She grins.

"If you must know, yes. I went through the area. There isn't much left. They didn't have a large footprint to begin with, but the place they used for a clubhouse is gone. Someone burned it down. I thought it might be Ryker, but now I'm not so sure." I pull my lip back in my mouth, glancing at his prone form. My heart stutters until his back rises with his next breath.

"You understand why he's not happy about it, right?"

"Frankly, I don't give a shit if he's happy or not. I'm just glad he's alive. And now I've confirmed they won't be coming back for me. At least, that's what I'm banking on."

"Okay, next time, call me. I'll go with you," she mumbles, pulling her phone out, then scowls at the screen.

My heart swells, and tears fill my eyes. I knew running to Ryker was the right choice once I got over my anxiety, but I never expected to find someone else who understood what my life was like. My only friend back in Rima didn't grow up in our world. She never fully understood what my life is like. I wonder if she and Sam will get along.

"Thanks. Is that the only reason you came? To bust my balls about going without you?"

Typing away at her phone, she shrugs. I turn back to the door, wondering if Ryker and I will get over all the shit that keeps derailing us. Most of the problems are of our own making. I'm furious at myself for all the insecurities I'm still carrying. Ryker accused me of going to talk to Maddox, and I didn't have the heart to see his face fall.

"What did Maddox have to say?" Swinging back to her, I narrow my eyes, but she merely smiles.

"He's still an asshole, saying I'm a bitch and will get what's coming to me." I roll my eyes. "As if he's in any position to throw out threats. I don't know what Ryker will do with him, though. Hawk wants to float him, but he won't without Ryker's say-so."

"I thought Helms said *you* were making the decision of what to do with him?" Sam raises an eyebrow.

"Fucking hell, Sam. Why are you constantly calling me out on shit?" I laugh softly.

She smirks. "Because I was exactly like you are, hiding from shit and not saying a fucking word about what I was feeling or what I wanted. The journey would have been a lot easier if I had sucked it up and talked to my guys before I was kidnapped, zip-tied to a pipe, and almost killed."

"That's . . . wow. That's not normal."

"Our lives aren't normal. Get used to it," she says, hopping off the counter. "Wait, you *are* staying, right?"

I hesitate, a stone dropping in my stomach. I don't know how to answer. Ryker talked a lot about being together, but he's been shot, almost bleeding out on the floor. My old fears rear their ugly heads, forcing me to choke back the questions crowding my mouth every time he wakes. I've been avoiding him, running from the room in the guise of fetching things. I wait until he's asleep again before I slip back inside to keep vigil. I'm not ready for his answer.

"Mac?"

"I'm not ready to ask Ryker yet," I whisper, trying to hide the pain stabbing me in the chest, but a look of pity comes over her face, and I realize I failed.

"He loves you. He's told you, like a lot. Why wouldn't he want you to stay?" Her logic is sound, but my heart isn't completely convinced, even if my mind is.

"Because he got shot. Ink said he . . ." I can't finish my sentence, clearing my throat and shoving the terror down deep inside. "I'll tell him what I want, but if he wants me to go, I'll have to live with his decision. This is his territory. I have to respect him as the president of the Reapers."

I don't know if she understands, but she nods, doubt still clouding her features. I can't explain it any better than I have. Words crowd my mouth to tell her not to say anything, to back the fuck off, to not make me feel any worse than I already do, but lashing out at Sam isn't what I need. I'm angry at myself. I'm pissed at a dead man. I'm livid at my half brother. Hell, I'm mad at Dante, too. He left without a fucking word to anyone, leaving us to deal with this whole fucking shit show. Anger at my brother burns away every other emotion trying to swamp me, and I glare at Ryker's sleeping form.

"Uh, I don't know what transformation you just went through, but I gotta go. Care if I go out the window? Doc is downstairs, and I swear he psychoanalyzes me every time I come within ten feet of him." She shudders.

"Be my guest. Don't fall, or I'll have three very angry men coming for me. I can't handle any more attitude than I'm already getting from Ryker." I lead us from the bathroom, her padding behind.

She grins and disappears out the window. Ryker clears his throat, and I rush to his side.

"What'd she want? Trying to smother me?" he grunts breathlessly.

"What? Of course not. She wanted to check in." I pull the comforter to his shoulders, covering the white bandage spanning the entirety of his waist.

The blood has stopped seeping through, which is a relief. Ink kept telling me it was normal to keep bleeding, but with the amount he's lost, it freaks me out every time.

"MacKenzie, come to bed." He sighs, closing his eyes again.

He never stays awake very long.

"Shh, go back to sleep. I'm right here," I murmur, smoothing his hair back, then pressing my lips to his temple. His body relaxes, sleep pulling him back under. I sink to my knees, resting my chin on the bed, content to watch him for a little while longer.

FORTY-ONE

Ryker

The last three days have been hell. I swear they're drugging me. There's no way I can feasibly sleep nineteen hours a day. Every time I wake up, Kenzie is sprawled out in the chair. She asks if I need anything and slips away. I cling to consciousness, waiting for her to return, but I never win the fight. I've tried to bring up her going to Rima, but she brushes me off, rushing from the room.

I watch her sleeping form covered in a thin blanket, and shame floods me. I tried to apologize, explain why I couldn't talk to her before, but she pretends I haven't said anything. The fuzziness isn't as thick in my brain now. I want to bask in the feeling, but a stabbing pain reminds me I have to pee.

I don't want to wake her. Like hell, I'm calling one of the guys to help me. Instead, I roll, smothering a groan with my pillow. My leg slides out, and I brace my foot, but when I shift again, I end up on my knees, clinging to the sheets so I don't end up sprawled on the floor. The burning sensation I felt before when Ink was working on my back is tenfold now, radiating across my body. I grit my teeth, resigning myself to crawling. Halfway there, I shuffle on my hands and knees when Kenzie clears her throat. I don't dare stop. I'll collapse if I don't keep moving.

"What the hell are you doing?" she asks, the scowl in her voice clear.

"Gotta pee," I reply through my teeth.

"Why don't you just ask for help, you stubborn asshole?"

Another wave of spasms wracks my body, and I pause, bracing my elbows on the ground and panting. I swear the toilet is farther away. MacKenzie won't be able to help me up, much less carry my ass in there. I hang my head, my overheated forehead resting on the cool hardwood. I shudder, swallowing nausea. The last thing I want to do is puke all over the floor, especially in front of her.

"You can't help me," I croak.

"There you go, pushing me out again. When are you going to learn it's okay to lean on me?" The tears in her voice send a twinge through my chest.

"Kenz, you physically cannot help me. You're not strong enough."

She snorts, and I glimpse her bare feet from the corner of my eye. Next thing I know, she's laying on her back next to me.

"Push up on your hands," she says.

I do as she asks, but it isn't easy. By the time I'm back on all fours, I'm out of breath. She slides between my arms, tucking her legs between mine. I have no idea what the fuck she thinks this will accomplish, but at least she's not running away anymore.

"Baby, I don't think I have the energy to fuck you, but I'm more than willing to watch you make yourself come." I chuckle, regretting the move when my back spasms.

She huffs, flipping on her stomach before growling. "Don't get any ideas."

Bracing my body with hers, she pushes up and tries to carry me on her back. I can't help it, I bust out laughing, grunting when my muscles cramp.

"What the fuck are you two doing?" Hawk's alarmed voice rings out, and I almost collapse on top of her.

"I'm trying to get him to the bathroom, but he's not helping."

"Uh, how about you let me, Mac?"

She shakes her head, determined to fulfill whatever asinine plan she's concocted.

"Kenz, I'm going to piss on us both if you don't move."

Abandoning her plan, she scrambles away, and I almost face-plant. Hawk seizes my arm, tugging me upright. When I have my feet under me, I sway, blood rushing to my head. I close my eyes, fighting the urge to puke. Kenzie's arm wraps around my other arm, and we shuffle to the bathroom. They both fight to stay, but I grumble until they finally leave, hovering by the door the entire time. I want to shower, but my energy is zapped. They help me back to bed, and I moan when my back hits the mattress. Hawk walks out when he gets a call, leaving me alone with her.

She turns to follow, but I capture her hand in mine, forcing her to face me.

"Kenzie, you can't keep avoiding me." My eyes are half-closed, and I'm fighting exhaustion again. I fucking hate this.

"I'm not avoiding you," she mutters, avoiding my gaze.

"Yes, you are, and I get why, but we can't keep doing this."

"I'm really not. I mean, I am, but I'm not," she babbles, squeezing my hand. "I just don't want to get in another fight when you're still hurt."

"We're not fighting. I didn't say anything because I *didn't* want to fight with you, regardless of Ink's fingers digging into an open wound in my back and trying to rip out my liver or not."

She scoffs. "He wasn't trying to take out organs."

"I don't like that you went to Rima."

"I know," she whispers, hanging her head.

I sigh. "No, I don't like you went to Rima without *me*."

The myriad of emotions flitting across her face are too quick for me to decipher. Her guilt remains. I hate having to do this when I'm incapable of moving. I don't want to fight with her. I want her to understand what it felt like to wake up and find her gone, not knowing if she'd come back. I want her to understand how it felt when I found out she went to accost another MC without me there to protect her.

"Kenz, this won't work if you take all the shit on by yourself. This won't work if you go off on your own, trying to fix your problems yourself. It just won't."

She rips her hand from mine. "I wasn't trying to take everything on myself, but I sure as hell should be the one to fix the problems I brought on the Reapers, on you. You got *shot,* Ryker. I thought you died. Do you know what it feels like to think the person you live for has died? And I did that."

She's waving her hands around, pacing back and forth. Sucking in a breath, I track her as she falls apart in front of me. Tears stream down her face, reliving the memory of when I was lying on the floor, not breathing. Imagining our roles reversed sends a shock wave through me, and I push away the thoughts before they can take root.

"You didn't do anything, Kenzie. None of this is your fault. You have to stop blaming yourself for other people's choices. Come here. I can't . . ." I reach toward her, but she's too far away.

Frustration boils through me. I hate being hurt. I hate being in this bed. I hate she felt like she had to take over and protect me and my club. She spins, planting her hands on her hips.

"Ryker Dain Helms, do not tell me what to feel. And do not tell me what to do with all my pent-up energy." She glares, nostrils flaring, and I can't fight back the grin. "What the hell are you smirking at?"

"I love when you put me in my place."

Her mouth opens and then snaps shut. "I . . . what a stupid thing to say."

"I only speak the truth. Now get your ass over here, so I can talk to you properly."

She huffs but comes close enough for me to hook a hand around her thigh, yanking her closer.

"Kenzie."

"Ryker," she mocks.

I raise an eyebrow until she huffs again, crossing her arms. "Kenzie, you shouldn't have gone alone to Rima. I wish you would have waited until I could go with you. I would have felt better about the whole thing then. But"—I stop her when she opens her mouth to protest—"I understand why you did it. I also wasn't shutting you out. I was upset and didn't want to take it out on you. See? I'm learning."

I grin until she caves and sinks to her knees next to the bed and draping her arm over my chest, tucking her head into my neck.

"I'm sorry," she says, voice muffled.

Kissing her forehead, I run a hand through her hair. "Me, too. Let's just get through this without killing each other."

She snorts, her breath sending goosebumps along my skin. I hook my arm around her, but I'm not able to haul her onto the bed. She pulls back, ducking her head.

"I can't," she mutters.

"You can't keep sleeping in the chair, MacKenzie." Frustration runs through me, and my back spasms, making my breath hitch.

"No, Ink said I shouldn't sleep next to you. I don't want to hurt you more."

"You didn't fucking hurt me, MacKenzie. You need to work through this shit because I'm not blaming you. We'll deal with the fallout together. That's what we do. I get you're used to doing this alone, but I'm here now. The whole point is to do this thing together."

"What thing?"

"Life," I explode, immediately regretting it.

My breath stalls again in my chest, and I can't suck in enough air. I imagine this is what drowning feels like. Kenzie leans over me, running her hands over my face, whispering words I can't make out over the roaring in my head. Helplessness engulfs me. I feel like I'll never be able to breathe again. Panic lines Kenzie's eyes, and her lips are moving. I reach up a trembling hand to brush it along her cheeks. Suddenly, something releases inside me, and I suck in a little air.

Sounds rush back in, along with her frantic words. "Relax. Just breathe. Don't you fucking dare."

Tilting my head, I brush my lips over hers. Tears fall, splashing on my cheeks, and she reaches up to wipe them away. My fingers delve into her hair, and I kiss her again. I pull back, sighing against her lips while her trembling fingers clutch at my face. I can't stand to see her this way again. I pull in another breath deeper than the last to steady my heart trying to leap from my chest.

"Never enough." I sigh, closing my eyes once she's pulled away.

"Why don't you sleep. I'll be right here if you need me."

"What aren't you telling me, MacKenzie?"

"Don't worry. We'll talk more when you're not about to piss yourself every two seconds."

I crack my lids open, eyeing her. "Tell me."

She sucks in a breath. "Imighthavetakenyourbike." Her eyes widen, sucking her lip into her mouth.

"You did what?"

"Um, I may have, maybe, taken your bike. When I went to Rima." She shuffles back, out of my reach.

"So, you went to Rima—alone. You went to Night Slayer territory—alone. And you took my bike to aid yourself in this little adventure? Is that what I'm getting?"

"Yes?"

"Okay." I close my eyes again, muscles relaxing one at a time.

"That's it? Okay? How are you okay with me taking your bike? That thing is the love of your life!" I don't know why she's arguing with me when I'm not upset about it.

"She isn't the love of my life. You are. My bike is important, but I don't care if you fucking ride her. She's as much yours as she is mine. I don't give a flying fuck what you do with her, but don't take her into Rima without me. At least for a little while." Peeking at her again, I find her staring off, tears streaming down her face again.

"What are you crying about now?" I grumble.

"I'm the love of your life?" she breathes.

"That's pretty fucking obvious, Kenz. I don't know why it's such a goddamn shock."

She sniffs, crawling next to me in the bed, trying not to touch me, but I haul her against me as much as I can.

"You're the love of my life, too," she whispers.

I listen as her breaths even out, peace settling over me, and I follow her into sleep.

* * *

Thank you so much for reading Ryker and MacKenzie's
story!
Not ready to leave the shadows of Synd behind?
Pre-order Hawk's story-out March 21, 2023

If you'd like to hear about the other stories that have been
living in my head, sign up for my newsletter, visit my
website, or follow me on social media visit:
emiliaabraham.com

Special Thanks:

K.B. Barrett Designs - Cover Artist
Miss Eloquent Edits - Editor and Interior Formatter

Also by E. Abraham:

Under the Shadows
Book 1: Shadows of Synd series

Running From Shadows
Book 2: Shadows of Synd series

Becoming Shadows
Book 3: Shadows of Synd series (March 2023)

Also by Emilia Abraham:
Stuck at Sundown

About the Author

After many years of dreaming of becoming a full-time writer, Emilia Abraham took the leap, bringing her words to print. From sweet contemporary romance to spicy why choose and everything in between, she focuses on the happily ever after.

Emilia lives in the Upper Midwest with her husband (who's probably sick of listening to her expound on fictional men) and three kids (who try to steal her post-it notes). When she's not writing, she enjoys reading, playing video games, and consuming copious amounts of energy drinks.